CONNIE BRISCOE

SISTERS & LOVERS

HarperCollinsPublishers

HarperCollins *Publishers*
77–85 Fulham Palace Road,
Hammersmith, London W6 8JB

A Paperback Original 1996
1   3   5   7   9   8   6   4   2

A catalogue record for this book
is available from the British Library

ISBN 0 00 649804 3

Set in Meridien
at The Spartan Press Ltd,
Lymington, Hants

Printed and bound in Great Britain by
Caledonian International Book Manufacturing Ltd, Glasgow

For my sister Pat,
her daughters, Simone and Camille,
and all my sisters everywhere

1

Beverly slammed the phone down so hard the nail on her index finger jammed the buttons. She shook the hand. The pain seemed to claw its way from the tip of the finger to the base of the nail. She screwed up her nose and squinted at the finger. The nail, once a perfect oval shape like all the rest, was split deeply on one end. The crimson polish she had applied so meticulously not more than thirty minutes before had chipped and peeled away and blood seeped over the cuticle.

She sank down on the edge of her bed and stuck the sore finger in her mouth. It was fitting that she'd do something like this to herself right now, she thought. That the frustration that had been building up inside her all these weeks would finally find its way to the surface. She'd known the minute the phone rang that it was him calling to disappoint her again, to say he wouldn't be able to make it. She wasn't sure why she'd sensed it. Women's intuition? Maybe. Although with most of these men it eventually reached a point where a woman didn't need intuition to know things were going downhill. It was as obvious as the grass under your feet was green. Vernon never broke off dates when they'd first started seeing each other six months before, but now he was canceling all the time. And each time he had the same sorry excuse.

'Bad news, baby . . . not going to be able to make it tonight.'
Mmm-hmm.
' . . . got to work late on this project.'
Mmm-hmm.
'I'll make it up to you, promise.'
Lies, all lies. She was sick and tired of these lying men. Didn't they know if they kept on lying, sooner or later they would get caught? The last time Vernon called from the office to break off

a date, it was some urgent last-minute business trip. She'd decided then and there that this crap had gone on long enough. The business trips and late nights at the office were popping up a little too much to suit her. She'd called him back on the pretext of asking him something. Spent ten minutes before making the call trying to think up a good excuse to phone him back, but she needn't have bothered. He wasn't at the office, and when she called his apartment a woman answered the phone.

A woman. With a deep, sultry voice. She acted like she thought she owned the damn place, asking who was calling and all. Vernon got on the line and made up some lame story about having his coworkers over to his place to finalize some papers before he left on his business trip. Uh-huh. Sure. And she was having Denzel Washington over next Saturday night for tea and crumpets. He must think she was a complete fool. Why would a coworker answer his phone? Why couldn't he just come out and tell the truth? That he was starting to see another woman. She was twenty-nine years old, a big girl. She could take it. What she couldn't take was all the lying. All the cheating. She wasn't about to play the role of fool. Not for him, not for nobody.

She stood and switched on the lamp next to her bed. She opened the drawer to the little oak nightstand and shoved aside pencils, papers, and old paperback novels until she found the knife lying flat in the back. The sight of it made her pause. It looked so strange sitting there among all her personal things. It was one of a set of four carving knives, not the biggest but the sharpest. She tucked it there one night after watching a scary movie about a mass-murdering rapist on TV. A single woman living alone in Washington, DC., even in a nice part of town, couldn't be too careful. But that was so long ago she'd forgotten the knife was there until recently.

She wasn't sure when this idea started forming in her head. Maybe it was when she first suspected Vernon was tipping out on her. Maybe it was even before that, when things started going sour with her last boyfriend. To this day, she didn't know what had happened between her and Michael. He just seemed to lose interest, for no reason. She'd suspected there was another woman in the picture then, too, but could never prove it. And of course he denied it. They all did. Michael's car didn't have a convertible top like Vernon's did, but it had tires, big, expensive ones.

Vernon, with his precious BMW convertible, would make an even better target. Miss Sexy Voice could have him. But sharks would swim across the desert before that woman would sit next to him in that fancy convertible again.

She pulled the knife out by its wooden handle and looked it over under the glare of the lamp. The bitterness on her face jumped out from the metal surface of the blade. It surprised her, and she turned the point away from her body and left the bedroom.

Her heels clacked loudly on the hardwood floor in the hallway until she reached the small dhurrie rug in the living room. She grabbed her black leather coat off the back of the loveseat and carefully placed the knife in the front pocket, blade down. Part of the handle stuck out over the edge of the pocket, but that would have to do, she reasoned. The pockets to her other winter coat – a black and white checkered affair – were even shallower. She draped the coat over her arm and picked up her shoulder bag and car keys from the wicker coffee table.

It wasn't until she had her hand on the door knob that she remembered she was still dressed for dinner and the Mary Wilson show at Le Pavilion. She looked down at the silk beige dress with its intricate embroidery and her satin heels. It would make sense to stop and change into jeans and tennis shoes. The dress could get dirty and the soft fabric could easily be torn. And she never was much of a one for heels. They were stupid – hard to walk in and bad on the feet. She only wore the things because men said she looked good in them. Vernon, for one, was always asking her to wear a skirt and heels when they went out. He thought her legs were her best feature.

Well, here she was standing around in her perfect little silk faille dress — a dress she'd spent hours running up and down Connecticut Avenue looking for just for him. But instead of leaving the apartment with her so-called boyfriend on her arm, she was standing here with a nine-inch blade in her pocket and mayhem on her mind. She would probably regret it in the morning, but right now she didn't care if the dress got ripped into a million pieces. She had business to tend to.

2

Hmmph. He was going to have to get his act together starting now or get the hell out of her house. Charmaine had made up her mind — she wasn't putting up with his trifling ways any longer. All he did was run the streets. She was sick and damn tired of all the bull and she was going to tell him exactly that tonight.

She glanced up from the keyboard to the clock on the wall. Thank goodness, only ten more minutes before quitting time. She needed to get out of this office and go pick up Kenny from the day care center. He was getting a head cold when she dropped him off that morning, and Charmaine was anxious to see how he was doing. That no-good husband of hers didn't even help much with her son, and the main reason she'd married the bum was so Kenny would have a father figure. Well, that wasn't the *only* reason she'd married Clarence. That beautiful bronze complexion and those sexy mustached lips played a big part. No doubt about it. And he had a body that just wouldn't quit, or at least certainly wouldn't let her quit daydreaming about it the whole time they were going together. Sometimes even now she got a little warm and tingly just thinking about those muscles wrapped around her shoulders. But she didn't care how cute a honey he was, he was going to have to start acting like he had some sense or she was kicking his ass out on the pavement.

Her eyes moved from the sheet of paper on her desk to the computer monitor, and she realized she'd done it again. The last few lines on the screen were nothing but garbage because she had her fingers on the wrong keys. She groaned and threw her hands up into the air. What the hell was the matter with her? Brain running in circles like a rat trapped in a cage. Thinking about everything except this budget report she was supposed to be typing. What she needed now was a cigarette. But that was out of the question since the boss had recently started a no-smoking policy in the office. She took a deep breath and hit the exit button. No point pushing it when it was almost time to go home anyhow. She would just finish this thing Monday. Right now, she was getting the hell out of here.

She removed her bag from the bottom drawer and set it on top of her desk. It was a big black shoulder bag by Liz Claiborne made of a plastic that looked and felt like leather. Stylish but not too expensive. She had long since stopped carrying the genuine leather ones. With a child, and a husband who acted like one, she just couldn't justify the expense.

She opened the bag and rummaged through it until she located her little Hallmark date book. Then she flipped the pages to October, where she'd placed a check mark in the square for the seventh. She counted forward, touching the square for each day with her forefinger. Just as she reached the end of the month and was about to turn the page, the phone rang.

'Shit.' She looked at the clock on the wall. It was 5:28. And it was Friday, for God's sake. Didn't these people ever go home? She debated whether to answer it or just let it ring. Her boss was in a late meeting upstairs and just about everyone else had already left. Susan would never know if she just ignored it. But on the third ring she picked it up. It was hard to ignore a ringing phone when you had a child.

'Good evening,' she said. 'Finance Department. Susan Tupperman's office.'

'Hello,' said a male voice unfamiliar to her. 'May I speak to Charmaine Perry, please?'

That was strange. Who would be calling her at this hour? Everybody knew she got off at 5:30 and was out that door instantly unless she couldn't help it. 'Speaking.'

'This is Charmaine Perry of 1621 Newton Street, Northeast, Washington, D.C.?'

That made Charmaine feel uneasy, and she narrowed her

6

eyes in anticipation. Where'd this dude get all that information? She knew instinctively that it must have something to do with that Clarence. 'Yes, it is.'

'Mrs. Perry, I'm calling for Sharp Sounds. You're a few months behind on your bill.'

Oh, shit. Should've let it ring. 'I don't have any bill from Sharp. Haven't bought anything from there in years.' As soon as she finished talking, she remembered the brand-new twenty-four-inch color television Clarence had brought in the house a few months ago and plopped down in the living room.

'Well, a Clarence Perry signed for it in July,' the man said. 'A color Zenith television set. None of the payments have been made yet.'

The lying sucker. Clarence said it was paid for. Charmaine figured he was lying, but what was she supposed to do? Pick it up and throw it out on the street?

'We've tried to reach Mr Perry at his job but haven't had any luck.'

Hmmph. That didn't surprise her one bit. She couldn't reach that man half the time herself, and she was his wife. 'He can be hard to catch up to.'

'Is there a problem paying the bill, Mrs Perry?'

You bet there's a problem, she thought. Clarence could have been raised by a band of gypsies for all he cared about something as mundane as paying a bill. Personally, she'd rather give the damn thing back than take money out of her pocket to pay for it, which was what this whole phone conversation was coming to anyway. What the hell did he need that big old TV for anyhow? He was hardly ever home to watch it. And the thing was so big it took up half the living room.

'I didn't even know we had a bill coming in. I mean, I know he bought a TV, but I thought it was paid for.' Lying. Since when did Clarence ever pay for anything in full?

'We have both your names on the credit card he used to purchase it.'

Well, of course, dummy. We're husband and wife. But that don't mean I bought it. 'How much is it?'

'Four hundred ten dollars. As of now you owe ninety-nine dollars.'

Oh, perfect. What the hell was wrong with that man? Didn't he know decent people just didn't go out buying stuff and not paying the bills? Sometimes he acted like someone had snatched all the sense out of his head.

'Can you put a check in the mail today, Mrs Perry?'

Did she have a choice? She knew the routine. It was that or this man would report them to the credit bureau or wherever the hell it is they report people who don't pay their bills. 'I don't have all of it, but I can send you fifty. And another fifty in two weeks.'

'That will be fine. That'll bring the account up to date. But try to see that it gets paid on time each month in the future.'

Easier said than done, Charmaine thought, dropping the receiver in the cradle. Now where in the hell was she going to find an extra fifty bucks? And another in two weeks? Maybe she could borrow it from one of her sisters. No, no, not from those two. They would bug her for all the details, and she would have to tell them why she needed it. They were on her case about Clarence and his trifling ways enough as it was. She would just have to ask her daddy. She hated to, but it was that or send the TV back, and that would be a mess on their credit. Their finances were shaky enough as it was. God. She couldn't wait to get her hands on that man tonight.

She saw the date book sitting on the desk and remembered what she was doing before the phone rang. She picked up the book and started counting again, beginning from the seventh of October. When she reached the end of the month, she turned the page and counted through to today's date. Then she looked up and slumped back in her chair. Yep, thirty-three days. Same as it had been when she counted this morning. One more than it was when she'd counted last night. She knew it was silly to keep counting. The number of days could only go up, never down. But this had so taken her by surprise that she didn't know what to do besides count. Except when she was pregnant with Kenny, she'd been right on the clock, down to the hour of the day practically. Now she was five days late.

This was what she got for not using that damn diaphragm like she was supposed to. She never added more jelly before act two. Who the hell could be bothered? It was enough trouble getting the stupid contraption in the first time. And with Clarence there was almost always a second act. Probably a wonder this hadn't happened sooner.

She took a deep breath and put the calendar back in her bag. Just have to be patient, she told herself. With any luck, she might not be pregnant. It was probably just all the worrying she did.

She reached for the answering machine they used during off-hours, but before she could get it set up, the door to the office suite opened and Susan rushed in. Shoot. She'd been trying to get out of here before that woman got back. As usual, Susan was in a hurry and had that look on her face that meant she was about to bark some order. Charmaine stood and made a point of slinging her bag over her shoulder to signal that the day was over for her. Not that she thought it would do much good.

'Oh, great,' Susan said, approaching Charmaine's desk. 'You're still here.'

Charmaine didn't know what kind of perfume Susan wore, but it must be expensive because its rosy scent clung to the woman all day long. Charmaine's own perfume, or cologne to be more precise, lost its fragrance almost as soon as it left the bottle. 'I was just about to leave though.'

'Did you finish typing the budget report?'

'You said you didn't need it 'til Monday afternoon.'

'I know. But it turns out from this meeting I just left that I'll need it first thing Monday morning. Can you stay a while and finish it for me?'

No, no, no. Type it yourself. She had a child to go pick up, food to cook, bills to check on, a husband to lay out. The only decent part of the day was going to get her son in the evening, seeing his eyes light up when she picked him up from the day care center, playing with him while dinner cooked, putting him to bed at night. Besides, the day care center would charge extra if she was late picking up Kenny, and she just managed to make the payments as it was. Now she had this fucking TV bill to pay. You'd think a woman boss with children of her own would understand these things. But of course Susan wouldn't. Susan could afford to pay the baby-sitter for an extra hour or two. Or her loving, dutiful husband could pick up the kids. How could she expect this WASP princess to understand?

Charmaine dropped her purse on the desk. It took a lot of restraint to keep the resentment she felt off her face. 'I guess I'll have to.'

Susan smiled. 'Oh, great. If you just type it on the computer and bring me the diskette, I'll print it out and then you can go. How long will it take you?'

'About an hour, maybe more.'

'Make up the time by coming in late Monday morning. I'll be here late tonight, so I'm going out to get Chinese. Can I get you something?'

'No.'

'You sure? It's on me.'

'I'm sure, but thanks.' Susan went into her office, and Charmaine flipped on the computer switch. Now she was feeling a little bad about the curt way she'd responded to Susan's request to work a little late. Susan was a workaholic, no doubt about it, demanding and sometimes thoughtless of others' needs. But Charmaine couldn't help admiring her. She was a woman who had climbed through the ranks over a horde of men to become vice president of finance. And she was willing to meet Charmaine and the rest of her staff halfway when things got tough. Well, maybe a third of the way. Like just now offering to print out the report so she could go home, offering to buy her dinner. That was more than some of these top-brass men walking around here would do.

Still, she had this problem with the day care center. She needed to get someone to pick Kenny up before six. Most evenings Clarence went home after work, changed his clothes, and hit the streets before she even got in. But maybe she could catch him and get him to pick Kenny up from the day care center so they wouldn't have to pay extra. Or rather, *she* wouldn't have to pay, since Clarence wasn't about to come up with the money. She dialed her home number while waiting for the computer to come up, but there was no answer. She dialed Clarence's work number at the Martin Luther King, Jr, Library even though she knew it was a long shot that he'd still be there.

The receptionist at the library, where Clarence worked stacking books, answered the phone. 'Hi, Brenda. Is Clarence still there?'

'No. He's gone for the day.'

'Shoot. He's not at home either. How long ago did he leave?'

'I can't say. Haven't seen him around here since this morning. It's a big place.'

'Okay. Thank you, anyway.' She pressed the button on the phone and held it with her finger. No doubt he was out fooling around with some of those no-good men he hung with. He was never around when she needed him.

The only other person she could call was Ma. She hated dragging her into this. Here she was thirty-five years old, married, with a four year-old child. She was supposed to be grown and independent. Her mama had retired a year ago, after teaching for thirty years in the D.C. public schools, but that didn't mean she had time on her hands. The woman was always into something – working in her garden, sewing quilts, attending club meetings. But Charmaine didn't think she had much choice. She released the button and dialed. 'Ma, can you do me a favor? I got to work late. Can you or Daddy go pick up Kenny from the Lemon Tree Center so I won't have to pay extra?'

'Your father's not home from work yet. But I'll go. Where's Clarence?'

'You know better than to ask me that. When you get Kenny, take him to your house. And check his temperature 'cause he seemed to be getting a cold this morning. I'll come get him when I get off, but I'll probably stop home first to change.'

'Don't worry about Kenny. I'll get him and feed him.'

'Thanks, Ma. Talk to you later.'

'Wait a minute. You're coming tomorrow, right?'

'Don't I always?'

'Good. Beverly's not sure she's coming and I was counting on her to bring a garden salad. Can you make one?'

'I was bringing a potato salad. I already got all the stuff to make it.'

'Your aunt Jeanine is bringing potato salad. And you know how much she makes. And Fred and Louise are bringing macaroni salad. But we won't have enough greens.'

'Why isn't Beverly coming?'

'You'll have to ask her. When I talked to her earlier, she was waiting for that man to pick her up. What's his name?'

'Vernon?'

'That's him. He was running late and she sounded upset about it. Have you met him yet?'

'Once. He's good-looking and seems nice. I just hope she doesn't dump him for being late.' Charmaine laughed at her own sarcasm. 'She always manages to find something wrong with every man she goes out with.'

'You're too hard on your sister.'

'I'm not. She's too hard on herself. She's looking for the perfect man and the perfect relationship, and believe me, Ma, there just ain't no such thing.'

'I wish you wouldn't talk like that, Charmaine. You know better.'

'Yes, Mother. Anyway, I got to go. I want to get this work done so I can get out of this place at a halfway decent hour.'

'You're bringing a garden salad tomorrow, right?'

'Uh, I'll talk to you about that when I get there.' Charmaine said good-bye and hung up. She pushed all the keys necessary to retrieve the budget report, then jumped up and headed for the ladies' room. She thought she felt a little drip down there while she was talking on the phone and wanted to check it out.

* * *

12

A stack of bills greeted Charmaine at the mailbox, which meant Clarence hadn't even bothered to come home and change. One of the bills caught her eye. It had the words 'Second Notice' printed in big, bold letters in the upper left corner. Seeing these notices always got to her. She tore at the flap. That man was always buying things and charging them and not paying the bills on time – that was why he usually came home from work before going back out. He wanted to get to the overdue bills before she did because he knew she'd get on his case about them.

This one was from Hecht's, one of the department stores. No doubt Clarence had bought more clothes for himself. The man was a fashion freak. She liked clothes, too, but she didn't go around buying them and then not paying for them. He had no business dressing the way he did, wearing two-hundred-dollar shoes and eighty-dollar neckties on a clerk's salary. Hmmph, was she going to let him have it when he got home tonight. All he had to do was pay the utilities and the credit card bills and buy groceries. But he couldn't even pay those few measly bills on time. What the hell he did with his money was beyond her.

She took care of the mortgage and car payments because she had learned early on in their three-year marriage that he couldn't be trusted to pay them on time. She'd bought the house herself a year before she'd even met Clarence, and she wasn't about to lose it because of his stupidity. Her father helped her with the down payment. It was small, only two bedrooms, but her life was pretty messed up back then, and her parents figured a house would help her get back on the right track. She'd been divorced for several months from her first husband when she discovered she was knocked up by her new boyfriend. But no way was she marrying that man. He was too much like her former husband. Good-looking and super in bed, but without an ounce of ambition. Why she always fell for men like that she just couldn't figure out. Clarence was the same way, only he was a smooth talker. He managed to fool her into thinking he was going to make something of himself. He made her think his job at the King

Library had real possibilities. And it probably did. The job wasn't the problem, Clarence was.

Her sisters had been hot with envy about their parents giving her all that money for the down payment on the house. Thought they should get some money, too. But, shit, Beverly was always getting a handout from them for a new car or a trip somewhere, and they had paid for Evelyn to go to that fancy all-girls' school, that Smith College or whatever the name was. Charmaine had gone to Howard University right here in the city, so it wasn't nearly as expensive, and she had dropped out in her junior year when she got married. Big mistake that was, though. She sometimes thought about going back to get her degree if she could ever save the money. She didn't want to be somebody's secretary for the rest of her life. But with the way Clarence spent every dime that came into the house that would never happen.

She put the Hecht Company bill in her purse. It was evidence she'd use to confront Clarence with later tonight. If he got ahold of it, she would never see it again in this life.

Now she had to change and go pick up her son, but first she went to check to see if she'd gotten her period yet. She took the stairs two at a time.

3

Evelyn DuMont turned the silver Mercedes-Benz sedan onto Windmill Lane. She loved the way her new car handled. It felt so luxurious compared to her old Volvo. Not that the Volvo had been a bad car. It had served her well for more than a hundred and fifty thousand miles. But the Benz had so many more luxury features, like leather seats and cruise control. Her job as a psychologist in D.C. was almost an hour's drive from her home in the Maryland suburbs. The Benz made that long commute much more pleasant.

As she approached her house at the end of the block, her eyes fastened on two bicycles sprawled in the driveway behind her husband's Saab. How many times did she have to tell those children not to leave their bikes in the driveway? To put them back in the shed where they belonged when they'd finished riding them. At eight and thirteen years old, they could at least do that much without constantly having to be reminded.

She eased the Benz partway onto the front lawn and shut off the engine. Evelyn lived in one of the hundreds of Maryland subdivisions that consisted of driveways with cars, usually two or more per family, front lawns, usually green and manicured, and big, modern houses rising stately in the background. If Norman Rockwell were painting the typical American suburban scene of the latter decades of this century, this is what would fill his canvas.

She stepped out of the car with her briefcase and walked quickly up the driveway, scanning the block as she always did to see what her neighbors were up to. The Weldons next door had raked their leaves since that morning. She would have to remind Kevin or Andre to be sure to rake theirs this weekend.

She reached the top of the driveway and looked at the house

three doors down. Two nights ago it had gone up in flames. Now it stood there, a mass of charred brick and scorched aluminum. She noticed that all the broken glass and other debris had been removed, probably by the insurance company repairing the house. Fortunately, the retired couple who lived there wasn't hurt seriously, although Elvin Johnson had given them all a good scare. His wife managed to escape before the fire trucks arrived, but there was too much smoke to go back for him. Regina stood on the front lawn, her nightgown and bathrobe blowing in the night breeze as she screamed and screamed, calling out to him. The neighbors gathered around and tried to calm her, and it took three of them to keep her from running back into the smoke-filled house to try to save him. The trucks finally came and rescued him and then rushed them off to the hospital. They were released later that night.

From what Louise Levinson across the street had told Evelyn and some of the others last night, Elvin was the cause of the fire. He'd dozed off on the sofa in the family room while smoking a cigarette. Evelyn had no doubt he was still drinking, even though Regina was going around telling everyone he'd quit. That would explain why he'd dozed off with a lighted cigarette in his hand and why he had been so slow to respond. It was exactly the kind of thing that happened when you were careless. The insurance company would pay to have the house rebuilt and for new furniture, but no one would be able to replace all their personal mementos — the family photo albums, the heirlooms, the souvenirs from their travels.

Then there was the problem of appearances. The Johnsons were the only other blacks in the subdivision, and his drinking embarrassed Evelyn to say the least. None of the neighbors said anything about skin color when they gossiped about Elvin Johnson's drinking habits, but Evelyn couldn't help feeling they somehow lumped her family with the Johnsons. Her husband always told her that it was a waste of time to worry about things like that. If anyone was narrow-minded enough to think that way, there wasn't a thing she could do about it. He was right, of course, but that didn't stop her from thinking about it. Well, maybe after this the man would get some help with his drinking problem.

She entered her house from the side door and stepped into the L-shaped country kitchen. One side of it was filled with shiny modern appliances — stove with built-in microwave, refrigerator with ice maker, double sink, dishwasher. The pantry and eating area sat in the other end, beneath a gleaming brass chandelier.

Evelyn was dying to kick off her heels and stretch her tired toes right there on the linoleum floor. Friday was always a long day for her, since she supervised a late therapy session with a group of women. But she would have to keep the shoes on until she got the children to remove their bikes from the driveway so she could park her car. She heard them arguing over the sound of the television in the family room, so she leaned over the stairs until she could just see Andre and Rebecca sitting on the leather couch watching a game show on the fifty-two-inch television screen. They stopped fussing with each other when they heard her at the top of the stairs. 'Hi, you two,' she said.

'Yo,' Andre said, never taking his eyes off the television screen. He had his sneaker-clad feet propped up on the chrome and glass coffee table and was wearing the black leather bomber jacket he'd gotten a month earlier for his thirteenth birthday.

'Mama,' Rebecca said, jumping off the couch. She walked around the table to the bottom of the stairs and looked up at her mother. 'Andre's hogging the remote control. And he keeps changing the channel.' She tossed her older brother a spiteful look. 'How are we supposed to watch anything with you flipping the channel every two seconds?'

Andre folded his arms across his chest and sank defiantly into the sofa.

'Right now,' Evelyn said, 'I don't want to hear about any TV shows from either of you. I'm too tired. Just go put those bikes in the shed where they belong so I can park my car.' She turned back toward the kitchen, thinking the matter was settled, but Andre's voice pulled her back to the top of the stairs.

'I'll get to it soon as I finish watching this,' he said.

'You'll do it now. And get those feet off my good table. What's the matter with you?'

'Can't we finish watching this first, Mama?' Rebecca asked.

'I thought you didn't even like this show, Rebecca. But never mind, you know the rules. Bikes in the shed when you finish with them.' She clapped her hands at them to show she meant business. 'Move. And I mean now.'

Rebecca ran all the way up the stairs in less time than it took Andre to remove his high-tops from the table and stand up.

'What are you?' Evelyn teased as he poked along up the stairs. 'An old man?'

He shoved his hands into his jacket pockets, and she followed the two of them as they walked into the kitchen. She noticed that the room was spotless, not a dirty dish in sight. That was a sure sign that no cooking had yet been done that evening.

'Have you eaten yet?' she asked.

'Daddy came home early and took us to McDonald's,' Rebecca said.

'Oh, no, not that place. Did you start on your homework?'

'I finished mine,' Rebecca answered, slipping into her jacket.

Andre reached the screen door and pushed it open. His pace had suddenly picked up a beat, as if he were a cat that had just discovered a dog was on its tail.

'Andre,' she called after him. 'Did you hear me just ask you a question?'

He paused, holding the screen door halfway open. 'I heard you.'

'And?'

'I haven't gotten around to it just yet.'

'Then after you move your bike and finish watching this one show, go do your homework. You know the rules.'

'Aw, Ma. It's Friday. There's this other show I wanted to watch at eight.'

Evelyn shook her head. 'You have to at least start your homework before TV on Fridays. And that's that.'

'Aw, chill out, Ma. It's only on a half hour. The homework's not going anywhere before Monday.'

'No, smartmouth. You think your father and I make rules just to have something to do?'

He kicked the door open and was out before Evelyn could say anything more, so she let his cheeky attitude slide. She just shook her head and followed with Rebecca at her side.

After pulling her car into the driveway, she came in and headed up the stairs to the bedroom. It felt good slipping out of her suit and heels and into a pair of jeans and one of her husband's sweatshirts. It drooped over her tall, slender frame, but she loved wearing it around the house because it was so roomy.

She went into the master bath and stood over one of the two sinks to wash the makeup off her face. Not that she wore much, with well-sculpted cheeks and thick eyelashes handed down from her father. Her sisters had them, too. Charmaine's were the prettiest, though, because she also had big almond-shaped eyes like their father. It seemed to Evelyn that Charmaine had gotten the best of about all the physical features, their father's eyes and their mother's shapely figure. Beverly had the best hair, though, thick and wavy like their father's.

She'd inherited the smarts. This hadn't seemed like much of a bargain until she got to graduate school and saw how far brains could carry her. Not that Beverly and Charmaine weren't smart, too. Evelyn just didn't think they used their intelligence as well as they could, especially Charmaine when it came to picking men.

She jumped when she heard a sound from behind her, and a bottle of bath oil toppled over on the marble vanity top. She looked up at her husband's dark brown reflection in the mirror as he stepped up behind her. The thing that had attracted her to Kevin besides his intelligence was his athletic six-foot three-inch frame. In fact, after graduating from Moorehouse College in Atlanta, he was recruited by the New York Jets to play wide receiver but never made the team. He wound up taking a job in D.C. and they met shortly after that. She was almost six feet tall, and he was one of the few men she'd dated who was tall enough so that she could wear her heels and still have to look up. He placed his hands on her upper arms and squeezed gently.

'Still as beautiful as ever,' he said.

She smiled and set the bottle upright. 'You startled me,' she said, holding up her cheek for his kiss. 'Where were you?'

He planted a warm kiss on her face. 'Downstairs in the den, going over some papers.'

'Mmm. How was work today?'

He shrugged his shoulders and turned back into the bedroom. 'Do you need to ask?' He sat on the edge of the bed and rolled a pencil he was holding across the handmade quilt.

She turned to face him, standing in the bathroom doorway. 'I guess I keep hoping your feelings will change again. Just a few months ago you were all excited about that new case you've been assigned to.'

'I have my ups and downs.'

She walked to the side of the bed and slipped her feet into her bedroom slippers. 'The leaves need raking.'

'I'll get to it.'

'It'll be dark soon. Why didn't you get Andre to do it earlier?'

He shrugged his shoulders. 'He had homework to do.'

'He wasn't doing any homework, he was watching TV.'

'I definitely told them to go do their homework after we ate.'

'They're always pulling the wool over your eyes, Kevin, especially Andre. You can't just tell them something and let it go. You have to keep checking on them.'

'I know that, but like I said, I got wrapped up in these papers.'

'You know as well as I do that if they think they can get out of something, they'll try, especially Andre. I don't know what's going on with him lately. He walks around the house

20

wearing that leather jacket all day and it's like pulling teeth to get him to do his homework. His whole attitude is terrible.'

'His grades haven't dropped, have they?'

'No, but he's . . . You're not going to give me that boys will be boys stuff are you?'

Kevin waved his hand in the air. 'The boy's fine. He's going through a phase, that's all.'

'Then I hope it's a brief one. I had two sisters, so maybe I just don't know. Did you go through that?'

'Don't remember. Probably.'

'Mmm. A lot of help you are.' She smacked him playfully on the top of his head and headed for the door. 'I'm going downstairs to eat. Is there anything besides that McDonald's food?'

'Some leftover lamb from yesterday, I think.'

'Provided Andre didn't beat me to it.'

'You got that right.' He stood up. 'Listen, uh, we need to talk.'

She paused in the doorway and turned to face him. 'I know.'

He looked surprised at first, then he nodded. 'I know you don't want to talk about this again but . . .'

'Then don't bring it up.'

He smiled reluctantly. 'I'm not letting you off that easy.'

'That much I figured. Let's go downstairs and talk then. I'm starving.'

She looked in the refrigerator for the lamb roast and whatever else she could find. Kevin sat at the table and rested his arms on top, twirling the pencil back and forth between his hands.

'The more I think about this, the better it seems,' he said. 'We could refinance the house to get our share of the money. But we wouldn't need to use all our equity, just part of it.'

'You're not serious? That would be a big extra payment every month, Kevin. And with you not working . . .'

'Working part-time,' he said. 'I would still work at the firm at least twenty hours a week until we start bringing in clients. Of course, it will take us a while to get to that point. We have to raise the money, find office space, support staff.'

'I don't know about this, Kevin.' She removed the plate holding the roast and a bowl of salad from the refrigerator and set them on the countertop. 'Doesn't look like enough here to make a meal.'

'Why don't you eat the fish sandwich and fries from McDonald's?'

'You know I hate that stuff. I'll have to make do with this.' She removed a knife from the drawer and turned the plate around, trying to find some meat. 'I honestly don't know how one family of four can devour a whole lamb roast in twenty-four hours.'

Kevin sat back and folded his arms across his chest. 'Can we get back to the subject at hand, please?'

Evelyn took a deep breath. 'I still don't get it. I know you've explained it to me, but for the life of me, I just don't understand why you want to leave one of the top law offices in the city to do something as risky as starting your own firm. You just made partner a year ago. They've been good to you.'

Kevin twisted his mouth up in disgust. 'I wouldn't call their treatment good by a long shot. They've been fair, but they've been a lot fairer to some of those white boys. You know that.'

'At least you're a partner. Now you want to give it up, after all that work.'

'Nothing compares to having your own firm, Evelyn. I'll be the senior partner.'

Evelyn frowned. 'Yes, but the senior partner of what? I read an article in *Black Enterprise* just the other day about the top black law firms in the country. There are only a few dozen, and they're all much smaller and bring in a lot less money than the firm you work for. That tells you something right there.'

'I saw that. Yes, they're small by comparison. But those firms are doing well enough. A few have thirty to forty partners and associates, with revenues in the millions.'

'But your firm has almost two hundred lawyers. Will they even let partners work part-time?'

'I can negotiate something, I'm sure. It'll be less money, of course.'

'That's what I know. I don't see how we can pay all our bills and a new loan with you working part-time. The only real money we have saved is Andre and Rebecca's college savings plan. You aren't thinking of using that, are you? Because we can't touch that.'

He shook his head. 'Of course not. You think I would risk that?'

'You're willing to risk the house.'

He dropped the pencil on the table and inhaled deeply, then released the air slowly. 'I keep telling you, it's not a risk. I've gone over everything on paper a thousand times the past few weeks. You make enough to cover the bills, with me working part-time. We'll just have to cut back on the extras, like big summer vacations and new things for the house. I wish we had held off on that new car. The Volvo was running fine.'

'Now you're ready to take my Mercedes.'

'Nobody's talking about selling your car.'

'We would have to if we couldn't make ends meet, Kevin. And we wouldn't be able to add to the college fund.'

'You keep bringing that up. Andre's thirteen, Rebecca's only eight. We have plenty of time to save for their college educations.'

'College costs a fortune these days. And I wasn't going to bring this up, but what about our plans to start saving to buy a bigger house, maybe in Potomac, in a few years?'

'We would still be able to do that. Eventually.'

'That's what I mean. It would take forever if we go through with this.'

'So what? This house is fine. You thought it was a dream come true when we moved here seven years ago.'

Evelyn shrugged her shoulders. 'It was then. You had just finished law school and started working at the firm. But it's nothing compared to living in Potomac or Bethesda or some of those places. And now that you've made partner we can afford them.'

'You make it sound like we'll be living in poverty for the rest of our lives. It's not like things will be tight forever.'

23

She placed her plate on the table and sat down across from him. 'And how long do you think they'll be tight?'

'It's hard to say.'

'That's what I know. That's part of the problem.'

'A year. Two at the most.'

Evelyn shook her head. 'It'll be longer than that, Kevin. It takes a very long time to get a law firm going. And that's if it's successful. What if it fails?'

'It won't. Trust me, Evelyn. I'm not going into this blindly. Jeremy and I have looked at everything carefully. We've talked to a couple of others about coming in with us. I know we can make it work.'

'And who's this Jeremy?'

'I told you, Jeremy Malone. Another attorney at the firm. Started in June. He was with a firm in Chicago before he moved here. You met him at the office picnic this summer. You don't remember?'

Evelyn frowned.

'He can't be all that hard to remember,' Kevin said. 'He's the only other black partner in the firm.'

Evelyn nodded. 'I remember now. How much is he supposed to be putting up?'

'The same as everybody else.'

'Well, how much is that? You haven't told me much of anything.'

'Only because you haven't seemed interested. Whenever I try to bring it up, you've got a million other things to do.'

'Well, I'm listening now.'

'If we get four people on board to start, about twenty-five thousand a piece.'

'That's an awful lot of money. Is anyone else thinking of getting a second mortgage on their house?'

'Jeremy made some money when he sold his house back in Chicago. He's using that.'

'And he's not buying a new one here? How does his wife feel about that?'

'He's divorced. She got her half from the sale of the house.'

24

'Mmm. I just don't understand why you want to do this. Maybe if we were younger and just starting out, but we're not. I don't want to risk everything at this point on some –'

'I told you, it's not a risk.'

'You keep saying that, but that's not the way I see it.'

'I keep hoping you'll come around. It means a lot to me.'

'I know. That's why it's hard for me to just come out and say no.'

'Is that your answer – no?'

She looked down at her plate and picked at a slice of tomato with her fork.

He stood up. 'Fine.' He walked to the back door.

'Where are you going?'

'Out to rake the leaves.'

'But it's almost dark now.'

'So I'll rake them in the dark.' He opened the door and a draft blew across her shoulders.

'You need a sweater,' she said.

He didn't say anything, just quietly closed the door behind him. She looked down at the plate of cold lamb and wondered why she wasn't hungry anymore.

4

Beverly couldn't remember ever being so pumped up. She didn't know if the thumping in her chest was fear or excitement. Probably a lot of both. Her heart had started beating wildly the minute she pulled up near Vernon's apartment and saw his BMW sitting there.

She cracked open the car window. The weatherman had said it was supposed to get cold tonight, down to the thirties, but it felt so hot sitting in this car that she was starting to sweat. She fumbled through her bag in the darkness until she found three big hairpins. She placed the bent ends of the pins between her lips, reached back and twisted her long brown hair into a knot at the back of her head, and secured it in place with the pins. She opened the window a few more inches. The cool night breeze felt good blowing across her face and neck.

She tried to prepare her mind for what she was about to do by concentrating on the BMW parked in the next block. At twilight, it had seemed to change colors, from green to blue. Now, in the moonlight, it gave off an eerie glow, much like the silver blade of the knife lying on the seat beside her. Or was it on the dashboard now? She'd moved the damn thing between the seat and the dashboard so many times, she was never sure where it was. She glanced down. The knife sat there on the passenger seat, only its blade visible in the darkness.

She looked back toward the BMW. It was now or never, she reasoned. She reached for the knife, paused, then pulled her hand back and wrapped her coat around her tightly. She was starting to feel cold now, so she shut the window. A few more minutes, she thought, hugging herself against the chill. She needed just a little more time to plan this thing carefully so she wouldn't get caught. Not that it would fool Vernon. He'd figure

26

out who was responsible the minute he saw his convertible top slashed to shreds. But he wouldn't be able to prove anything unless she was careless enough to slip up and let someone see her.

She had worked everything out in her mind down to the last detail. Since this was a dead end street few cars drove by. Only two had approached since she'd been sitting there in her little Mazda Protege, and they both seemed to be people who lived on the block, probably coming home late from work. The last person she'd seen was an older woman who'd come out of Vernon's apartment building and walked her dog around the block. The street was so quiet that if she hadn't been so busy planning the details she would have dozed off long ago. She'd been sitting there for more than two hours, waiting for it to get dark and trying to get up enough nerve to go through with this thing.

The BMW was parked across the street from Vernon's apartment complex, in front of a single-family house. She figured she would stand on the side of the car facing the curb and away from the apartment building. That way, if someone came out of the building or a car came down the street, she could duck out of sight. The house nearest the car was dark, and she would just have to gamble that no one was home. If someone came out of one of the other houses, she'd have time to run around the BMW and hide on the other side before they saw her. She wished she'd changed into her Reeboks. These heels would slow her down.

She glanced up and down the street one final time. Then she picked up the knife, dropped it in her shoulder bag, and opened the car door. Just as she put her foot on the pavement, a bright light flashed behind her, and she looked into the rearview mirror. Two headlights were coming her way. Shit. She quickly closed the door and slid down in the seat, throwing her bag onto the passenger seat. She could see the headlights creeping slowly toward her. After a few seconds the lights passed, and the car continued toward the dead end. She stretched up on her elbows and peeked out over the dashboard. The car had stopped. Those dummies must be lost, she thought. She wished they'd get a move on. The backup lights came on as she watched, and the car began to crawl back in her direction. She ducked down as it continued on past her and back down the block. Then she sat up and watched it in her rearview mirror. At the intersection it stopped, turned around, and headed down another street.

She let out a long, deep breath. The sound of the air echoed through the dark silence, and she realized just how tense she was. She sat up and leaned her head back on the headrest, but only for a moment.

She opened the door and stepped out. She tried not to make too much noise as she shut the door, then she crossed the street to the sidewalk and walked toward the BMW. Her heels clacked loudly on the pavement, so she tried to soften her step by putting her toes down first. This slowed her down, but she reasoned it was better than all the noise.

As she got closer to the house nearest the BMW, she noticed that a light was on in a back room. She stopped dead in her tracks. If one of the neighbors saw her, that was it. They would definitely phone the police. She could see the headlines in the *Washington Post* now. SCORNED WOMAN CAUGHT SLASHING BOYFRIEND'S CONVERTIBLE TOP. She twisted her mouth. Don't be silly, she thought. The *Post* had better things to write about. Still, if word got out, it might cost her her job as an editor at the *Environmental Review* magazine. Everyone, including her family and friends, would think she'd just plain flipped. Some of her girlfriends would probably cheer her, but they'd still think she had gone a little batty and would probably talk about her behind her back.

She looked at the car. She was not more than five feet from the rear. It was small and low, so the top would be easy to reach. But could she get away with it? Was it worth the risk? Yes, yes, yes. Hell, yes. She could already feel how the anger would lift from her body as she plunged the knife in and ripped it through the fabric. All she had to do was walk up, jab the knife into the hood a few times, run back to her car, and

28

take off. She wouldn't see Vernon's face when he saw the damage, but, boy oh boy, could she imagine the horror on it.

She reached for her shoulder bag, but her hand slapped against the side of her leather coat. She felt on the other side. No bag there either. She lifted both arms and looked down. Nothing. She whirled around on her heels and looked down the street. It was too dark to see the ground clearly, but she was sure she hadn't dropped the bag anywhere. Well, almost sure. She realized now that she'd been in such a daze as she'd walked toward the car that she could barely recall getting there. Then she remembered her coat pockets. Maybe she'd put the knife there. She gripped them both at once, then shoved her hands inside. Empty.

How stupid, she thought. How asinine. She threw her hands up in the air. Not only had she lost the knife, her bag was missing. She had about fifty dollars in the bag, but more important than that were her driver's license, credit cards, and goodness knew what else. She looked at the BMW. She was so close she hated to have to turn back now. But she had no choice. She couldn't do a thing with her bare hands.

She retraced her steps down the street, scanning the ground for her bag with each step. She crossed over to her Mazda and looked around, then stooped on her hands and knees to look underneath the car but couldn't see a thing in the dark. As she stood up and brushed off her hands, she felt a ripple slide down her leg. She looked to see a big fat run in the front of her stocking, extending from the knee to her ankle. Oh, that's just perfect, she thought. A ten-dollar pair of hose ruined the first time she wore them.

She approached the door on the driver's side, praying that the bag was inside. She grabbed the door handle and pulled, but the door didn't budge. A sharp pain shot up from the pit of her stomach to her breast. Oh, Jeez! She tugged at the door again. Nothing. She ran around the back of the car to the passenger side and yanked the handle. It didn't budge an inch. She bent down, put her head up to the window, and squinted to see inside. There, lying on the passenger seat, was her bag.

29

She could even see the tip of the knife blade protruding from the top, glowing in the dark. She also saw her car keys dangling from the ignition.

She straightened up, whirled around, and fell back against the side of the car. What a mess. Here she was standing outside Vernon's apartment, locked out of her car in the middle of the night while he was in there screwing the panties off some bitch. Jeez. She wanted to turn around and kick the car, but the way her luck was running, she'd probably break her foot. How had she gotten herself into such a jam over some no-good two-timing man?

She straightened up and looked down the street at the apartment building. She'd thought Vernon was different when they met, that he was special. He had the best body of any man she'd ever dated. Broad, muscular shoulders, slim waist and hips. Beautiful copper complexion. When he showed up at her office door in his suit and tie with an article on blacks and the environment, she thought the angels had sent him from heaven. He'd just started working as an engineer for an environmental firm in the city. He'd grown up in Charlottesville, a small city in Virginia. That was another big plus right there. The native D.C. men were so rotten. She was fed up with their shaky asses, and Vernon had seemed like a breath of fresh air. He had a corny little Southern accent, but she decided she could overlook that. Easily. Here was a good-looking country boy come to the city to seek his fortune, and she was lucky enough to be one of the first women he met.

She showed him the ropes of the big city, even helped him pick out his apartment. It wasn't long before he was buying all his clothes in Georgetown, and she had never thought anyone could drop an accent so fast. The only problem was keeping him away from all the hungry women in town, no small feat in a city where black women heavily outnumbered decent black men.

He didn't take her when he picked out the BMW last month. Maybe he took the little whore he was cozying up to now. Well, the sister could have him. She was through with this mess. But before she made her exit, she was going to teach him one more lesson about big-city life.

She walked up the street, passed his car, and turned onto the walkway in front of Vernon's apartment building as fast as her heels would carry her. She entered the lobby and climbed the stairs to the second floor, then walked down a long hallway. She banged on his door, then stepped to the side so he couldn't see her through the peephole. A sound came from some-where, but she couldn't be sure it had come from Vernon's apartment. Then she heard a noise that had definitely come from his apartment – the squeak of the cover moving over the peephole. She heard the bolt lock turning and then the door knob. It seemed to take an eternity, but the door finally swung open and Vernon stuck out his head. The color drained slowly from his face. The look of total shock in his eyes was about the sweetest thing she'd seen all evening.

She stood there with her arms folded under her breasts and smiled sweetly up at him. 'Surprised?'

He was wearing the navy bathrobe and leather bedroom slippers she'd bought him for his birthday in August. He pulled the robe tighter across his broad chest and smiled weakly. 'Uh, yeah. You could say that.'

'Going to invite me in?'

He tightened the belt around his waist and glanced quickly inside the apartment. He turned and looked at her with a funny smile on his face. 'Ah, this is really unexpected.'

'I'll bet it is.' She tried to push the door open but he reached out and stopped her. He stepped into the hallway and closed the door behind him, oh so very softly.

'This isn't a good time, Beverly.'

'How long did you think you could get away with this shit?'

'With what?'

'You know what I'm talking about. All the lies.'

'I haven't been lying. I'm –'

'Then why don't you let me in?' She tried to step around him but he spread both arms and rested his hands on the door jambs. The robe fell away from his chest, but instead of

31

arousing her as something like that normally would, it only made her angrier. The beautiful body she had once thought was all hers, wasn't. It felt like the ground had suddenly been snatched out from under her feet. By another woman.

'Who is she?' she asked, backing away, trying to keep her composure.

He dropped his arms and tightened his jaws.

'Someone who works with you?'

'No.'

'Then who is she? And don't lie to me, Vernon.'

'She's from my hometown.'

'From Charlottesville?'

He nodded.

Beverly paused, trying to remember what he'd told her when they first started seeing each other about an old girlfriend from back home. She recalled something about a woman named Harriet or Heather or something. 'So you were lying when you said you broke up with your old girlfriend.'

'No I wasn't. We did break up.' He pointed his thumb toward the door. 'This visit was totally unexpected.'

Beverly's eyes narrowed. 'You mean she just popped up unannounced?'

He nodded and shoved his hands into the robe pockets. 'She was waiting in the lobby downstairs when I got home from work.'

Maybe he was telling the truth. Beverly wanted so much to believe him, but that was no excuse for lying to her. 'Why didn't you tell me that when you called instead of lying about working late?'

'Because I knew you wouldn't understand. I figured it would be better for you not to know. At least not until I had more time to explain it to you.'

'Well, now you've explained it. Tell her to leave. Tell her you have other plans.'

'I can't just kick her out.'

'Why not?'

'Because she drove nearly three hours to get here, that's why. She's got nowhere else to stay.'

Beverly threw her arms in the air. 'Send her to a damn hotel.'

Vernon took a deep breath of air and rubbed his hand across the top of his forehead as if trying to figure out the best way to deal with her. That was when she noticed that his hair, cut very close on the sides, a little longer and curly on top, was looking curlier than usual. The only time Beverly had seen his hair looking like that was when she ran her fingers through it. And the only time she did that was when they made love.

She fixed her eyes on him, on the little curls on top of his head, the bathrobe, the bare chest. Only putting her up for the night, huh? Then why was he half naked? Why was he letting the bitch run her claws through his head? The juices in her stomach started to boil.

'Look, why don't you just go back to your place,' he said. He reached out and touched her arm. 'I'll call you . . .'

She slapped his hand away. 'If you expect me to just go home and forget about this, to sit around waiting by the phone until you finish screwing your old girlfriend, then you're a bigger fool than I've been.'

'There's nothing going on here. I'm just putting her up for the night.'

'If nothing's going on, why can't you let me in?'

'Because you're all worked up. Look at you. What happened to your panty hose?'

'What happened to your hair?'

'My hair?'

'Someone's obviously had their hands in it.'

He looked away. 'I don't know what you're talking about.'

'Why can't you just come out and say you're seeing someone else, Vernon? Instead of doing all this lying.'

'Because I'm not seeing anyone else.'

'Oh, please, Vernon. I don't want to hear any more of your bull. The only thing I want now is to use your phone.'

'My phone?'

33

'Yes. I'm locked out of my car. And I don't want a lot of questions about how it happened. Just let me use the phone to call triple A. After they come, I'm gone. For good.'

'I definitely don't think it's a good idea for you to use my phone now.'

'I'll just go in the kitchen, use the phone, and come right back out. I'm not going to do anything crazy. I got that out of my system before I came up here.'

'What do you mean, you got that out of your system?' He looked at her suspiciously. 'How'd you get locked out of your car?'

'Just let me use the phone, Vernon.'

He shook his head with finality. 'I can't do that.'

'You're going to leave me stranded in the middle of the night?'

'There's a phone in the lobby. Or give me the number and I'll call triple A for you.'

'And what am I supposed to do until they come? Stand outside and freeze to death? It can take them as long as an hour.'

'Wait near your car. They prefer that you wait near the car, anyway.'

Beverly stared at him as if he was turning into a monster right before her eyes.

'Or you can wait in the lobby,' he said.

She turned on her heels and walked away.

'Where are you going?' he called after her.

She kept walking down the hallway.

'Do you want me to call triple A for you or not?'

She turned and yelled at the top of her lungs. 'The only thing I want you to do is go to hell, you cold bastard.'

She opened the door to the stairwell and ran down the steps.

The sound of the front door shutting woke Charmaine, and she opened her eyes to see Arsenio Hall doing his stand-up comedy act on the portable television screen and the light from

34

the pole lamp next to her bed glaring in her face. Hmmph. It was about time he got here, she thought, struggling to a sitting position in the double bed. She puffed up the pillows beneath her tired back, then reached for the remote control and snapped the television off.

She lit a Salem Light and listened as her husband moved around downstairs. Her bones were so weary she wasn't even sure she still wanted to get into a discussion with Clarence tonight. It would probably just turn into an argument. She'd worked until seven that evening, gone home to change, then picked up Kenny at her mother's. She'd gotten back home around 9:30 and put Kenny to bed, but it took an hour to get him to go to sleep because his sinuses were all clogged up. Then she'd straightened up the living and dining rooms a bit. It was a small house, and any little bit of clutter looked a mess. Now she was plain worn out. But she was up, so she figured she might as well get this over with. Besides, it was no telling when she would see the man again.

He came in the bedroom with one of his brown More cigarettes dangling from his lips and walked straight to his chest of drawers. 'You still up?' he said, emptying his pockets of keys and coins and dumping them in a pile on top. She could hear it scattering across the wood chest. She'd bought him a little tray just to hold that stuff, but he never used it. He just dumped it all up there in a heap. She'd just straightened it up that evening, putting his papers and gadgets away in the drawers, and now he was messing it all up again. But she didn't say a word. It would only start an argument and she already had enough to fuss about. 'What does it look like? Yeah, I'm up, even though I don't want to be. But it's the only way to catch you, and we got to have a talk.'

He put his cigarette out and turned to face her, smiling. 'Sounds like I'm in trouble again.'

She ignored his little joke. 'I got a call today from a bill collector.'

He twisted his face into a grimace and sat on the foot of the bed to remove his shoes and socks, his back facing her.

'Don't you even want to know what they called about?' she asked.

'Not particularly.'

'I know you don't. Our credit's a joke and you don't even care.'

'It's not that, Charm. Those assholes always calling and hassling people.'

'Not if you pay your bills, fool. Do you even know which bill they called about?'

He pulled out his shirttail and started unbuttoning his shirt. She smashed her cigarette out in the ashtray on the night table, then kicked at him from beneath the covers. 'You heard me. You got so many overdue bills out there you don't even know which one it is, do you?' She kicked at him again.

'Quit kicking me, woman. I know what it was.'

'Which one was it, then?'

'The one for the big TV downstairs. Satisfied?'

'Hmmph. That was just a lucky guess.'

'It was not a lucky guess. I know 'cause that's the only bill I didn't pay this month.'

'You're lying, Clarence. We got a notice today from Hecht's. I'm surprised you didn't sneak in here to get it before I got home.'

'I paid that bill earlier this week. They must have sent that notice out before they got the money.'

'Don't jive me, Clarence.'

'I'm not jiving. I paid it, and I'll pay the TV bill, too.'

'When?'

'When I get paid week after next.'

'They want the money now. They wanted it months ago. You haven't paid on the thing since you took it out the store.'

'That's not true. I —'

'That's what the man said when he called. You owe ninety-nine bucks and they want it now.'

'Well, I can't pay it now. Can't pay it before the library pays me, can I?'

'You just got paid this week. What the hell did you do with all that money?'

'What do you think I did with it? I paid bills. Shit. You got lights on over your head, don't you? And the heat's running.'

'That's only about a hundred dollars this time of year, fool. I don't understand it. I've never seen anybody blow money the way you do.'

He stood up and stretched. 'I don't know why we have to go through this every month.'

''Cause you don't ever pay your bills, you lazy bum, that's why. When you going to grow up?'

He walked toward the door. 'Turn out the lights and get some shut-eye. I'll take care of it.'

'I'm not finished with you. Where are you going?'

'To take a leak if that's all right with you.'

'Have you heard anything I've said? What about the TV bill?'

He frowned impatiently. 'I said I'll pay it. How many fucking times do I have to say it?'

'But they need it now. Not in two weeks.'

'I'll send it Monday.'

'Where you going to get the money by Monday?'

'Guess I'll have to rob a bank. Anything to get you to shut your damn mouth.'

'You think I'm jiving, don't you? That this is all a big joke. But I'm dead serious. If you can't pay it, we should just return the TV. We don't need that big old thing anyway. You hardly ever watch it.'

'We're not returning no TV. I like the big screen for the games on Sunday. I'll get some money from one of my sisters or somebody this weekend.'

'For your sake, I sure hope you telling the truth for once in your life, 'cause I'm going to tell you something else. I am sick and tired of you buying things and not paying and then having to pay myself. And I'm not putting up with this shit any longer. I want to go back to school one of these days. And I –'

37

Clarence chuckled. 'You just talking. You been saying that crap about going back to get your degree ever since I met you. Ain't done a damn thing about it.'

Charmaine glared at him. 'You make it impossible, wasting every penny I make.'

'You don't need to go back to no school. You make enough money.'

'You think I want to be a secretary for the rest of my life? Or live in this house? That's your problem, Clarence – you don't have a drop of ambition. All you want to do is run the streets, but you keep it up and you'll find yourself living out there.'

'I know, I know.' He left the room.

'You think I'm jiving, don't you?' she shouted after him.

She plopped her head down and pulled up the bed covers. 'We'll see about that,' she muttered into the pillow. 'Your butt will be out on the sidewalk so fast . . . you'll be taking those leaks in a gutter somewhere.'

She was so tired she dozed off almost the second her head hit the pillow. But a few minutes later, she felt Clarence's hands on her ass under the covers. She reached back and pushed them away. 'Stop it. I'm tired.'

He wrapped his arms around her waist and pulled her toward him. 'Come here, Goldy.'

'I mean it, Clarence. And stop calling me that.' He always called her Goldy when he was in a playful mood though she never understood why since nothing about her was yellow. She had brown hair, brown eyes, a brown complexion. So she always pretended not to like it, but a part of her thought it was affectionate.

He tugged at her. 'C'mon, Charm, it's Friday. I don't get to see you much.'

She protested with her mouth but didn't resist much with her body as he turned her to face him. 'And whose fault is that?' she said, looking at him.

'I'm trying real hard to make up for it now.'

'It would take a century.'

'Then we better get us started.'

38

He planted wet kisses on her neck and slid his fingers down the length of her nightgown. Then he slipped his hand underneath the gown and ran his fingers up her leg to the inside of her thigh. He was lazy, undependable, and immature, but he sure knew what buttons to push to get her juices flowing. It was about the only thing the man was good for, so if she was going to be married to him, she might as well enjoy it. She would just have to be sure to remember to get up and put that diaphragm in before things heated up too much. He had a way of making her forget to do that. Probably on purpose, since he wanted to have a baby anyway. She just hoped it wasn't already too late to be using the damn thing.

5

Evelyn plunged the shovel deep into the earth and turned the soil. Kevin came up behind her with a big sack of manure and sprinkled a generous portion over the hole. They had been working together on the garden for nearly two hours, since nine that morning, and had reached the last corner. Evelyn turned, Kevin dumped.

She loved working the vegetable garden in the fall, loved feeling the cool, dry air on her face and the satisfaction of enriching the soil. In the winter, she planted seeds indoors and watched over them anxiously until it was time to set them out in the spring. But the greatest joy was in summer. Hers was the biggest vegetable garden in the area, and friends and neighbors from all over stopped by to see the fat red tomatoes, shiny green bell peppers, and luscious golden squash. And each year she planted something a little unusual. This year it was pumpkins that she gave away to a few of the neighbors just before Halloween. They'd gotten a big kick out of that. Next summer she was going to try a fruit, probably cantaloupe since she'd heard they were the easiest of the melons.

Kevin missed a small area with the manure, and Evelyn stopped digging and pointed with her foot. 'You missed that spot.'

'I got it,' Kevin said, moving on.

'It needs more.'

He went back to the spot and dumped on more manure. When he finished, Evelyn turned it over with the shovel. Kevin dropped the sack on the ground and clapped his hands together to brush off the dirt. 'Whew,' he said, arching his back to stretch the muscles. 'I don't see where you get so much energy.'

'Don't just stand there,' she said, turning over the soil in the

40

last corner. 'Or we'll be late leaving for my mother's. It needs to be smoothed over with the rake.'

'I'm going in for a minute. I need to make a phone call before we go to your mother's.'

'Come on, Kevin. I need your help out here so we can get ready to leave.'

'You're doing fine,' he said, walking toward the house. 'I'll come back when I get off the phone if you're not finished.'

She stopped digging and looked at him, squinting in the bright fall sunlight. 'Who do you have to call that's so urgent?'

'Jeremy,' he answered without stopping.

She bent over and picked up a big stone with her gloved hand and tossed it out in the yard. 'What are you planning to tell him?' When he didn't answer, she turned and looked across the lawn. He was already halfway to the house. 'Try not to be on the phone long,' she yelled after him. 'We need to finish this so we can get dressed and leave.'

She removed a glove and wiped the perspiration from her forehead. She hoped he was calling Jeremy to say he wouldn't be going through with the plans to start a law firm of their own. Kevin hadn't said a word about it since the night before, and she thought it best not to bring it up herself. She had long since learned he was not the kind of man who could be pushed. The independence and determination that she admired in him could turn into downright stubbornness when he thought he was being pressured. The best thing to do was wait while he worked it out himself and hope he came to the right conclusion. Besides, he already knew how she felt about the idea.

But sitting by quietly, hoping he made the right decision, was tough. The thought that he was even thinking of taking such a big chance with their lives scared her silly. They had come so far. They weren't *black* middle class, they were *middle class*. And if all went well, they'd soon be upper middle class. How could he think of jeopardizing things now? It was something she'd wanted ever since her parents moved the family from D.C. to the suburbs, and she discovered how whites and

41

a few lucky blacks lived. Even though it had been a step up for them, the Jordan house was the smallest in the neighborhood. Evelyn had resolved that her family would one day have one of the finest homes around.

Kevin wanted the same things, so she just had to be patient. His family was important to him, and sooner or later he would realize that this idea of his wasn't right for them.

Charmaine turned off the vacuum cleaner and put it in the living-room closet, back behind all the coats and boots. Then she went around the room and started picking up things — a sweater, a hat, yesterday's newspaper. She emptied the cigarette butts from the ashtrays. She had just straightened up the night before, picking up Kenny's toy soldiers and trucks from the floor. Now it was the things Clarence had left lying around after he came in last night. It was like she had two four-year-olds instead of one, the only difference being that when she asked Kenny to pick up his things, he did it. That was what she got for marrying a bum who had four older sisters and whose mother did everything for him. Not to mention all the ex-girlfriends and live-in lovers. Bottom line: He was a spoiled rotten, lazy, good-for-nothing fool.

She'd tried to get him out of his sloppy habits once. For five whole days she'd refused to pick up after his lazy ass. It hadn't done a bit of good. After his morning shower, he always dropped his towel in the most convenient spot — on top of the clothes hamper, on the bathroom floor, anywhere except on the towel rack. The week she went on strike, whenever he went into the bathroom and didn't see his towel folded nice and neatly on the rack, courtesy of his little cleaning fairy, he just went to the linen closet and got a fresh one. Every day. Twice a day. They ended up with five days' worth of muggy towels lying around on the bathroom floor.

It was pretty much the same thing all around the house. Clothes on the backs of chairs, dirty dishes all over the kitchen table and countertops. And he never emptied an ashtray. She originally planned to try her no-cleaning experiment for seven days but after five she couldn't stand the mess anymore. It took a whole weekend to get the house back in shape. They say a lot of men are color-blind. Well, Clarence was dirt-blind.

She picked up his jacket from the seat of the armchair in the living room, where he'd dropped it when he'd come home the night before, and shoved it into the closet. All of them were so tiny they were stuffed to the point of bursting, mostly with Clarence's things. She looked inside a small paper bag from an auto shop that was lying on the glass table in the dining room. It was empty. 'Shit,' she muttered aloud, crumpling the bag up in her fist. Clarence had taken out whatever he bought and dumped the bag on the table. What the hell did he think was going on around here? That the table was a trash can? That the whole house was his private dump and she was his personal maid? Here she was straightening up after that lazy bum and he was still in bed. And it was after eleven o'clock. She turned on her heels and marched through the house to the stairs. She took them two at a time.

She paused at Kenny's room and stuck her head in the door to see what he was up to. As she expected, he was on the floor making another mess with his toy cars, trucks, and airplanes.

'I'll be back in a minute to help you get dressed to go to Grandma Pearl's house. Okay?'

Kenny nodded without ever taking his eyes and hands off his toys. She walked down the hallway into her bedroom and right up to the bed. Clarence was lying on his back, fast asleep, his mustached mouth hanging open just a bit and snoring loud enough to wake the dead. He wore only his shorts to bed, and the covers were turned back enough to expose the top half of his bronze-colored chest. He looked so cute lying there that she almost changed her mind about what she planned to do. Almost. He didn't look cute enough to change it completely. An angel when he was sleeping, a devil when he was awake.

She pulled the quilt off the bed and dropped it in a heap onto a chair. Clarence didn't budge. She couldn't believe it. The man was in such a deep sleep that he didn't even feel it.

She grabbed the sheet and pulled to free it from under the edges of the bed. This time, Clarence jumped and opened his eyes.

'What the hell are you doing, woman? You crazy or something?' He reached for an end of the sheet, but she yanked it out of his reach before he could grab it. Charmaine couldn't help but giggle at the look of frustration on his groggy face. 'I'm washing the sheets.'

'Can't you see I'm sleeping on 'em?'

'It's after eleven o'clock,' she said, dropping the sheet on top of the quilt. She picked up her pillow and shook off the cover. 'Way past time for any decent human being to be sleep.'

'Ah, woman.' He turned onto his side, his back to her, and folded his arms around his bare chest.

'Get up out of that bed, Clarence.'

He closed his eyes and buried his face deeper into his pillow. She dropped her bare pillow on the bed and walked around to his side of the bed. She reached for his pillow and yanked it from underneath him. He opened his eyes and lunged after her, but she jumped out of his reach. She backed away and shook the pillow from its cover, then threw the pillow at him. 'Shit. I'm working my butt off and you got your lazy ass in that bed like there's no tomorrow.'

He smiled sheepishly and stretched his long, muscular body across the bed.

'God, you're one lazy bum,' she said.

'I'm not lazy. Hell, you go to bed at nine o'clock every night. I guess you're not tired.'

'How would you know when I go to bed? You're never here.'

'I'm here now, ain't I?' He sat up on the edge of the bed and rubbed his eyes.

'I want you to wash my car before we go to Ma's house.'

'It's too cold to be washing some damn car. Besides, I got to do some work on my car today. It's not running right.'

'You don't have time to be starting that stuff. You get to working on that dumb car of yours and you'll never stop. I have to be over at my mama's by two o'clock.'

'Go ahead. I'm not stopping you.'

'Clarence. You said you were going with me.'

'That was before my car started acting up.'

'That stupid car's always acting up. I don't know why you don't get rid of that piece of junk.'

He stood up. 'You going to give me the money for a new one?'

'You not getting a dime out of me.' She picked up the sheets and pillowcases.

'Then shut up about it. I got to work on my car or I won't have nothing to get to work in next week.'

'You mean you won't have nothing to run the streets in.'

He waved his hand at her and walked toward the door.

'Clarence, work on your car tomorrow. It's Daddy's birthday today. I wanted us to go as a family.'

He stopped and turned to face her. 'I know, but I need to go over to Lemuel's and do the work in his garage. He's got the tools I need, and he won't be home tomorrow. Besides, I got to get some parts and the store's closed on Sundays.'

She waved him away. 'Go on then, you always got some excuse whenever I want you to do something.'

He sighed. 'Look, I'll wash your car before I go over to Lem's, okay?'

'I wish you'd come with me. Everybody will be looking for you.'

'It can't be helped, baby.'

'Can you try to finish up at Lem's early and stop by Mama's on your way back?'

'I don't think so. I got to get parts. I'll probably be most of the day.'

'You could try.'

'Okay, okay. I'll try.'

'And don't forget to get the money for the TV bill from your sister or whoever you supposed to be getting it from.'

'Yeah, yeah.'

45

6

Somewhere between the state of waking and cracking her eyelids open, the previous evening whizzed through Beverly's brain. Driving to Vernon's building, locking the keys in the car like an idiot, confronting him, pacing the lobby until triple A came to rescue her. She pushed her eyes open all the way. Everything was so vivid, it felt like it had happened just minutes earlier instead of a whole night's sleep ago. She'd acted like someone else – wild and crazy. Getting locked out of her car was probably just what she deserved for thinking about cutting up somebody's convertible top. What if she'd gone through with it? Jeez. The cops would probably be banging on her door right now. Just the thought of it made her stomach turn.

She moved from her side onto her back and realized she had an awful cramp in her neck, probably from sleeping so fitfully. She rubbed it, staring up at the ceiling. There was something else, something she was supposed to remember. She frowned, focusing on the light globe in the ceiling, trying to think what it was. Then it hit her. The family get-together was today. Ma was having a big celebration for Daddy's sixty-fifth birthday, and the whole extended family would be there. The house would be filled with grandparents, aunts and uncles, cousins, even a few distant cousins.

She was almost scared to look at the clock on the bedside table. She knew it was shamefully late, and she always felt guilty about sleeping past nine on weekends. She turned her body toward the clock, being careful not to twist her neck. Jeez. Two-thirty already. She'd slept almost thirteen hours but it felt more like thirteen minutes.

She inhaled deeply and let the air out. Everyone was starting

46

to arrive at her parents' by now. There was a time when she loved these family get-togethers, all the laughing, teasing and joking, the storytelling. No matter where they were held, the routine was always pretty much the same. The men would have drinks and talk about politics and the Redskins while the women prepared the food. The adult cousins would get a game of Bid Whist going, and the kids would run around the house playing games. Everybody would ooh and aah over how much they'd grown, and at about four o'clock they would all drop everything and eat, buffet style. Grandma and a few lucky others got chairs and tables. The rest would sit on armrests, the stairs, and footstools, balancing plates piled high with fried chicken and ham, sweet potatoes baked with marshmallows, macaroni and cheese, garden salad, kale and collards, and the prize of every feast, Ma's homemade rolls.

She wondered if cousin Sylvia would be there – Beverly hadn't seen her in over a year. Last she'd heard, Sylvia was back from Los Angeles after taking her kids and running off with some man from out there. They were supposed to get married, but that never happened, and now Sylvia was back in D.C., living with her parents. Beverly had twenty-three cousins, fifteen within eight years of her in age, and they were an interesting bunch to say the least. When they were little, they always had a ball running around the house and yard of whoever was hosting the get-together. As they got older, they'd bet each other about who would be the first to marry, the first to have kids. Sylvia won, since she got married and had a baby right after high school. And one by one, all the others followed. In June, little Jamie, the youngest of the group, tied the knot. His wife was already pregnant. Little Jamie! He was only twenty-one, eight years younger than Beverly. She could remember holding him on her lap not long after he was born.

She sat up slowly and slid her legs over the edge of the bed. The cramp bit into her neck whenever she turned it or put any kind of strain on it. She rubbed it some more and slid her feet into a pair of old slippers at the side of her bed. She had a mind to skip this get-together. She didn't know why they even bothered inviting her anymore, her life was so different from theirs now. All they seemed to do these days was sit around talking about whether cloth diapers were better than disposable ones. What the hell did she care about stuff like that? Do what's right for the environment or whatever, but why spend an hour yakking about it?

She went down the hall to the bathroom and turned on the hot water full blast, adding just a trickle of cold. She liked her bathwater steaming hot, the kind where you had to ease in gingerly, toes first. She tucked her hair into a shower cap to keep it from frizzing up in the steam, then stepped into the tub. That was the easy part. She lowered herself in very slowly. The water was so hot it made her bottom tingle, and she sat there stiffly for the few seconds she knew it would take for her body to adjust, for the water to go from stinging to soothing. Then she sat back and rested her head on the tile wall, being careful not to strain her sore neck.

The only problem about skipping the get-together was that she would feel guilty about missing Daddy's birthday party. But then, his birthday wasn't actually until Tuesday. She could take his present over that evening after work and wish him a happy birthday in private, without all the fuss. She already had the present. Vernon had taken her downtown to pick it out last weekend.

Vernon. It always came back to him. She was trying hard not to think about the man, to think of other things, but it was just impossible. He'd been such a big part of her life the past six months. Hell, he'd been everything. He was even supposed to go with her to the family get-together today. Well, that wouldn't be happening now − she was through with him. Lying and cheating were bad enough, but leaving her stranded outside his apartment in the middle of the night all alone. How could he do that to her?

She picked up the washcloth, held it up over her breasts, and squeezed until all the warm water ran out. She shut her

eyes tightly and swallowed hard. No crying. She was determined about that. She'd done enough boo-hooing over
Michael to last a lifetime. These men weren't worth one more
drop of her precious tears.

The phone rang, and her eyes popped open. Vernon! No, not
Vernon, he was with that woman. But then again, maybe he
wasn't. Maybe she was on her way back to Charlottesville by
now and he was calling to . . . to what?

She decided to stop wondering and get to the phone and
find out. She stood up, threw on her robe – her sore neck all
but forgotten – and ran down the hall in wet feet. She grabbed
the receiver on the fourth ring. 'Hello?'

'Beverly? What are you doing still home, girl?' Charmaine
asked.

The familiar voice felt like a ton of bricks landing on her bare
toes.

'Beverly, you still there?' Charmaine asked.

'I'm here.' Beverly plopped down on the edge of the bed.
She was probably fooling herself thinking Vernon would call
after the way she'd acted last night.

'Why you all outta breath?' Charmaine asked.

'I was in the tub when the phone rang.'

'You're just getting dressed? When were you planning to get
your behind over here?'

'Maybe never. I don't feel so hot.'

'What's wrong?'

'Just tired I guess.'

'That's no reason to miss Daddy's birthday party, girl. Take a
couple aspirin and get on over here. Everybody's been asking
for you.'

Beverly started to protest but then she heard her mother's
voice in the background. Her parents would be very disappointed if she didn't go. 'She's fine, Ma,' Charmaine said away
from the receiver. 'Just tired or something. Okay.' Charmaine
put her mouth back to the receiver. 'Beverly, Ma wants to talk
to you for a minute. Hold on.'

Beverly braced herself for what she knew was coming. Their

mama always worried when one of them wasn't feeling one hundred percent.

'What's wrong, Beverly? You coming down with something?'

'No, Ma. I'm just a little tired, that's all.'

'Were you out late last night?'

'Yes, but that's not why I'm tired.'

'Well, if you don't feel like coming, I'll have your father or somebody bring you a plate of food. It would be a shame for you to miss all this good cooking.'

'You don't have to do that, Ma. I'll come.'

'You sure you feel up to it?'

'I'm okay, really.'

'We'll be looking for you, then. Here's Charmaine.'

Beverly heard Charmaine and her mother talking but couldn't understand what they were saying. She thought she heard Vernon's name being mentioned.

'Beverly?'

'Yes?'

'Well, get in the car, girl, and bring Vernon with you. I'm the only one in the family who's met him so far.'

'No.'

'No, what? No, you not coming or no, you not going to bring him?'

'He's not coming.'

'Why not? When's everybody going to get to meet him?'

'Probably never.'

'Oops. Guess that's that then. Well, hurry up and get yourself on over here.'

Beverly said good-bye and hung up. Now, how had she managed to talk herself into that? One minute ago she was pretty sure she wasn't going, now she was. Well, maybe it would do her some good. At least it would keep her mind off Vernon.

'I pass,' Beverly said.

'That's all you been doing all evening,' Charmaine said.

50

'What am I supposed to do? I haven't had any decent cards.'

'You were sitting there with two aces last time,' Charmaine said.

'And nothing else.'

'Four,' Sylvia said.

'Umph,' Charmaine said. 'What's the matter with you-all? Five low.'

'I pass,' Jamie said.

'Hearts,' Charmaine said, picking up the kitty. She spread it out on the table. There was one heart, the four. 'Shit.'

'I hope you have something to back that bid up with this time, partner,' Beverly said. 'Last time you couldn't make a four, even with my two aces. I'm getting tired of losing.'

'Don't worry, I got us covered.'

'I hope so, 'cause I don't have a thing to help you with this time.'

'What the hell's this?' Sylvia said, sitting up in her chair.

'Yeah,' Jamie said. 'Quit yakking across the table.'

The four of them sat around a small square table in the back room of the basement, playing Bid Whist. Most of the other members of the family were upstairs.

As Charmaine got her hand together, Beverly and Charmaine's mother came into the room. She picked up the plate at Beverly's elbow. 'Did you get enough to eat, Beverly?'

'Plenty, Ma. I'm about to burst out of these jeans now.' She shouldn't have worn the darn things. She reached under her sweater to undo the snap and was tempted to undo the zipper, too. In her rush to get out of her apartment, she'd forgotten her rule never to wear these tight jeans when she was going to be stuffing her gut. But after the night she'd had, she certainly wasn't in the mood to get all dolled up – even if she was the only family member here in jeans and Keds. Her cousin Sylvia, as usual, had on gobs of makeup and every inch of her hairdo was neatly in place. She'd put on quite a bit of weight since the last time Beverly had seen her, most of it in the hips, but she obviously wasn't trying to hide it. She was dressed in a red wool suit with a short tight skirt, white blouse, and red pumps. Jamie had on a shirt and tie. Charmaine was dressed a little more casually, although in her usual sexy style. She had on leather slacks and a multicolored mohair sweater, both fit to emphasize her shapely figure. Beverly didn't see how Charmaine stayed in such good shape; she was already thirty-five and had a son. Beverly sucked in her tummy and placed a card on the table.

'That the best you can do?' Charmaine asked, turning her nose up at the card.

'I told you I didn't have anything.'

'You got that right,' Jamie said. He stood up and slammed the ace of hearts on the table. Then he picked up the four cards and followed with the joker.

'Whoo!' Sylvia shouted. She and Jamie slapped a high five across the table.

'What you got in that hand over there?' Beverly asked, frowning at her sister.

Charmaine smiled and batted her eyelashes coyly.

'Sure you don't want more to eat?' Beverly's mother asked, picking up Charmaine's empty plate.

'Positive, Ma.'

'How about you, Jamie?'

Jamie sat back and rubbed his stomach. 'Nah. I had about five of your rolls already, Aunt Pearl, and I'm putting on too much weight as it is these days.'

'I noticed you've put on a few pounds,' Beverly said.

Sylvia snickered. 'A few? He's starting to look like the Pillsbury doughboy there.'

Jamie chuckled. 'I don't need you to remind me.'

'Too much of that good home cooking,' Charmaine said.

'Shoot,' Pearl said. 'He could afford to put on a few. He was skinny as a beanpole before.' She carried the pile of plates out of the room.

'How's married life been treating you?' Sylvia asked.

'Fine,' Jamie said. 'I just didn't know getting fat was part of the bargain.'

52

'It shouldn't be,' Charmaine said. 'Especially at your age. What are you? Twenty now?'

'Twenty-one.'

'Still a baby,' Charmaine said. 'You just need to get some exercise. Clarence shoots baskets to stay in shape.'

'What do you do to stay in shape?' Sylvia asked Charmaine.

'Me? Nothing. With some of us it just comes natural.'

'Well, excuse me for asking.'

'It's true,' Charmaine said. 'Beverly doesn't have a weight problem either. Neither does Evelyn. Slimness runs in the family. I don't know why.'

'But I don't look like you do,' Beverly said. 'And I'm starting to get a little bulge. Is this what turning thirty is all about?'

'Where?' Sylvia said, looking at Beverly doubtfully.

Beverly patted her stomach. 'In places I don't need it.'

'Beverly, please,' Sylvia said. 'None of you Jordan women have a weight problem worth speaking about.'

'You don't see it 'cause I suck it in,' Beverly said.

'Girl, if it was a real weight problem you wouldn't be able to suck it in.'

'I used to shoot baskets every weekend, too, before I got married,' Jamie said. 'But Imani won't let me go hardly nowhere without her.'

'C'mon,' Charmaine said. 'She can't mind you getting a little exercise.'

'She don't mind me exercising. She just wants me to do it in the house.'

They all laughed.

'And that's boring,' Jamie said.

'I can't imagine trying to keep that tight a rein on anybody,' Beverly said. 'Or anybody letting someone else keep that tight a rein.'

Jamie shrugged his shoulders. 'Don't want to rock the boat.'

'Ain't that sweet?' Charmaine said teasingly. She reached over and tickled him. He jumped and smacked her hand away.

'They've only been married a few months,' Sylvia said. 'Just wait a while.'

53

'You think things will change?' Beverly asked.

'Shit, yeah,' Sylvia said. 'They're still in the honeymoon phase, but that won't last forever. With my second marriage it took about six months before we were getting on each others' nerves. The first one, we started to bug each other from day one.'

'Pretty soon she'll be glad to get his butt out of the house,' Charmaine said. 'Or he'll get sick and damn tired of her keeping tabs on him.'

This kind of talk always bothered Beverly. She thought something was wrong if you could get so tired of the one you loved. People just chose mates without considering it carefully enough, that was all. 'Maybe they'll have a perpetual honeymoon,' she said.

'Never happen,' Sylvia said.

'No such thing,' Charmaine said.

Beverly didn't want to believe that. 'Look at Evelyn and Kevin.'

'Shoot,' Charmaine said. 'They got problems just like the rest of us do.'

'But they do seem to get along pretty good,' Sylvia said.

'Where's Clarence?' Jamie asked Charmaine. 'Haven't seen him around here.'

'He's working on his car. Said he might stop by later.'

'Which means he's not coming, no doubt.'

At the sound of this new voice, all four of them turned. Evelyn entered the room holding a glass of punch. As usual, she was dressed elegantly, this time wearing gold earrings and a casual but expensive-looking raspberry-colored pantsuit that made the most of her tall, slender frame.

'Who the hell asked you?' Charmaine said, turning back to the card table.

'That's what it usually means when Clarence says he's coming later,' Evelyn said. She pulled up a chair and placed it between Beverly and Sylvia, across from Charmaine.

'Here comes another skinny minny,' Sylvia said sliding over a little for Evelyn. 'I swear, girl, you look like you went and lost weight since I last saw you.'

'She's about the same,' Beverly said. 'Evelyn has been the same height and weight since she was at Smith.'

'Umph,' Sylvia said. 'You-all are disgusting. Where'd you get that outfit, Evelyn?'

'Oh, this? One of the shops out at White Flint Mall. Maybe Ann Taylor. But it's been so long, I'm not sure.'

'For your information,' Charmaine said to Evelyn. 'Clarence is working on his car. And he'll be here if he finishes on time. Unlike some husbands, he doesn't mind getting his hands a little dirty to save some money.' She slung the last card in her hand across the table.

'And what's that supposed to mean?' Evelyn asked.

Charmaine sneered. 'Figure it out. You're the one with all the fancy degrees.'

'Cut it out, you two,' Beverly said. 'We were having a nice little card game a minute ago.'

'Evelyn's right though, Charmaine,' Sylvia said. 'Lately, Clarence hasn't been coming to our get-togethers.'

'How would you know? You been running around in California with some Hispanic dude for a year. Where is he, anyway?'

Sylvia's eyes widened. 'Where the hell did you hear that? He was as black as they come.'

'That's what I heard, that he was Puerto Rican or something.'

Sylvia rolled her eyes skyward. 'I swear, the way news travels through this family. Only problem is it's always wrong. He's part American Indian, but that's from three or four generations ago. And stop trying to change the subject, Charmaine. I been back more than two months now. Aunt Sarah had that cookout when I first got back in August and Clarence didn't come to that. Neither did you, come to think of it.'

'That was just one time we didn't come. Clarence's car broke down and he used mine to run an errand. By the time he got back, it was too late.'

'I don't mean nothing, just wondering.'

'Well, you can stop wondering. We been having a few problems with the car, that's all. No big deal.'

'Get a new one if it's giving you so much trouble,' Evelyn said.

Charmaine rolled her eyes heavenward with exasperation.

'I mean, even a newer used one would probably be better,' Evelyn said. 'If you can't afford a brand-new one.'

Jamie slid down in his seat. 'Uh-oh. Here we go.'

Sylvia laughed a bit nervously.

Charmaine ignored them both. 'That's not the problem. He just likes working on the one he has. Okay?'

'Mmm-hmm,' Evelyn said. She picked up her glass and took a sip. Charmaine folded her arms across her waist. Sylvia and Jamie looked at each other across the table, trying to keep their faces straight.

'Uh, Charmaine,' Beverly said. 'I don't know if you noticed, but we didn't make that bid. Not by a long shot.'

Charmaine didn't say anything, just cut her eyes. Beverly was going to tease her sister about losing another bid, but she could see this was not the time for that. Charmaine was plenty pissed off as it was. Beverly looked around the table at the quiet, downturned faces. 'Whose deal is it?'

'Charmaine's,' Sylvia answered. She gathered the cards and held them out, but Charmaine kept her arms folded, so Sylvia dealt them herself as Jamie's very pregnant wife entered the room, walked over to the table, and gently placed her hands on Jamie's shoulders. 'Jamie, it's after seven. You about ready to go home?'

'One more hand, baby, then we'll leave.'

Imani frowned.

'Okay, okay, we can go now.' He stood up. 'Evelyn, you want to take my hand?'

Charmaine snickered. 'Hmmph. She don't hardly play no Bid Whist.'

Everyone looked at Evelyn.

Evelyn smiled. 'She's right. I don't.'

'See if you can get John to come down when you go up, Jamie,' Beverly said.

'Okay. See you-all later.'

''Bye, Jamie. See you next time, Imani.'

'Never thought I'd see the day Jamie would be henpecked,' Sylvia said after they'd left.

'He's just trying to be a good husband,' Evelyn said.

'Beverly, you missed that cookout at Aunt Sarah's, too.' Sylvia said. 'Where were you?'

'She was in St Thomas with Vernon,' Evelyn answered. 'Where is he, by the way?'

Beverly picked her cards up off the table. They weren't ready to play yet, but she needed a moment to regroup. She'd known the conversation would get around to this topic sooner or later, and on the drive over she'd rehearsed what she would say when it did. A part of her wanted to be brief, to get the subject changed as quickly as possible. Another part wanted to share her pain and frustration. 'He's probably at his place,' she said casually.

'When are we going to get to meet him?' Evelyn asked. 'Charmaine's the only one in the family who's met him. She said he's nice-looking and that he's an engineer.'

'Ooh,' Sylvia said. 'Big time. Where does he work?'

'For an environmental firm. But it doesn't matter. It's over between us.'

'Oh,' Evelyn said, looking surprised.

'Uh-huh,' Charmaine said. 'So that's why you were acting so funny when I called this afternoon.'

'I was mostly just tired.' Beverly wondered why she was lying. She'd been on the verge of tears when the phone rang. 'I had a long night.' Well, at least that much was true.

'Why'd he call it off?' Sylvia asked.

'Why do you assume he broke up with her?' Evelyn said.

'I just . . . That's just what I thought,' Sylvia said.

'It didn't happen that way,' Beverly said. 'Nobody's really called it off. Not yet, anyway.'

'Well, tell us what happened, for God's sake,' Charmaine said.

Beverly breathed deeply and set her cards on the table. She

looked around at the three of them. All eyes were fixed on her, waiting. 'I think he's still seeing his old girlfriend from Charlottesville.'

'Oh, no,' Evelyn said.

Charmaine's eyes narrowed. 'He told you that?'

'Of course not. But he didn't have to.'

'That sucker,' Sylvia said. 'How'd you find out?'

'He broke off our date last night, saying he had to work late. I knew he was lying, so I drove over to his place to, ah . . .' She paused. Maybe someday she'd tell her sisters about the knife and all, but the feelings were too raw to talk about now. 'When I knocked on his door, he wouldn't let me in, but he admitted a woman from his hometown was there, probably for the weekend. He tried to act like her visit was all unexpected and innocent.'

'Maybe it was,' Charmaine said. 'He could've –'

'Now, wait just a minute here,' Sylvia said, cutting Charmaine off and crossing her ample thighs. She held both hands out, palms facing Beverly. 'I just want to get this shit straight. You mean you drove over there knowing he might have some bitch there and? . . .'

'I knew he was lying, and I can't stand that.'

'Still, I never, ever, would have been able to do that. You just went up to the door and knocked?'

'What's wrong with that?' Beverly asked.

'I'd a been scared he'd hit me or something. Or that she would.'

'Vernon's not the type to do that.'

'At least she knows where he's coming from now,' Evelyn said. 'Have you talked to him since then?'

'No.'

'It's just possible, you know, that the man was telling the truth,' Charmaine said. 'I mean, there's a lot of crazy-assed chicks out there. I could imagine him having someone from his past that he can't get rid of.'

'You mean like a fatal attraction kind of thing?' Sylvia said, giggling.

'Laugh if you want, but it does happen, you know.'

'Believe me, it wasn't like that,' Beverly said. 'He practically threw me down the hall.'

'The nerve of some men,' Evelyn said.

'You can be pretty hard on guys, though, Beverly,' Charmaine said. 'At least give him a chance to explain if he tries. Decent black men are hard to find.'

'You call his behavior decent?' Evelyn said.

'At least he's got a good job,' Charmaine said.

'Be careful,' Evelyn said. 'With some men, the lying and cheating are habits.'

'It doesn't matter,' Beverly said. 'There's nothing left to explain. He had his chance and he blew it.'

'I agree,' Sylvia said.

'You listen to these two and you'll be spending the rest of your days alone, Beverly,' Charmaine said. She turned to face Evelyn. 'Everybody can't find a perfect little man like yours.'

'Who says Kevin is –'

'There's nothing wrong with trying to find an honest man, is there?' Beverly said, interrupting Evelyn. 'I personally don't intend to settle for anything less than what I want. If I have to spend the rest of my days alone, so be it.'

'There's one thing I'll say about Kevin,' Evelyn said. 'He's honest and dependable. But he's not perfect.'

'That's not what you'd have everybody believing,' Charmaine said. She twisted up her nose and lips and rocked her shoulders up and down in exaggerated imitation. 'Kevin did this. Kevin did that. We just bought that.'

Beverly and Sylvia laughed.

'Come to think of it,' Charmaine said, 'you and Kevin had some problems before you got married. You even broke up once.'

'Everybody has problems,' Evelyn answered. 'All I'm saying is, she should be careful. The last thing you want is to get involved with a man who can't be trusted.' Evelyn stopped speaking when Sylvia's almost two-year-old son Floyd burst

59

into the room crying and ran up to his mother. 'What's the matter, honey?' Sylvia asked him. He climbed into her lap and she lifted him and sniffed at his pants. 'He pooped.' She stood up. 'I'll be right back.'

'Have you started potty training yet?' Evelyn asked.

Sylvia nodded while trying to hold onto a squirming Floyd, who wanted to get down. 'He's pretty good at home. But with all the excitement here –' She headed for the door.

'See if you can find John or somebody up there to play cards with us,' Beverly called after her.

'I definitely do not miss having toddlers, cute as they are,' Evelyn said.

'You're not having any more?' Beverly asked.

'No, indeed. Two is enough.'

Beverly looked at Charmaine. 'And you?'

Charmaine looked away. 'Not if I can help it.'

'This is the 1990s,' Evelyn said. 'Women have control over that kind of thing. Why wouldn't you be able to help it?'

Charmaine didn't answer, just pursed her lips tightly. 'Charmaine's so impulsive,' Beverly said. 'She could lose control of herself.'

'You got so fucking much mouth.'

'At least *her* mouth's clean,' Evelyn said. 'When are you going to stop all that cursing?'

'When you two stop giving me so much shit to cuss about,' Charmaine said. She stood up. 'I need to go check on Kenny. Haven't seen him for a while.'

'He was up in the living room with Daddy when I came down,' Evelyn said. 'He's fine.'

Charmaine hesitated, then sat back down.

'I can't believe Daddy's sixty-five years old,' Beverly said.

'I think it's hard to believe because he and Ma are in such good shape,' Evelyn said.

'Thank God,' Charmaine said. 'We don't have to worry about them.'

'This house has a way of making *me* feel old,' Beverly said, looking around. 'Seems like eons ago that we all lived here.'

60

'It *was* eons ago,' Evelyn said. 'Do you even remember when we moved here from D.C.?'

'Of course I do. I remember you two carrying on like the end of the world was coming.'

'It was,' Charmaine said. 'Moving out to Maryland with all those white people.'

'It was like moving to a foreign country,' Evelyn said. 'There were a lot fewer black people out here then. You remember the first day of school?' she asked Charmaine. 'It was awful. We were the only black people in most of our classes.'

'What about gym class?' Charmaine said. 'Those white chicks couldn't understand why we didn't wash our hair every time we showered after gym. Or why we put so much lotion all over our arms and legs afterwards. Evelyn started waiting until she got out of class to sneak into the girls' room and put the lotion on.'

'I did not.'

'Yes, you did. Me, I got that big old bottle of Jergen's out and slapped that stuff all over my ashy body right in front of their faces.'

Charmaine and Evelyn giggled. 'She made a spectacle of herself just so they'd have something to gossip about after class,' Evelyn said.

'It was harder for me,' Charmaine said. 'You just became a bookworm, Evelyn. Me, I went from getting B's and C's to C's and D's.'

'You wouldn't apply yourself,' Evelyn said. 'Too busy chasing boys. The few you could find, anyway.'

Beverly giggled. 'Remember that time I caught you around the side of the house after school necking with that boy, Charmaine? What was his name? Robert or something. He had his hand all up your blouse, and I threatened to tell Ma unless you took me shopping out at Wheaton Plaza.'

'Shit, how could I forget it? I was never so embarrassed when you came around the house and showed your face.' A sly smile creased the corners of Charmaine's lips. 'Old Ralph, my first real boyfriend. He was a cute honey.'

'I was only about ten,' Beverly said. 'I was shocked when I saw his hand up your blouse. But he was cute. You always got the cutest guys.'

'I never heard about that one,' Evelyn said. 'But Charmaine was so fresh I can believe it.'

'The fastest chick outside the beltway,' Beverly said, laughing. 'And you didn't know about that, Evelyn, 'cause Charmaine threatened to beat my behind if I ever said a word. A terrible way to treat your baby sister.'

'You weren't a baby then. Mainly just a thorn in my ass 'til you got a little older and started liking boys yourself. Come to think of it, after you turned about fourteen you weren't exactly an angel.'

'I was trying to keep up with you two,' Beverly said. 'And between Evelyn getting all A's in school and Charmaine getting all the cute boys, it was hard. Remember when I cut my hair into that real short Afro?'

'Oh, Lordy, I remember that,' Charmaine said. 'Ma like to had a fit.'

'I guess so,' Evelyn said. 'She was practically baldheaded.'

'I didn't cut all of it off.'

'All but about a quarter of an inch,' Evelyn said.

Beverly giggled. 'I was trying to attract this guy at school. He was the star basketball player, and he was soooo cute. Everybody in the county knew him. All the girls wanted him, black and white. He was going with this cute girl who wore a short Afro for the longest time, then he broke up with her. So I cut my hair like hers. Only it didn't do much good. About a month later, he started going with that Cynthia Lawson. She had hair down to her waist.'

'Them's the breaks,' Charmaine said. 'Only I don't understand why you always pin it up like that now.' She reached up to touch the bun at the back of Beverly's head, but Beverly slapped her hand away.

'I like it like that,' Evelyn said. 'Makes her look demure. She's lucky. Her hair's nicer than ours. Like Daddy's.'

'Still, she should wear it down over her shoulders more

often. Looks sexier, and men like that. Sexy will beat out demure every time.'

'It's so thick it's hard to do much with it like this. I'm thinking of getting a relaxer and getting it cut. Where do you get your's done, Evelyn?'

'Downtown Silver Spring. A woman named Denise. She's absolutely the best. Only problem is it takes forever to get out of that place. But I'll give you the phone number.'

'Don't cut your hair,' Charmaine said. 'Men like long hair.'

'But I'm tired of fooling with it. And I don't need to be bothered with some guy who's interested in me 'cause my hair's long. If he's not interested in my personality, forget it.'

'You got to attract them first, honey. Then you can let them see your glowing personality.'

'Is that why you wear all your skirts and slacks so tight?' Evelyn asked.

'Honey, if you got it, flaunt it,' Charmaine said, crossing her legs.

Evelyn laughed. 'You were lucky, though, Beverly. By the time you reached high school there were more black guys out here.'

'Still wasn't anything to get excited about, though,' Beverly said. 'But things have really changed out here now.'

'Haven't they?' Evelyn said. 'Some parts of Prince George's County are majority-black now. Can you believe it?'

'Nothing wrong with that,' Charmaine said. 'My neighborhood is probably about sixty or seventy percent black.'

'Your block isn't so bad,' Evelyn said. 'But the area around it . . .'

'Mine isn't so bad, huh? Just what does that mean?'

'Some of Landover's got a lot of crime and drugs now.'

'That's true,' Beverly said.

'Everybody can't afford to live in uppity Montgomery County like you do,' Charmaine said.

'You're right,' Evelyn said. 'And most neighborhoods in Prince George's are all right once you get outside the beltway. Like this one.'

'You just think this one's nice 'cause it's still mostly white.'

'That's not what I meant. Although I admit it sometimes works out that way.'

'You act like you think all our people form street gangs and sell drugs.'

'Some of them have. Look at . . .'

Beverly had heard them argue about this and a million other things so many times it all blended together in her mind. How these two could go from reminiscing to arguing so fast she'd never been able to understand. She knew that whole deal about P.G. versus Montgomery County was a big thing with some people, but she just couldn't get worked up over it. She was a city girl through and through. P.G., Montgomery – what was the difference? They were both the 'burbs.

' . . . I could never understand why anyone would pay all that money for a house in P.G. County, when for a little more you can get something in Montgomery County. Property values are better there and appreciate faster.'

'It's obvious,' Charmaine said. 'Some blacks when they get a little money still want to live around their own kind.'

'There's plenty of blacks in Montgomery County.'

'Shit. Where? One every five or ten miles?'

Beverly leaned back and stretched her arms. 'You-all are about to wear me out with all this fussing. I'm going to get ready to go home.'

'You can't go yet,' Sylvia said, coming into the room. 'Some of the children are going to put on a rap show in a few minutes. Sing some rap songs.'

'Oh, no,' Evelyn said. 'Not another one of those? We'll be here half the night.'

'Count me out of this one,' Beverly said. 'I'm just too tired.'

'I like 'em,' Charmaine said. 'They're cute.'

Evelyn stood up. 'I think I'm going to try to get out of here before it starts.'

'Too late,' Sylvia said. 'Andre is one of the top performers.'

'Andre?' Evelyn asked. 'And just what does he think he's doing?'

'An imitation of Kris Kross, with Eric, I think.'

Evelyn glanced at her watch as she started out of the room. 'Where is that boy?'

Beverly stood up.

'You should stay for the show, Beverly,' Charmaine said.

'Nah, I'm just going to tell Mama and Daddy good-bye and leave.' She pushed her chair under the table. She'd paid her dues. When she'd left the apartment earlier, her intention had been to wish her father a happy birthday, grab a bite to eat, and return home. She'd ended up staying for hours, talking and playing cards. It was just as well, though. She'd enjoyed it. But she was tired now and needed some solitude. 'Tell Clarence I said hi.'

Charmaine stood up and they walked toward the doorway with Sylvia. 'Maybe next time we get together, you and Vernon will have kissed and made up,' Charmaine said.

Beverly folded her arms. 'Don't hold your breath.'

Charmaine took hold of Beverly's arm and held her back. They stopped just inside the doorway and faced each other as Sylvia went on. 'Don't be so hard on him. Anybody can make a mistake.'

Beverly's eyes got wide. 'A mistake? I wouldn't hardly call this a mistake. He knew exactly what he was doing.'

'Even if it's what you think and he was with this woman, come Monday morning, or whenever it is she leaves, he'll probably wake up wondering why he did it and if it was worth it. She'll be gone and he'll be worried that he lost you. I bet he calls you right after she leaves.'

Beverly shrugged her shoulders. 'That's not good enough. I mean, I jump every time the phone rings, but I don't think I can deal with him after this. He should have thought about the consequences before he screwed up. Any man who takes that long to smell the coffee is wrong for me.'

'You did the same shit with Michael just because you *thought* you smelled another woman's cologne on him or something.'

'It was more than that. I don't believe in hanging around once the trust is gone.'

Charmaine shook her head with disapproval. 'I hope you meet this super dude you're looking for someday.'

'I'm not looking for some super anything. What would you do if you found out Clarence was cheating on you?'

'Kill the bum. No, just kidding. It would depend. If it just happened one time and he was really sorry, I'd get over it. Fortunately, nothing like that has ever happened. The one decent thing in our marriage is the sex.'

Beverly shook her head. 'I'll bet Evelyn would never put up with it. Like she said, what kind of relationship have you got if you can't trust somebody?'

'Later for Evelyn, this is you. Just 'cause somebody messes up once doesn't mean they're untrustworthy, does it?'

Beverly thought about that for a second. 'Probably. Yes, it does.'

Charmaine shook her head. 'You got a lot to learn, sis.'

7

The phone rang just as Beverly put a spoonful of cherry-chocolate chip ice cream to her lips. It was the first time the phone had rung since she'd returned home from her parents' house the night before, and it sort of startled her. Not so much the ring as who might be on the line. She wasn't sure she was ready to talk to Vernon. She wanted him to call but didn't want to talk to him; she wanted to break up with him but didn't want the relationship to be over. About the only thing she was sure of was being thoroughly confused.

She put the ice cream on the coffee table, got up from her lounging position on the sofa, and walked to the phone. Her heart pounded a little faster with each step. She placed her hand on the receiver, took a deep breath, and waited for the fourth ring.

'Hello?'

'Beverly, hi.'

It wasn't him. She breathed a little easier. 'Hi, Ma.'

'I was just calling to see how you're doing. You left so early last night.'

'I was tired. How did the show turn out?'

Pearl laughed. 'Oh, fine I guess. You should have stayed. What are you doing today?'

Sitting around the apartment in an old robe and pajamas, eating everything in sight and feeling sorry for my pitiful self, she thought. But she didn't want her mama worrying about her love life. 'Nothing much. Probably just clean up around here. Go to the grocery store later.'

'Shoot. Don't do that. There's a lot of food left from last night. Stop by and get some.'

'I might.'

'Good. What happened with Vernon yesterday? I thought you were bringing him with you?'

Beverly took a deep breath. 'We kind of broke up.'

'That's what Charmaine said. What happened?'

Oh, no, Beverly thought. What else did Charmaine say with that big mouth of hers? Beverly could just imagine Charmaine, Sylvia, and Evelyn sitting around after she'd left talking about poor old Beverly and worrying Mama. 'He's just not right for me, Ma.'

'Well, you should know best. Are you okay?'

'I'm fine.'

'Try to come by later, then.'

'I will. 'Bye, Ma.' Any other time she would have been eager to get some of that food. There was probably enough that she wouldn't have to cook for a week. But she doubted she'd be going anywhere today.

She went back into the living room and plopped onto the couch. She picked up the ice cream and cuddled the cold bowl in the palm of her hand. Ice cream for breakfast – or lunch really, considering it was almost noon. She must really be in a bad way, as her mother would have said if she could see her.

The television was turned on with the volume blasting. The Redskins didn't play until later this evening, and Sunday afternoon programming being what it was, she wasn't really watching it. She just needed some noise to break the silence. Music would only make her think sad thoughts about Vernon. Not that she wasn't going to be thinking about him anyway. It was just that her thoughts tended to be irrational when she was in a sour mood and played music.

Sundays would be especially difficult without him, she could sense that already. They had fallen into a cozy routine of watching the Redskins together every Sunday afternoon. It had seemed like such a simple thing, but boy was she going to miss it. She loved the 'Skins, and watching them with Vernon was even more fun, even though he wasn't a 'Skins fan. He preferred the Giants or the Eagles or the Cowboys. Anybody, it seemed, but the Redskins. Sometimes she thought he pretended to like all those other teams just to irk her. But those were some pretty passionate Sunday afternoons when they'd make up after all the shouting.

Why was she sitting here torturing herself like this after what he did to her? She must be a masochist or something. She banged the empty bowl on the coffee table. The thing that got her the most was when he'd refused to let her use the phone, even knowing she was locked out of her car in the middle of the night. This was a man she'd shared everything with – her secrets, her dreams, her bed – because she thought he was different from the others and she was crazy about him. She thought he felt the same way about her. Yet look at the cold way he'd treated her. Just thinking about it made her blood boil.

She wrapped her bathrobe around her tightly. This was the second time a man had really, really hurt her in less than a year. First Michael, now Vernon. But she'd learned something from Michael – that it didn't pay to try to patch things up once a man started stomping all over you like you were no better than an ant in the dirt. She never really understood what happened with Michael. He just changed on her, started treating her like she was the edge of midnight. She'd tried everything she could think of to get his interest back. Being extra sweet and sexy, ignoring him, making him jealous. Nothing worked. Oh, he was always ready to hop into the sack with her, but toward the end that was all he wanted to do with her. She was pretty sure it was another woman even though he always denied it.

Why was she so good at her career and so lousy at her love life? Here she was, almost thirty, with not a thing to show for it except a halfway decent paycheck. No man, no kids, no house. Nothing that really mattered. At the rate she was going, she'd be an old-maid aunt all her life.

She picked up the empty bowl from the table and carried it into the kitchen. She opened the refrigerator. Jeez, the thing was almost as empty as her life. Bacon, a couple of eggs, a chunk of sharp cheese, grapefruit juice. About the only thing in there she wouldn't have to cook was salad fixings. But she didn't even feel up to making a salad – all that chopping and slicing took too much energy. She closed the refrigerator door and opened an upper cabinet to see if she had any crackers to go with the cheese. Just as she suspected – all out.

She shut the cabinet as the front doorbell buzzed. Oh, no. What if it was Vernon sticking to their Sunday routine as if nothing out of the ordinary had happened? She looked down at her robe and slippers. It wasn't exactly one of those pretty little things you didn't mind greeting guests in. It was ancient and in desperate need of some good old soap and water. The slippers were ready for the trash bin. And her hair – it was tied up in a red bandanna she'd slept in for years, except, of course, when she didn't sleep alone. If she were out on a street corner someone would probably hand her a quarter.

The doorbell buzzed again, and she reached up and yanked the scarf off as she ran down the hall. In the bedroom, she glanced in the mirror and tucked a few loose strands of hair up into the bun at the back of her head. She quickly added a couple more hairpins, then wet her fingertip with her tongue and smoothed her thick eyebrows. She moaned. Jeez. She could be such a slut sometimes. She wanted to get rid of the robe, but there wasn't enough time.

She ran out of the bedroom and down the hall. The buzzer sounded again just as she crossed the living-room rug. She didn't know which was racing faster, her feet or her heart. At the door, she paused for a second to catch her breath, then took off the locks and turned the knob. She was so sure it was Vernon she didn't bother looking through the peephole.

She couldn't have been more wrong. Standing in the hallway was her old college friend Valerie. Beverly tried to return Valerie's smile, tried to seem happy as she invited her friend in. But it was hard. Suckered again, she thought, taking Valerie's jacket. But she had nobody to blame but her own sorry self. The man could send her emotions on a roller-coaster ride from clear across town. She was going to have to do something about that.

'Took you so long to answer the door, I was about to leave. What are you doing home on a nice day like this? Especially since the Redskins don't play until four.'

Beverly shrugged her shoulders as they sat on the couch.

'I tried to call you last night but you were out,' Valerie said. 'Probably with Vernon. How's he doing? I started not to even stop by just now, 'cause I assumed you'd be out with him. But you're not even dressed. The weather's so nice, I don't see how anybody can be cooped up in the house.'

'Where's that man you met a few weeks ago?' Beverly asked.

'Jackson? Oh, he always, always stays in on Sundays to watch the games. He watches them from one to seven or eight at night. And since I can't stand to watch that stuff I have to find other things to keep myself busy. I don't know why he . . .'

Beverly smiled. Valerie was a dear, old friend, but she had some mouth on her. Beverly had been listening to that mouth since she and Valerie had met at Hampton University in Virginia. Nothing like a dose of Valerie's nonstop talk to bring a girl back down to reality. Valerie was an elementary school teacher, and Beverly always wondered if her students ever got a chance to speak up.

' . . . You know, they say it's one of the warmest Novembers on record,' Valerie said.

'So I heard.'

'Where were you last night? Out with Vernon?'

'No. My family had a get-together for my father's birthday.'

'Oh. That's nice. How are your parents doing these days? Haven't seen them for a while.'

'They're fine. How's Olivia?'

'Oh, she thinks she's so grown-up since she'll be thirteen next month. And she looks so much like her daddy I can't stand it. Believe me, the two of them could be twins. I may have divorced that man, but I still have to look at him through her.'

'She's getting so pretty. She'll probably have boys all over the house in a couple of years.'

'Believe me, she would now if I let her. Anyway, enough of that. Olivia's out at a movie with some of her girlfriends. I was going downtown to do some shopping. Don't have a penny to my name, but I had to get out. I've been cooped up in the house all morning, mostly running my mouth on the phone. By the way, you'll never guess who I talked to.'

'Who?'

'Guess. Someone from Hampton.'

'I don't have the faintest idea. And you know I hate it when you do that.'

'Andrea Johnson. You remember her?'

Beverly frowned. Valerie had this strange knack for remembering every person she had ever met and everything that had ever happened to that person.

'You don't remember her? She's a Delta. Kind of short. From New York.'

Beverly shook her head. No, she didn't remember. And she was in no mood to try to remember.

'That's funny. I was sure you'd remember her. Anyway, she's back in New York now, but we talk on the phone from time to time. I called her last night 'cause it's her birthday today. She's getting married in June.'

Don't say that word.

'This is her third marriage.'

Beverly moaned. 'Jeez. How does someone find three husbands? I can't even find one.'

'Tell me about it.'

'At least you've been married once.'

'Believe me, it was the biggest mistake of my life. Only good thing to come out of it was Olivia.'

'At least you have something.'

'Yes, well, you should get dressed and come downtown with me if you're not doing anything. We can look around, have a late lunch at the Shops or the Pavilion. I hardly ever see you since you started going out with Vernon. How is he, by the way?'

If one more person mentions that man's name, Beverly

thought, she would start screaming. She looked away. She had to figure out the best way to handle this. Once she told Valerie the details, the woman would go on and on about it. And Beverly wasn't in the mood to hear her endless chatter right now. 'He's okay.'

'Okay? Just okay? I thought you'd be the next one walking down the aisle.'

'I don't know what ever gave you that idea, Valerie. It's only been a few months.'

'It's been longer than that. You started seeing him last May. Remember when you showed up with him at that barbecue around Memorial Day? You had only been seeing him a couple of weeks then. I've hardly seen you since. When I talk to you on the phone it's always "Vernon this" or "we that." I was so jealous until I met Jackson, 'cause I lost my club-hopping partner. I'm expecting to get a wedding invitation any day now.'

'Valerie, please.'

'Well, we're not getting any younger, you know. I'll be thirty-two in a couple of months. You'll hit the big three-oh yourself in May.'

'I'd love to get married someday. But I doubt Vernon will be involved.'

'I thought you were crazy about him. You never stop talking –'

'Valerie,' Beverly said, cutting her off. She had to stop this woman's mouth or her head would fall off from spinning. 'I'm not seeing him anymore.'

'I didn't know that.' Valerie's voice dropped to a whisper. 'What happened?'

Beverly swallowed hard. 'He really hurt me.'

'What in the world did he do? If you'd rather not talk about it now . . .'

'No. You're going to have to hear it sooner or later. I found out he was still seeing his old girlfriend from back home.'

Valerie's eyes popped open. 'Oh, no.'

Beverly nodded. 'Oh, yes. Unfortunately.'

73

Valerie touched her cheek with her forefinger thoughtfully. 'Well, you know, a lot of the outer planets are passing through Capricorn and conjuncting your Venus and opposing your moon right now. They're also trining your sun in Taurus. They're just whacking your personal planets to death.'

Beverly stared wide-eyed at Valerie. But she shouldn't be surprised. Valerie was an astrology nut. Always had been. Beverly burst out laughing.

'What's so funny?' Valerie asked.

'I don't know. Here I am expecting you to say something about Vernon and you're just going on and on about that astrology stuff. You're one in a million, you know that? What does all that mean, anyway?'

'Well, you're going through a trying emotional period, especially with one-on-one relationships.'

'I could have told you that much. I just did.'

'But this explains why.'

'I think you're putting the cart before the horse or something here.'

'Well, I'm not an astrologer. I just dabble. But my astrologer could tell you more. You should go see him.'

'So he can tell me more of what you just told me? Thanks, but no thanks.'

'I think he would be able to help you. I don't want to scare you, but when the outer planets are involved, things usually go on for a long, long time.'

'Just what I needed to hear.'

'It's not necessarily all bad. Depends on how you handle it. But a good astrologer can help you with that. That's why you should see him.'

'Uh-uh. He'd probably just tell me I'm doomed to a life of loneliness.'

'I doubt he would tell you something like that. So what are you going to do about Vernon?'

'I wish I knew. When it first happened, I didn't want to have anything else to do with him. But Charmaine thinks I should give him a second chance. And I miss him so much already.'

'I don't know about that. Considering what he did.'

'Did Frank ever do anything like that?'

'My ex? No, indeed. Who else would have him? The only one who ever got out on me, at least as far as I know anyway, was Darnell. That guy I was seeing right after my divorce.'

'I remember him.'

'I guess you do. You're the one he was two-timing me with. That's how we met.'

'God, he was a bum. What's the matter with these black men? Charmaine says I should stick with Vernon even if he slipped up once because decent black men are hard to find, da-da, da-da, da-da. And it's true in a way. Most of them are unemployed or on drugs or in jail. Pitiful. And the ones who don't have all these problems are married.'

'That's no reason to put up with a guy who cheats on you. Believe me, once they start that stuff they don't stop. There's got to be a few good ones left out there. Single ones you can trust. You just have to keep digging.'

'I'm about ready to give up. What's the point, anyway? I only know one person in our generation who's in a good marriage. And that's my sister Evelyn. Everybody else is either divorced or having problems.'

'I know this other couple who seems to be doing good, but believe me, there aren't too many of them.'

'Downright depressing.'

'Yep.'

'Wonder what the secret is? How do you find that one right person out there in that jungle?

'Believe me, if I knew I'd tell you.'

8

Monday mornings were always the pits as far as Beverly was concerned. But this one was pure agony. Crawl out of bed, bathe, dress, gulp down some grapefruit juice. Hit the subway station, jam the ticket in the machine, fuss with the attendant, run up the escalator, slip onto the train just before the doors slam shut. Standing room only. She shifted her briefcase to her left hand and grabbed a pole in the aisle with her right just as the train jerked forward. It picked up speed and roared out of Union Station. She told herself to look on the bright side. At least she was finally doing something besides sitting around the apartment moping.

Three stops later she exited at Metro Center, the main downtown station, onto 13th Street and made her way through the morning rush-hour crowd — commuters preoccupied with reaching their destinations, street vendors peddling their wares, homeless people begging for change, construction crews. But she'd made her way through all of it so many times that she hardly noticed anymore. She had other things on her mind. Her thoughts had been so focused on what had happened Friday night that she couldn't even remember the subject of the article she'd been editing Friday evening. She entered her building through the glass doors and pressed the button for the elevator up to the sixth floor. She cocked her head to the side. Was it the one about the hole in the ozone layer? No, no. She'd finished that one earlier in the week and had handed it in to the managing editor.

She entered the office suite and stopped at the receptionist's desk to see if she had any messages from that morning, since she was arriving about thirty minutes late. The only one was from Marie Walker, a scientist at the National Zoo who was studying big cats. Now she remembered what that article was about. It was the one she was writing herself on the cheetah. How could she have forgotten that? Get a handle on things, Beverly Jordan, she told herself. Or you'll end up an *unemployed* old-maid aunt.

In her office, she dropped her briefcase on top of her desk and hung her coat on the hook on the back of the door. She'd just picked up the phone to dial Marie when Zelma, the managing editor's executive assistant, tapped on her open door and pranced into the office. Beverly looked up and smiled. Zelma had a way of swishing her hips when she was excited, and it was kind of comical, especially since she was more than a little on the plump side. Her saving grace was that she was always dressed to kill. In fact, Zelma never seemed to wear the same thing twice and she had a knack for picking out things that made her look good. But Beverly often wondered how an executive assistant could afford such an extensive wardrobe. Beverly tried to make her own meager wardrobe seem more interesting by mixing and matching coordinates. She had a lot of black in her closet since it went with everything else.

Today, Zelma was decked out in a beige suit with a red silk blouse that set off her pretty brown face. Her heels were the exact same color as the suit. Beverly put her finger over the button to hang up the phone. 'What's got you so hyper?'

Zelma closed the door behind her and sashayed over to Beverly's desk. She leaned in conspiratorially. 'Have you met the new editor?' she asked, almost in a whisper. 'Byron Peterson?'

'No, not yet,' Beverly whispered back, wondering why they were speaking so softly. 'What about him?'

Zelma whirled around with a dreamy look on her face. She plopped down in the chair across from Beverly's desk, crossed her ample thighs, and fanned her face with her hand as if she'd just run a marathon and was about to pass out. 'Oh, Lordy, child, help me. Mr. Stern took him around this morning and introduced him to everybody and all. I guess you weren't in your office.'

77

'And what?'

'He's black, that's what. Afro-American. And cute, too.'

'He's black?' Beverly dropped the phone in the cradle. Up until now, she'd been the only other black professional on the staff. A few years ago they had had a black graphic designer, but he was so good he was offered a job at a major publication in New York City. Even though D.C. was mostly black, there just weren't many black editors out there.

'What was he doing before he came here?'

'I don't know,' Zelma said, waving her hands in the air. 'And who the hell cares? He's here now.'

Beverly laughed and snapped her fingers at Zelma. 'Hey, hey. Snap out of it. You're getting married in a few weeks, remember? What would your fiancé think about you drooling over another man?'

'I can still dream, can't I?' Zelma said, batting her eyelashes. 'No, seriously, it's just nice having another black body on the staff.'

'It is. I just can't believe it.'

Zelma stood up and walked to the door. 'Mr Stern will probably bring him in here to meet you. I just wanted to warn you.' She paused at the door. 'I wonder if "you know who" will go after him like she does all the other good-looking men around here.'

'Is the new guy single?'

'I don't know. But that never stopped Linda before. She's married herself.'

'I know. But the new guy's black. Linda's white. Maybe she'll stay away.'

'She went after that Hispanic guy, remember? He was married, too. Didn't stop her.'

'How could I forget. We had our own little "Knots Landing" around here until he left. Maybe this new guy will be able to resist her.'

Zelma twisted up her nose. 'Most of them don't seem to be able to. Not once she sets her mind on getting them. I can't stand the thought of that woman messing with him. If it

78

wasn't for Vernon, I'd tell you to go after him. Hell, if it wasn't for Jessie, I'd go after him.'

'Vernon's out of the picture.' Beverly realized she was getting awfully tired of saying that.

Zelma came back to Beverly's desk. 'You broke up?'

'You could say that.'

'Why'd he end it?'

Beverly put her hands on her hips in mock indignation. 'Why does everyone assume *he* was the one who decided to end it?'

An embarrassed smile crossed Zelma's face. ''Cause. That's the way it usually happens, don't it?

'Not necessarily.'

'You were so crazy about him. I didn't think you'd be the one to end it. What happened?'

'It's a long story. I'll tell you about it later. I need to make a phone call now.'

Zelma sashayed to the door. 'Let's do lunch, then. I want to hear about this, child.'

'You're on.'

As soon as Zelma left, Beverly picked up the phone and dialed Marie. Busy. She dropped the receiver in the cradle. The thing to do was work on the cheetah article and try Marie again in a few minutes. That was what she *should* do, but she just couldn't bring herself around to it. It was so hard to get down to business as usual when her personal life was so screwed up.

She'd forgotten until this morning that Vernon was supposed to go to Chicago on business this evening. He'd be gone until next Sunday afternoon. That meant if he didn't call her at work today she wouldn't hear from him until next weekend at the earliest. She was so sure he would have called by now. Even if he knew she would give him a hard time, he was still supposed to call. She was curious about what he'd have to say, and certainly didn't want to have to go a whole week to get things off her chest.

She looked at the phone again. Maybe she should just call him. He might be hesitant to contact her because of the way she'd acted Friday night – ranting and raving and carrying on.

That kind of behavior turned off a lot of men. Then again, that woman could still be there. No law said she had to leave on Sunday. If she called and that old girlfriend of his was still around, Beverly knew she'd just get angry all over again.

She turned away from the desk to face her computer. She was not going to put herself through this one more second. Letting some no-good man control her thoughts. It was bad enough thinking about him all the time at home; now she couldn't even get her work done.

She turned on the computer. Work. Work. Work. Save the cheetah from extinction. She pressed buttons until the cheetah article came up on the monitor. She would force herself to concentrate on it until noon, then she would go out for lunch with Zelma. This afternoon, she had a long production meeting that would help get her through the rest of the day. If he called, he called. If he didn't, he didn't. So be it. It wasn't like he was the last man on earth.

'Oh, Lord. Guess who just walked in with who,' Zelma said. They were seated across from each other at the American Cafe, a popular downtown eating spot. Beverly started to turn. 'Who?'

'Don't turn around,' Zelma said excitedly. 'She'll see you.'

Beverly turned back to face Zelma. 'Who is it then?'

'Oh, God,' Zelma said. 'They're coming this way.'

Beverly was dying to turn and see who had Zelma squirming on the edge of her seat. She didn't have to wait long to see. Linda, the office flirt, walked by near their table with a black man following her. Beverly never saw their faces, only their backs as they passed by. She couldn't see what he looked like, only that he was tall and very slim. 'Is that him?' Beverly asked, watching their backs as they crossed the restaurant.

'Yes. God, that little whore doesn't waste any time does she?'

Beverly giggled. 'She didn't even speak to us. You think she saw us?'

'Oh, she saw us, alright. She looked right into my face. She doesn't want to take any chances introducing her man to the enemy before she stakes her claim. What are they doing now?'

Beverly peered over Zelma's shoulder. 'They're sitting down looking at the menus.' The way they were seated, Beverly still couldn't get a good look at him.

'Isn't he good-looking? What he wants to mess with her for, I don't know.'

'I can't really see his face.'

'You mean you haven't met him yet?'

'No. Mr Stern was in that meeting all morning.'

'Believe me, the man is gorgeous. Nice and tall. And can dress, too. He's paying good money for those suits he wears. Linda wouldn't be wasting her time if he didn't look good. But I'm kinda surprised she's going after him so fast.'

'She probably considers him an exotic challenge.'

'Disgusting.'

'I know.'

'Ain't it enough white men around for her to mess with? Leave the black ones alone. There's not enough of them as it is.'

'Maybe it's not what we think. Maybe he's just being sociable.'

'Ha. I don't know what it is, but men just can't seem to say no to that woman.'

'Probably those forty-inch boobs.'

Zelma burst out laughing. 'It ain't just that, honey. Mine are just as big as hers.'

'But you don't throw yourself after men like that. And I have to admit she's kind of pretty, and sexy.'

Zelma shrugged. 'If what you like is white and dyed blond. Anybody could look sexy wearing their skirts halfway up their ass. Even though hers is as flat as an ironing board.'

Beverly giggled as the waiter walked up with their orders. He placed ginger chicken and hot tea in front of her and a broiled hamburger and fries in front of Zelma. 'Enough about them two,' Zelma said, taking a generous bite out of her hamburger. 'Tell me about you and Vernon.'

Beverly picked up her fork and slid a morsel of chicken around on her plate. 'Well, I went to his place Friday night and . . .'

'You were going to see Mary Wilson with him.'

'Yes. Well, he called and said he couldn't make it to the show 'cause he had to work late. But I didn't believe that so I went to his place. He had another woman over there.'

Zelma gulped. 'Oh, Lordy. I never would have thought Vernon would do that – not from the way you talked about him being this sweet guy from the South and all.'

'He *was* sweet and sort of innocent when he first got here. But this town will spoil any man rotten.'

'Ain't it the truth. You wouldn't believe the women I have to fight off to hold onto Jessie.'

'I believe it.'

'So . . . What are you going to do?'

Beverly took in a deep breath of air and let it out. 'I might not have to do anything. He hasn't even called yet.'

'That's just like a man. He's trying to force you to call him.'

'I'm not doing that. I refuse.'

'I don't blame you. You wait, he'll call you sooner or later.'

'He must be planning on doing it later, then. He leaves to go out of town on business this evening. He'll be gone all week.'

'Then call him.'

'A minute ago you said not to.'

'A minute ago, I didn't know he was leaving town for a whole week. You got to play hard to get, but not that hard.'

'I'm not playing hard to get or anything else. It's probably over, but I still want to talk to him. We couldn't talk much Friday night, and I think I'm due an explanation.'

'You actually caught him in bed with another woman?'

'I didn't see her. But I know she was there.'

'That's disgusting.'

'I know.'

'You might never be able to get that out of your mind.'

'That's what I know.'

'It would be hard to learn to trust him again.'

82

'Almost impossible.'

'Now having said that, let me say this.' Zelma paused and put her half-eaten hamburger on the plate. She dabbed a corner of her lips with her napkin. 'Not long after I got together with Jessie, he started seeing another woman. I said, "Forget it. I'm not dealing with this shit." So I broke off with him.'

'You never told me that.'

'I try not to think about it. I know I've got him now, so I don't worry about it, not much anyway.'

'How did you find out? Did he come out and tell you about her?'

'No, indeed, child. His sister did. I don't get along with her too good. She told me about this other woman, thinking it would break us up. It worked for a while, but we got back together about a month later, after he finally dumped this bitch. Been together almost a year now.'

'But do you trust him? I guess you must, you're marrying him.'

'I trust him. I just make sure I know where that sucker is every minute of the day.'

They both laughed. 'See,' Beverly said. 'I couldn't deal with that.'

Zelma shrugged. 'A woman's gotta do what a woman's gotta do. I'll do anything to hold onto my man. If it means checking up on him and chasing other women away, that's what I'll do. I hardly let him go anywhere without me, except to work. And I call him at work three, four times a day.'

Beverly shook her head in disbelief. 'That would drive me crazy.'

'It drives *me* crazy. But I'd be crazier without him.'

'How are the wedding plans coming?'

'I'm going outta my mind. This was supposed to be a small affair. You know, sixty, seventy people. Mostly just family. I didn't even invite people from the office. Just you. But every time I turn around my mama's adding somebody to the list.'

'Weddings are like that. They seem to be more for the parents than the people getting married.'

'I'm telling you. My mother tried to get us to wait until spring. Thought we was crazy wanting a wedding in December. But I had enough trouble just getting this man to propose. I don't want to give him enough time to change his mind. Men are so fickle. Don't know what they want 'til we tell 'em.'

'That's why I dread getting back into the dating scene. It's dog-eat-dog out there.'

Zelma leaned over the table with a glint in her eye. 'Maybe you won't have to. What do you think of the new guy?'

'Byron? I haven't even met him yet. And we don't even know if he's married.'

'Oh, yes, we do. I asked around. He's single.'

'You mean he's never been married?'

'That's what I heard.'

'Wonder how old he is.'

'Thirty-eight.'

Beverly stared at Zelma. 'You've really been busy, haven't you?' Zelma giggled as Beverly glanced over at Byron and Linda. 'Thirty-eight and never been married. I wonder what's wrong with him.'

'Maybe he just hasn't found the right person yet. But with you and Vernon having problems . . .'

'Zelma, please. I'm not ready to start thinking about other men. I need a rest. A long one.'

'Don't rest too long, child. Otherwise you'll be scraping up Linda's leftovers.'

When Byron walked into her office late that afternoon, Beverly was so deep into the cheetah article that at first she didn't realize anyone had entered. She glanced up from her computer to see this tall, lean figure towering over her desk and nearly jumped out of her chair. She was startled not so much because he had sort of snuck up on her, but because it was strange to see a black man dressed in a suit and tie standing there. She saw many on the street but none in this office.

She stood up and shook his extended hand, and he smiled,

exposing the whitest set of teeth she'd ever seen. This man obviously had never smoked a cigarette or drunk a cup of tea in his life.

'I didn't mean to scare you. I'm Byron. The new assistant editor.'

She smiled. He spoke in a very soft voice, barely above a whisper. 'Nice to meet you, Byron. I'm Beverly.'

'You weren't in your office when Mr Stern introduced me to everybody this morning, so I thought I'd come in and do that myself. You're a senior editor, right?'

Beverly nodded. 'I was hired as an assistant editor like you, though. Promoted from associate editor a year ago.'

'Congratulations.'

Beverly indicated the chair in front of her desk. 'Why don't you sit down?' She sat down herself and waited as he folded his long, lean body into the chair. 'What were you doing before you came here?'

'I was with the Park Commission in Maryland and before that a ranger at Yosemite.'

'That's an interesting background. You have hands-on experience with wildlife. I'm impressed.'

He smiled broadly, obviously pleased at her compliment. 'Haven't done any editing, though I've written a few articles for newspapers and small magazines. I'm sure I can get the hang of it. Mr Stern thinks I can.'

'And Mr Stern's usually right.'

'I've already got several ideas for articles I'd like to see in the magazine.'

Beverly nodded. 'I'm sure you do, but Mr Stern will assign you to work with a senior editor for now. You have to be promoted to associate editor before you get to handle your own articles.'

He nodded enthusiastically. 'That's what Mr Stern said. I'm hoping I can do that within a year.'

Beverly raised her eyebrows. This cat was definitely not short on ambition. 'I wish you luck, but it takes most people a bit longer than that.'

He smiled. 'I'm not like most people. At least I don't think I am. It's never taken me much more than a year to get promoted on my other jobs. How long did it take you?'

'About two years to associate. And another three to get to senior editor.'

He shook his head. 'I don't mean to sound pushy or anything. But my pocketbook can't afford to wait that long. This assistant editor salary is the pits, to tell you the truth.'

Beverly smiled and shrugged her shoulders. 'Maybe you'll do it faster.'

'How's a senior editor different from an associate editor?'

'We assign articles to the associate editors. And decide on the content of each issue. We do some editing, usually on the main feature. And approve everything before it goes to Mr Stern.'

'Sounds like I need to get in tight with you. He said you were working on something on the park system now.'

'Uh-huh. But there's two other senior editors, Jane and Jack. Mr Stern will decide which one of us you work with.'

'I told him I wanted to work on that with you. He said it was no problem.'

'You don't waste any time, do you? I spent my first week just doing a lot of reading about wildlife. It was a couple of weeks before I was assigned to any material.'

He shook his head. 'I don't need that. I learned all I need to know working in the field.'

'Fine. I'm also writing an article on the cheetah. So I can use some help on the park piece, double-checking figures and making some phone calls. Give me about an hour to finish what I'm doing now, and then I'll get everything together and bring it to your office before we get off at five.'

'Take your time. I'll be around the office for a while.' He stood and smiled down at her. 'I'll let you get back to your work now. Maybe we can have lunch one day this week.'

'Good idea.' Beverly smiled as he left. She wasn't exactly sure what to make of him. He was attractive, as Zelma had said, but not drop-dead cute. He was a little too thin for

Beverly's taste. She liked them more broad in the shoulders, more muscular. The most noticeable thing about him was the way he carried himself. A lot of confidence and poise. Maybe an overdose of the confidence. Even though he wasn't married, she would be surprised if he wasn't involved with someone. Successful, unattached black men were about as common as palm trees in this city.

She glanced at the phone on her desk. Vernon would be leaving for Chicago in a couple of hours. Maybe she could just call and wish him a safe trip. No. That would be too corny. He'd think she was looking for an excuse to talk to him, and he'd be right. She had to let it go. If he wanted to speak to her, he would call. If he could just walk away from their six months together, without even a second thought, then so be it. She didn't need to be bothered with a man who thought so little of her.

She swung her chair back toward her desk and opened the bottom file drawer. She would put the cheetah article off for now and get the stuff together for Byron. That wouldn't take a lot of concentration, and it was better than waiting for a call that was probably never coming.

9

Beverly found an empty spot among all the paper and books spread out on the dining-room table and placed her cup of tea on it. She'd been bringing work home every night that week. Monday evening she'd finished the cheetah article. Tuesday and Wednesday she'd worked on the park piece. She should be able to wrap it up tonight so her weekend would be free. Although to do what she wasn't sure – she didn't have a thing planned, but she'd have to find something to keep her busy.

She crossed out the last line on the page and flipped to the next one. It was a wonderful article about the deterioration of the national park system over the years, thorough and provocative. Byron had been a big help, suggesting areas that needed more detail and contacting the sources to get them. All it needed now was her touch to make the writing flow smoothly. By the time she was finished with the piece, it would sing off the page. She planned to try to convince Mr Stern that it should be the lead article in the February issue, instead of the toxic waste piece they were considering. If she finished the editing before tomorrow's meeting, there would still be enough time to make the switch.

She was in the middle of the page when the doorbell rang. Oh perfect, she thought, looking up. She threw her pencil down on the table. The last thing she needed now was company. Whoever it was, she was going to get rid of them fast so she could get back to work.

It rang again. Shoot. No slippers and no time to find them. She pushed her chair back and stood up quickly. She rounded the table and banged her left thigh on the corner. 'Ow,' she shouted as the pain ripped through her flesh and down to the bone. She jumped back and massaged it. The doorbell blasted.

'Damn. I'm coming, I'm coming,' she muttered, rubbing her leg as she limped out of the dining room. At the door, she put on the safety chain and undid the bolt lock. Before opening it, something told her to look through the peephole. She slid the cover back and peered through. She jumped back and covered her mouth with her hand. It was Vernon.

She stomped her foot on the cold floor, her sore thigh practically forgotten. She looked down at her robe and bare feet. What on earth was he doing here now? He was supposed to be in Chicago. She looked so bad a part of her wanted to run into the bedroom and hide. Then she remembered the night at his apartment and began to feel downright foolish at the way she was behaving. This man had gotten her so pissed off she was ready to slash his convertible top. What did she care what she looked like? She reached up and tucked a few loose strands into the French twist at the back of her head. She opened the door.

He was standing there smiling and looking as confident as ever. She hoped she looked just as sure of herself. It had only been a week since she'd last seen him, but strangely, it felt as if it had been much longer. She'd forgotten how good-looking he was, especially when he was dressed like this. He had on gray slacks and a navy double-breasted blazer under a tan all-weather coat.

'Hell-lo,' he said, stringing out that Southern voice the way he usually did when he knew he was on her bad side. In the past, its soothing sound had always brought a quick smile to her face, melting her anger like butter in a warm pot. But not tonight.

'You should have called,' she said, tugging the collar on her robe.

'I would've, but I came straight from the airport.'

So he was just getting back from Chicago. She wanted to ask him why he'd returned so early, since he was supposed to stay until Sunday and it was only Thursday. And why had he waited so long to contact her? She wanted to ask him a million things, but she didn't.

'You going to invite me in?' he asked.

'I'm thinking about it.'

The smile disappeared from his mouth. 'I guess I deserved that. But, you know, at some point we have to talk.'

She wasn't so sure about that anymore. Not after all this time. But she stepped aside. He entered the living room, and she shut the door behind him. He removed his coat and held it out. She walked past him and sat down in the far corner of the couch. When he realized she wasn't going to take the coat, he draped it across the back of a chair. He sat down at the other end of the couch. She tucked her legs up under her hips and pointed her knees away from him. Her thigh still hurt and she was dying to rub it, but didn't dare. That would just start small talk about what was wrong with it, and she wasn't in the mood for that. She folded her arms across her waist and stared at the little geometrical shapes in the dhurrie rug under the coffee table.

He leaned back, laid his arm over the back of the couch, and turned to face her. The tips of his fingers brushed her shoulder. 'Something to drink would be nice. A glass of water or something. It was a long flight.'

She twisted her shoulder out of his reach. 'There's iced tea in the refrigerator. I just boiled some water if you want hot tea. You know where the kitchen is.'

He got up and went to the kitchen. He wasn't really thirsty, she thought. Probably just nervous about this, although you'd never know it by looking at him. She rubbed her thigh until she heard the refrigerator door bang shut. When he came back into the room, she had her arms folded back across her waist. He sat at the other end of the sofa and took a long gulp of iced tea, emptying the glass of all but the ice cubes. Then he held the glass over his knee with one hand and loosened his tie with the other. 'Isn't it kind of warm in here?'

'I'm fine.'

He smiled at her. 'I don't ever remember us having temperature differences before.' When he realized she wasn't going to return his smile, he continued. 'This past weekend was really something. First, Henrietta shows up on my door-step totally unexpectedly. I was about to leave to pick you up for dinner and the show when she knocked on my door.'

He shook the glass and raised it to his lips again, letting one of the little cubes slide into his mouth. Beverly tightened her arms around her waist as she listened to the ice cubes rattling around in the glass. So the name was Henrietta. Just hearing it got her juices boiling again. She wanted to slap that glass out of his mouth and ask him where the hell this Henrietta had suddenly come from.

Vernon set the glass on the coffee table and fixed his eyes on it. 'And when she shows up, she's all upset with me because last month I . . . Well, we'll go into that in a minute.' He turned and looked at her. 'Then you showed up.'

'How inconvenient for you,' she said, staring straight ahead.

He smiled weakly and returned his gaze to the glass. 'Look, I'm going to come straight out with it. If you still hate my guts . . . well.' He shrugged his shoulders. 'I don't know what else I can do at this point.'

She looked straight at him for the first time that night. 'Don't you think it's a little late for honesty?'

'Maybe. But better late than never, I guess you could say.'

She rolled her eyes. 'Please, Vernon.'

'What do you want me to do, Beverly? Should I just get up and leave and we forget everything?'

A big part of her wanted to say, 'Yes, get the hell out of my apartment, get the hell out of my life.' She was just starting to get a grip on herself, so why let him drag up all the grimy details at this point? But another part wanted to hear what he had to say. 'That's up to you.'

'I would have called you earlier, but I was busy getting ready for this trip. And I figured you needed a cooling-off period. We both did. But that's why I came back early. It's been gnawing at me, and I wanted to try to explain.'

She was silent, and he picked up the glass of ice cubes again and popped one into his mouth. 'You remember me telling you when we first started seeing each other about . . . How long has it been since we started seeing each other? Six months?'

Beverly rolled her eyes to the ceiling. 'You can't even remember that?'

'Okay, six months then. Well, I told you that before I moved here I was seeing this woman from my hometown, from Charlottesville. You remember that?'

'Yes. You were with her for two years or something. But you told me you broke up with her.'

'I did after I started seeing you. Or I tried to, anyway.'

'Tried to?'

'Well, Henrietta can be pretty stubborn and she didn't want to end it. She kept calling, and whenever I went home to see Ma she was always hanging around.'

'So you were still seeing her after we started going out? Is that it?'

'In the beginning.'

'Vernon, I thought you were going to start being honest.'

'I am being honest. Our relationship wasn't the same after I met you. But, yes, I did see her from time to time in the beginning. You can't really blame me for that. I was just starting to see you. I didn't know we would hit it off like we did. When I did realize it, I told her I was involved with someone else, and that we would have to stop seeing each other. But see, we go way back. She knows all my family and they love her. Every time I went home, she was hanging around. It was hard trying to cut it off completely. Like I said, she's determined when she wants something.'

'Let's get to the big question.'

He looked at her, puzzled. 'What's that?'

'Do I have to spell it out for you?'

He raised his eyebrows as a look of understanding crossed his face. 'Do you really want me to answer that?'

'Yes! Who the hell cares if she dropped by your parents' house when you were there, or if she called you long distance a few times. Or even a lot of times. What I want to know is if you slept with her while you were seeing me. But never mind, you answered the question for me.'

'Wait a minute, don't go jumping to conclusions. Okay, I admit that when you and I first started dating, I was with her a couple of times. But only in the beginning of our relationship.'

'You expect me to believe that?'

'It's the truth.'

'Then what was she doing at your apartment last Friday?'

He took a deep breath. 'I'm getting to that. Anyway, after I stopped being involved with her, she convinced me that all she wanted was to remain friends. That worked for a while, a few months maybe, but then she started coming on to me again. She wanted us to go away to the Bahamas together. She was calling and writing a lot. So about a month ago I told her I couldn't have anything else to do with her, friendship or otherwise. And she knew I was serious because I wouldn't talk to her when she called, and the last time I went home I insisted my family not tell her I was coming. Anyway, this past Friday night she popped up just as I was about to pick you up. I had no idea she was coming.'

'God, she's persistent.'

'She's the most persistent woman I know.'

'What does she do?'

'She's a model.'

'A model? How old is she?'

'Twenty-two.'

'Twenty-two?' Beverly nearly spit the words out. Jeez, she thought, gimme a break. Here she was only twenty-nine and already being challenged by a younger woman. 'You're thirty-three years old. Don't you think that's a little young for you?'

'She's very mature for her age.'

Beverly ignored him. 'No wonder you couldn't keep your pants on. You men and your baby bimbos.'

'C'mon, Beverly. It has nothing to do with that.'

'Why couldn't you just tell her you were busy Friday night and send her home?'

'That's a two-, three-hour drive. I couldn't send her back late at night —'

'Oh, please,' Beverly said, interrupting. 'You couldn't send her back, but you could lie to me about breaking off our date and then leave me stranded outside your apartment.'

'I didn't think it would be a good idea to tell you the whole story over the phone. You can be pretty hot-headed, too, Beverly. In that way you're both alike.'

'Don't give me that bull. I'm nothing like her from what I'm hearing. You're about to realize that.'

'Oh, I am, huh?'

'Damn right. I'm not some clinging vine and I can't stand lying . . .'

'I never lied to you. I . . .'

' . . . and I'm not about to put up with someone leaving me stranded in the middle of the night when I'm locked out of my car.'

'What was I supposed to do? You know the city much better than she does. And you were acting like a nut. Admit it. No way was I letting the two of you get together that night. I let her stay the night and sent her home in the morning.'

'Why didn't you just tell me what was going on instead of lying?'

'I'm telling you now and look where it's got us. Would you have understood and gone back quietly to your apartment?'

'Maybe.'

'I doubt that.'

'So do I, to tell you the truth.'

He laughed and Beverly smiled despite her bitter feelings. 'Still,' she said, getting serious again. 'That would have been better than all this.'

'I know that now. I shouldn't have let my concern for her welfare get in the way of my feelings for you. And I'll say this, because I know you're wondering.'

'What now?' she asked, looking away from him.

'I did not, I repeat, did not, sleep with her that night.'

She looked at him. 'You expect me to believe that?'

He stared back. 'Yes.'

'Where did she sleep?'

94

'In my bed but . . .'

'And you.'

'Same place. But nothing happened.'

She laughed. Not because it was funny, but because it was so damn pitiful. 'You must think I'm a complete fool.'

'It's the truth. What do I have to say to make you believe it?'

She looked up at the ceiling. 'I'm not sure you can. I'm not sure it makes any difference since you've been . . . been screwing her all along.'

'Not since things got serious between us.'

'How come you get to decide when things got serious? I thought they were serious from the beginning. Now I find out you were still sleeping with your old girlfriend.' She paused because her voice was beginning to crack. 'And this weekend she was here. This is too much. I can't take it.'

She stood up with her back toward him and crossed the rug to the bare floor. Until now, she'd clung to a thread of hope that he'd dance in here and magically explain away all her doubts. That thread, frayed though it might be, was what kept her hanging on the past week. Now it had broken. She covered her mouth with her hand. She had made it this far without crying, and she was determined not to start now. Not in front of him. She took a deep breath.

He picked up his glass from the table. Out the corner of her eye, she saw him raise it to his lips and open his mouth to take an ice cube, but then he realized they had all melted. He held the glass on his knee and stared at it. 'I can't change what's already happened. Are you going to punish me for one weekend?' When she didn't respond, he stood up. 'We had a good thing going, Beverly. Can't we just get past this and . . .'

She wheeled around to face him. 'No. Because it's not just one weekend. You've been screwing around all along. And I can't forget it just like that.' She snapped her fingers. 'Every time I look at you, I'll think about it. Maybe it's nothing to you, but to me it's a big part of the history of our relationship.'

She turned away from him again. He went into the kitchen, returned almost immediately without the glass, and picked up his coat from the back of the chair. 'This isn't going anywhere right now. Maybe we both need a little more time.' She didn't say anything, just stood with her back to him.

'I'll call you next week, okay? By then . . .'

'You just don't get it, do you?'

He came up behind her. 'Maybe I don't want to get it, 'cause I don't like the idea of losing you.'

'You did that last Friday night.'

He put his hands on her shoulders. 'Bev . . .' She jerked her shoulders free and took a step away from him.

'I see. I'm just wasting my time here, is that right?'

She answered with a stony silence. He put on his coat and straightened the collar. 'You're a tough woman, Beverly.'

'I'm not so tough. I'm just no pushover. If that's what you want, go back to Charlottesville or just step outside and look around. But you won't find one in here.'

He let himself out, closing the door softly. She sank into the chair at the dining-room table and looked down at the page she'd been editing. How she could take someone else's flawed writing and prune and polish it to perfection but fail so miserably at her own affairs was beyond her understanding. She used to think she wasn't investing enough of herself in her personal life, that if she put as much time and energy into her love life as she did into her profession, she'd have it all. When things failed with Michael, she vowed to do just that with her next relationship. So she tried to shower Vernon with the attention men seemed to crave. That was one reason she was late with this national park article. Her job almost demanded that she bring work home to compete and get ahead, but when she was seeing Vernon she rarely did that. She'd decided he was more important, that her career could be put on hold for a while. Now she was behind in both areas. She folded her arms over the table, buried her head in them, and had herself a good cry.

10

Charmaine pulled the black sequined dress over her head and pushed to get it down over her hips. She slipped her feet into a pair of high-heeled suede mules as Beverly frowned from her lounging position on Charmaine's bed. Beverly was lying on her side, in blue jeans and a Hampton University sweatshirt, her head propped up on one hand.

'I don't see how you can walk in that skintight skirt and those heels, Charmaine.'

'What do you mean? I'm a woman, ain't I? You learn these things if you want to look good for your man.'

Beverly giggled. 'I don't mean that. I can walk in heels. But I stopped wearing those four-inch ones 'cause they're murder on your feet.'

'Might be murder on my feet, but they put a lot of spice into my sex life. Clarence thinks they're so sexy.' Charmaine wiggled her buttocks and they both laughed.

'So where's the big Saturday night bash?'

'At some clubhouse over in Southwest.' Charmaine leaned across the dresser and applied a generous coating of royal-ruby lipstick. 'We'll probably be out pretty late. I can't never get that man home when he's out partying with his buddies. But I shouldn't complain. At least he's taking me with him this time. You sure you don't want to stay overnight? We can put Kenny in the bed with us when we get back and you can sleep in his room.'

'Nah. I want to go back to my place so I can get up early tomorrow morning and finish an article I'm working on. I'm really behind.'

'Suit yourself,' Charmaine said, sitting at the foot of the bed. She began transferring things from her shoulder bag to a small evening purse. 'So you told Vernon to go . . .' She stopped talking when she heard Clarence calling her name from the bottom of the stairs and got up and went to the door. 'I'm coming in just a minute. Quiet down or you'll wake Kenny.'

'If you don't get a move on, woman, the damn thing'll be over before we leave the house.'

Charmaine rolled her eyes to the ceiling and returned to the bed. 'Just 'cause it's his 'Bama friends, he can't wait to get there. If it was something one of my friends was having, he'd have some lame excuse for not going.'

She sat back on the edge of the bed. 'So, you told your man to go take a hike?'

'That's what I told him, but I'm not sure it was the right thing to do. That's why I'm so behind at work. I was supposed to finish up last week. But I can barely concentrate since he came by Thursday night.'

'Nothing wrong with playing a little hard to get. Just don't overdo it. Before you know it, some other chick will have her claws in him.'

'I'm not sure one already doesn't. And even if she doesn't, I'm not so sure I'll decide to take him back.'

'If you don't, you're a fool.'

Beverly sat up. 'How can you say that? The man cheated on me when we started dating. Then he kicked me out of his apartment building while the woman was up there with him, even knowing I was locked out of my car.'

'Oh, grow up, Beverly. You think you're the first woman that's ever been cheated on? At least he told you the truth. Most men wouldn't have done that. And what's this about getting locked out of your car? I didn't know nothing about that.'

'Oops,' Beverly said, covering her mouth with her hand. 'I wasn't supposed to say that.'

'C'mon, tell me what happened.'

'If I tell you this,' Beverly said, shaking her finger at Charmaine, 'you have to promise never to tell anyone.'

'I promise.'

'I mean it. Not a soul. Not ever. It's so embarrassing. Maybe I shouldn't even tell you.'

'You better tell me, girl.'

'Okay, okay.' Beverly told her about going to Vernon's apartment intending to slash his convertible top. It was hard to get the story out, Charmaine was laughing so hard. Especially at the part about Beverly locking the keys in the car.

'That don't sound like you at all, Beverly,' Charmaine said between fits of laughter.

'You're right. I don't know what came over me. Sounds more like something you would do.'

''Scuse me? I have never, ever, done anything that crazy. And you not even married to the man. I'd hate to see what you'd do if you found out your husband was getting out on you.'

'I talked to Evelyn on the phone this morning. She thinks I did the right thing by breaking up with him.'

'What the hell does she know?'

'She must know something. She's got a good marriage.'

Charmaine threw her compact into the evening bag. 'If I hear one more thing about Miss Perfect Marriage, I'll scream.'

Beverly moved across the bed, closer to Charmaine. 'Look, I've seen too many women put up with this kind of thing. A friend at work is getting married in a few weeks to a man she knows cheated on her. That's the dumbest thing I ever heard of. That's why the men in this town are so stinking rotten. We let them get away with too much.'

'You make everything so complicated. Just 'cause he slipped up a few times, you think he's the devil reincarnated. And like I said, at least he was honest about it. Would you rather he had lied?'

'No. I'm not saying that. And I know decent people make mistakes. It's just . . . I don't know. I expected more from Vernon. He seemed so different, so special when I met him.'

'He may be special. But you're not giving him much of a chance to show it.'

'What do you expect me to do? Just ignore . . .'

They both turned to look toward the doorway when they heard Clarence's voice from downstairs. 'Charm, will you come on here?'

'You'd better get going,' Beverly said. 'Your husband is ready to jam.'

Charmaine stood up. 'It's been so long since we went out together for a night on the town, I'm not sure I remember how to dance.' She twirled around. 'How do I look?'

Beverly smiled. 'You'll knock 'em dead. I could never make a straight black dress look like that.'

Charmaine put her hand to her forehead as if to steady herself, then sat back on the bed.

'What's the matter?' Beverly asked, reaching out to touch her sister's arm.

'Nothing. Not a thing. Got a little dizzy from spinning around too fast, that's all.' She stood back up. 'And what are you talking about, girl? You have a nice shape. You just don't have the nerve to wear something like this.'

'Well, yeah. There's that, too. You sure you're okay?'

Charmaine leaned over and kissed Beverly on the cheek. 'I'm fine. Thanks for giving up one of your Saturday nights to look after Kenny for us.'

'Ha. Not like I had anything exciting planned.'

'If things don't work out with Vernon, you have to start getting out more. Maybe we'll go to a club one night or something. You can't meet any men sitting at home. What about work? Any interesting men there?'

'Well, there is this new guy who seems interested.'

'Already? Go for it, girl.'

'We've only gone out to lunch a couple of times. But he asked me out for dinner.'

'What did you tell him?'

'I told him I don't date men I work with. Besides, I'm not ready for that.'

Charmaine rolled her eyes to the ceiling. 'Why on earth did you do something stupid like that? Is he cute?'

'Not bad.'

'Damn, Beverly. What's the matter with you?'

'I'm not so sure about him, you know? There's something that makes me uneasy. He seems very nice, but a bit on the conceited side, I guess.'

'You don't have to marry this . . . what's his name?'

'Byron.'

'Byron. Just go out with him and have some fun. Maybe he just has a lot of confidence. Could be just what you need to help you get through this Vernon thing.'

'Charm!' Clarence shouted.

Beverly stood up. 'Look, you go on and have a good time. I'll call you tomorrow and we can talk some more.'

Charmaine nodded. 'Coming, dear,' she said loud enough for Clarence to hear. She and Beverly laughed as they walked through the bedroom door.

Charmaine knew the minute Clarence pulled his old Ford into the gravel-covered parking lot that this was not going to be her kind of thing. The dance hall was a huge dilapidated warehouse along the waterfront at the far end of the main drag. One side of the building was surrounded by a small wooded area, the other by several old abandoned buildings. Charmaine didn't even think they had spots like this in the nation's capital anymore, with so much building going on all around town lately. Leave it to Clarence Perry and his friends to find the last remaining one.

'You mean I put on this dress and you put on a suit and tie to come to this giant outhouse?' she said as Clarence pulled into a parking space.

'Quit complaining,' he said, extinguishing his More cigarette. 'The boys couldn't afford one of those fancy hotels downtown.' He opened the car door and got out, but Charmaine didn't budge. She sat there with her bottom lip poked out and her arms folded under her breasts. Clarence watched her as he rounded the front of the car to her side. He opened her door. 'The thing will be over by the time you get your ass outta that seat, woman.'

'Shit, Clarence, I'm not going in that dump. I don't believe this hole in the wall was the best they could come up with.'

'I'm sure they fixed it up nice inside, baby. C'mon.' He stuck his hand out and she took it reluctantly.

Hmmph, they fixed it up all right, she thought as they entered the building. Oh, the people were dressed nice enough. She suspected some of the women had spent a week's wages on their shiny new dresses. Still, there was something seedy about the whole affair. It looked to Charmaine like a couple of men had just slapped a coat of paint on the walls, mopped the cement floors, and hung a few glittery decorations from the ceiling. There weren't even enough tables and chairs for everybody. Many of the people were standing around the edges of the room near the walls, and out in the lobby.

She grabbed Clarence's arm after he finished checking their coats. 'Clarence, you got to be kidding me if you're planning on staying.'

'We just got here.'

'Look at this place. It's depressing.'

'Give it a chance. I laid out forty bucks to these people for those tickets.'

'You mean you laid your hand out for forty bucks from my pockets.'

'Same difference. What's yours is mine and vice versa. Right?'

'Hmmph. Only problem is you ain't got nothing.'

Clarence smiled. 'I knew you were going to say that. C'mon, let's go find a seat.' He took her hand and she followed him as he made his way through the crowd. She almost hoped they wouldn't find any empty seats. If they were forced to stand all night, maybe Clarence would get tired sooner and want to leave. Almost nobody was dancing, the band was so bad. But it was probably just as well, Charmaine thought, since the dance floor was about the size of her kitchen.

Charmaine's hopes of an early departure were dashed when she saw that some of Clarence's friends had saved a spot for them at one of the big round tables scattered throughout the room. Clarence introduced her to a couple of his friends standing around the table. She smiled and nodded even though she was barely able to catch the names over the loud music. Their table was right near the band and the speakers, so normal conversation was almost impossible. If it were good music, it wouldn't be so bad. But the stuff had no rhyme or rhythm. It just blared. She sat down, and since everything looked so shabby, she found herself lifting the frayed red tablecloth to peek under the table, fully expecting to be greeted by one of the nasty little rodents the waterfront was famous for.

Clarence looked down at her and said something she couldn't hear, but she could tell by his gestures that he wanted to dance. That was Clarence for you. He would dance to anything. Once, when they first started dating and were shopping downtown, Clarence grabbed her in the middle of the street and started dancing to the beat of the construction noises. She thought it was funny and cute then, though she doubted she would find it so funny and cute if he did something like that now. But those construction tools had more rhythm than this.

'If you think I'm dancing to that sorry excuse for music,' she said, practically shouting, 'think again.'

'It is pretty bad,' Clarence shouted into her ear. He sat down next to her. For once, Charmaine thought, they agreed on something. He lit a cigarette and offered her one. She took it and held it between her lips while he lit it for her. She took one drag and made a face. 'Damn.'

'What's wrong?'

'This cigarette tastes like shit,' she said, smashing it out in the ashtray.

He touched her forehead. 'Maybe you're coming down with something. You want a drink?'

She couldn't pick up his last few words over the music. 'What did you say?'

He cupped his hand near his mouth like he was holding a glass. 'I saw a cash bar when we first came in.'

103

She nodded. 'I guess. But just a Coke.'

He leaned near her. 'Huh?'

'Yes!' she shouted. 'A Coke!'

'Okay,' he said, jumping up. 'Be back in a New York minute.'

As Clarence walked off, Charmaine looked around at the other people at their table. The oddest thing, she thought, was that despite the dreary atmosphere, everyone seemed to be having a good enough time, everyone except her. Two women, one in her thirties and the other probably in her early forties, sat at the opposite end of the table and were deep into some kind of private conversation. The older woman was talking animatedly into the younger woman's ear as the younger woman nodded her head eagerly in agreement.

Two chairs away, to the left of Charmaine, a stocky man wearing a too-tight suit and puffing on a fat cigar stood behind his chair talking to a man with a bushy mustache. Every so often, the big man would lean down and say something to the thin woman seated between him and Charmaine. She was wearing a bare-shouldered dress that no woman that skinny should have the nerve to put on. Charmaine could see the bones sticking out of her shoulders. The woman was smoking a cigarette and nursing a drink and her eyes were sort of drooping, but Charmaine couldn't tell if the poor thing was drunk or just bored to death.

Who the hell were these people? She didn't recognize a damn soul. She and Clarence didn't share many friends, but it seemed she would at least recognize somebody, any old body. D.C. was such a small town, you always ran into somebody at things like this. The two men on her left slapped high fives and the one with the mustache took off. Mr Cigar sat down next to his droopy-eyed date. Charmaine turned her body slightly away from them, trying to be discreet so as not to offend them. But she had to get her legs out from under this creepy table and her nose away from the cigar smoke.

The band stopped playing, probably to everyone's relief, and one of the band members walked up to a microphone and announced that they were taking a ten-minute break. The older woman glanced around the table with a look of disbelief on her face. 'That's the third break they've taken since we got here. Seems like they take one after every number.'

The younger woman nodded. 'As bad as they sound, they should just take one for the rest of the night.'

The others at the table laughed, but Charmaine did not find it particularly funny. She failed to see anything amusing in this pitiful setup. How had she let Clarence talk her into this shit? And knowing how Clarence was when he got around his buddies, it was going to be a long evening. By the time it was over, Clarence would be more than a little tipsy – not roaring drunk, but high enough for her to be scared to let him drive home. Then they would argue about who was going to get behind the wheel until he finally gave her the keys. That was the main reason they stopped going out to parties together as much as they used to. She just hated the way Clarence got at these things.

She stretched her neck, looking for him. He seemed to be taking an awful long time getting those drinks. She didn't see him or anyone else she knew, but she saw a sign for the rest rooms, so she decided to go there. It would give her something to do besides sitting here looking stupid.

When she stood up, her head felt a little light, like she was about to float off into space, so she put her hands on the back of her chair to steady herself. Shit. What was the matter with her? Probably all the smoke, she thought, glancing at the odd couple. The woman was using one cigarette to light another. The man was relighting his cigar. Charmaine shook her head and picked up her purse. As she made her way through the crowd, she kept an eye out for Clarence, even though she was headed in the opposite direction from the bar. Knowing Clarence, he was nowhere near the bar by now anyway. Probably met up with some of his buddies and forgot all about . . .

'Well, well, well. If it isn't Miss Charmaine Perry.' Charmaine turned and looked for the source of the voice calling her name. Out from the crowd stepped Lemuel Marshall, or Lem, as he was always called, one of Clarence's hanging buddies. As always, Lem was looking like a million bucks. He had the kind of gorgeous looks that turned every female head in a crowd, and he knew it. One of his many girlfriends probably bought the sharp suit he was wearing.

'Hello, Lem. It's been a long time.'

He leaned over and kissed her cheek. 'You're looking good, sweetheart, as always. And still got the most beautiful figure I've ever seen on any woman.' He stepped back and looked her over in that way he always did, especially when she was wearing a short, tight skirt. 'That dress was made for you, Charm.'

She smiled. 'Thank you. You don't look half bad yourself.'

He patted the jacket to his double-breasted suit. 'Well, I do try to keep myself up.'

'So, Lem, still haven't settled down, I hear.'

'Whoa,' he said, stepping back with a big smile. 'Why do women always ask me these provocative questions?'

She nudged him teasingly in his side. 'You know I always thought you'd make some woman a good catch.' Lying through her teeth. Heaven help the woman who ended up marrying Lem. He was one of those men that no sensible married woman wants her husband hanging around. Charmaine always got a sinking feeling when she knew Clarence was out with him. He attracted women the way a picnic table attracted flies.

'You know me, sweetheart,' he said, putting one hand in his pocket. 'But then it's just a matter of finding the right one. Not too many women out there like you. Clarence is one lucky brother. I'm always telling him that.'

Sure he was, Charmaine thought. Was that before, during, or after he was trying to turn Clarence on to the chicks in his harem? She smiled at him. 'Have you seen him, by the way? He was supposed to be getting me a drink, but that was a while ago.'

'I saw him out in the lobby a few minutes back.'

Charmaine was about to excuse herself and head in that direction when a pretty young thing in a tight red dress sauntered up to Lem and wrapped her hand around his arm quite possessively. Charmaine figured she couldn't be more than twenty. Despite her sweet, innocent looks, though, she managed to toss off one of those woman-to-woman 'he's mine, back off' looks that the chicks with Lem always seemed to have mastered.

Lem patted the woman's hand as if to reassure her. 'This is Charmaine, Clarence's wife. Charm, Robin.'

The woman's expression immediately softened and she smiled sweetly. Charmaine smiled back. Don't worry, hon. Wouldn't want your man even if it wasn't for Clarence. She looked at Lem. 'I'm going to go find that husband of mine. You take care, Lem. Nice meeting you, Robin.'

Robin nodded and Lem kissed Charmaine on the cheek. 'If I see Clarence, I'll tell him you're looking for him,' he said.

Charmaine turned back toward the lobby and the rest rooms. The music was starting up again. She hoped the walls in this place were thick enough to drown out some of the noise once she got outside the main room.

'Hey, miss,' someone said at the ticket table near the entrance. He held out a used ticket. 'If you're coming back in you need this.' Charmaine wished she could tell him to keep it, that she wouldn't be needing the thing because she didn't plan on coming within ten miles of this place again anytime soon. But she took it, then stepped out into the big entry lobby. It was as crowded and stuffy as the dance hall, with people standing around talking, drinking, and smoking.

As Charmaine made her way toward the rest rooms, located in a poorly lit corner of the lobby, she realized the people out here were doing something else as well. The smell of marijuana was faint but unmistakable, and it made her stomach turn. She thought she was going to be sick right then and there. She didn't actually see anyone smoking, but a blind person would know what was going on here. She suspected that the odor hit her with such force because it had been years since she'd smoked the stuff – since before Kenny was born.

She made her way through the crowd and pushed open the door to the ladies' room, expecting to find relief from the nausea building up in her stomach. Instead, she found that the odor was even worse here. A woman was bent over the vanity, and for a second Charmaine thought she was feeling out of it, too. But she didn't spend much time thinking about it — combined with the stench of the poorly vented bathroom, the smell of marijuana was unbearable. Rotten odors seemed to be coming from the walls. The queasiness in her stomach rushed up through her chest so fast that she barely had time to get into one of the stalls before the big lump reached her throat. In her haste, she almost knocked over the other woman in the room, but there was no time to stop and apologize. She threw the seat up with a bang and bent over the toilet just before everything in her stomach gushed out of her mouth.

By the time she came out of the stall several minutes later, the other woman had left. Charmaine wiped her mouth and tongue with the wad of toilet paper in her hand and looked into the mirror over the vanity. She felt drained and about twenty pounds lighter. She couldn't put it off any longer. First thing Monday morning, she was going to have to call her gynecologist and schedule a pregnancy test. But she knew what the results would be without some doctor telling her. She'd vomited almost every day for a month when she was pregnant with Kenny. It was the only other time in her life that she'd been this sick to her stomach.

She didn't want to think about what it all meant or what it would do to their lives. Not yet. She would get the test before she started worrying, to be absolutely certain. She had to take this one step at a time.

She was about to place her purse on top of the vanity when she noticed tiny bits of a white powdery substance lining the bowl. She couldn't believe what she was seeing, so she leaned closer to be sure. So that's what that woman was up to. These people had no shame. Smoking and snorting out in the open. Did they think this was still the sixties? Someone could call the cops. She made up her mind then and there that she was getting out of this crazy place as soon as she could find Clarence. It wouldn't have made any difference if they had paid four hundred dollars apiece for the tickets.

She rinsed the pasty taste from her mouth and applied a fresh coat of lipstick. When she came out, Clarence was the first person she saw. He was talking to a bunch of men she didn't recognize, nursing a drink, and smoking one of his brown Mores. She walked up behind him and tugged at his jacket sleeve. He turned to face her with a big smile on his face. 'Oh, hey, baby. I want you to meet –'

'Not now.' She pulled him away from the group of men, who looked a little disappointed that they wouldn't get to meet her, and dragged him out of earshot.

'What's going on?' Clarence asked. She held onto his arm and continued to pull him along behind her. 'Wait a minute. You're making me spill my drink.' He freed his arm from her grasp, and she whirled around to face him. 'I have to get out of this place. Now. This instant.'

'We just got here. I brought you your Coke. It's on the table.'

'To hell with the Coke, Clarence. I want to go home.'

'Well, I'm not ready just yet, if you don't mind. What's gotten into you all of a sudden?' He put his cigarette out in an ashtray stand near the wall.

'There's drugs all over this place. And I don't plan to be here when the police come and raid it.'

'Is that what this shit is all about? So there's a little grass. The police aren't coming 'cause a couple people smoking joints.'

She threw her arms in the air. 'A little? What the hell's the matter with your nose? The place is reeking with it. And that's not all. I saw coke in the bathroom. And I don't mean the kind you brought to my table.'

'Calm down, Charm.' He reached out to her. 'Calm –' She jerked away and looked at him furiously. He stuck one hand in his pocket and took a sip of his drink. 'You're getting all worked up about nothing. You're also embarrassing me acting like this. Go sit at the table, and I'll join you in a minute.'

'Have you heard a thing I been saying to you, Clarence? I don't approve of that stuff in my house, and I don't approve of it out here in the open. If you won't take me home, I'll get a damn cab.'

'Okay, okay. I'll take you home. Just give me a few minutes.'

'No, Clarence. If you're not coming now, just say so and I'll call a cab.'

'Okay, I'll take you home now. But I'm coming back.'

'Fine with me.'

'Stay here a second. I have to talk to Lem about something.' He turned toward the dance hall.

'Wait a minute,' she shouted after him. Some of the people in the lobby turned to look in her direction, but she didn't give a damn. Let 'em look. 'I just saw Lem and he didn't say nothing about needing to talk to you. If you go in there, you'll never come back out. I want to go now.'

Clarence turned back to face her, and it was apparent that his patience had worn thin. He grabbed her arm and marched her to the entrance. He looked so pissed off, Charmaine fully expected him to throw her out the door. But he stopped just inside the entrance. 'Look, I'm tired of this bullshit. I said I would take you home and I will as soon as I talk to Lem. You just park your ass here and shut up 'til I get back. Or do something useful, like getting our coats.' Charmaine snatched her arm away and straightened her dress. Clarence walked off.

Hmmph. She looked at her watch. She was giving him exactly five minutes. And if he wasn't back, she was leaving his sorry ass here.

But for once in his life, Clarence was true to his word. He returned in a few minutes, smiling and dangling his car keys in his hand. 'Okay, let's go. Where are our coats?'

'Uh, I forgot. I never thought you'd get back so soon.'

'What good are you, woman?' He smiled. 'Never mind. Wait here while I get them.'

He skipped off and Charmaine rolled her eyes. What did he have to be so damn cheerful about? Strutting around and twirling his keys. Probably planning on coming back here and getting into something he had no business with. When they'd first started going out together, he'd used drugs occasionally. A little grass on weekends. Coke once in a while. Nothing heavy.

But she didn't like the stuff, especially around Kenny, and after they were married she forbid it in her presence. He swore he'd stopped using the stuff, and since she'd seen no signs of it, she'd believed him. But after seeing what was going on here around his friends she wasn't so sure.

He returned and helped her with her coat. 'I'm not getting up out of bed to bail you out of some jail if they come raid this place tonight. You hear me?'

'Yeah, yeah,' he said, holding the door open for her.

'I mean it, Clarence,' she said, following him across the gravel-covered parking lot. 'What do you want to come back here for, anyway?' He was walking so fast, weaving through the maze of parked cars, that she had trouble keeping up with him in her spiked mules. 'You hear me talking to you, Clarence Perry?' she asked, shouting over the sound of gravel crunching under their feet. 'All those people doing is getting high. That what you plan on doing when you come back?'

'No, I'm not,' he said without slowing down or turning back to look at her.

'Then what the hell are you coming back for?'

'To be with my friends. That's all.'

'Hmmph. Your friends who are probably in there snorting their noses off right now and goodness knows what else.' It seemed the faster they walked, the more gravel they kicked up. She could feel pebbles slipping into the toes of her shoes. 'Can you slow down some? Why you so anxious to get back to this dump to be with these sorry-assed bums I don't understand.'

'You the one that couldn't wait to get out of there. Now you want me to slow down. Make up your damn mind.'

'I can only walk so fast across this muck. Maybe if they had found a place with a halfway decent parking lot I wouldn't be holding you up from your precious goons.'

He spun around in front of her so quickly she nearly fell backward. She had to put her hand on the hood of their car to steady herself.

'Why don't you shut the hell up?' he shouted. 'You been on

111

my case, putting my boys down ever since we got here. I'm sick and damn tired of listening to your fucking mouth.'

She put her hands on her hips. 'If you got some decent friends, you wouldn't have to hear my mouth, 'cause I wouldn't have so much to complain about. All most of them do is chase women and sit around getting high. Half of them don't even have jobs. You don't need to hang around people like that, Clarence. You're better than that.'

He thrust his finger in her face. 'If it's anything I don't need right now, woman, it's you. And if you don't stop dissin' my boys, your fat ass'll be walking home. Now get your butt in the got-damn car.'

She stood beside the car and gave him her worst evil eye as he walked around and opened the door on the driver's side. Hmmph. Who the hell did he think he was, talking to her like that? She wheeled around on her heels and marched back toward the building.

'Where the hell are you going now?' he yelled after her.

She ignored him.

'Will you come on back here, woman?'

She kept walking. She heard the car door slam shut, but she wasn't sure if he'd gotten in and was about to drive off or if he was coming after her. She was determined not to turn and look. Then she heard footsteps cracking in the gravel behind her. He grabbed her arm and turned her around to face him. She yanked it out of his grasp.

'What is the matter with you?' he asked. 'You want to go home or not?'

'You mean what's the matter with *you*. I don't need anybody talking to me like that, including you. *Especially* you. I'll get a cab.' She stomped off toward the building.

He ran up in front of her and walked backward. 'No wife of mine is getting a cab home in the middle of the night when she's out with me. I don't care how mad you are.'

'Watch me.' She moved to the right to pass him but he stepped in front of her. She tried to go the other way, but he moved to block her.

112

'I mean it,' he said. 'Get in the car.'

'Out of my way, Clarence.'

He raised his hands in mock defeat. 'All right. All right. I said some things I shouldn't have. I'm sorry. Now get in the car.'

She stood there and stared at him, her eyes furious.

'Please, Charm. You know this part of the city is no place for a woman to be hanging out alone.'

He was right about that.

'I won't be able to enjoy myself in there worrying about whether you got home safe,' he said.

She rolled her eyes at him and turned around and walked back toward the car. He caught up and walked beside her.

'If you ever talk to me like that again, Clarence Perry, so help me it'll be the last time.'

'Right.'

'I mean it.'

'I know you do.'

11

A cool November breeze greeted Charmaine as she walked out of the doctor's office. She turned the collar to her leather jacket up around her neck, shoved her hands in the pockets to keep them warm, and headed toward the Foggy Bottom metro stop.

There was no denying it anymore. She was pregnant. For about the next thirty weeks she'd have to put up with vitamins, swollen feet, and a fat stomach. Shit. The fucking diaphragm should be outlawed. What good was it?

She'd always wanted another child, but not under these shaky circumstances. As much as she adored Kenny, having and raising him those years before she met Clarence had been the pits. She never wanted to go through anything like that again. She could remember the night in the delivery room as if it had happened last week. She'd long since broken up with the baby's father and had never felt so scared and alone in her life. Sure, her mama and daddy were outside in the waiting room, but that wasn't how it was supposed to be. Her husband was supposed to be there, and she had vowed to get it right the next time.

She stepped off the curb into the busy intersection at Washington Circle. Now she had the hubby, but in some ways things were worse than before. That husband of hers was such a big baby, it felt like she had a third child on the way. How were they ever going to earn the money to feed another mouth and clothe another body? And she could forget going back to college. They would never be able to save enough for that.

A car whipped by so close her pleated wool skirt flew up in the air. She froze in her tracks and looked up. She was in the middle of the street, and cars were whizzing by her. In the center lane where she was standing, several cars had stopped because she

114

was in the way. The occupants had their heads stuck out the windows and were staring at her curiously. She glanced up at the street signal and realized she was crossing against the light. Shit. How the hell did that happen? There was no time to figure it out now, though. Drivers were starting to honk their horns. She had to get out of this busy intersection before someone flattened her simple ass to the pavement. But how? There was one lane behind her, one in front, and cars were flying by in both. She was stuck in the middle, holding up a line of irate drivers waiting for her to get the hell out of their way. Finally, she saw a break in the lane ahead of her. She clutched her shoulder bag to her side and darted to the opposite sidewalk.

It was then that she realized her heart was thumping wildly against her chest and beads of perspiration had broken out across her forehead. She spotted a bench under some trees shedding the last of their leaves and sat down. She unbuttoned her leather jacket and fanned her face with her hand. She needed a moment to collect herself. She was so lost in thought that she had damn near gotten herself killed back there.

She couldn't take too much time, though. She promised her boss she'd be back in two hours, and knowing that woman, she was counting the minutes. She hadn't told Susan or anyone else at the office where she was going, just that she needed a long lunch break to take care of some personal business. Susan hated that kind of thing, thought she had a right to know about everybody's affairs when they took time off from work. But Charmaine wasn't ready to tell anyone about this just yet, not before she decided what to do.

Knowing Clarence, he would want the baby. He'd been trying to get her to stop using the diaphragm since the night they got married. But to him a baby would be like a new toy, something he could play with until he got bored. Then he would drop it in her lap and go out partying with his boys, like he did with Kenny.

Maybe she should just have an abortion without telling him she was pregnant. Why bring another baby into this crappy family? As it was, there were days on end when she was about ready to give up on the marriage and tell Clarence to get the hell out. Like last Saturday night when he'd insisted on going back to that stupid dance. He was so afraid he'd miss out on some fun.

Then there was school. She might never be able to manage that if she went through with this pregnancy. And if the baby is a girl, where will she sleep when she gets too old to share the room with Kenny?

She closed her eyes. So many problems. If only Clarence would get his act together and start being more responsible, they could work out all these things. They were adults, they both had jobs. There was no excuse for this foolishness.

Maybe a baby was just the medicine he needed to cure his chronic case of immaturity. If anything could make somebody grow up in a hurry it was a baby. She'd found that out herself with Kenny. Okay. She would give him that chance. Tonight she was going to sit that thirty-one-year-old adolescent down and tell him in no uncertain words that if he wanted her to have this baby, fine, but he was going to have to help out. She wasn't raising his kid alone. Either he would promise to show a change for the better in the next few weeks, or she would have an abortion. No more of this fooling around like it was Christmas 365 days a year. She hadn't insisted with Kenny, 'cause Clarence wasn't Kenny's father. But this was different. This was Clarence's doing.

She stood up and buttoned her jacket. Now that she'd worked that out in her head, she was ready to get back to the office.

'Uh-huh,' Charmaine said, nodding her head and writing her boss's instructions in a stenographer's notebook. Susan had a 5:20 P.M. flight to Grand Cayman for a conference and would be gone for two whole weeks. Heaven, Nirvana, Charmaine thought in between scribbles on the pad. For everybody. Susan would get a chance to rest her frayed nerves in the Caribbean, and Charmaine and the rest of the gang in the department would get two weeks of peace and quiet. She could come in an hour or so late, leave an hour or so early, and take two-hour lunches. Charmaine couldn't wait. When Susan was here, she never got a moment's rest and almost never took time off. And the days just before Susan left for a business trip, the madhouse was even madder than usual. Xerox this, call that person, type this, find that. By the time Susan stepped out the door on her way to the airport, Charmaine could actually feel her blood pressure drop.

'. . . don't forget to mail the Jacobs report by first thing tomorrow morning. And send it Federal Express. He has to get it on Friday.' Susan was standing behind her desk packing a briefcase and munching on a salami sandwich at the same time.

'I won't forget,' Charmaine said, writing it all down. 'I'll print it out before I leave today.'

Susan sifted through the clutter on her desk. 'Where's the audit report? I need to take that with me, too.'

'At my desk. Just have to put it in a folder.'

'Well, get it. It should be in here with my other things. I leave for the airport in ten minutes.'

Brother, Charmaine almost said aloud. She only had two hands and this one body. The woman got her away from the audit report to take notes on what to do while she was gone. Or didn't she remember that? 'You want it in a clear cover or solid?' Charmaine said, forcing a bright smile. Ten minutes, ten more minutes, and this woman would be gone. Then she could get on the phone and try to find Clarence. She wanted him home at a decent hour tonight so they could talk about her condition.

'Uh, clear, I guess. Whatever you think is best.'

Charmaine turned toward the door.

'Oh, one more thing.'

She turned back to face Susan.

'Stanley's in charge of things while I'm gone, as usual, but he'll be in and out of the office a lot, attending some meetings. I'm counting on you to keep an eye on things for me. If there are any problems, call me. You have the number?'

Charmaine sifted through her steno pad. 'Yep, right here.'

'Oh, and one more thing.'

Charmaine looked up.

'The conference is over next Wednesday, and John and the children are coming up that evening for a few days. John's coming by the office Tuesday evening to pick up a paper that Bob's still working on for me. Can you? . . .'

'I know. Bug Bob to make sure it's ready by Tuesday.'

'Right.'

'Anything else?'

Susan looked around her desk. 'No, just the audit report.'

Charmaine went back to her desk and wrapped the report with one eye on the wall clock. Susan said she was leaving in ten minutes, which meant she should be gone by 4:15. That would leave fifteen minutes to call Clarence before he got off work. If she didn't catch him, she'd have to sit up half the night waiting for him to get home or put off talking to him until tomorrow morning.

And she needed to talk to him about more than just the new baby. When she returned from her doctor's appointment, a message from the bill collection agency was sitting on her desk. Charmaine hadn't bothered returning the call. She was sure they wanted to know what happened to the payment for the television set. It had been a couple of weeks since she'd talked to them and agreed to send a check. Since Clarence had promised to borrow the money from one of his sisters and pay the bill, she'd held off. But she should have known better than to rely on that sucker. She eyed the little pink message slip sitting on the corner of her desk. It was marked 'Urgent.' Of course, those people thought everything was urgent. But they would just have to wait until tomorrow to hear from her. She had more important things on her mind now than some bill for some stupid TV she didn't even want.

She finished wrapping the report and was about to take it into Susan's office but noticed that the light to Susan's telephone extension was on. She sat down and looked up at the clock. It was already seventeen minutes after. 'Come on, boss,' she said aloud, 'let's get cracking.' You got a plane to catch. I got a husband to catch.

She stood up. Sometimes Susan got so wrapped up in what she was doing that she lost all sense of time. She walked into Susan's office, placed the report in front of her boss, and pointed to her watch. Susan covered the mouthpiece. 'I'm coming. It's John calling to say good-bye.'

'Oh.' Charmaine nodded and went back to her desk. She called up the Jacobs report on her computer but couldn't concentrate on it. She looked at her watch again – 4:22. If those two lovebirds didn't get off the phone . . . The light to Susan's extension finally went out, and Charmaine turned to face her computer, pretending to work. After a couple of minutes, Susan came out of her office carrying a briefcase in one hand and a large garment bag in the other.

Charmaine stood. 'You want me to get someone to help you to a cab?'

'No, I can manage. You got everything straight now?'

'Yep,' Charmaine said. Go, go, she thought. 'Any problems, I'll call you.'

'Okay. Oh, wait a minute,' Susan said. She placed the suitcase on the floor. 'I wanted to speak to Bob before I left.' Susan walked off toward Bob's office, and Charmaine sank into her chair. She looked at the wall clock. Shit. 4:26. She would never catch Clarence at this rate. Her whole future, the future of her family, was hanging in the balance, depending on whether Clarence could convince her that he was up to behaving like a decent father. The biggest personal crisis Susan would probably face all day would be which meal to have on the plane. Beef or chicken. Next week, after her meetings, it would be whether to lie on the beach or go shopping with her family. Not whether they would still *be* a family.

She was thinking of picking up the suitcase and carrying it to the front door, just to have something to do, when Susan came out of Bob's office. Charmaine snuck a peek at the clock. She had two more minutes before Clarence got off. 'Everything okay?' Charmaine asked.

'I think so,' Susan said, smiling. She picked up her suitcase. 'See you in two weeks.'

'Okay. Have a good trip.' Good-bye, good riddance. Charmaine had the telephone receiver in her hand before the door closed behind Susan.

'Brenda? Mrs Perry. Is Clarence still there?'

'Hold on a second.' Brenda came back on. 'Mrs Perry? Clarence took off sick. He hasn't been in all day.'

Charmaine clenched her fist to keep from pounding the desk. The lazy bum didn't even go in. Again. 'Oh, uh, well, he said he wasn't feeling well this morning. But I didn't know if he decided to stay home or what. 'Bye.' She hung up. Sick my ass. There wasn't a thing wrong with that man this morning. She'd told that fool a hundred times, he better stop taking off so much or he was going to find himself unemployed. He acted like he thought jobs grew on trees.

She picked up the phone and dialed her home number. The line was busy. Well, at least he was home. She turned her computer off, grabbed her purse from under the desk, and flew to the closet for her jacket. She didn't have to pick up Kenny from the day care center until six. If she hurried, maybe she could catch Clarence before he went back out.

The music was so loud she could hear it as she came up the walkway to her house. Just as she reached the porch, a man who couldn't be more than twenty opened her front door. He was short, not much taller than Charmaine, kind of stocky, and a total stranger. The man nodded and smiled as they passed each other on the porch. What was going on in her house, she wondered. A party?

She opened the screen door and was about to insert the key in the lock when she realized the door was ajar. She pushed, and the odor of marijuana crept out. The same smell that had made her so ill at the dance last Saturday night, and here it was in her home. She couldn't believe her nose. She stepped into the foyer and looked toward the living room, ready to lash out at Clarence.

They didn't even notice her at first. Clarence, his head resting on the back of the couch, was staring at the ceiling with his long legs stretched out across the carpet. She noticed he had on a brand-new pair of shoes and that a marijuana butt dangled loosely from his fingers. Lem was sitting on the armchair across from the couch with his back to Charmaine. He was talking, but Charmaine couldn't hear what he was saying over the rap music. A woman sat on the couch next to Clarence, leaning forward and listening intently to Lem. All three of them were dressed casually in jeans, and it was obvious that none of them had put in a hour's work that day. Charmaine recognized the woman from the dance last Saturday night. The woman was the first to notice Charmaine, and she got this strange look on her face, like she wasn't sure whether to smile or what. She signaled to Lem.

'Uh, Lem,' she said with a half smile, half frown on her face.

Lem followed the woman's gaze to Charmaine. Clarence sat up and immediately glanced at his watch when he saw her. Lem stood while Clarence smashed his reefer butt in an ashtray on the end table. He tried to fan the smoke away without being seen as Lem took a step toward Charmaine.

'Charm, baby,' Lem said, forcing a smile on his face. He reached out to kiss Charmaine on the cheek, but she turned her face away and stepped out of his reach. She went to the CD player and turned off the music.

'What the hell is going on here?' she asked, pitching her shoulder bag into a chair. She didn't bother to remove her jacket.

'Whoa,' Lem said, backing away and looking at Clarence.

'Ain't nothing going on,' Clarence said, standing up. 'Just sitting around talking, listening to some notes. What are you doing home so early, anyway?'

'You lying, Clarence,' Charmaine said, her hands on her hips, her eyes fixed on him. If looks could kill, Clarence would have been spread out bleeding on the floor.

'I'm not lying. I —'

121

'Shut up. I'm sick of your damn lies. I told you about drugs in my house. You think I don't know what's been going on here?' She turned toward Lem. 'And you. You ought to be ashamed of yourself. I thought you was one of the few halfway decent friends Clarence had.'

Lem started to say something but stopped when Clarence held up his hands to silence him. 'We was just about to go over to Lem's garage to help him —'

'Oh, no, you're not. I want to talk to you. Alone.'

'I'll be back as soon as —'

Charmaine shook her head emphatically. 'No. I need to talk now, and I mean now.'

'I told you, wasn't nothing going on here.'

'It's not about this. Although I'm pissed enough to shit about you sitting around getting high in my house. I want to talk to you about something else.'

Clarence frowned. 'What's so important it can't wait 'til tonight?'

'Damn it!' Charmaine screamed, jerking her hand in the air. 'You'll just have to stay and find out, won't you?'

The woman, who had been sitting quietly on the couch through all of this, stood and took a step toward Lem. 'Uh, honey,' she said. 'Why don't we go on? Clarence can catch up with us later.'

'Good idea, sweetheart.' The two of them eased out the door as Clarence and Charmaine stared each other down. 'I don't appreciate you talking to me like that in front of my friends,' Clarence said.

Charmaine ignored his comment. 'Who was that guy who just left here?'

Clarence looked puzzled.

'The one who left just before I came in,' Charmaine said impatiently. 'Don't act dumb with me.'

'Oh, you mean Stud.'

'Who?'

'Real name's Jeffrey.'

'What was he doing here?'

'What do you mean? He was visiting. I can have company, can't I?'

'He looked young enough to be your son.'

'He's not as young as he looks.'

'I bet. How old is he?'

'How would I know? Late twenties, early thirties, I guess.'

'I don't believe that for a minute, Clarence. Was he selling drugs?'

Clarence paced around impatiently. 'Nah. Hell, no. Is this what you had to talk to me about that was so urgent? 'Cause if it is . . .'

'I'ma tell you something, Clarence Perry,' she said, pointing her finger at him. 'If I ever in my life catch you using drugs again in my house, it's over. You hear me? I will not put up with drug parties in my house. I'm trying to raise a son. A decent one.'

Clarence looked to the ceiling. 'I know that.'

'I thought you stopped using them anyway. You told me you stopped.'

'This is rare. A one-time thing.'

'It better be. Where'd you get it, anyway?'

'Uh, Lem's girlfriend.'

'Oh, sure. Blame it on her. This really bothers me. I don't know what to say about you.'

He looked away, and Charmaine took a deep breath. She took off her jacket and sank into the armchair. Clarence sat on the edge of the coffee table in front of her. 'Okay,' he said, looking at her. 'I know it was wrong. Bad judgment on my part. It won't happen again. I swear.'

'You've said that before about so many things, Clarence. And you just keep on doing them. I don't know what the hell to believe anymore.'

'I know how you feel about drugs. I would never do that around Kenny. I swear.'

'It's not just this. You're always saying one thing and doing something else. Did you ever send the money in for the TV bill?'

123

'I said I was, didn't I?'

'Then you tell me why I got a call from the collection agency today.'

'They called? Again already? Damn.'

'Answer the question, Clarence.'

'I guess the check must still be in the mail then. I only sent it a few days ago.'

'If you paid it, which I seriously doubt, where'd you get the money? And where did you get the money for those new shoes?'

'Why am I getting the third degree here?'

'Because you're always lying, that's why. Did you go to work today?'

He looked away. 'I went in for a few hours this morning.'

'See what I mean? You're lying again.'

He stood up. 'Look, I don't have to put up with this shit.'

'Yes, you do. Unless you want to be out on the street tonight. I called your office today and they said you were out sick.'

'Well, I went in for a few minutes and told them I wasn't feeling –'

She stood up and faced him. 'Stop it. I swear you got a lie for everything. First it was a few hours, now it's a few minutes. Brenda said you never came in.'

'She must didn't see me, then. I was there.'

She waved her arm at him. 'Forget it, Clarence. It's hopeless. Everything that comes out of your mouth is a lie.' She put on her jacket and grabbed her bag from the chair. She walked to the door and opened it.

'Hey, where you going?'

'To pick up my son, that's where.' She opened the screen door.

'I thought you had something to tell me that couldn't wait.'

She turned back to look at him. 'I lied.' She turned back around, walked out, and slammed the door shut behind her.

12

Evelyn rammed the shovel into the dirt one more time, then put her foot on the end of it and pushed. She'd gone through this last year with the same weed. The roots were so deep it was impossible to get to the bottom, and each year it sprang back bigger and tougher and uglier than the year before. She was hesitant to use weed killer because the monster was only a few feet from her garden. But it was beginning to look like she would have no choice.

She twisted the shovel up and got a big chunk out but knew that wasn't the last of it. Tomorrow she was going to Hechinger's and get the strongest can of weed killer she could find. She dropped the weed into her homemade composter and scattered fertilizer over the pile.

The door to the kitchen opened, and Rebecca's little head popped out. 'Mama, the phone,' she yelled.

Evelyn looked up and frowned. 'Who is it?'

'Aunt Charmaine.'

'Okay. I'll take it out here.' She peeled off her work gloves as she walked to the patio. She picked up the portable phone. 'Charmaine?'

'Hey, girl.'

'Hi. I was just doing some yard work. How are you doing?'

'Oh, surviving.'

'Is this about Thanksgiving dinner?' Evelyn asked. 'Did Mama tell you?'

'Tell me what?'

'I'm having dinner here. Mama does all that cooking every year for Thanksgiving and then again for Christmas. I thought I'd give her a break.'

'I thought about having the gang here one year, but this

125

house is just not big enough for all of us. Besides, I didn't think Ma would go for that. She likes doing all that cooking.'

'She resisted at first. But I put my foot down.'

'Good for you.'

Andre came out the back door, pulling on his leather jacket and cradling a basketball in his arm. 'Hold on a second, Charmaine.' Evelyn covered the mouthpiece. 'Where are you going? It's almost dinnertime.'

'Up to the court.' He jumped and aimed the ball at the back door as if it had a basket on it but stopped short of throwing the ball. 'I won't be long.'

'Come here, your collar's not right.' He walked over and she pulled his collar up out of the jacket. 'Be sure you get back here by six for dinner.'

'Six o'clock? Lately, Daddy's been staying out 'til, like, eight or nine.'

'Never mind that. I still want you back by six. If he's not here, we'll start without him.'

'Yeah. Yeah.' He walked around the side of the house and disappeared. Evelyn put the phone back to her ear.

'Sorry to keep you. That was Andre. For some reason, he decides he's going out to play basketball just before dinner.'

'I hate to even bother you with this, Evelyn. But I'm coming up a little short of money to pay the bills this month. I don't want to go to Ma. I owe them enough as it is. And Beverly said she doesn't have it 'cause she has to put her car in the shop.'

'How much do you need?'

'A hundred dollars. Clarence gets paid in two weeks. He said he'd give me the money to pay you back then.'

Evelyn wasn't so sure about *that* plan, but she thought better than to say anything. Besides, it was only a hundred dollars. It didn't matter whether she got it back. 'Fine. You can get it when you come for dinner on Thursday.'

'Uh, I need it before then. I would pick it up, but you live so damn far, girl. Especially if I got to come back out there on Thursday. So, can you drop it in the mail? I should have it by Monday or Tuesday if you mail it today.'

'I'll take it to the post office after dinner.'

'Thanks. I really appreciate this. You'll get it back in two weeks.'

'Whenever you can is fine.'

'Oh, it'll be in two weeks. No question.'

'Fine.'

Evelyn hung up the phone. She needed to add a layer of soil to the compost pile to keep it from smelling like a garbage heap, but first she wanted to check on dinner. She went into the kitchen from the side door. As she removed the roast, the aroma of beef and bay leaves floated out of the pot. She looked at the thermometer, then pushed it in a little deeper. It needed a few more minutes. The kids liked their roast beef well done. Just as she placed it back in the oven, the phone rang. She closed the oven door and went to the phone on the kitchen wall.

'Hello?' she said.

'Evelyn? Hi,' Kevin said.

'Where are you? Dinner's almost ready.'

'Start without me. I'm still at Jeremy's.'

Evelyn let out a deep breath. 'Kevin, don't you think this is going a bit far? You've been over there every night this week.'

'I'll see you a little later.'

The abrupt tone of his voice indicated that he didn't want to go into it now. She supposed Jeremy was in the room with him. 'How much later?'

'I don't know. A couple of hours maybe.'

They said good-bye, and she stood there, staring out the big picture window in the kitchen. Mr Levinson across the street was raking the last of the fall leaves, something Kevin had always done with Andre in years past. But she'd helped Andre get them up earlier this afternoon, since Kevin was nowhere to be seen. That was becoming a pattern lately. On Saturdays, he was up and off to some meeting before the rest of them turned over in bed. Why he would even think of leaving his job – a good job, a job lots of other black people would kill for – to start from scratch was beyond her. It just didn't make sense.

127

She went back out to the patio. Even though it was November, it had been unusually warm for this time of year. If she didn't add soil to the compost pile, it would start giving off rotten odors. Flies and goodness knew what other kinds of creatures would swarm around it. She went back to the compost box and spread soil over the pile.

She'd known Kevin was not all that happy with his job when he was an associate. He hated research and writing briefs, which was what he always got stuck with, especially the first couple of years. He felt he was being assigned to just the crummy cases and was constantly having to prove himself. But they had worked so hard to get him there. Those four harrowing years at Georgetown University had cost them a fortune. She'd even taken on a part-time job, working in the evenings so they could keep up with the bills while he read and reread majority opinions, concurrences, and dissents. 'Just give it a little time,' she kept telling him after he started working. Once he made partner, she was sure he would start liking the job better. So he stuck with it and finally, after six long years, he made partner. Now he wanted to bolt. It was crazy. How many other thirty-nine-year-old black men were partners in prestigious Washington, D.C., law firms? *Not many.*

She picked up the garden tools and put them away on the shelves Kevin had built inside the storage shed for her. After Rebecca was in bed and Andre was in his room listening to music or watching TV, she and Kevin would have a nice, long talk. Maybe he was just bored. He'd worked with the same corporate clients for years, but it was such a huge firm that he could probably get himself reassigned to other cases. Or maybe he just needed to develop more outside interests. He was always talking about taking up golf but could never find the time when he was an associate and putting in as much as eighty hours a week. That had slacked off since he'd made partner, so maybe now was the time. She wasn't sure what the answer was, but somehow she had to make Kevin realize there were other, less risky options.

* * *

Andre was late for dinner, of course. He strolled in the kitchen door with his jacket swung over his shoulder and the basketball cradled under his arm as Rebecca was setting the table and Evelyn was slicing the roast.

'You're late, Andre,' Evelyn said. 'We could have used some help around here.'

'I know. But I couldn't just cut out in the middle of a game.'

She waved him away. 'Go on and get cleaned up.'

'Make him do the dishes,' Rebecca said.

'It's not my turn to do 'em,' Andre said. 'It's your turn.'

'You were supposed to set the table, and I don't see you doing that,' Rebecca said.

'What about that day you were supposed to do the dishes last week,' Andre said, 'but you had that tiny little cut on your finger and acted like it had been chopped off or something. Your big brother stepped in to the rescue. And I set the table that day, too. You forgot all about that, didn't you?'

'That was different,' Rebecca said. 'I *couldn't* do the dishes because my hand was sore. You were out goofing off.'

'I was out getting exercise. You know how Grandma Pearl's always saying a growing boy needs plenty of food and exercise? Well, I'm a growing boy.'

Evelyn smiled. 'If I remember correctly, Andre, I had to practically twist your arm to get you to do the dishes for your sister that day.'

'So? I did 'em, didn't I? Now she's doing the table for me. And she can still do the dishes. It's payback time.'

'We'll see,' Evelyn said, bringing the roast to the table. 'Go wash up.'

'You're not going to fall for that, are you, Mama?' Rebecca asked, banging a glass on a place mat as Andre took off.

'Fall for what?' Evelyn asked, looking at her.

'Andre smooth talking you into making me set the table and do the dishes.'

'He has a point, Rebecca,' Evelyn said, picking up a dish filled with green beans from the countertop. 'He did them for you last week.'

129

'But that was different. I was sick.'

'Never mind that now,' Evelyn said, putting the beans on the table. 'Put some ice in the glasses.'

Rebecca groaned and went to the freezer. 'You're letting him get away with murder.'

'You know me better than that.'

'Know you better than what?' Andre asked, walking into the kitchen.

'Never mind,' Evelyn said. 'Let's eat, gang.'

'What happened to Pops?' Andre asked as they sat at the table.

'He's meeting with some people about business,' Evelyn answered.

'You mean about ditching his job?' Andre asked, piling potatoes on his plate.

Evelyn stopped putting beans on her plate and looked at him. 'What did he tell you about that?'

'Said he was thinking about changing jobs. Tired of the old one.'

'Does that mean we'll be poor and have to sell our house?' Rebecca asked.

Evelyn sat the dish down and looked at Rebecca. 'Where did you get that idea?'

'A girl at school. Her father lost his job and they had to move away. He was a lawyer, too. His whole company got fired.'

'You mean it went out of business,' Evelyn said. 'A lot of companies are having money problems now because the economy is bad. That's not the same thing. Anyway, your father is not leaving his job.'

'According to him, he is,' Andre said, shoving potatoes into his mouth. 'He's fed up with that crap they be dishing out.'

'I don't want you talking like that, Andre.'

'Well, that's what it is. And I don't blame him. Whiteys don't give us our propers, don't treat us right, we don't need 'em. Daddy can take his skills and get it going on someplace else.'

'It's just a phase your father's going through.'

'What's a phase?' Rebecca asked.

'Uh, it's when people think and act differently for a short period of time,' Evelyn said. 'Then they go back to being normal.'

'I hope Daddy stops having his phase soon,' Rebecca said. 'I miss him at dinner.'

'We all do,' Evelyn said. 'But don't worry. I think he'll snap out of it soon.'

It was almost midnight when Kevin returned. Rebecca was in her room asleep, and Andre was in the family room catching the end of a Saturday night movie. Both of the children had thirteen-inch color televisions in their bedrooms, but Andre preferred the big screen in the family room for movies and football games. Evelyn was sitting up in bed reviewing the file of a new client, a woman who would join one of her therapy groups the following week. The bed covers were pulled up to her waist, and she was wearing a silken knee-length nightgown and reading glasses.

Kevin entered the room without speaking and placed his briefcase on the floor near his chest of drawers. He sat at the foot of the bed, facing away from Evelyn, and took a deep breath of air.

'Tired?' Evelyn asked.

'I'm beat,' he answered, rubbing his eyes.

'Did you eat?'

'A little something much earlier.'

'Do you want me to fix you a plate?'

He shook his head and reached down to remove his shoes.

'You should eat something. You've been over to Jeremy's every night this week and not eating right.'

'I'm not really hungry.'

Evelyn removed her reading glasses and placed them on the nightstand next to the bed. 'Kevin?'

'Yeah,' he said, dropping a shoe on the carpet.

'What exactly has been going on over at Jeremy's?'

131

He stood and emptied the contents of his pockets onto the top of the chest of drawers. His back was facing Evelyn. 'I told you.'

'All you've said is you're going over there to talk about setting up a practice. Are you making much progress?'

'Some.'

'Well, tell me about it. You haven't told me much of anything.'

'You haven't asked.'

'I thought if you were really planning to go through with something this drastic, you'd tell me on your own. Besides, you know how you can be if you think I'm pushing you.'

'Yeah. Well, nothing's definite yet. That's why I didn't say anything.' He pulled his shirt out of his trousers and unbuttoned it.

'But what have you come up with so far?'

'Right now we're just talking to people, trying to come up with different ways to raise the money.'

'Such as?'

'Don't worry. I'm not planning on getting a second mortgage on the house, since you're dead set against it. A loan from a friend, maybe. We're working on a business plan.'

'Kevin, what do I have to say to get through to you? It's not just the idea of getting a second mortgage that bothers me.'

'Don't I know it.' He snatched his shirt off and tossed it onto a chair.

'It's this whole idea of throwing everything away and starting over. It scares me.'

'I'm not throwing anything away,' he said, unzipping his trousers. 'I'm taking everything I've learned, all my experience, and putting it to better use. That's the way *I* see it, anyway.'

'Well, it doesn't make sense to me. There must be other things you can do if you're tired of working where you are. Have you considered other options?'

'Like what?'

'I don't know. There must be a million alternatives. Like getting them to reassign you to other cases for one.'

'That's not the answer.'

'What about changing firms?'

'I am changing, to one of my own.'

'Why are you being so stubborn about this? I don't understand it.'

'Evelyn, if you don't understand by now, I can't make you. And I've given up trying.' He threw his trousers on the chair and headed for the master bathroom in his shorts.

'So I'm just supposed to sit back quietly for the ride, huh? Is that it? No matter how bumpy things get.'

He stopped at the door and turned to face her directly for the first time that night. 'This is why I didn't bring it up, see? I knew it would start something. And there's no point in arguing about this stuff when it's not even definite yet. When I know more, I'll tell you.'

'We're not arguing. We're talking.'

'Yeah. Well, we'll have to talk some other time. I'm dead tired and all I want to do now is crawl under the covers and get some sleep.'

'Then just when do you —' Evelyn stopped in midsentence as Kevin turned on his heels and shut the bathroom door firmly. She picked up the papers she was reading, jammed them into a folder, and threw them down on the carpet next to the bed. A couple of papers fell out of the folder, but so what. She turned off the lamp on the nightstand and slipped under the covers, facing away from Kevin's side of the bed. A few minutes later, she heard him come out of the bathroom, then felt him tossing the bed covers back on his side of the bed.

'Will you go tell Andre to turn off the TV and go to bed?' she asked without turning to look at him.

'It's Saturday night, for Pete's sake. Let the boy watch TV.'

'But it's after midnight.'

'If you want him to go to sleep, you go tell him.' He pulled the covers over his head and faced away from Evelyn.

133

This wasn't going well at all, Evelyn thought. She closed her eyes, and it was then that she remembered Charmaine's call. With all the worrying about what Kevin was going to do, she had completely forgotten to mail the check, and Charmaine was counting on getting it by Monday or Tuesday. She would have to take it to Charmaine's after church tomorrow. She was planning to go to a jewelry store in town, anyway, and could stop by Charmaine's on the way. She and Kevin had a dinner party tomorrow night, so it would be a busy day. But at some point, she was going to have to find the time to try to get him to talk.

13

After church, all four of the DuMonts went upstairs to change. Evelyn and Kevin dressed in almost complete silence, just as they had that morning. Evelyn slipped into an ivory-colored turtleneck, navy wool slacks, and a peach-colored blazer. She draped a silk peach and navy scarf with a maritime pattern around her neckline. Kevin slipped into his jeans.

'I'm going over to Charmaine's,' Evelyn said, standing in front of the dresser brushing her short hair flat around the ears. She set the brush down and inserted a gold-rimmed pearl earring in one ear. 'Will you be here a while?'

'I'm watching the game with Andre at one.'

'Good. I'm also going to stop at Sun Gallery Goldsmiths after I leave Charmaine's to have the clasp repaired on that bracelet you gave me for our anniversary. I'll probably be gone a few hours.'

'Don't forget we're expected for dinner at Nathan's at seven.'

'I would never forget that. He's the senior partner at your firm. And I'm dying to see their new house. It's in Potomac?'

Kevin nodded.

'Don't worry,' she said, inserting the other earring. 'I'll be back in plenty of time.'

He walked toward the door.

'Kevin.'

He stopped and turned toward her.

'About last night,' she said, looking at his reflection in the mirror.

'I know, I know. I wasn't in the best frame of mind. I was very tired.'

'I understand. But we need to talk about this sooner rather than later.'

135

'I'll be here when you get back. We can talk then.'

'Good.'

'Evelyn,' he said, coming back into the room and approaching her.

She turned away from the mirror to face him.

'I would never go through with something as big as this without your consent.' He tried a smile. 'As much as I want it, I know I couldn't live in the same house with you unless you were behind me. I thought if I worked out all the details, it would be much easier to get you in my corner. That's the only reason I didn't talk to you about it sooner. Now, if you're still dead set against it after I work out all the details . . .' The smile dropped from his face and he shrugged his shoulders. 'I'll have to live with that. But don't expect me to give up easily on trying to persuade you.'

She nodded. She *was* dead set against it and didn't think any amount of detail would change that. But she would at least give him a chance to explain his plans to her – and then try her best to convince him that it wasn't a good idea for them. It wasn't going to be easy. Kevin could be determined when convinced he was right. But then, so could she. 'I would never expect you to give up easily. Not Mr. Attorney himself.' She reached up and kissed him on the mouth, and they hugged warmly.

'I'll see you when you get back,' he said, kissing her on the forehead. He went off to find Andre, and she breathed a sigh of relief. At least they'd called a truce. And he'd said he wouldn't go through with it without her blessing. That was more like the Kevin she knew. The past week he'd been behaving so unlike himself – not talking much, out at odd hours almost every evening. When he was at home, they tiptoed around each other as if the carpet under their feet were made of bone china. She was glad they'd gotten past that.

She picked up her navy Coach shoulder bag from the bed and went downstairs, stopping in the kitchen to straighten the Sunday newspaper spread out on the table. Then she went to the garage and slid into her Benz. It was another one of those unusually warm November days, and Rebecca was riding her bike with some of the neighborhood children. Evelyn honked and waved at them as she drove up the street.

This thing obviously meant a great deal to Kevin, and he wasn't going to drop it easily. He thought it would succeed, and *maybe* it would – Kevin was quite an attorney, one of the most successful black lawyers in the city. Only a few others practiced at bigger and better firms. Given a few years, he could easily be at the top of his field.

But she hated the risks involved in starting over. Most new business ventures failed within the first year. The odds were probably even worse for black businesses. How many whites would give their business to a firm headed by blacks? Some *black* people would even hesitate to do that. Kevin knew this, of course. He was always complaining about how few black law firms there were with more than four or five attorneys and how hard it was for them to get good-paying corporate clients. Even corporations with black chief executives were afraid to trust black firms to handle their legal affairs. Many black doctors and dentists had the same kinds of problems getting patients when they tried to set up their own practices. It wasn't fair, but that was the reality. The chances that a black law firm would be really successful and make lots money were slim. Even if Kevin's firm made it to the top, it could take years getting there. And that would mean years of sacrifice and struggle for the family.

Why couldn't he see that? All he had to do was look at Steve and Regina. Steve had started his own law firm several years ago with one or two others, and he and his wife and kids were still living in an apartment, for goodness sakes. And in Prince George's County, too. It was one of the nicer sections, but P.G. County was P.G. County – no two ways about it. It was nothing compared to Montgomery County. When you did find a nice section in P.G., it was usually miles and miles outside the beltway. Take Charmaine's house. It was right on the eastern edge of one of the worst parts of the city. The crime and drugs in that neighborhood weren't much better than they were in parts of D.C. The only difference was that it had a few more trees than the city did.

She exited the beltway and headed southeast. Kevin couldn't have really given this a lot of thought or he would realize just how much they stood to lose. Not so much what they had now as the things they had planned for the near future. Good colleges for the children, preferably ivy league. A bigger and better house in Potomac. She'd dreamed about moving there. They'd even talked about buying a summer place somewhere on the Cape in Massachusetts. And she'd been wanting to go back to school for her Ph.D. for the longest time.

All that took money. Lots of money. All these years, they'd been putting it off until Kevin made partner. And now that they could afford these things, he wanted to start over. Goodness. She was thirty-seven years old, he was thirty-nine. Both much too old for this nonsense. She smacked the steering wheel. He wasn't going to get away with upsetting their lives like this. When they talked later this evening, she had to make certain he understood just what was at stake. Especially when it came to the children. Heaven forbid, Andre would have to go somewhere like the University of D.C. because they couldn't afford to send him anywhere else.

She turned onto Landover Road and a short time later she pulled onto a side street of small brick houses lined with trees. Three girls about the same age as Rebecca were jumping rope on the sidewalk just a few doors from Charmaine's house. Their singing and laughter filled the air as she drove past them. Evelyn was always surprised to see how quiet and well kept this block was, considering the roughness of the surrounding neighborhood. It was like an oasis in the middle of a Desert Storm battlefield.

She got out of the car and made sure all four doors were locked. She always felt uneasy parking her car here and tried to get a spot right in front of the house. She just knew that one day she would come out of Charmaine's house and find the spot empty – horror of all horrors.

As she went up the short walkway to the house, Charmaine came out wearing a bathrobe with a sweater slung over her shoulders. She was holding a small, flat pan, and Kenny stood behind the screen door watching as Charmaine placed the pan down in a far corner of the porch. As soon as Charmaine backed away, three cats appeared out of nowhere and descended on the pan. Kenny squealed with laughter and clapped his hands. 'Here, kitty,' he said. Charmaine smiled and looked up the walkway at the sound of footsteps on the pavement.

'Evelyn,' she said, her eyes wide with surprise. 'What brings you here, girl?'

Evelyn stood at the bottom of the short flight of steps that led up to porch and put her hand on the iron railing. 'Can't I come visit my sister?'

Charmaine smiled. 'Well, sure you can. I'm just surprised, that's all. C'mon up, girl.' Charmaine turned toward the front door as Evelyn came up the stairs. 'Kenny, come on out and say hi to your aunt.'

Kenny came out and stood in front of Evelyn.

'Hi,' he said, smiling up at her.

Evelyn smiled back. He had the cutest little dimples. And he was so well behaved. It always amazed Evelyn that Charmaine could do such a good job of rearing Kenny despite the neighborhood and the lack of help from Clarence. Evelyn bent over him and pointed to her lips. 'Give me a kiss.' He reached up and kissed her. Evelyn ran her hand over his head and looked at Charmaine. 'He starts kindergarten next year, right?'

'Yep. He can't wait and neither can I. Those day care payments are killing me.'

'Where will you send him? Not anywhere around here, I hope.'

'Probably one of the Catholic schools or maybe a private school, with a little bit of luck. Depends on my financial situation at the time.'

'You need to get started if you want to send him to a private school. Competition at the better ones is fierce, and I do mean fierce. *Washingtonian* magazine did an article on private schools in the area. I keep meaning to give it to you, but I always forget.'

'You read that?'

Evelyn nodded. 'It's a good magazine.'

'Too uppity for my taste. Any schools listed in there would probably bust my budget.'

'Not necessarily. You can get it when you come Thursday.'

Charmaine put her mouth near the screen door. 'Beverly, Evelyn's here,' she shouted.

'Beverly's here?' Evelyn asked.

'Uh-huh. I got her back in the kitchen washing my greens. We're cooking up a storm for dinner, girl. Fried chicken, collards and mustard greens, potato salad. I'm baking a cake. You should stay.'

Evelyn shook her head. 'That's too many calories for me.'

'Shoot. You can afford it.'

'Thanks, but I have another run to make when I leave here. And Kevin and I are going to a dinner party to-night. How did Beverly get here? I thought her car was in the shop.'

'She took the subway over to the Landover Road stop, and I picked her up after church.'

'We went to church this morning, too. I even got Kevin to go for a change.'

'How's he been?'

'Fine, just fine.' Just going a little nuts, that's all.

'What you want me to bring Thursday? I was thinking of making macaroni and cheese.'

'Oh, you don't have to bring anything. I'm having it catered.'

'Catered? For just nine or ten people?'

'It'll be a few more than that. Kevin's parents are coming and his sister and her family. I figured why bother with cooking for all those people. There's enough to worry about with getting the house ready and all.'

'Well 'scuse me. Never heard of nobody catering no Thanksgiving dinner. What do we wear?'

'Casual. Same as usual. I think it'll be nice. They come in and do everything. They even clean up after —'

'Kenny,' Charmaine shouted suddenly. Evelyn paused and followed her sister's gaze. Kenny was on his hands and knees, sneaking up on the cats. Evelyn laughed as Charmaine ran up and grabbed Kenny from behind. Charmaine picked him up and planted his feet firmly on the porch, away from the cats. 'Stop trying to scare them,' she said. Kenny looked up at his mother as if to say, 'What's wrong with scaring them?' Charmaine opened the screen door. 'Go on back in the house before you catch cold, anyway.'

Kenny went in and stood inside the screen door and watched them.

'When did you get all these cats?' Evelyn asked.

'They're not mine. I just feed 'em every now and then.'

'You feed stray cats?' Evelyn was horrified.

'She feeds stray cats, dogs, birds, everything,' Beverly said, appearing at the door behind Kenny. She was wiping her wet hands on her jeans.

'Hi, Beverly,' Evelyn said.

'Hi. I like that blazer you're wearing. It's a beautiful shade of pink.'

'Peach,' Evelyn said.

'Oh, peach then. 'Scuse me.'

'It's nice, isn't it?' Charmaine said, eyeing the jacket and everything else Evelyn was wearing.

'Where did you get it?' Beverly asked.

'Ann Taylor, probably,' Charmaine said.

'Bloomingdale's,' Evelyn said.

'See?' Charmaine said. 'They'll probably rename those stores Evelyn Taylor and Evelyndale's the way she spends money at 'em.'

Beverly giggled. Even Evelyn had to smile at that. 'I catch sales, mostly.'

141

'Hmmph,' Charmaine said. 'Sales or no sales, I couldn't afford the gift wrapping in those stores.'

'You know those animals can carry diseases,' Evelyn said, pointing at the cats. 'Like rabies.'

Charmaine waved her hand at Evelyn. 'Aah. Do these cats look diseased to you? All they want is a decent meal.'

Wasn't that just like Charmaine? Evelyn thought. Worried about these three cats when there were thousands of stray ones running around the city. Evelyn noticed that one of the cats stood out from the others, with a coat of hair that looked healthy and fairly clean. 'That one on the end there . . .' Evelyn said, pointing.

'Yeah,' Charmaine said. 'Gorgeous thing, isn't it? That one just started coming around last week.'

'It looks like a Birman,' Evelyn said.

'A what?' Charmaine said, frowning.

'A Birman. It's a kind of cat. A friend of mine has one. You can tell by the white paws. The owner's probably looking for that one.'

'Call the animal shelter,' Beverly said. 'The owners may be trying to find him.'

Charmaine shook her head. 'Uh-uh. If nobody claims 'em, they put the poor things to sleep.'

'If nobody claims it, they'll probably let you keep it,' Evelyn said.

'I'm not keeping no cat in the house. You saw how Kenny was. He's too young. He'd probably terrorize the thing. Why don't one of you take it?'

'I can't have pets in my apartment building.'

Charmaine looked at Evelyn.

'Don't look at me. I'm not taking it.'

'Why not?' Charmaine said. 'Rebecca would probably love a cat.'

'I'm not taking any wild cat from the street.'

'That one's not wild yet. Watch.' Charmaine stooped and signaled the cats, snapping her fingers and smacking her lips. The other two ran off and hid in the bushes, but the Birman walked right up to within a foot of Charmaine. She put out her hands and let him approach her.

Evelyn's eyes grew wide with alarm. 'You better stop that before it scratches your hand off.'

Charmaine rubbed the cat's back, and it stretched its hind legs leisurely. 'The fur's so soft. Feel it.' She gestured to Evelyn.

'No thank you.'

'C'mon. It won't bite.'

'Are you sure about that?'

Charmaine took Evelyn's hand. 'C'mon.'

Evelyn let Charmaine guide her hand to the cat's head, and she patted it lightly. The cat walked right up to her feet and snuggled against her legs. Evelyn laughed and stooped and rubbed its back. The cat purred.

'It likes you,' Beverly said. 'You should take it — Rebecca would love it.'

Evelyn stood up straight and shook her head firmly. 'It's a nice cat. But we don't need it.'

'Let's go inside and let them eat, then,' Charmaine said. 'I'm feeling a little chilly out here.'

The two of them went into the living room with Beverly and Kenny. The aroma of collards boiling in bacon fat drifted out from the kitchen, reminding Evelyn of her childhood days when their mother always seemed to be cooking greens. Evelyn rarely cooked greens that way now, and when she did, her house was big enough so that the odors didn't drift into the living room.

Beverly sat on the sofa and propped her bare feet up on the coffee table as Charmaine bent and scooped the toys off the floor. She handed them to Kenny. 'Take these to your room and play up there for a while.'

'You don't have to do that because of me,' Evelyn said.

Charmaine picked up a jacket from the back of the armchair. 'You wouldn't believe I just straightened this place up yesterday.' She hung the jacket in the closet as Evelyn sat down.

'Oh, before I forget,' Evelyn said, reaching into her purse. She removed her checkbook, and her credit-card holder fell on the floor, spread open right on the page holding her gold American Express card. Charmaine bent over and picked up the leather card holder. Evelyn expected her to say something sarcastic, but Charmaine handed it over without saying a word, then sat on the couch next to Beverly.

'How much do you need?' Evelyn asked, her Mont Blanc fountain pen poised over her checkbook. 'A hundred dollars?'

'Uh, can you make it for one-fifty? I need to get a few winter things for Kenny and . . .'

'That's fine,' Evelyn said. As she wrote the check, the thought crossed her mind that if Kevin had his way, writing a check for a measly hundred and fifty dollars wouldn't be so easy in the future. They would have to scrimp and count every penny. Just the thought of that sent chills through her body. She handed the check to her sister.

'Thanks,' Charmaine said, placing the check on the coffee table. 'Like I said, you'll get it back next week.'

Evelyn waved her hand. 'Pay me back whenever you can.' She sat back in the chair and crossed her legs. 'So, what's been happening with you two?'

Charmaine squirmed in her seat. 'Not a damn thing.'

'Is Clarence here?'

'No,' Charmaine said.

'Didn't you tell her yet?' Beverly asked, looking at Charmaine.

'Tell me what?'

Charmaine shot Beverly a warning glance. 'I don't know what the hell Beverly's talking about. So, where you going when you leave here? You said you had to make a run.'

Evelyn was puzzled. Charmaine was obviously hiding something. The first thing that came to her mind was that maybe Charmaine had asked Clarence to leave the house. Finally. 'Uh, I need to stop at Sun Gallery Goldsmiths.'

'I've heard of that place,' Beverly said.

'What's Sun Gallery Goldsmiths?' Charmaine asked.

'A jewelry store owned and run by blacks. They sell silver and gold jewelry with stones from Africa. Mostly amber but also some onyx and malachite.' Evelyn was tempted to ask Charmaine outright if she had made Clarence pack his bags, but a question like that would only upset Charmaine if Evelyn was wrong.

'My girlfriend Valerie talks about that place,' Beverly said. 'I've been meaning to go there and have a look around. But you know how I hate shopping. Is it expensive?'

'Shit,' Charmaine said. 'If Evelyn shops there, do you need to ask?'

'It's really not,' Evelyn said. 'You'd be surprised.'

'What are you planning to buy?' Beverly asked.

'The whole store, probably,' Charmaine said.

Beverly slapped Charmaine's arm playfully.

Evelyn smiled. 'Let her talk smart all she wants. It doesn't bother me one bit. For your information, I'm not buying anything. I'm taking a bracelet Kevin bought me to have the clasp repaired. He didn't get the bracelet there, but they do good repair work.'

'You mean that ruby and diamond bracelet he bought you a few years back?' Beverly asked.

Evelyn nodded.

'That's some bracelet,' Beverly said.

'Wait a minute,' Charmaine said. 'What ruby and diamond bracelet? I never saw no bracelet.'

'He got it for her for their tenth wedding anniversary,' Beverly said. 'You never saw it?'

'No. Evelyn never tells me nothing.'

You mean, you never tell *me* nothing, Evelyn thought. 'I thought I showed it to you.'

'You have it here or is it in the car?' Charmaine asked.

Evelyn blinked. She would have to be plain crazy to leave a diamond and ruby bracelet in the car in this neighborhood. 'No. I have it here.' She reached into her purse and pulled out a black velvet pouch. The bracelet was a wide gold bangle with small diamonds and rubies scattered throughout the design.

145

Charmaine gasped as Evelyn handed it to her. 'Whew! You want to switch husbands, sis?'

Beverly and Evelyn smiled as Charmaine slipped the bracelet around her wrist. She couldn't fasten it, because of the broken clasp, so she used her hand to hold it in place as she held out her arm to admire it. 'Girl, this is something else. You know how much he paid for this?'

'No. I'm not sure.' Evelyn knew he'd paid close to five thousand dollars but she certainly wasn't going to give Charmaine an excuse to make one of her sarcastic comments.

'Probably thousands,' Beverly said.

Charmaine handed the bracelet back to Evelyn. 'It's nice, but I'd be scared to wear the damn thing. 'Fraid somebody would rip it right off my arm.'

'I only wear it when we go out in the evenings, to parties and things like that.'

'That's the very place somebody would snatch it,' Charmaine said.

Evelyn started to explain that jewelry like this was common at the dinner and cocktail parties she went to, where the women were wives of doctors and lawyers and corporate executives or were doctors, lawyers, and corporate executives themselves, but she thought better of it. 'Well, yes, you do have to be careful,' she said, placing the pouch back in her purse. She looked at Charmaine. 'But it's insured. Now, what was Beverly talking about that you haven't told me?'

Beverly looked in the same direction.

'It's nothing,' Charmaine said.

'Jeez, Charmaine. Why don't you just tell her?'

'I'm not ready to tell people yet. So just drop it.'

'But she's family. You told me.'

'That was a mistake. I can see that now.'

'Will somebody please tell me what's going on here?' Evelyn asked.

'Charmaine's pregnant.'

Evelyn didn't think she'd heard right. 'What?'

146

'Damn. I swear I'll never tell you nothing else, Beverly Jordan.'

'She's your sister. Why wouldn't you want her to know you're pregnant?'

'Never mind,' Charmaine said. 'She knows now.'

Evelyn was having trouble digesting this news. Why in the world would Charmaine get pregnant? She was having enough trouble trying to support Kenny, always having to borrow money and ask their parents for something. Although Charmaine tried to hide it, Clarence obviously was not much help. What was she thinking of? 'I'm shocked,' Evelyn said.

'I'm sure you are,' Charmaine said.

'But why were you trying to keep it from me?'

'Because I'm not sure what I'm going to do about it yet. And I don't want the whole world knowing about it if I decide not to keep it.'

So she didn't want the baby, Evelyn thought. That was perfectly understandable.

'Oh, come on, Charmaine,' Beverly said. 'You can't even turn in a stray cat, worrying about it being put to sleep. No way you're going to have an abortion.'

'Don't be so sure about that. And I could always put it up for adoption.'

'How did this happen if you didn't plan it?' Evelyn asked.

Charmaine looked at Evelyn like she thought Evelyn had just stepped off a flying saucer.

'Well . . . I mean, don't you use birth control?'

Charmaine rolled her eyes with exasperation. 'Of course I do.'

'What kind?' Evelyn asked. 'The rhythm method?'

Beverly giggled.

'Hell, no. The diaphragm.'

'I use the diaphragm,' Evelyn said. 'I've never had any problems with it.'

'Knowing you, Evelyn, you probably get up and put more jelly in every time you do it again,' Charmaine said.

'And you don't?' Evelyn asked.

By now, Beverly was cracking up. Evelyn looked at Beverly. 'What's so funny? What do you use?'

Beverly stopped laughing. 'Nothing, right now.'

Charmaine burst out laughing.

'You know what I mean,' Evelyn said, smiling.

'Normally the diaphragm,' Beverly said. 'I'm afraid of the pill.'

'Then, don't you add jelly in between?' Evelyn asked.

'Tell the truth,' Charmaine said.

Beverly giggled. 'Of course I do.'

Charmaine looked at Beverly doubtfully.

'Okay,' Beverly said. 'I admit there have been times . . .'

'See? Who the hell can be bothered getting up in the dark in the middle of the night to do that? Shit. It's enough trouble getting the damn thing in right in the first place.'

'It is a pain in the neck,' Beverly said. 'But most of the time I do add jelly. Unless, you know, it's right around my period, and I know I can't get pregnant. Or at least I think I can't.' Beverly looked at Evelyn and pointed to Charmaine. 'But let this be a warning to you.'

'I didn't need a warning. The directions on the package make it very clear. You can get preg –' Evelyn stopped when the front door opened and Clarence entered the house. All three of them turned to the hallway and looked at him.

He noticed Beverly on the couch next to Charmaine and waved to her without stopping. 'Hey, Beverly,' he said heading for the stairs. Then he noticed Evelyn and stopped at the bottom of the stairs. 'Hey, Evelyn. What brings you here?'

Evelyn smiled. 'Just stopped by. It's been a long time since I've seen you, Clarence.'

He smiled and entered the living room. He was dressed in slacks, shirt, and a brown leather bomber jacket. 'You know me. I try to keep things hopping.'

'So I've heard. Congratulations.'

Out of the corner of her eye, Evelyn could see Charmaine and Beverly giving each other strange looks. Clarence stared at Evelyn, his brows raised in a puzzled expression.

'About the new member of your family,' Evelyn said, seeing the confusion on his face. 'Isn't this your first? . . .'

Charmaine bolted out of her seat. 'Uh, Clarence, could you go up and check on Kenny for me. He's been up there by himself for more than half an hour now.'

Clarence looked at Charmaine, then at Evelyn, then back to Charmaine. 'What's she talking about?' he asked Charmaine, eyeing her suspiciously.

It was then that Evelyn realized Clarence knew nothing about the pregnancy. She sat back in her chair and covered her mouth with her hand.

'It's nothing,' Charmaine said, pushing him by the arm toward the stairs.

He pulled his arm out of her grasp. 'Wait a minute.' He turned to Evelyn. 'What new member of our family?'

Evelyn looked away and shook her head. 'I've already said too much.'

He faced his wife's other sister.

'Don't look at me,' Beverly said.

He looked at Charmaine. 'You pregnant, or something?' he asked, half joking. 'That would explain why you been so cranky these past few days.'

Charmaine looked away and didn't say anything. Neither did Evelyn or Beverly.

Clarence's eyes narrowed as he looked at the three of them. 'Come to think of it, that would explain a lot of things. Like that smell in the bathroom this morning. I thought Kenny had taken sick. And why you can't smoke cigarettes lately.' His eyes got big as he realized he was zeroing in on the truth. 'It was you that got sick, wasn't it?'

Charmaine slumped down on the sofa.

'Was it you?' he asked.

All three of them looked at Charmaine. She nodded reluctantly.

A big smile crossed Clarence's face. 'You're pregnant? That's it?'

Charmaine nodded again. 'Yes.'

Clarence threw his hands in the air. 'Hallelujah! I can't believe this. When were you planning on telling me? Seems everybody in town knows except me.'

'Just my sisters. I was going to tell you next.'

'When? After you announced it in the newspapers?'

Charmaine rolled her eyes at him.

'You something else, Charm. If you wasn't pregnant with my son, I'd be plenty pissed off.' He grabbed her shoulders and planted a big wet kiss on her cheek, then headed for the stairs. 'I'll go check on Kenny for you right now.' He bounded up the stairs, three at a time.

'Thanks a lot, Evelyn,' Charmaine said. The look she shot her sister could have been fired from an AK-47.

Evelyn smiled sheepishly.

'You can't blame anybody but yourself,' Beverly said, defending Evelyn. 'You should have told her just what you were up to. Then this wouldn't have happened.'

'You should have kept your damn mouth shut,' Charmaine shot back. 'It wouldn't have happened if you had kept it to yourself like I asked you to in the first fucking place. Clarence may be old enough to knock me up, but he's not ready to be a father. I wanted to tell him in my own way, if at all. Well, so much for that.' Charmaine folded her arms tightly under her breasts.

'It's probably for the best,' Beverly said. 'I mean, he's tickled to death. Maybe he'll settle down now.'

'Maybe,' Charmaine said. 'But it's going to take some doing. I wanted time to think about the best way to handle it with him. But you're right, if anything can get him to change, it's a baby.'

Evelyn was appalled at the direction in which this conversation was moving. 'I hope you two don't think a baby is going to make him change.'

Charmaine glared at her. 'Who asked for your advice?'

'It might,' Beverly said. 'A baby is a big event.'

Evelyn shook her head firmly. She felt bad about spilling the beans to Clarence that way, but Charmaine needed to get something straight. 'That's not the way it works. People don't

150

change after they get a certain age, not unless they really want to. If you go through with having this baby, Charmaine, you'd better plan on doing everything on your own. Just like with Kenny.'

'That situation was nothing like this one,' Charmaine said. 'I wasn't married then. And Clarence isn't so bad. He's got a big heart. He just needs some direction.'

Evelyn twisted up her lips. 'He's thirty-some years old, Charmaine. If he hasn't found his way by now –'

Charmaine cut her off. 'Please, spare me the sermon. The last thing I need now is advice from a spoiled rich bitch.' She looked at Beverly. 'Now do you see why I didn't tell her? I got enough problems without having to put up with her mouth.'

'I wish you two would cut it out,' Beverly said impatiently.

'I'm just trying to help,' Evelyn protested.

'You want to know the best thing you can do to help me?' Charmaine shot back. 'Keep your prissy attitude to yourself.'

Evelyn stood up. 'If that's the way you feel . . .'

'Damn right that's how I feel.'

'I'm leaving,' Evelyn said, walking toward the door.

Beverly looked at Charmaine sitting stiffly at the end of the couch with her arms folded across her waist. Charmaine looked the other way. Beverly stood up and followed Evelyn to the foyer. 'I'll walk you to your car.'

Just then, Clarence came down the stairs. 'You two leaving without getting some chow?'

Evelyn nodded and tried to smile.

'I'm just walking her to the car,' Beverly said.

'Wait a second. I'll walk out with you two.' He stepped into the living room. 'I'm going over to Lem's for a few minutes,' he said to Charmaine.

'What about the leaves? You haven't raked them once all fall.'

'I'll get them when I get back.'

'You been promising to do it for a month.'

'Why you want to bug me about that now? I want to go out and spread the good news about my baby.'

151

'You keep fooling around with me, there won't be any good news to spread, you hear?'

Beverly and Evelyn looked at each other.

'What's that supposed to mean?'

Silence.

'Look, I'll be back in a New York minute and your leaves will be raked. I promise.'

The three of them walked out of the house toward Evelyn's car. 'You be sure to come back and get the leaves up like you promised,' Beverly said to Clarence. 'Charmaine's going to need your help now that she's pregnant.'

'Yeah, I'm gonna come right back. Don't want her getting all upset now.'

When they stopped in front of the Benz, Clarence's eyes grew wide. 'This is yours?'

Evelyn nodded. 'Just got it a couple of months ago.'

He whistled. 'Nice.'

'You like that, huh?' Beverly said, smiling at him.

'Yeah. I could get used to this real easy.'

He walked up and down looking it over as Evelyn went around to the driver's side and got in. She pushed the button to open the window on the passenger side, and Clarence leaned in. 'This is really nice. Tell Kevin and those two little monsters I said hi.'

Evelyn smiled, wondering if he even remembered the children's names. He so rarely came to the family get-togethers. 'You coming over Thursday?'

'Thursday?' Clarence asked. 'What's happening Thursday?'

'It's Thanksgiving, silly,' Beverly said.

'Oh, right,' he said, snapping his fingers. 'And dinner's at your place?' he asked Evelyn.

She nodded.

'We'll be there. Count on it.'

Evelyn waved good-bye and headed into town. She didn't know what to make of what had happened back there. For some reason, she had a knack for setting Charmaine off when she tried to help. Instead of being appreciated, she was accused of being this or that. In grade school, whenever she'd tried to get Charmaine to study more Charmaine had called her a square. After high school, she'd tried to convince Charmaine to go somewhere, anywhere, besides Howard University. Charmaine had accused her of being a snob and a traitor to her race.

When she'd tried to talk Charmaine out of dropping out of college to get married, she'd been accused of meddling in something she knew nothing about. But Evelyn figured even a degree from Howard was better than no degree at all. And there was no need to drop out of school just because she was getting married. Needless to say, Charmaine had not taken her advice; she'd dropped out of Howard right in the middle of her junior year. Three years later she'd left her husband, although it was several more years before they were divorced. Charmaine decided to make it legal when she realized she was pregnant with Kenny. At first, she was going to marry the father but called it off at the last minute, saying he was no better than her former husband. Evelyn was so relieved when she did that. It was one of the few things they'd agreed on.

Now Charmaine was pregnant. Again. She'd take one step forward, then two back. She seemed to be digging herself farther and farther into this pit. It was a shame, because Charmaine had so much potential. She was pretty and smart and funny. She could really make something of herself if she'd give it half a try. Sometimes it was hard to believe they were sisters, had grown up in the same household with the same parents. They were so different. Take their husbands. Those two men couldn't be more dissimilar if they had been born on opposite sides of the globe. Kevin was smart, successful, a good father. Clarence was . . . well, he was good-looking and seemed to be a nice enough man. But he wasn't very dependable and had absolutely no ambition. Truth was, she really didn't know much about Clarence. She'd never had a real conversation with him because she'd never been comfortable around men like that, the smooth talkers who seemed to have nothing going for them but their looks.

* * *

153

'White people do things like this all the time,' Kevin was saying as he tucked his necktie under the collar of his freshly laundered white shirt. He was standing in front of the dresser mirror. 'You'd better believe it.'

'Mmm-hmm,' Evelyn said, pulling a tan camisole over her head.

'That's why they're so successful and we're not,' Kevin continued. 'They take risks. We're too scared we'll get burned.'

'But they have things to fall back on.' She pulled a matching half slip over her hips, then went into the master bath. 'Like inheritances, parents with money. We don't have that. My mother's retired. Daddy will probably retire next year. I could never go to them asking for a large sum of money if we got into financial trouble.' She wet the tip of her finger to test the curling iron sitting on the marble vanity. 'And your parents – Ouch!' She snatched her finger away from the hot metal.

'What's wrong?' Kevin asked. He let go of his tie and looked at her.

'Nothing,' she said poking her finger in her mouth. 'It's this old curling iron. Sometimes it overheats. I need to replace it.'

He shook his head and went back to his tie. 'The things you women will do for your hair.'

'You want me to look nice for a dinner party with all your superiors, don't you?' She picked up a comb and looked in the mirror over the vanity as she separated several strands of hair at the top of her head.

'It looks fine without all that. Anyway, what were you saying about my parents?'

She picked up the curling iron and curled the lock of hair with the precision that comes from many years of practice. 'Well, they're still working. But even after a lifetime, you know a security guard and a government receptionist can't have a lot saved. Would you go to them and ask for what little money they have if things went wrong?'

'No. We'd go to your parents. The way your father's always bragging about how much he's got invested in the stock market.'

154

'That's not the kind of money we're talking about. He's got maybe a few thousand.'

'I'm just kidding. But I would have thought it was more, the way he talks.'

'Maybe it is. But it doesn't matter, because he worked long and hard to save it, and I would never dream of asking him to give us any.'

'I'm not planning to use your old man's money.'

'Good, because it's out of the question.'

'My point is, that's how whites, and now these Asians, get ahead. They take risks and the families pitch in and help each other out. Us? We get a few bucks and we're scared to death of losing it.' He sat on the edge of the bed and picked up one of his shoes. 'Look at my father. The man saves every penny he earns . . .'

'What's wrong with that?' She set the curling iron on the vanity top and looked at Kevin's reflection in the mirror.

'Everything. It's just sitting in a bank somewhere making the white man richer while my father earns a few pennies in interest. I try to get him to invest it in some kind of business – a store, his own security firm, something. But he won't hear it. He'd rather take the change the white man gives him and sit on it.'

'Everyone doesn't have your burning desire to be an entrepreneur,' she said, picking out another lock of hair. 'And there are other ways of getting ahead. You could always look for a job at another firm if you're unhappy where you are.'

Kevin stomped his foot on the floor a little harder than necessary to get his heel in the shoe. 'You haven't been listening to a thing I've been saying. I don't want to work for another firm. I want my own.'

'Why do you have to be so stubborn about this?'

'I don't think I'm the one being stubborn.'

'And I wanted to go back to school next fall and get my Ph.D.'

'That wish list of yours is getting bigger by the minute.'

'I've always wanted to go back to school, you know that.'

'You've talked about it, but nothing definite. Now you have to go back starting next year.'

Evelyn set the curling iron down and turned it off. 'I was waiting for you to make partner.'

'I made partner a year ago. But, no, you wait until I start talking about launching my own firm to bring this crap back up.'

She yanked the plug out of the socket, even though she knew better. 'I'm afraid if you go through with this, I'll never be able to go back.'

'Yes, you will. Waiting a couple more years won't kill you. I mean, you act like I'm asking you to suffer along in dire poverty for the rest of your life. You know how many other people would love to be in your shoes right now?'

She turned to face him. 'I'm not other people. We always talked about how we wouldn't settle for what most people have. About all the things we would have and do after you made partner – me going back to school, a new house, a nice place to spend the summers. Didn't we?'

'Yes, and we'll still do all of that and more. All I'm asking for is a few more years.'

'We've already waited almost fifteen years, Kevin. First you were in law school, and we struggled through that. Then we waited for you to make partner. I'm tired of putting things off.'

Kevin stomped his other foot into the shoe. 'See, that's the difference. White women, these Asian women, they back their men up. Black women . . .' As soon as he saw her face, he regretted saying it. He stood up and stretched his hands out to defend himself as Evelyn stormed out of the master bath. She stood facing him with her hands on her hips.

'What the hell is that supposed to mean? Are you saying I haven't backed you up? All these years I put everything on hold, even worked two jobs for a while, and this is the thanks I get?'

'Wait a minute. Don't get me wrong. I appreciate all that. But when it comes to something a little risky . . .'

156

'A *little* risky? You want to put our welfare on the line. Not only mine, but the children's, too.'

'I wish you'd get some perspective on this. Nobody's welfare is going to be put on the line.'

'Maybe you should have married that little white tart you were dating when we met. Her family had plenty of money, and she seemed to go along with everything you ever said and did.'

Kevin frowned. 'You mean Chrissy? She wasn't white. She was mixed. We all are, for that matter.'

'You know what I mean. Her mother was white.'

'Her mother's mother was white. All her other grandparents and her parents were black.'

'Whatever.' Evelyn went to her side of the double closet.

'Strange that you'd mention her now. I didn't even think you remembered her. You never met her.'

'No, but I remember her all right. How could I forget? She bought you a brand-new Nissan shortly after we started dating, trying to get you back.'

'Yes, she did.'

She turned to face him, holding the navy velvet suit with silk trimming that she planned to wear to the dinner party. 'You say that so wistfully. Well, if that's the kind of woman you wanted, you should have married her. I'm not like that.' She pulled the plastic dry cleaner's bag off the suit.

'Don't I know it.'

'Well, I'm not. Do you wish I was?'

'This is getting silly,' he said, walking to the door.

'You always do that.'

'Do what?'

'Walk away whenever we get into a disagreement.'

'That's 'cause we never get anywhere once we start arguing. I'll wait for you downstairs.' He left the room.

Evelyn sighed and sat down on the edge of the bed, holding the velvet suit in her arms. Why was he being so difficult? He was obsessed about this. He was hardly ever home now, and when he was he locked himself in that den working on papers or talking on the phone to that Jeremy. Or he argued with her. They couldn't have a conversation these days without arguing.

She absentmindedly ran her hand across the smooth surface of the suit. And forget about sex. They hadn't done anything in almost three weeks. He wasn't around long enough. Or he was too tired. The only other times they'd gone that long without each other was during her pregnancies. And even then they'd managed to be caring and romantic with each other. This whole thing was getting out of hand, and nothing she said seemed to matter. He was as determined to go through with it now as he was when they first started talking about it. Maybe even more determined.

She stood up and removed the skirt and jacket from their hangers. She was going to have to come up with something. They'd had a good healthy marriage for almost fifteen years now, and she wasn't about to let things fall apart over this silly idea of his.

14

Evelyn opened the miniblinds and the early evening sun skidded across the bare floor and up to the lone wall decoration in the room, a handmade poster with the words *God grant me the serenity to accept the things I cannot change, the courage to change the things I can, and the wisdom to know the difference.*

On a small table near the window a fresh pot of coffee brewed, filling the air with its aroma. Next to that Evelyn placed a glass pitcher filled with ice water. No one would ever have suspected that the room she used for her therapy sessions was once the office storage room, its walls dulled with dust and its floors cluttered with old discarded chairs, file cabinets, and bookshelves that nobody wanted. She'd had all the junk removed and the walls repainted in pure white. She laid the white floor tile herself with help from her secretary. There were no tables, no phones, no drapes. It was bright, open, and uncluttered, perfect for probing damaged minds and spirits.

She began to arrange white hardbacked chairs in a neat semicircle around the middle of the room, one for each member of the group. Tonight a new woman was joining, so Evelyn added a sixth chair, then placed one for herself facing the others.

And what a group it was. They called themselves the Half Circle, a reference as much to how they felt about their lives as to the arrangement of the chairs — half full, half empty, halfway there. Three of the women were black, one Filipino, and one Hispanic. They represented a variety of occupations and social standings — two secretaries, a personnel manager in the D.C. government, a junior accountant, and a grade-school teacher. As different as the women were, they had one thing in common — problems with the men in their lives. Two had never been married, one was divorced, and two were in the process of divorce.

The coffee finished brewing and Evelyn filled her mug, adding a half teaspoon of sugar. She wrapped her hands around the cup and blew into it. She didn't especially like this office coffee, but it helped her stay alert for these late sessions. She had two groups. This one met every Tuesday and Friday at 5:30. Another group met on Wednesday evenings. Her secretary and other coworkers didn't understand why she bothered with the evening sessions, since her psychology practice had a steady stream of daytime clients. But Evelyn realized that many women in the city simply couldn't afford to spare the money or time for single counseling sessions during the day. And she thought it helped the women to be around others with similar problems, because even though she was trained to counsel them, she could not escape the fact that her life was nothing like theirs. Her relationship with Kevin had its ups and downs, all marriages did, but basically it was sound. Thank goodness.

One by one, the women filed in from their jobs across the city and chatted over coffee and ice water. Evelyn sat in her chair across from the semicircle while waiting for everyone to arrive and read through her notes from the last session. She also glanced at the file of Wanda Green, the woman who was joining the group today. Evelyn had met Wanda the previous week, when she'd come in for her first office visit. After seeing her for an hour, Evelyn thought Wanda would fit right in with this group. She was a pretty black woman, thirty-five years old, and worked with one of the congressmen on Capitol Hill. She'd been married briefly when she was in her late twenties and had never had any children or been remarried. And she was having trouble with a man.

As soon as everyone had arrived, Evelyn asked them to take their seats. Then she looked around at the group and smiled. 'How were your weekends?'

'Okay, I guess.'

'Could have been better. That's for sure.'

'I sat around holding my dog, feeling sorry for my pitiful self,' Laverne said. 'Only time I got my butt up was when the damn phone rang.' Laverne, a legal secretary in her late forties, was the oldest member of the group. Her husband had recently run off with a twenty-two-year-old white woman when their only son had gone away to college, and now Laverne lived in their big old house alone.

'I thought you were going to start going out more,' said Merlinda, the teacher. She had emigrated from the Philippines years earlier to go to college in the United States. Her pretty baby face and diminutive five-foot three-inch frame belied her feisty disposition. She had made the most progress of all the women in the group. She was in her late thirties and had never been married, and when she first started therapy with Evelyn about a year ago, she was absolutely despondent – lonely, bitter, and frantic about her biological clock ticking away. She was getting out more now and was even considering adopting a child from the Philippines. She had taken on the role of helping the others along.

'Not so easy when you got nobody to go out with,' Laverne said. 'All my girlfriends are married or they've got steady boyfriends.'

'You can go out alone,' Merlinda said. 'You'll meet other people like yourself.'

'Where the hell am I supposed to go by myself?'

'Lots of places. Museums, restaurants.'

'No thanks. That's not for me.'

'Okay, ladies,' Evelyn said. 'Tonight, before we start, I want to introduce you to our new member. Her name is Wanda Green and . . .' Evelyn paused and looked at Wanda. She was seated in a chair on one end of the semicircle. 'Do you want me to briefly tell them about you, or do you want to do that yourself?'

All eyes turned in the direction of the new face. Wanda had the kind of exotic features that men fawned over and women fought about. She looked at least ten years younger than her thirty-five years, with a smooth coconut complexion and gray

161

eyes. She wore a short, simple black dress that showed off long, shapely legs and a figure that rich women would gladly give up their diamonds and furs for. When she'd first come to Evelyn's office, she'd worn her long reddish hair down over her shoulders. Today she had it swept up in a modified French twist, with wispy bangs dangling seductively around her eyes. With her hair like that, she reminded Evelyn of Vanessa Williams. Wanda looked at Evelyn and smiled a little nervously. 'I'm not sure where to start.'

'Start wherever you want. We're very informal and spontaneous here.'

'I find it kind of hard to believe she even needs to be here,' another woman said, looking Wanda up and down sharply. That was Dora, the other secretary. She was the most vocal member of the group. She had recently discovered that her husband had a common-law wife and three kids Dora knew nothing about tucked away in another part of the city. She was going through a messy divorce and was often testy and argumentative.

'Why is that?' Evelyn asked.

'I mean, look at her. Hard to believe she has man trouble.'

'Her problem is probably too damn many men,' said Laverne.

Wanda smiled. 'No. Not by a long shot.'

'Wanda's problems center around a single man, just like most of us here,' Evelyn said. 'Give her a chance to talk.'

'Then cut to the chase, girl,' Dora said, crossing her legs. 'I want to hear this.'

'C'mon, you guys,' Merlinda said. 'She probably needs some time to get used to us before she tells us everything.'

'Maybe you can start by telling us a little about your background,' Evelyn said.

Wanda let her small purse drop from her shoulder to the floor. 'I'm from Atlanta. I moved here about two years ago.'

'What brought you to D.C.? A job?' Merlinda asked.

Wanda shook her head. 'I moved here after I got my divorce.'

'To get away from your ex-husband?' Laverne asked.

'Not really. This is kind of complicated. See, I was engaged to a different man years before I got married, then after I got my divorce . . .'

'Ah,' Dora said. 'You moved to be with this old flame?'

'C'mon, Dora,' Merlinda said. 'Let her tell us.'

'No, it's okay,' Wanda said smiling. She tossed her head to shake a lock of hair from her gray eyes. 'The reason I didn't marry the first man I was engaged to was that he left and moved here. He ended up marrying someone else.'

She paused and the other women exchanged knowing looks.

'Then when my marriage didn't work out, I moved up here.'

'To be near him?' Merlinda asked.

Wanda nodded. 'I never got over him. He's part of the reason my marriage didn't work.'

'But he was already married to someone else by that time?' Dora asked as if she wanted to be sure she had that part straight.

'Yes.'

'Is he still married to this person?' Tracy, the junior accountant, asked.

Wanda nodded.

'Are you seeing him?' Angela, the Hispanic woman, asked.

'From time to time. We're just friends, though.'

'But you have something more in mind?'

Wanda smiled weakly. 'Like I said, I never really got over him, but . . .'

'Girl,' Dora said, uncrossing her legs, 'the solution to this problem is really quite simple, the way I see it. Forget him. He's married.'

'Does he have children?' Laverne asked.

Wanda nodded. 'I tried to get over him at first. That was why I got married when I really shouldn't have. But I just can't seem to do that. We knew each other for years before he met this . . . this other woman. We went to high school together . . .'

'Wait a minute, honey,' Dora said, cutting her off. 'Let's get something straight. She's his wife now. *You're* the other woman.'

'I don't see where she's got much choice,' Merlinda said, looking around at the other members of the group for approval. 'She's got to get over this man and move on.' They all nodded in agreement.

'I can't,' Wanda said, twisting her fingers in her lap. 'I can't seem to function when I'm not around him. Before I moved up here, I was having trouble with my job, my personal life. Nothing was going right.'

'Good grief,' Laverne said. 'You'd think a woman like you could have just about any man she wants, but here she is all worked up over this one guy. If I looked like you, I wouldn't even care about that bum husband of mine running off with some white woman.'

'I want to know just where you think you fit in up here?' Dora said, her voice rising. 'He's got a wife and children.'

'As a friend. Wherever I can. I'm not trying to break them up. I just want us to be friends.'

'Oh, c'mon,' Dora said. 'I don't believe that for a minute.'

'Are you dating other men?' Merlinda asked.

'Nothing serious.'

Dora threw her hands into the air. 'Listen here, girl,' she said, jumping up and pointing her finger at Wanda. 'Let me tell you something. 'Cause you just don't seem to get it.'

'Wait just a second,' Evelyn said, holding up her hand. 'Why don't you sit and calm yourself, Dora.'

'Nah,' Dora said, shaking her head and wagging her finger. 'I got something to say here and I'm standing up to get my point across.'

'All right,' Evelyn said. 'But first take a deep breath and get ahold of yourself.'

Dora paused and took a deep breath, but it didn't seem to have calmed her much. 'Look, I can't even feel a little sorry for someone like you. I might've in the beginning, when he left you for that other woman. But not now. 'Cause see? You lost out. And you've had all this time to get over him and get on with your life but you haven't.'

'I tried. That's why I got –'

'I'm not finished,' Dora said, cutting her off. 'You're going to have to try harder, until you get it right. 'Cause a woman like you can cause a lot of damage in a marriage. I know because I'm going through it myself now, honey. My husband had a woman on the side for damn near ten years before I found out about it. Although she don't look half as good as you. In fact, I don't know what he sees in the ugly bitch. But you got to think about somebody besides your own precious hide. Like this man's wife and children.'

'I can't cause problems if he's got a good marriage.'

'What's a good marriage? All of 'em have problems. And what are you doing? Standing in the wings waiting for something bad to happen so you can jump in. And even if you do get him, how could you ever trust him? The only satisfaction I get out of my own situation is that I know sooner or later that bastard husband of mine is gonna do the same shit to this other woman that he did to me.'

Wanda tossed her head and folded her arms in defiance.

'Hmmph. You can shake that head all you want. But know this, no matter how good you look, there's always somebody out there better.'

'Dora,' Evelyn said. 'That's enough. Give someone else a chance to speak.'

Dora let out a deep breath of air. 'Good idea,' she said, ''Cause this really got me pissed off. I'm wo' out.' She plopped down into her chair and the others laughed. Except Wanda. Wanda stared straight ahead at Evelyn.

'That was good, Wanda,' Evelyn said. 'I know it wasn't easy, but at least you got it out. We'll work on it more in the future. And the rest of you, don't forget, it's not always easy to change. Wanda's going through some of the same things the rest of you are, trying to break self-destructive old patterns.'

165

15

'I told you, you didn't have to bring anything, Ma. The caterer is handling everything except the beverages.' Evelyn stepped aside to let her mother in the front door. Pearl was carrying a big brown paper bag.

'You know your mother better than that,' her father said, stepping into the foyer behind Pearl. He planted a kiss on Evelyn's cheek, and his thick mustache grazed her skin, giving her a warm, tingly feeling. Evelyn smiled as she shut the front door.

'I don't feel right not making anything for Thanksgiving dinner,' her mother said. 'Anyway, it's only a ham. You said you were having roast duck.' She held the package out to Evelyn.

'Only a ham? Goodness,' Evelyn said, taking it from her mother. She carried the bag into the kitchen as her parents removed their coats and hung them in the closet.

'Here, let me carry that down to the family room,' her father said, following her into the kitchen.

'No, no,' Evelyn said, waving him away. 'The caterer can do it later. That's what they're here for. I'm just going to unwrap it for them and put it on the table with all the other food. You go on down with the others. They're in the rec room shooting pool and playing Ping-Pong.' She carried the package across the kitchen to the countertop and removed the bag. 'Mmm. Smells delicious,' she said, lifting off the aluminum foil.

'That's the cloves,' Pearl said, coming into the kitchen.

'I'm going on down,' Franklin said. 'You coming, Pearl?'

'In a minute.'

He went downstairs, and Pearl placed her purse on the floor. She looked at all the goodies spread out on the kitchen table.

'My, you sure have enough food here. What's this?' She pointed to a dish.

'Chicken puffs. An appetizer. Some of that is already downstairs.'

'Well, I'll be.' Pearl walked on through the breakfast area toward the section of the kitchen that held the appliances. 'Who's here?' she said, standing next to Evelyn.

'Everyone except Charmaine and Kenny. And Clarence if he's coming. Which I seriously doubt.'

'Where's Kevin?'

'Out getting some orange juice. I'm making that fruit juice drink you always make that everybody loves.'

'You already have the grapefruit juice and lemon?'

Evelyn nodded toward two half-gallon jars of grapefruit juice and two lemons sitting in a bowl near the kitchen sink. 'Everything except the orange juice.'

'I'll squeeze the lemons,' Pearl said, reaching for one. Evelyn gently slapped her hand away.

'I've got everything under control. You go on down and enjoy yourself. The caterer is serving appetizers and setting up the tables in the family room, but when they get ready to serve the food at six, we'll all have to get out of the kitchen anyway.'

'If you're sure you don't need any help.'

'I'm positive. The only thing I have to do is the juice. I'm going to start now and hopefully Kevin will get back here soon so I can finish before the caterer comes back up. I don't know what's taking him so long. He's been gone more than an hour already.' She removed an automatic juicer from a bottom cabinet, trying to think how a ten-minute trip to the store could take her husband so much time. Obviously, he had stopped somewhere else. But where and why she couldn't begin to figure. Just about everything was closed on Thanksgiving Day.

She set the juicer next to the sink just as Andre bounded into the kitchen. He had just changed out of tennis shoes at his mother's insistence. 'Yo, Grandma Pearl.' He put his arm around his grandmother and kissed her on the cheek.

167

'My goodness, you get about a foot taller every time I see you, Andre. But it's about time for you to be getting a haircut, isn't it?' She reached out to touch her grandson's hair, but he ducked away. It had grown to about two inches, the longest Andre had ever worn it, and he had twisted it all over the top.

'I'm letting it grow out for dreads,' he said, backing toward the doorway leading down to the family room.

Evelyn rolled her eyes to the ceiling as she plugged the juicer in.

'For who?' Pearl asked, frowning at him.

Andre stopped in the doorway. 'Not a who, Grandma. A what. You know, dreadlocks. It's an African do.'

'Oh, Lordy,' Pearl said.

'It's really Jamaican,' Beverly said, pushing Andre out of the doorway to enter the kitchen. He pretended she'd shoved him much harder than she had and threw himself against the wall. Then he doubled over in mock pain. Beverly laughed and stuck her tongue out at him.

'Jamaican, African,' Evelyn said. 'Makes no difference. Andre DuMont's father is taking him to get a haircut this weekend.' She picked up a lemon and sliced it in half.

Andre walked across the floor and stood in front of the sink, next to his mother. 'Daddy said I could wear 'em if I want.'

'I don't care what he said. No son of mine is going around without washing his hair and looking like a freak.' She picked up the other lemon and sliced it.

'Ma, you got it all wrong.'

'How did you get it to twist around like that, Andre?' Pearl asked. She walked to the breakfast area and sat at the table.

'Easy. You'd be surprised at the things you can do with your hair if you wear it in its natural state.'

'I think he puts vinegar in it,' Evelyn said.

'Dreadful,' Pearl said.

Beverly chuckled. 'Probably got something to do with the name.'

'And he doesn't wash it,' Evelyn said.

'That's wack, Ma. You think I'm crazy enough to go around without ever washing my hair?'

'Well, it's *something* you don't do with it,' Evelyn said.

'You don't comb it,' Beverly said. She stood at the counter on the other side of Evelyn and picked at a corner of the ham. 'Did you bring this, Ma?'

'Yes,' Pearl said.

'And get your grubby fingers out of it,' Evelyn snapped. 'That's for dinner.'

Beverly jerked her hand away. 'Meanie,' she said. She turned and leaned her backside against the counter, licking her fingers.

'What you got against dreads, Ma?' Andre asked. 'Everybody's wearin' 'em.'

'You're not.'

'Why would you want to go around without combing your hair, Andre?' Pearl asked.

He shrugged his shoulders. 'Because I want to go back to my roots.'

'If you don't comb your hair, it'll fall out at the roots,' Evelyn said.

'No it won't,' Andre said. 'Lots of people wear 'em and their hair doesn't fall out. It grows.'

Evelyn pushed Andre away from the sink and turned on the faucet.

'C'mon, Ma. Be reasonable.'

Evelyn pretty much ignored him as she rinsed off the knife. She didn't have time to worry about this boy. She was trying to decide whether to go ahead and juice the lemons and mix everything or wait until Kevin got back. She didn't want the mixture sitting too long before he brought the orange juice. Where in the world was he? He was going to ruin her dinner if he didn't hurry and get back.

'Sounds to me like when the Afro first came out back in the sixties,' Pearl said. 'You wanted to wear one and I wouldn't let you at first. Remember that, Evelyn?'

Evelyn looked up at the sound of her name. She hadn't heard a thing her mother had just said. 'What?'

169

'Oh, ho,' Andre said smiling brightly. 'Ma wore an Afro?'

'Of course,' Beverly said. 'Everybody did then.'

'That was nothing like these dreadlocks,' Evelyn said. She put a lemon half in the juicer and turned it on. 'We combed our hair every day and kept it neatly trimmed.'

'But the idea of not straightening your hair was a big thing at the time,' Pearl said. 'It frightened us older folks at first, just like this dreadlocks stuff now, I guess.'

'This dialogue is gettin' real interesting,' Andre said.

Evelyn turned off the juicer and shot her mother a warning glance.

Pearl smiled and stood up, smoothing her skirt across her thighs. 'Guess I've said enough. I'll mosey on down to see the folks.'

Andre leaned across the counter and stuck his face directly in front of his mother's. 'Daddy said it would be okay, Ma. Why you got to be such a drag?'

'Get out of my face, Andre,' she said, waving him away. She poured the grapefruit juice into the blender, followed by the lemon juice. Then she turned the blender on. Where was that father of his? Everything else was ready now. She was beginning to think something bad might have happened to Kevin. It was so unlike him not to do what he said he would. But then he had not been himself lately, so edgy and out of character. When they'd left the dinner party last Sunday night and she'd commented on how nice Nathan and Brenda's new house looked, he'd jumped all over her, saying she was too concerned about material things. She reminded him that there was a time when he admired things like that, too.

'It's only a hairdo,' Andre said, sticking his face into his mother's again.

'He'll probably just wear it a couple of months and get tired of it,' Beverly said, raising her voice over the blender. 'Kids go through these phases.'

Evelyn turned off the blender and gave Beverly a sharp look. 'He's getting a haircut Saturday and that's final.'

'Whoa,' Beverly said, raising her hands in mock defense.

'Excuse me for being alive.' She picked up the ham and put it on the table, then sat down.

The doorbell rang and for a second Evelyn thought it might be Kevin. Then she realized he would have used his key and come in the kitchen door. 'Get the door, Andre.'

Andre sighed and sulked out of the room.

'You trying to make my job harder?' Evelyn asked Beverly after he left. She licked her fingers without thinking and the tart taste of pure lemon hit her mouth. She frowned and smacked her tongue.

'What do you mean?' Beverly asked.

'It's enough trouble trying to raise a boy these days. I should think my own sister would at least back me up.'

'It so happens I don't have a problem with dreadlocks. Okay?'

'That's not the point. You wait until you have a family of your own. Then maybe you'll understand how difficult it is.'

'Evelyn, all I was doing was . . . Oh, never mind. What's wrong with you? You're making a federal case out of nothing.'

Charmaine walked into the kitchen carrying a big cardboard box with holes punched in the sides. Andre followed her, carrying Kenny on his shoulders.

'How's it going?' Charmaine said, dropping her big shoulder bag in the middle of all the food.

Evelyn flew across the room. 'Don't put that thing there. Can't you see all the food?' She picked up Charmaine's bag and dropped it under the table.

Charmaine looked at Beverly as if to say, 'What's eating her?' Beverly merely rolled her eyes to the ceiling. 'What's in the box, Charmaine?' Beverly asked.

Charmaine set the box on the floor and opened it. She lifted a Birman cat up out of the box.

'Oh!' Beverly said. 'You brought it.'

'Oh, no,' Evelyn said. 'You didn't.'

'I brought it for the kids.'

As if on cue, Rebecca entered the kitchen. Her little face lit up like a Christmas tree when she saw the cat. 'Where'd you get that, Aunt Charmaine? Can I hold it?'

Charmaine handed the cat to Rebecca, and she gathered it in her arms.

'Charmaine, I thought I made myself clear about the cat,' Evelyn said.

'If you don't want it, I'll take it back. But I contacted the animal shelter and so far nobody's claimed it.'

'Can't we keep it, Ma?' Rebecca asked, rubbing the cat's fur against her face.

'Otherwise I'll have to turn it in,' Charmaine said. 'They'll probably put it to sleep.'

'Did you hear that, Ma?' Andre said. He sat Kenny down on the floor and rubbed the cat's neck.

'It's too much trouble,' Evelyn said. 'Who's going to look after it?'

'I will,' Andre said.

'Me, too,' Rebecca said. 'Cats are easy to take care of. All you need is some food and a litter box.'

'How do you know so much about cats?' Evelyn asked Rebecca.

'Some of the girls at school have them.'

'Okay, then. If I let you keep it, who's going to clean out the litter box?'

'Clean out the litter box?' Andre asked.

'You have go in and scoop the cat's do out of the box several times a week, you know. And change it every once in a while.'

Andre turned up his nose at that. 'Personally, I'd rather have a dog.'

'Uh-huh. That's what I thought.'

'I don't mind,' Rebecca said.

'You say that now, Rebecca, but when the time comes, I'll be the one that ends up doing it.'

'No, you won't. I promise. I'm going to take him downstairs and show him to Granddaddy.'

'Take Kenny with you,' Charmaine said.

Andre picked up Kenny and hoisted him over his shoulders again.

'But don't get any ideas about the cat,' Evelyn said. 'And Andre, ask Mama if it's one part orange juice and two parts grapefruit juice or one part orange juice and three grapefruit.' Andre frowned.

'Just ask her. She'll know what I mean.'

The three of them went downstairs with the cat.

'Are you going to let them keep it?' Beverly asked.

'I probably don't have much choice now that they've seen it. I wish you hadn't done that without asking me, Charmaine.'

'I knew you'd say no if I did.'

'Well, maybe we'll try and see if it works out. Rebecca really seemed taken with it.'

Charmaine winked at Beverly.

'I saw that,' Evelyn said, smiling. 'You think you're slick, don't you?'

'I knew you wouldn't be able to resist it if the kids saw it.'

'We'll see.'

'How are you doing, Charmaine?' Beverly asked.

'As well as can be expected considering the circumstances.'

'You tell Mama and Daddy about the baby yet?' Beverly asked.

'I haven't told anybody yet,' Charmaine said, sitting at the table next to Beverly.

'Have you decided if you're going to keep it?' Beverly asked.

'Haven't got much choice now that Clarence knows all about it.' She gave Evelyn a sideways glance.

'I'm sorry about that,' Evelyn said. 'But you have no one to blame but yourself. You should have told me you didn't want Clarence to know you were pregnant.'

'I never got much of a chance. Shit. I wasn't expecting him back home so soon. And any other time you hardly ever say two words to my husband.'

'How can I when he's never around?'

'Even when he is, you avoid him.'

'I do not.'

'Yes, you do, Evelyn. You never have much of anything to say to him. Even Kevin talks to him more than you do.'

173

'Evelyn and Clarence get along better now than they used to,' Beverly said to Charmaine.

Charmaine put her hands on her hips and looked at Beverly. 'Since when?'

'The last couple of times they've been together, I've seen them talk a bit.'

'Hmmph. You must've been seeing things.'

'Where's Clarence now?' Evelyn asked.

'He's coming later.'

'Mmm-hmm,' Evelyn said. She picked up the empty jar of grapefruit juice from the counter and threw it in the trash. 'He's always coming later.'

'Look, I'm not getting into this shit —' Charmaine stopped talking as their mother entered the room. Pearl looked around at her daughters. 'What are you girls arguing about now?'

The three of them looked at each other.

'Nothing,' Evelyn said, leaning her backside against the counter. She crossed her arms over her waist.

'Who's arguing?' Charmaine said, crossing her legs away from Evelyn.

'It's the usual, Ma,' Beverly said. 'Men. What else?'

Pearl looked first at Charmaine, then Evelyn. 'I thought you two had grown out of that by now.'

'Some things never change,' Beverly said. 'One thing, listening to these two always makes me feel better. Seems to be so many problems with being married, they make me almost glad I'm still single.'

'I don't have problems,' Evelyn said. 'Charmaine's the one with the problems.'

'Who the hell are you to judge? I wish you'd —'

'All right, all right,' Pearl said. 'That's enough. I didn't come up here to listen to you two bicker. Evelyn, Andre said you had a question about the juice.'

'Yes. Is it one part orange juice to two parts grapefruit juice?'

'I'm not sure. I just do it by eye. Is Kevin back with the orange juice yet?'

'No. And I don't know what's keeping him.'

'So where's Mr Perfect?'

'Charmaine,' Pearl said reprovingly.

Evelyn walked toward the door leading out of the kitchen. 'I'm going to make some calls to try to find him.'

'It's only been an hour,' Pearl said.

'It's been almost two hours now, Ma. I'll be right back.' As Evelyn left the room, she could hear Charmaine's voice.

'Hmmph. If I worried about where Clarence was after just two hours, I'd have a head full of gray hairs by now.'

'Kevin's not like Clarence,' Pearl said.

'Now *you* going to start getting on my case, too, Ma?'

'I'm not saying a word. That's a beautiful cat downstairs. Where'd you get . . .'

In the bedroom, Evelyn went to Kevin's night table and rummaged through the drawer until she found his personal address book. She opened it and a slip of paper fell on the table. She picked it up. It had the initials C. C. and a Washington telephone number on it. Evelyn frowned, wondering who or what C. C. was, but nothing came to mind. She replaced the slip of paper, then turned to Jeremy Malone's phone number. Lately, Kevin had been spending so much time with Jeremy. Too much, as far as she was concerned. Maybe he had stopped over there. She couldn't understand how a trip less than a mile up the street would end up five miles away in Takoma Park, but Kevin had been acting so irrational these past few weeks. She sat on the edge of the bed and picked up the phone. Jeremy answered on the second ring. 'Hello?'

'Jeremy? Hi, this is Evelyn DuMont.'

'Evelyn,' he said, clearly surprised. 'How are you?'

'Fine. Are you enjoying your Thanksgiving?'

'Pretty much. I was just on my way out to a friend's for dinner.'

'I won't keep you, then. I just wanted to ask if you've heard from Kevin.'

'Not today. Something wrong?'

Her heart sank. Now she was starting to really worry. 'I hope not. He went out a couple of hours ago to pick something up

175

for dinner, and everyone's here waiting for him to get back. I just thought he might have stopped by there.'

'He probably stopped somewhere else and got held up.'

'But that's just it. Everything is closed today.'

'You're right. Maybe he's stuck in traffic.'

For two hours? 'That's probably it. Well, I'll let you go. Have a nice Thanksgiving.'

'You too. And if I hear from him before I leave here, I'll tell him he's holding up your turkey.'

'Thanks, Jeremy. 'Bye.'

She hung up and flipped through the address book, trying to find someone else who might know Kevin's whereabouts. There was Jimmy, Kevin's best friend, but he lived all the way in town. She couldn't imagine Kevin would go that far on the spur of the moment. Then again, who knew? With the way he'd been acting these days, anything was possible. She picked up the receiver, then realized that the chatter coming from the kitchen was a little louder, as if someone had just come in. And she hadn't heard the front doorbell ring. She put the receiver down. God, she hoped it was Kevin.

She left the bedroom and walked down the hallway, straining to hear the chatter coming from the kitchen. It wasn't until she reached the top of the stairs that she was certain she heard his voice. She didn't know whether to shout with joy or scream in anger.

She walked into the kitchen, fully intending to get an explanation for his long absence. But he was standing near the table laughing and talking with her sisters, so this was not the time to get into it with him. She would put it on hold and bring it up later tonight. She tried hard to smile as she passed Kevin and her sisters and walked toward the section of the kitchen where the appliances were. Her mother was standing near the sink adding sugar to the blender. The smile disappeared from Evelyn's face. 'Why are you adding sugar? Where's the orange juice?'

'He couldn't find any,' Pearl said.

Evelyn stared at her mother, then looked across the room at

176

Kevin. So much for holding it until later. 'You go out of the house for two hours to get orange juice, holding up everyone and everything, and don't even come back with it?'

Everyone stopped talking and looked at her. 'Everything's closed because of the holiday,' Kevin said.

'What about Seven-Eleven? They're always open.'

'I didn't see any along the way.'

'There's always a Seven-Eleven somewhere, Kevin.'

He shrugged, and Evelyn threw her hands into the air. 'My drink for dinner is ruined.'

'No, it's not,' Pearl said. 'We'll improvise. I'm adding sugar to dilute the sour taste from the lemon.'

Evelyn twisted up her nose in disgust. 'It won't be right without the orange juice.'

'It'll be fine,' Pearl said. 'Just get me some ice cubes.'

'I did the best I could,' Kevin said.

'It's not his fault all the stores are closed,' Beverly said.

'I don't believe that for a minute.'

Beverly and Charmaine exchanged glances. Pearl picked up a spoon and stirred the juice. Kevin shoved his hands into his pockets.

Evelyn walked to the refrigerator and yanked the freezer door open. She removed the ice bucket, then banged the door shut. She dropped the ice bucket on the countertop next to her mother, then looked at Kevin. 'Well, are you going to tell me what you were doing all that time?'

'I was trying to find you some juice.'

'For two hours?'

He removed his hand from his pocket and looked at his watch. 'Has it been that long?'

Evelyn bit her bottom lip and glanced at Beverly and Charmaine. It wasn't often that they saw her engaged in a spat with Kevin, and she was trying to determine just how absorbed they were. Beverly was looking out the picture window even though it was pitch black outside, but Charmaine was looking directly at them. Obviously, she didn't plan to miss one iota of this unusual episode.

'It's been at least that long,' Evelyn said, her voice a little calmer.

'I went to Giant and Safeway but both of them closed early today.'

Kevin knew better than to expect her to believe that. Giant and Safeway were both within two miles of the house. It was impossible for anyone to be gone all that time and drive only two miles up the road. But it seemed pointless to try and get more out of him now. 'Fine, Kevin. If that's the way you want to be.'

She picked up the ice bucket and reached across her mother to drop several ice cubes into the blender. Pearl snapped the top on and pushed a button. Its whirring sound filled the room just as Kevin spoke to Evelyn, drowning out his voice from across the room. She was so fed up with him that at first she thought she wouldn't even bother to ask him to repeat what he'd just said. She was so tired of all this nonsense. But she signaled her mother to turn off the blender for a second. 'What did you say?' she asked as the noise died down.

'I said I also stopped by Jeremy's, but I didn't realize it had taken so much time. We . . .'

Evelyn didn't hear the rest. She was trying so desperately to make sense of what Kevin had just said that she barely heard the blender when her mother switched it back on. She put her hand to her head, trying to reconcile Kevin's words with what Jeremy had told her on the phone not five minutes before. If Kevin stopped at Jeremy's, why would Jeremy say he hadn't seen Kevin today? Did Jeremy mean *all* day? She was so absorbed with these thoughts that she forgot she was holding the ice bucket until it slipped from her fingers and crashed to the floor. Cubes of ice scattered everywhere.

'Damn it.' She picked up the empty bucket and threw it into the sink.

'Don't be so rough,' Pearl said. 'You'll scratch the sink.'

'Who cares?' She bent over and picked up several ice cubes from the floor and threw them into the sink. 'Nothing else is going right today.'

Kevin came across the room and bent over to help her.

'Never mind,' Evelyn snapped. 'I'll do it myself.' The look she gave him was as hard as the ice cubes.

Kevin straightened up. 'Fine,' he said. 'I'm going downstairs with the others.' He left the room.

'What's the matter with you?' Pearl asked.

'She's been edgy all day,' Beverly said.

'I swear,' Charmaine added, 'she acts like the whole damn dinner is ruined just 'cause one ingredient in her perfect little recipe had to be changed.'

16

Beverly tapped her foot on the Persian rug as she sat in the small waiting area of the hair salon. The place was nice enough, she thought, located on the ground floor of a big old Victorian house in downtown Silver Spring, Maryland, not in a modern chrome and glass building, as she had expected it to be. It had a homey feel to it.

The waiting area was a small, sunny room at the front of the house. Probably used as a sitting room or something, she thought, before the house was remodeled into a hair salon. A receptionist sat behind an oak rolltop desk adorned with a white and gold-trimmed antique telephone and a thick leather appointment book. The large picture window behind the couch was covered with sheer white curtains that let in the sunlight. A handmade patchwork quilt was tossed over the back of the couch. Two stuffed armchairs faced it.

From her position on a corner of the couch, Beverly could look through French double doors into a huge room that looked as if it had once been the living and dining rooms. Several women sat in salon chairs having their hair styled, and the hardwood floor was littered with dark hair clippings.

All very nice, she thought, sinking back into the couch. Nothing less than what she would have expected of a salon recommended by Evelyn. What she hadn't been prepared for, though, was all the waiting. She looked at her watch. She was on her lunch break and had wanted to be in and out of this place in an hour and a half. But that was beginning to look like wishful thinking. When she'd first arrived, the receptionist told her that Denise, the stylist Evelyn had recommended, would be with her shortly, but that had been twenty minutes ago.

Even more surprising to Beverly, though, was the way the

three other women seated in the waiting area were taking it. They looked so patient, and two of them had been waiting longer than she had. For the life of her, Beverly couldn't understand it. The two sitting in the armchairs across from her were flipping ever so calmly through hairstyling magazines. The woman seated next to her on the couch seemed to be napping, with her head reclined on the stuffed pillows and her eyes closed. Every now and then she sat up and watched the beauticians through the French doors.

Beverly looked at her watch again, then crossed her arms. How could they be so calm? Didn't they have things to do besides sit here and wait? She had a mind to forget this and walk out. It took her only thirty minutes at the most to wash and blow her hair dry at home. Sometimes she ran a hot comb through it for a different look, but most of the time she took advantage of her hair's natural wave. Still, pressing it only took an extra ten to fifteen minutes. She'd been sitting here just waiting twice that long.

She should have listened to Valerie when they'd talked on the phone last night. Valerie had tried to talk her out of getting a perm, telling Beverly to count her blessings. She went on and on about how they trapped women into returning to salons over and over, again and again. When the new nappy hair grew out after six to eight weeks, a woman was almost forced to return for a touch-up, since it was hard to manage a head of hair that was half nappy and half straight. Valerie had calculated that she spent about twenty-four hours a year in these places and about half of it waiting. When she was able to get a word in edgewise, Beverly admitted to Valerie that she had a point. But she was determined to try it, at least once. This seemed to be an exciting time for black women and their hair. They were having it permed and relaxed, braided and weaved, pressed and wrapped. Beverly had never had any of it done and felt left out. Some of the women leaving here looked really nice.

So Beverly guessed she was here to stay no matter how long it took. She picked up a copy of *Black Hair* magazine from the coffee table in front of her. Halle Berry was on the cover, looking great in a sassy short cut. Beverly studied the picture, trying to determine how it would look on her. If it looked half as good as this, she thought, she'd be happy.

As she flipped through the pages, a petite black woman about her age approached. 'Miss Jordan?' the woman asked.

'Yes,' Beverly said, closing the magazine. About time, she thought.

The woman smiled. 'I'm Denise. I'm not ready for you yet, but I'll be with you shortly.' She turned and beckoned one of the women seated in the armchairs. Beverly watched with dismay as the woman got up and followed Denise through the double doors. Now she was really thinking about getting up and leaving. She was beginning to get an idea of what 'be with you shortly' must mean around here. No hairdo was worth this.

'Don't feel bad,' said the woman seated next to her on the couch. Beverly turned and faced her. She was around fiftyish and dressed impeccably in a wool suit with a brightly colored scarf at the neckline. Her black and silver hair looked as if it had been done just yesterday. The woman smiled. 'I'm waiting on Denise, too. And I arrived after you did.'

She had a nice smile, Beverly thought. 'Unbelievable. Are you on your lunch hour, too?'

The woman chuckled. 'No, indeed. I always take the rest of the afternoon off when I come here.'

'I'm beginning to see why.'

The woman looked Beverly up and down. This made Beverly feel woefully underdressed in her simple wool skirt and red pullover sweater. She twisted the silver chain around her neck.

'This your first time here?' the woman asked.

Beverly nodded. 'First time at any salon.'

'Really? I couldn't imagine my life without them. But you really don't need them. You have beautiful hair.'

'Thanks. But I'm starting to get bored with it. I wanted something different.'

'You couldn't have come to a better place. Denise is really good. But let me give you some advice. Unless you're one of those people who can afford to take very long lunch breaks,

182

don't try to cram it into your lunch hour. It'll probably be more like two to three hours before you get out of here.'

Beverly rolled her eyes to the ceiling. 'I can't say I wasn't warned. Why don't you try other salons? Find one that's faster?'

The woman smiled knowingly. 'I have, and they're all like this. Some are even worse. But my hair was falling out around the edges when I was doing it myself. Rather let the experts fuss with it.'

'So you just got used to the waiting, huh?'

'You never get used to it. But you learn to live with it. By the way, I'm Marie.'

'I'm Beverly.'

The two of them smiled at each other and shook hands. 'So,' Beverly said, 'I guess I'll stick around and try it, at least this once.' She picked up the copy of *Black Hair* magazine from the coffee table. 'How do you think this style would look on me?' she asked, showing the cover to Marie.

'Oh, it's perfect for you.'

'You really think so?' Beverly said, pleasantly surprised at Marie's enthusiasm.

Marie nodded. 'Very sophisticated but youthful. Looks like it may be a wrap.'

Beverly held out the photo at arm's length. It was radically different from the way her hair was now – much, much shorter. And once it was cut this short, she wouldn't be able to pin it back in a twist the way it was now. But then so what? The style she wore now wasn't exactly breathtaking. She could probably use a dose of sophistication. And even though she was only twenty-nine, she'd just been dumped for a twenty-two-year-old. So a shot of youthfulness probably wouldn't hurt either. Since breaking up with Vernon about a month before, her life wasn't exactly hopping. A new hairdo might be just the thing to perk it up a little.

Weddings. Beverly thought if she never got invited to another one as long as she lived, it would be fine with her. Especially

183

since it seemed like she was never going to have one of her own. She rested her arms on the sides of the tub, raised her big toe to about an inch below the faucet, and waited for the next drop of water to land on it. She had a little time to kill before she had to leave for Zelma's wedding. Although with the icy conditions on the road today, she should probably allow herself extra time or . . . Or what? Or she'd be late? So what. Big deal. These things never started on time anyway, and then they took up the whole afternoon and evening. She leaned back in the tub and closed her eyes.

She had once thought that as she got older and everyone was married off, there would be fewer of these affairs. But now it just seemed like everyone was having their second and third go-rounds. Personally, she thought anyone getting married for the second or third time should be banned by law from having a big wedding. Spare guests the agony of trying to decide what to buy someone who already has one set of blenders and automatic juicers. And she was appalled at the number of repeat brides who wore frilly white dresses.

She leaned over and pulled the stopper from the drain, then stood and reached for a towel. If she ever got married, she was definitely not wearing white. Off-white maybe, but then only in something mature, not all frilly and childish-looking. And she was only inviting family and close friends. Although why she was even thinking along these lines she didn't know. At the rate she was going, she would never walk down anybody's aisle. Since breaking up with Vernon, her social life was about as active as that of a bear hibernating in winter.

Valerie had been pressing her to go out for drinks, but she just wasn't in the mood yet to mingle. In fact, she wasn't sure she'd ever be ready to get back into the rat race again. Once you reached a certain age, the singles scene was downright gloomy.

She'd thought about calling Vernon more times than she cared to admit to anyone. Men like him couldn't be found around every corner. Even with what he'd done to her, he was

184

still a pretty good catch. The problem was she didn't think she'd ever be able to completely trust him. If he cheated on her once, what was to stop him from doing it again? And a second time would kill her. First one damn nearly did.

Sometimes she wished she could be more like Charmaine. She wasn't sure Clarence had ever gotten out on her, but even if he had, Charmaine would probably just toss it off and not let it worry her. No, she was more like Evelyn, she guessed. No way Evelyn would put up with something like that. Kevin would be out of that house in a minute if he ever cheated, though he probably would never consider it. That was the kind of man and the kind of marriage Beverly wanted. And she'd rather be single forever than settle for anything less.

She stepped from the tub and opened the door to let the steam out of the room, then wiped the fog from the mirror with the towel. She removed her shower cap and peered into the mirror. At first, her new short hairdo always sort of surprised her when she saw it. But now she was getting used to it. And since it was a wrap, it was unbelievably easy to care for. Just wash it and wrap it with a scarf. Zelma and the others at the office loved it. So did Charmaine. She had yet to get out to Evelyn's house to let her see it. Now, barely a week after getting her hair cut, it felt commonplace. So much for a new hairdo adding some pizzazz to her life.

She didn't know a soul here other than the bride, she thought, standing near the gift table and sipping some too-sweet pink punch from a plastic cup. Zelma said she'd invited Byron, the new editor, at the last minute, but so far Beverly hadn't seen him.

The bride looked radiant. Of course, the dress was somewhat corny, making Zelma's already wide hips look wider than a river, especially standing next to her new husband. Beverly had heard a zillion stories about Jessie but this was the first time she'd ever seen him. He was about as short and thin as

Zelma was short and wide. The way Zelma talked, as if every woman in the city was after her man, Beverly had expected a bit more of a hunk. Especially since Zelma, even though overweight, was very pretty and stylish. But then who was she to judge? Miss Old-maid Aunt. The important thing was that they looked happy.

Beverly took one more look toward Zelma and Jessie. They were linked arm in arm, and moving toward the cake with the photographer and a half dozen others in tow. No need for her to hang around any longer. No one would miss her in the slightest.

Just as she turned to leave, Byron from the office popped into her face. He smiled, showing off those beautiful white teeth. Zelma thought he was the finest thing since silk. And he *was* the best-dressed man in the office. He had on a dark gray wool suit with a white shirt and burgundy tie. But there was something about him that made Beverly uneasy, besides the fact that he was a little too skinny for her taste.

'I knew I'd find you sooner or later,' he said, smiling down at her.

'I looked for you in the church but didn't see you,' she said.

'I didn't make it to the church, and I just got here about ten or fifteen minutes ago.'

'Did you get a chance to talk to Zelma?'

He nodded. 'Briefly.'

'Nice wedding, isn't it?'

He shrugged. 'If you like big affairs like this. Personally, I'm not too crazy about them. Were you about to leave?'

'Yes. I don't know anyone here.'

He nodded. 'Same here. I know a nice restaurant not far from here, on the Hill. How about joining me for an early dinner?'

'I don't think so. I told you before, I don't date men I work with.'

'Who said anything about dating? I'm just trying to be friendly, to get to know you a little better.'

'Isn't that what dating is?'

'You wouldn't assume that if I was one of your female coworkers or one of the white men you work with and they suggested dinner after work or something like this. Would you?'

She stared at him for a moment as she thought about that. According to Zelma, he'd been asking a lot of questions about her lately around the office. But Zelma liked to play the office matchmaker, and it could be that she'd blown things out of proportion. 'Maybe not, but . . .'

'Then why make assumptions just because I'm a black male?'

She smiled at him. 'Okay, Byron. I'll have dinner with you.' Why not, under those terms? She enjoyed male company and found herself missing it.

'Good.'

'But only as one coworker with another coworker.'

'Fine.'

'And I'm paying for myself.'

'That's not necessary.'

'I insist. Now. How are we going to work this out? Did you drive here?'

'Yes. Tell you what. Why don't I drive us to the restaurant and bring you back to your car afterward? It's only about ten minutes from here. If that's okay with you, of course.'

'Sounds fine.'

They left the reception and headed for the parking lot. Byron was every bit a gentleman. He held doors open for her, helped her with her coat, and let her walk ahead of him in crowds. That was one of the things she'd liked so much about Vernon. 'You said you were from Los Angeles?' she asked as he held the door open to his silver Maxima.

'I was born in Birmingham, but I've moved around a lot, lived mostly in California. Been in the D.C. area for about four years now.'

She nodded. That explained it. Southern men were so courteous and considerate. Obviously, Byron hadn't forgotten what he'd learned back home.

The restaurant was a small, informal place with a friendly staff. 'It's not fancy,' he said as they studied the menu. 'But the food's very good and they have a fair selection of wines.'

'What do you recommend?'

'The baked chicken. It's always cooked just the right amount of time. Very tender.'

'Then that's what I'll have.' She placed her menu on the table.

He ordered the chicken for both of them when the waiter returned, along with a bottle of white Zinfandel. When the wine arrived, the waiter poured a small amount in Byron's glass. Byron handed the glass to her and she took a sip. It had a mildly sweet taste.

'It's good.'

Byron smiled, pleased that she liked his choice, and nodded toward the waiter, who filled both their glasses. Beverly picked hers up and settled back in her chair. Only three other groups were dining in the small restaurant. It had a relaxed, un-hurried atmosphere. She took a sip of her wine and smiled at Byron. She had forgotten how nice it was to dine out. She could definitely get used to it again in a hurry.

He looked at her and smiled. 'I know I already told you, but I really like your hair like that. It brings out your eyes.'

She patted the back of her head, feeling a little shy. She wasn't used to getting compliments on her hair. 'Thanks.'

'So,' he said, putting his glass on the table. 'Zelma tells me you recently broke up with your old man.'

Beverly frowned. 'When did she tell you that?'

'About a week ago.'

'It's true.'

'Have you started seeing anyone else yet?'

'No, it's only been a month since we broke up.'

'Still, I'm surprised.'

'About what?'

'You're a very attractive woman. I would have thought you had several men waiting in the wings.'

'Not exactly,' she said, relieved to see the waiter arrive with their food. The topic of this conversation made her uncomfortable.

'Go ahead, try the chicken,' Byron said, holding his fork and knife.

She cut a piece and popped it into her mouth. It was some of the best baked chicken she'd ever tasted. 'Mmm, this is delicious.'

He smiled and took a bite. 'Cooked perfectly,' he said. 'Always is. So what is it you have against dating men you work with?'

Uh-oh. 'I just don't like the idea of it.'

'Ever tried it?'

'No. The truth is, I haven't exactly been around a lot of datable men at the office. I've always been in private industry, so the men have been mostly white or ethnic.'

He nodded. 'I know what you mean.'

'Good. Now can we please change the subject?'

'Fine, but I'm curious about something.'

'What?'

'How do you know you don't like it if you've never tried it?'

'I don't need to try it. It's the principle of the thing.'

'You know what I think?'

'No.' And she wasn't so sure she cared.

'I think you probably never gave it much thought, since, as you say, the opportunity never presented itself. But the truth is, now that more women are working, office affairs are becoming common. They're not the taboo things they once were.'

'You're probably right. But I thought we weren't going to get into things like this, that this was supposed to be a meal between coworkers.'

'Sorry, but it seemed to be the only way to get you to have dinner with me. I don't come across the kind of woman I like, women like you, very often. So when I do, I'll try just about anything to get to know her better. Some men say there are a lot of available women in this city, but that's only because those men will get involved with anything that wears a skirt. I'm a lot pickier. That's why I don't hesitate to go out with coworkers. The office is one of the few places to meet smart, goal-oriented women.'

'But what happens when you decide to call it quits? I mean, you still have to work together. Doesn't that get awkward?'

'I'm sure it does for some people. But that's never been a problem for me.'

'Never? I'm surprised.'

'It's all in how you handle it. You have to set rules in the beginning – a framework for before, during, and after the relationship, if it comes to that.'

'You mean you say something like, "If this doesn't work out we'll do such and such at the office." Like that?'

'Exactly.'

'And it works?'

'Has for me. 'Course it has to be the right type of woman. You know, stable, levelheaded. Like yourself.'

Beverly thought about Vernon's convertible top and her kitchen knife and what might have been, and it was all she could do to keep from laughing. 'How can you be so sure I'm stable and levelheaded?'

'I've watched you, worked with you for a month now. I can always tell.'

'You never know. People can be so different at work than they are in their personal lives.'

'True. But somehow I think I'm right about you.'

Beverly smiled.

'So. Have I convinced you that office romances are in vogue or are at least acceptable in the 1990s?'

'I don't think so.'

'Hey, don't knock something before you try it. I mean, don't you think you know more about me than the man you'd meet at a party or nightclub and then go out on a date with the next weekend?'

He had a big point there. 'You're right.'

'I'm not asking you to elope with me. At least not yet. Just to go out with me, see if we like each other socially. If we do, fine. If not, we end it. Agreed?'

He wasn't her type physically. But then look what she'd gotten with her so-called types – two broken hearts and a lot of loneliness. Byron seemed so rational and sure of himself. And she enjoyed being out eating tasty food and drinking good wine. Certainly beat the hell out of those microwave dinners she'd been eating so much of lately. 'Okay. We'll give it a try.'

'Good,' he said, picking up his wineglass. He lifted it, and she raised hers. 'Here's to a new and long-lasting relationship,' he said. They clicked glasses. 'Do you want dessert? The cheese-cake is very good here.'

She smiled. 'Then I'll have to try it.'

He looked around for their waiter. Even though she wasn't all that attracted to him in a physical way, she thought, he seemed nice enough and interesting as you got to know him. He certainly knew about food and wine. Maybe there were other pleasant surprises in store.

He turned back toward her, not having much luck finding the waiter. 'I have another idea,' he said. 'What are you doing later tonight?'

He sure didn't plan to waste much time getting started with this dating, did he? She reached for the bottle of wine, trying to buy some time to think of what to say, but he grabbed it. 'Nothing special,' she said as he filled her glass. She picked it up and took a sip.

'We could swing by my place. You seem to like this wine. We can take the bottle and finish it off in my king-size brass bed while we make love. Have each other for dessert instead of cheesecake.'

Beverly almost choked on the wine. She placed the glass on the table, then picked up a napkin and wiped the corners of her mouth. She looked directly at him. 'To be honest, I'd prefer the cheesecake.' She threw the napkin on the table.

He looked crestfallen. Then a big smile crossed his face, baring those white teeth. He chuckled. 'That was a joke, right?'

Beverly glared at him.

'Right?' he said.

She stared at him intensely. Dirty double-crosser.

He looked away, then back toward her. 'I thought my suggestion was a good idea. Isn't that what all this has been leading up to?'

'Not for tonight, it hasn't.'

'Why not? Don't you find me attractive at all?'

'That has nothing –'

'And like I said, I think you're very attractive. I have from the first time I laid eyes on you.'

'I have to have time to get to know a person first.' Besides, two minutes ago, I wasn't even sure I wanted to date you.

'That's so old-fashioned. Like you were about dating coworkers.'

'Call it whatever you want, but I won't be changing my mind about this one. Jeez, give you an inch, you try to snatch a mile.'

'I didn't mean to offend you. But I believe in being direct.'

'Brutal's more like it.'

'What usually happens when you meet someone you like? You probably go out with him a few times, or maybe its several times with you, but sooner or later you have sex. Right?'

Beverly looked at him but didn't say anything. So what was his point?

'But all that time until you have sex, things are sort of awkward. You both know what it's leading to and you're anxious and horny anticipating it. You don't really become comfortable with each other until after you've been intimate. Why not reverse that? Have the sex first, get it out of the way. Then it's much easier getting to know each other socially.'

'How many women have you used this line on before?'

He laughed lightly. 'I don't call it a line. But if by that you mean have I used a direct approach in my relationships, yes. It's been my credo for several years now to be up-front about this.'

'As my nephew would say, "That's wack." In fact, it's the dumbest argument I've ever heard in my life.'

'It may sound dumb to you but a lot of women go along with it. You need to free your mind of outdated habits and beliefs. They hold you back from experiencing and enjoying life.'

'Are you saying you're involved with a bunch of women at the same time?'

'I didn't say a bunch.'

'A few?'

'They're all women I get along with very well and that I'm attracted to. And vice versa. I tell them up-front that I won't limit myself. They're free to do whatever they want, too. We're good friends as well as lovers. Only we don't kid ourselves that this person is the one and only for all time.'

This had to be a joke of some kind. 'And women actually go along with this?'

'Some do, some don't. You'd be surprised at some of those who do. Many of them are successful women like yourself. I meet a lot of them around the office.'

'Our office?'

He nodded with a kind of smirk on his face. This was supposed to impress her? 'What about AIDS and all the other things floating around these days?'

'I'll use a condom if you want.'

If *she* wanted? What did *he* want? He was the one screwing around. She looked at him. How had she so misjudged this man? 'Forget it. I don't want any part of your little harem. Or big harem, as it may be.'

'This is obviously too much for you.'

He was right about that. But she didn't say a word. She didn't think anything else needed to be said.

'Fine.' He dropped his napkin on the table and turned to call for the waiter. This time he found him. 'Check, please.' So much for dessert, Beverly guessed. They avoided each other's eyes as they waited for the check. She doubted he'd be asking her out on any more dates and it was just as well. She should thank him for revealing the true color of his stripes before she got too involved. Most of these men were so good at deception, it took forever to realize that what you thought was a polished diamond was really nothing but a warped chunk of glass. When it was this obvious, a woman had nobody but herself to blame if she got burned.

A part of her couldn't help being disappointed – and annoyed – that he wasn't the man he seemed to be shaping into. She felt like someone had presented her with a beautifully wrapped box and when she'd opened it, a weasel had popped out. She'd almost dropped her wineglass when he asked that question. Damn Vernon for forcing her back out here with these clowns.

' . . . Beverly.'

She jumped and looked at him. She was so far gone, she hadn't even seen the waiter come back to the table, but there Byron was, waving the check in her face. 'Your part comes to $12.50 including tax and the tip.'

Obviously, they were back on coworker terms.

17

'Astrologically speaking,' Valerie was saying as she shifted her red Volkswagen Cabriolet into fourth and gave it some gas, 'I think you're just going through an unpredictable and erratic period because all these outer planets – Uranus and Neptune mainly – are conjunct – that means they're next to or at least close by – and opposite your personal planets. And Saturn is squaring your sun. But I think the main problem is Uranus. Believe me, Uranus is a killer of a planet. Especially for you, 'cause you're so down-to-earth.'

Was that why they were roaring up Wisconsin Avenue on a December night with the convertible top down? Because she was going through an unpredictable, erratic phase? Beverly glanced in the backseat at Valerie's thirteen-year-old daughter, Olivia. All three of them were dressed from scalp to toenails in wool slacks and coats, scarves and hats. Still, she could barely catch her breath with all this wind racing by. She must be losing her mind, agreeing to go along with this. She pulled her scarf tighter around her neck and pushed it deeper under the collar of her coat.

'But it's only temporary,' Valerie said. 'Won't last forever even though it seems like it to you now, probably. The problem is knowing just how long it will last. Can't tell that without looking at your chart.'

'Are these planets bothering you? Or anybody besides me?' Beverly shouted across the wind.

Valerie nodded. She had a deep voice that carried real well, even against this wind, so she didn't have to shout. 'Well, some. But I'm an Aquarius and my moon is conjunct Uranus, so I'm a lot more used to the unpredictable side of life than you are. In some ways, I crave it.'

'That explains why you suggested this race around the city in the middle of winter.'

Olivia laughed and sat up in the backseat so she could be heard above the wind. 'That explains a lot of things about Mama.'

Valerie glanced back at her. 'You have your seat belt on, young lady?'

'Of course,' Olivia said.

'You needed to get out of that house,' Valerie said to Beverly. 'Sitting around moping and feeling sorry for yourself just because your first date since you broke up with Vernon didn't go well. Shame on you. It's a beautiful night.'

Beverly wrapped her arms snugly around her waist and looked up at the sky racing by. It was a pretty heady feeling, she had to admit. It felt like she was floating along on an endless sea of calm, leaving all the craziness of life behind. She closed her eyes, trying to absorb the sensation. If she could wrap her arms around this aura, this sea of tranquillity, and take it with her, she could survive anything life might toss her way.

'You know, you really should go see my astrologer. I think he would help you get through this period.'

Beverly opened her eyes slowly. 'No thanks. I don't need someone telling me I'm doomed to a life of loneliness, with no man and no children and no grandchildren.'

'Don't be so pessimistic. He's not going to tell you that. No decent astrologer would ever say something like that.'

'Okay, okay. But still. What I need at this point is a man, not some astrologer.'

'I liked Vernon,' Olivia said. 'He was so cute.'

'So did I,' Beverly said. They all laughed. 'And after last night with Byron, it's beginning to seem like Vernon's one of the last sensible men left on this earth.'

'Then why don't you go back with him?' Olivia asked.

Beverly shook her head. 'I'm still so mad at him.'

'I'm not sure you need to be bothered with him anymore, anyway,' Valerie said.

'Have you heard from him?' Olivia asked.

'Not since the night he came by about a month ago and we had it out. He's called a couple of times and left messages on my machine. But I haven't called him back.'

'It's not good for your system to have someone around who aggravates you,' Valerie said. 'You'll meet somebody else. Just be patient.'

'Speaking of aggravation, did I ever tell you what I did, or almost did, to his car that night?'

'No,' Valerie said. 'You didn't want to talk about it earlier and I didn't press.'

Beverly giggled, still embarrassed, and told them how she'd gone to Vernon's place intending to slash his convertible top only to lock her dizzy self out of her car. And how she'd confronted him at the door of his apartment and he'd refused to let her inside because she was raving mad and he had another woman there. She was surprised she could laugh as she told the story. They all laughed. Valerie laughed so hard she could hardly keep the car on the right side of the road.

'Well, I don't blame him for not letting you in,' Valerie said, trying to catch her breath and keep the car off the pavement. 'Is he still seeing her? Do you know?'

'I don't know and don't care to know,' Beverly said. 'Although he said he wasn't.'

'Isn't life about forgiving and moving on?' Olivia asked, holding her arms up to the sky, trying to sound philosophical.

'You can forgive and move on,' Valerie said. 'But that doesn't mean you go back to your old ways. Sometimes moving on means trying something new.'

'Your mother's right, Olivia. What I need is to meet someone else. Someone kind and sweet and honest. With a capital H. Even though that seems impossible in this crazy town.'

'Maybe not,' Valerie said. 'I have a suggestion. Whether you'll like it or not, I don't know.'

'What?' Beverly asked. 'Not more about going to see your astrologer?'

'No. Not that. Although that's not a bad idea.'

'What then?'

'Hear me out before you say no. Okay?'

Beverly eyed Valerie suspiciously. 'Go on.'

'How about a blind date?'

Beverly sank down in her seat. 'Forget it.'

'See? There you go. Saying no when you don't even have all the details yet. I told you to hear me out. I'm trying to help you out here.'

Beverly sat up. 'Go on then. I'm listening.'

'Well, next Friday night I'm supposed to go out with this guy from New York but I can't make it. That's —'

'Wait a minute,' Beverly said, interrupting. 'What about the guy you just met? Jackson.'

'He's history,' Olivia said.

'No he's not,' Valerie said. 'I still see him sometimes. But he's such a slouch. I mean, he's sweet, but all he wants to do is watch football on TV. So I've started going out with this other guy every now and then.'

'You should get interested in football so you can watch it with Jackson.'

'Why should I make myself suffer through that every Sunday afternoon? Besides, I don't like the way he dresses.'

'What's wrong with the way he dresses?'

'Everything. Wears his pants too short, and these cheap polyester shirts and neckties. It's getting so I'm embarrassed to be seen with him.'

'And I thought I was picky.'

'I don't think you're picky. You just know what you want. Anyway, back to the subject at hand. The reason we stopped by tonight was to ask if you wanted to take my place next Friday. But you were acting so depressed when we got there, I wanted to get you out of the house and cheer you up first.'

'Uh-uh. You think I want to go out with some dude you don't want to mess with?'

'It's not like that. You remember Andrea from Hampton University? Lives in New York now. She set me up with him. He just moved to Baltimore. I'm supposed to show him around

198

the D.C. area but I just found out about an astrology convention next weekend in Houston that I want to attend.'

'I don't know, Valerie. What's he look like?'

'I've never met him.'

'Oh, no,' Beverly said, sliding back down into her seat. 'Forget it.'

'But Andrea said –'

'No. End of discussion. Get somebody else to do your dirty work.'

'Wait a minute. Andrea said he's nice-looking, and I've talked to him on the phone. He seems intelligent, successful. He's a systems analyst. Whatever that is.'

'Has to do with computers,' Olivia said. 'Go on and go, Beverly.'

Beverly was still shaking her head.

'Oh, come on,' Valerie said. 'His job transferred him to Baltimore. He's already bought a condo there.'

'I don't care if he's bought a palace there.'

'Look, if it makes you all that uncomfortable, you don't have to go.'

'Well, thank you very much.'

'I'll just have to call him and cancel it. But I think you're missing a good chance to get out and meet somebody and have some fun. We were supposed to meet at the Florida Avenue Grill for dinner after work. I thought that would be a nice place to start him off. Good soul food cooking. Then we were thinking of catching a movie. Doesn't that sound better than sitting around the house all alone on a Friday night?'

'It does sound nice,' Beverly said. 'But with someone I've never met . . .' She shook her head. 'I just don't know.'

'If you don't like him, you don't have to see him again for goodness sakes. You make everything out to be a federal case.'

Beverly took a deep breath.

'So, what's it going to be?' Valerie asked, looking at Beverly out of the corner of her eye.

'Maybe I'll go. But if this doesn't turn out right, I'm blaming it all on you.'

Valerie and Olivia laughed. 'Fine,' Valerie said. 'You'll probably go out and have a ball. Fall in love, get married, and have a whole bushel of babies. Then I'll be pissed that I gave him to you.'

'I should be so lucky.'

As they got farther up Wisconsin Avenue, near Georgetown, the traffic thickened and they slowed to a crawl. Valerie glanced in the rearview mirror. 'So, what's it going to be, Olivia? American Cafe or that ice cream place you like?'

'Ice cream? No way tonight,' Olivia said, hugging her shoulders. 'I'm already freezing.'

'Too cold,' Beverly said. 'Even as much as I like ice cream. What are your bones made of, Valerie? Goose down?'

'Okay, okay,' Valerie said. 'American Cafe it is then.'

They spent ten minutes looking for a parking space on one of the side streets. As usual on a Friday night, Georgetown was bursting with windowshoppers and late-night eaters. But the American Cafe was a big place, and they only had to wait about ten minutes for a table. Beverly and Valerie ordered carrot cake and coffee. Olivia, chocolate cake and hot cocoa.

'Whew,' Olivia said, removing one of her sweaters, 'I'm burning up.'

'It's not really that cold out tonight. But we were so wrapped up, trying to keep up with your crazy mother.'

'I thought we were having fun,' Valerie said. 'You're definitely in better spirits than you were when we got to your place. Sitting in front of the TV in your robe and slippers on a Friday night. Pitiful.'

'I admit I'm having fun,' Beverly said, pulling the hat off her head. 'But we're keeping the top up when we go back. Or we'll all have the sniffles tomorrow.'

'I love your hair,' Olivia said.

'Thank you,' Beverly said, trying to fluff it up from being smashed by the hat. 'I'm surprised you're with us tonight, Olivia. No hot Friday night dates?'

'Dates?' Valerie asked, banging her mug on the table. 'She's only thirteen. Don't go putting ideas into her head.'

'I wanted to go to this party tonight,' Olivia said, 'but "you know who" wouldn't let me.'

'That's all she ever wants to do. If I let her, she'd go to a hundred and six parties every weekend.'

'No, I wouldn't,' Olivia said, licking chocolate icing off her fingers. 'You never let me go out.'

'I'm letting you go to that other party tomorrow night, aren't I? And you went to one last weekend. Actually, she went to two on the same night.'

'It's the Christmas season, Ma. A lot of people are having parties. What's the big deal?'

'Christmas season nothing. This goes on all year. And in the summer. Forget it. She'd go to a party every night of the week if I allowed it. I made a rule, because this stuff was getting out of hand. One party a week. That's it. So she has to pick the one she thinks she'll like best.'

Olivia rolled her eyes to the ceiling and took a sip of her cocoa. Then she stood up. 'I'm going to the bathroom.'

'Sit down a minute, young lady.'

'Ma, I'm just going to the bathroom.'

'Sit.'

Olivia sat.

'You're not letting her go to the rest room?' Beverly asked, shocked.

Valerie gave her friend a look that said shut up. 'I know what she's up to. There's two boys sitting over there next to the rest rooms.'

Beverly stretched her neck to look across the room. Sure enough, two black guys about fifteen or sixteen years old were sitting at a table near the entrance to the rest rooms.

'Ma, I have to pee. I can't help it if two guys are over there.'

Valerie eyed her daughter suspiciously.

'You want me to piss in my pants?'

'Watch that mouth, young lady. Okay. But you'd better go straight to the ladies' room and . . .'

Olivia jumped up and was gone before her mother could finish.

'You're lucky you don't have to deal with this,' Valerie said, 'because I tell you, the teen years are something else. Boys, boys, boys. And at that age they seem to be everywhere we go. Restaurants. Shopping malls. Movie theaters.' She looked across the room, checking on her daughter. 'She's not at their table now. But I'll bet she stops on the way out.'

'Let her enjoy it while she can. Before she knows it, they'll all be spoken for.'

'I don't think the problem is only that men marry off as we get older. There are single and divorced men out there our age. It's just that we eliminate a lot of them because we know they're no good. If they haven't amounted to something by now, it's obvious they never will. But when you're Olivia's age, it's harder to tell what you're getting because they haven't developed fully yet. They all look good. You could be with a potential failure and not know it. Like my ex. I was seventeen when I met him and I thought he was it. Said he wanted to be a doctor. Ha. Dummy never even finished college. I would never go out with somebody like him now.'

'You have a point. I never thought about it that way.'

'Well, neither did I until Olivia started bringing all these boys home and I'm trying to figure out if they're good enough for her. Nothing serious yet, but she's got a lot of male friends.'

'How did you even see those young guys sitting way over there? I never would have noticed them.'

'Believe me, when you have a teenage daughter you learn to notice these things, because she always does. And she's getting so flirtatious. She just bats those eyelashes. Sometimes I don't know what I'll do with that girl. Most days she's the light of my life, gets almost all A's. But others . . .' Valerie shook her head. 'Consider yourself lucky.'

'I don't think I'm so lucky. If I was in your shoes I wouldn't mind getting older so much. You've been married. You have a beautiful daughter. You'll have grandkids. You've done the things you're supposed to have done at your age. Things I'm beginning to wonder if I'll ever do.'

'Oh, stop being silly. You're not even thirty yet. And I had to drop out of college when I got pregnant. Took me two whole years to get myself organized and back in school. And I may have been married, but it didn't last.'

'But at least you've done those things. Here I am about to turn thirty, and what do I have to show for it? I could take not getting married. But I definitely want children.'

'You still have plenty of time. You're . . .' Valerie paused and stretched her neck. 'I knew it,' she said, looking toward the rest rooms. 'She's over there with those boys. The minute I let her out of my eyesight, she's flirting.'

Beverly looked and, sure enough, Olivia was standing at the table laughing and talking with the boys. 'I say let her go for it.'

'They're too old for her. Must be at least sixteen if they're here alone. The subway doesn't come to Georgetown.'

'Maybe they got the bus. Leave her alone. How much can she get into, knowing you're right across the room?'

'Enough. They'll probably exchange phone numbers and goodness knows what else. I guess she's okay, though. Can't keep my eye on her every second, can I? What were you saying?'

'I think you were talking. Anyway, my doctor's always saying, 'Have your first child before you're thirty.'

'Oh, shoot. A lot of women wait until they're over thirty these days. Some even over thirty-five or forty.'

'But he says it's best to have the first one before thirty. Decreases the chances of having problems if you have one later.'

'But you see all these women having the first one after thirty and they're fine. You remember Janel from Hampton?'

Beverly shook her head.

'You remember her. She was a lot older than us. Already in her late twenties when she started college. Lived off campus.'

Beverly shook her head again. 'How do you remember all these people? That was ten years ago.'

'I just do. Anyway, she just had her first baby and she must be about forty. She's doing fine, baby's fine. So I wouldn't worry about it if I were you. You have plenty of time. But Janel didn't marry the father. Thought he was too immature.'

'Too immature at forty?'

'I think he was a little younger. Around thirty-five. But he didn't have a steady job.'

'What is it with these black men out here? Most of them are so pitiful.'

'At least it's easier to tell who's really pitiful now.'

'Sometimes I think I should just go ahead and have a baby without getting married. Then I could take my time looking for a husband.'

Valerie's eyes got wide. 'Now wait a minute . . .'

'Well, why not?' Beverly asked. 'The main reason I want to get married is to have children. Or one of the reasons anyway. What do I need a husband for? I have a good job. And I think I'd make a good mother.'

'I know you would. But this just takes me by surprise. How would you go about finding a father?'

Beverly shrugged. 'Any male with a healthy dose of sperm would do.'

They both laughed.

'No, really,' Beverly said, getting serious. 'I'd look for a lot more than that. Someone who has physical features I like. He doesn't have to be gorgeous, but he should be someone I can at least stand to look at after we turn the lights back on – tall and well-built in case it's a boy. And he would have to be smart and successful. You know, growing up, I wouldn't want to have to tell the child its daddy was a street sweeper. And no drugs or criminal background. No chronic illnesses.'

'If you meet somebody like that, you should marry him. And find out if he has a brother.'

Beverly laughed. 'It doesn't always work out that way. Just because somebody has those traits, it doesn't mean I'll want to marry him, or that he'll want me. But you know, I wouldn't settle for anything less in a husband, so why should I for the father of my child?'

'What about Vernon?'

'Not him. It would have to be somebody I could walk away from easily after I got pregnant.'

'That sounds so cold. Would you tell the father or father to be you were trying to get pregnant?'

'Now that's the part I haven't worked out yet, but probably. I mean, I don't think I could do that without telling the guy. But we would have to work it out so that this baby is mine, all mine. No tricky stuff after it's born. All I want from him is the sperm.'

Valerie frowned and shook her head. 'See, that's the problem. I don't think you can find somebody like that. Think about it. A man with all those good traits is not going to be willing to father a child and then just walk away.'

'You're probably right – it's just an idea I've been tossing around. I'm sure it will never happen, but with my track record with long-term relationships, I can't help thinking about it.'

'Ever consider adopting?'

'Why adopt when I can have my own?'

Valerie shrugged her shoulders. 'There's a lot of black babies out there that could use a good home.'

'I want my own.'

'Then have your own. But give it time. You'll meet someone right for you sooner or later.'

'That's just the problem. If it's much later, I'll be too old and dried-up.'

'I figure you've got at least ten years.'

'Ten?' Beverly shook her head vigorously. 'No way I'm having a baby at forty. And I've gone the last ten years without finding Mr Right. Why should the next ten be any different? If anything, they'll be worse. There's fewer and fewer men out there.'

'God, Beverly. Sometimes I wonder why I hang around you. You can be so pessimistic, it's downright depressing. Makes me almost hope this guy I'm setting you up with turns out to be perfect. So I don't have to listen to this anymore.'

18

Beverly was standing in front of the bedroom closet in her underwear trying to decide what to wear to the office – it had been so long since she'd had a dinner date after work – when the doorbell rang. She frowned. Who the hell could that be at this early hour? She slipped into her robe just as the bell rang again.

'I'm coming, I'm coming,' she shouted. She yanked the door open to face a young white man peering from behind a bouquet of ruby-red roses in a crystal vase. 'Miss Beverly Jordan?'

'That's me,' she said, still staring at the roses.

He shifted the vase to the side and held out a slip of paper and a pen. 'Can you sign this?'

She tore her eyes from the flowers and signed the paper. The man smiled and handed her the roses. They were so heavy she had to cradle them in her arms. 'Enjoy them,' he said, and was off.

She shut the door and carried the flowers into the living room. She looked around for a place to put them and finally settled on the dining-room table. She ran her hand across the petals gently and bent down to sniff them. They were so fragrant and beautiful. She'd never had flowers delivered to her before. It was funny. All those dates, all those men, and none of them had ever sent her flowers.

Now, wasn't there supposed to be a card or something? Her best guess was that they were from Byron, apologizing for coming on so rudely at dinner. They both had managed to put the episode aside and continue to work together the past week, but the little bit of camaraderie they had established was gone. Maybe this was his way of warming the chill in the air. But then again, that seemed far-fetched. Byron probably didn't have a single sympathetic bone in his skinny little body. Maybe they were from someone in her family. She fished around in the bouquet until she found a small white card and opened it.

Did I ever say, 'I'm sorry'? Love, Vernon

She took a deep breath. Of all people. Yes, Vernon could be very romantic when he wanted, like the time he'd fixed that dinner for her. It was only take-out sushi, but with the candlelight and the wine and soft music, it turned out to be a beautiful evening. But he'd never sent her flowers. Then again, he'd never done anything so despicable as cheating on her either. She folded the card. Why did men think they could screw up, then all they had to do to straighten things out was apologize? It would take a lot more than a bunch of roses to soothe the bitterness in her heart.

She stuck the card back in the flowers and returned to the bedroom. She removed a blue rayon skirt and navy blazer from the closet. Probably no point in getting all worked up about what to wear. This blind date was just going to disappoint her like all the others.

Zelma knocked and opened the door at the same time. She wore the big smile on her face that all recent honeymooners have. At least the women. 'Hi, girl. What you know good?'

Beverly smiled. 'What are you doing here? I thought you didn't come back to work until Monday.'

Zelma sat in the chair across from Beverly's desk. 'I don't. But I was running out of money, so I came in to get my check.'

'So how was the honeymoon?'

Zelma bobbed her head from side to side. 'It was okay. We started getting a little bored, though, after the first couple of days.'

'Bored?' How could a honeymoon cruise be boring?

'Well, you know, it's not like we've never had sex or nothing before. And daytimes are nice, because you're on the islands. But at night they have these dances, and most of the people on the ship are white, so the music . . .' Beverly nodded with understanding as Zelma waved her hand from side to side. Still, she would have thought being with the man you loved would be enough to keep a woman from being bored on her honeymoon.

'I spent most of the evenings reading a novel while Jessie lost all his money in the casino.'

Beverly shook her head with disbelief. 'How were the ports?'

'Oh, they were nice. Especially Grand Cayman and Cancun. Beautiful beaches. I spent a fortune in Cancun. That's why I'm flat broke now. Only problem is you don't spend nearly enough time on the islands. You have to get back to the ship by dinner, just when island nightlife is warming up. Food on the ship was delicious, though.'

'I thought a cruise was supposed to be the perfect honeymoon.'

Zelma turned up her nose. 'For white people maybe. If I had to do it again, I'd just go to one of the islands and stay there.'

'Maybe someday I'll need that advice. At least you look good, well rested. And as usual you're dressed to kill.' Zelma had squeezed her plump but shapely figure into a black body-hugging jumpsuit with a gold belt.

'It's about the only thing I can get into now, child, since it's stretchable. I must've put on fifteen pounds eating on that ship. Food twenty-four hours a day. All you do is eat, eat, eat. It'll take me a month to get rid of it. So, anything interesting happen while I was gone?'

'Have you talked to Byron?' Beverly asked.

'No. Why?'

'You're not going to believe this. I went out with him after your wedding. To dinner.'

Zelma hopped up and did a little dance around the room. 'I knew that would happen sooner or later.' She stood in the middle of the floor with her hands on her hips. 'So how was it?' she asked, smiling.

'I hate to disappoint you, but it was lousy.'

Zelma sat down. 'How could a date with that hunk be lousy?'

'He comes on a little too strong for me. No, a lot too strong.'

Zelma's face pleaded with her. 'Oh, Beverly. Don't be so hard on him. That's because he likes you.'

'Please. Spare me. First thing out of his mouth, he's asking me to sleep with him.'

Zelma smiled slyly. 'That's not necessarily a bad thing.'

'It is for me. Especially in this day and age.'

'Okay, I admit that's a fast piece of work. But lots of men are like that. So what? Just tell him no, you want to get to know him first.'

Beverly shook her head. 'This was different. The way he did it was cold and calculated. Right in the middle of dinner, you know? I got the feeling it was a regular little routine with him. Dinner, screw, then get to know each other. He was trying to chalk me up as one of his conquests.'

'Maybe you could be the one to bump all the others. He was always asking me about you.'

'I don't care. Why would anyone want to get involved with someone who's got women all over the place?'

'For the challenge.'

'Thanks, but no thanks. I can think of better ways to be challenged.'

'You're so picky. He's good enough for all these other women.'

'That sounds like something my sister would say.'

'No man's going to be handed to you on a silver platter, carved perfectly, just the way you want him. You got to get out there and fight for what you want, child. You know how many women I had to pave over to get Jessie.'

Yes, Beverly thought. Zelma scratched, groveled, and begged with no shame to get Jessie down that aisle. That was exactly what Beverly planned never to go through. 'But I don't want him. And even if I did, all those women would be enough to turn me off.'

'Suit yourself. But a man like that doesn't come around often.'

Thank God, Beverly thought.

'So how is he acting around the office?' Zelma asked. 'Is it awkward?'

'He's cool about it. We both act like it never happened. So I can say that much for him. But then, he's probably had a lot of experience with this.'

Zelma laughed. 'You're so hard, child. He really seems nice when I talk to him.'

'Zelma, you probably think every man on the face of the earth is nice.'

'You think all of them are rotten.'

'I do not,' Beverly said. 'Just most of them.'

'See what I mean? You're hopeless. Anyway, I'm out of here, child.' Zelma stood up. 'I've got to get to the bank to cash my check before it closes.'

Beverly's phone rang just as Zelma left the office. She picked it up on the first ring. 'Beverly Jordan here.'

'Hi. This is Charles.'

'From Baltimore?'

'Yes, I got your number from Valerie yesterday before she left. We're supposed to meet for dinner today at the Florida Avenue Grill.'

And he couldn't make it, Beverly thought. She didn't know whether to be happy or disappointed. She hadn't wanted this date in the first place, but now she'd gotten used to the idea. 'Is something wrong?'

'No. Everything's fine. I just wanted to ask you something. Do you like tennis?'

She loved tennis. It was her favorite sport after football. 'Yes. But only to watch. I don't play.'

'That's what I meant. I played in college and I'm a big fan. At nine tonight there's two exhibition matches with some of the top female players at the Baltimore Coliseum. If you're interested, I'll get tickets and we can come back here after we eat to see the matches.'

Ooh, a tennis player. This might turn out to be an interesting evening after all. 'Sounds nice. But isn't that kind of far to be going back and forth? It takes about forty-five minutes. And I

210

don't know if I'll want to be driving back from Baltimore alone at night.'

'You could ride to Baltimore with me.'

'And you'll bring me back after it's over?'

'I don't mind. Or you could stay the night in my spare bedroom and I'll bring you back in the morning.'

Staying the night was out of the question. Tennis player or no tennis player. 'Fine. But only if you bring me back tonight.'

'No problem.'

'You're sure you don't mind all that driving?'

'Not at all.'

'I'll see you at the restaurant at six then.'

'Make it six-thirty. I have to stop to get the tickets.'

'Six-thirty then.'

'Okay. I've been looking forward to this all week.'

Beverly hung up. That was nice of him, she thought. Dinner, then a tennis match. How different from the usual date. Hmm. So far, so good. Still, she wasn't going to get her hopes up too high.

Beverly sat at a booth near the wall and watched the front door. Despite its reputation as the best soul food restaurant in the city, the Florida Avenue Grill was a tiny place, so she didn't have to look far. She wasn't really expecting Charles quite yet, since it was only 6:15. But knowing how hard it was to get a seat in this popular restaurant during dinner, she'd decided to arrive a little early to get a table, especially important if they planned to get to Baltimore by nine. It had been a wise decision. Already people were starting to pile up outside the door.

The place was amazing when you looked at it. Her first time here, she was shocked. Everyone had raved about the Florida Avenue Grill, and she'd been downright disappointed when she'd walked in and seen the decor. If you could call it decor, since it looked like no one had ever given much thought to how the place should look. It was kind of dark – not romantically dark but unintentionally dim – because the lighting was so poor. On one side of the room were several old booths barely adequate to hold four people. On the other stood a long bar lined with rickety-looking stools.

Behind the bar, lined up against the wall, was the secret to the place. Several huge pots rested on old iron burners, and the food in those pots was worth its weight in gold. Waiters scurried up and down behind the bar and in the narrow aisle in front of the booths bearing trays full of baked and barbecued chicken, chitterlings, pigs' feet, potato salad, greens, sweet potatoes, baked beans. The customers just couldn't get enough of it. It attracted people from all over the country. The last time she was here, for lunch about six months before, Jesse Jackson had been sitting at the booth right behind her.

Beverly glanced at her watch. Charles should be here any minute now. Her experience was that first dates usually showed up when they were supposed to. It wasn't until after a few more dates that they got careless about the time. And after sex, forget it. Some of them thought that gave them the right to show up whenever they felt like it. Or *if* they felt like it.

She wondered again why she bothered with this. Why she didn't just resign herself to a life of being single. These days, that didn't necessarily mean she couldn't have children. Being born out of wedlock was no longer a big deal. Probably half the kids in the schools were products of unwed parents or divorced parents and had no fathers living at home. There was no need to wait around for Mr Right just to have a baby.

Unless, of course, her dream man was about to enter that door. Wouldn't that be something? He'd slide in and he'd be absolutely gorgeous. Hell, he didn't even have to be gorgeous. She'd settle for pleasant-looking if he had a nice body – tall, broad-shouldered, slim-hipped. Maybe one facial feature would stand out, like nice intelligent eyes or soft sexy lips. He'd walk in and fix his eyes on her from across the room, and they both would know instantly who the other was. He'd glide on up the aisle and slip into the booth across from her. He'd smile warmly. Sparks would fly. There would be an instant rapport between them, as if they'd known each other for ages. Two kindred spirits finally crossing paths.

The door opened and she looked up. It was some potbellied man wearing a suit. He said something to the waitress, then walked past the others standing in line and went directly to the bar. From the way that gut jutted out over his belt, he was probably a Florida Avenue Grill regular.

She picked up her menu. Maybe she should go ahead and decide what she wanted to order. That was always a difficult decision for her here. She wanted a taste of everything. What she really wanted was the barbecued chicken wings, but they might be a little tricky on a first date. It was impossible to eat them with a fork, only the fingers would do, and the sauce ended up everywhere. She didn't want to look like a pig, scare the man off before they got a chance to know each other.

She was still trying to decide what to order when an attractive man with a thick mustache walked through the door. He wove his way through the line and looked around. If this hot honey was her date, she definitely was not ordering the barbecued chicken wings. She sat upright in her seat and was about to wave to him when she felt a presence at her side. Thinking it was the waitress, she turned to say she was not yet ready to order. But a potbelly hanging over a belt greeted her.

Her eyes followed the beach ball-sized gut up to the face. They didn't have to go far, since the man couldn't have been more than about five and a half feet tall. He seemed wider than he was long. He smiled down at her.

'Hi.'

She glanced back toward the door, looking for the mustached dreamboat. She caught sight of the back of his head just as he slipped into a booth with a small group of people.

'You must be Beverly,' said the mouth above the potbelly standing at her side, and she like to died right then and there. Uh-uh. Not today. Please no. 'Uh . . .'

213

'I recognized you from Valerie's description. And the people at the bar said you were waiting for someone. I'm Charles.'

Beverly wanted to crawl under the table and hide. This was a former tennis player?

'Is this the right place?' he asked, sliding into the booth across from her. She was slightly amazed that he could fit that gut in there.

'What do you mean?'

'Not exactly what I was expecting,' he said, looking around. 'A little depressing, isn't it?'

Took the words out of my mouth, she thought. Maybe he'd be so turned off by the decor he'd leave. She smiled. 'A lot of people have negative reactions the first time they come. Some don't even stay.'

'Ah, well. I won't let a little dinginess bother me. The food must be damn good for people to overlook this atmosphere.'

So he was staying. Beverly tried to keep the smile from falling off her face. Just wait until she saw that Valerie. She was going to kill the woman.

'And I've been looking forward to it all week.'

He'd also said something about looking forward to this when they talked on the phone. At the time, she'd thought he meant he was looking forward to meeting her, now she thought it was probably the food.

A long, awkward moment of silence passed between them. She'd stopped trying to hold a smile on her face. She was trying to think of an excuse to get up and leave without seeming too rude.

'Nothing like some good Southern cooking,' he said, resting his hands on his belly. At first Beverly thought he put his hands there in anticipation of the food, then she realized that was probably his way of resting his hands, considering that he had no lap to speak of.

'Do you come here often?' he asked.

'About two or three times a year. I'd come more but it's not the best of neighborhoods.'

'This place must be okay then, if you come here even that often. Valerie seems like a real nice person on the phone. Do you know Andrea?'

Valerie was a nice person, but Beverly still had every intention of killing her. 'I'm having trouble remembering her, although we were at Hampton at the same time.'

'So you went to Hampton, too? Sometimes I envy you folks who went to the black colleges. I missed out on that cultural experience.'

His face wasn't half bad, he was just too big. And he dressed well enough. That suit he had on wasn't cheap. She imagined he was probably an attractive man before that stomach got so out of control. 'Where did you go to college?' she asked.

'A small school in the midwest, then MIT for graduate school.'

She was impressed. 'Good school.'

He nodded as the waitress approached the table. 'Ready to order?'

Beverly supposed she could stay just for dinner. But forget the tennis match. She was getting out of that even if she had to fake a heart attack. 'Yes.' She looked at the waitress. 'I'll have the barbecued chicken wings with extra sauce, sweet potatoes, and collards. And another Coke, please.' And she was going to clean every morsel off those bones. That was the one positive thing about being out with a man like this – no need to worry about how she looked. Charles ordered chitterlings and potato salad and wanted to order kale or collard greens, but after a long discussion with the waitress about how much bacon fat they were cooked in, decided on green peas.

'You're eating chitterlings and you're worried about a little bacon fat?'

He spread his arms out to the side. 'Got to curb it somewhere.'

Kind of late for that now, she thought.

'By the way,' he said, reaching into the inside pocket of his jacket. He pulled out an envelope. 'I got the tickets for the tennis match. It says the gates open at eight-thirty. We should

215

try to get there a little before nine.' He held the tickets out as if he wanted her to look at them, but she didn't feel like even pretending to be interested when she had no intention of going. She knew she had no reason to be such a bitch just because the man was fat. He was still a person, and maybe an interesting one at that. But she couldn't help it. What if they ran into somebody she knew?

She looked away and took a sip of her Coke. He put the tickets back into his pocket, then placed both hands flat on the table and looked at her. Beverly turned her face farther away from him, looking out into the crowd and sipping on her Coke. Even though she could barely see him, she could feel his eyes boring into her and it made her uneasy.

She turned to face him, ready to say something sarcastic, but he quickly averted his eyes as if he was embarrassed that she'd caught him. He actually looked kind of shy, and she began to feel a little bad about the way she was behaving. She should try to be nicer or get up and leave. She set her glass on the table. 'Do you watch a lot of tennis?' Obviously, he didn't play much anymore.

His face brightened. 'All the Grand Slam matches, Wimbledon, the U.S., Australian, and French opens. I think I mentioned I played when I was in college. Was pretty good if I must say so myself. Should have stuck with it, I guess, huh?' He patted his belly and smiled.

She smiled back, but didn't know how to respond to a comment like that.

'I hope my being overweight doesn't bother you.'

'Ah, not really.' It was true in a way. The man was perfectly harmless sitting across from her at a restaurant table, and she had no intention of letting things go any farther. So why let it bother her? It was his problem, not hers.

'Good. Because some women are turned off by it. Wouldn't give someone like me the time of day. Fortunately, not all of them.'

'I think it frightens some of them. You don't meet a lot of overweight people. We're not used to it.'

'How do you expect to get used to it if every time you meet one you run the other way?'

'You have a point, I guess.'

'Of course. I assure you there's no reason to be scared of us. We can be just as good or better as friends and lovers or anything else as the next person. Obviously, the reason we're overweight is that we have insatiable appetites for the things that give the most pleasure. Not only food. Show me an overweight person and I'll show you a great lover.'

His self-satisfied smile at the end of this little sermon was almost a smirk. Jeez. How had they gone from tennis to sex so fast? She turned around and looked toward the kitchen. Where was that waitress with their food? When she turned back to him, she saw that he was watching her again. She was tempted to remove her blazer. He was making her so uncomfortable, it was starting to get hot in here. But she was afraid he might find it suggestive. One thing was for sure. She was not going to start feeling sorry for him again. If he said one more word along those lines, she was getting up and walking out of here so fast he'd think she'd been a figment of his imagination.

'What are some of the things you like to indulge in?'

She eyed him sharply. 'What do you mean by that?'

'Everyone has a weakness for something. Chocolate? I know – shopping. You women love buying clothes.'

'Not me. I like ice cream. I'm a nut for Edy's cherry-chocolate chip.'

'Ah. That's a good one. But obviously it doesn't do you any harm. You're a nice size.'

She wanted to tell him that was because she knew when to stop, but thought better of it. They had to get off this whole subject of cravings. 'Do you think Jennifer Capriati will ever win one of the Grand Slams?'

He nodded. 'Probably. She's still young. But she's got to make her move now. The women tend to peak much earlier than the men.'

'And they dominate much longer once they reach the top.

217

Monica Seles and Graf are just about unstoppable. Before it was Evert and Navratilova.'

He smiled at her, obviously pleased that she knew something about the sport. 'Exactly. They peak in their teens and then play well into their thirties. The span for men is usually shorter. That's why the men's finals are usually up for grabs. Almost anyone can win.'

The waitress brought their food, and they dug in and chatted about tennis and other things. She told him about her years at Hampton as she worked on her chicken wings. This wasn't so bad, she thought. The food was good enough to make just about anything bearable. And since she wasn't concerned about how she looked in front of this guy, she could eat them the way she would at home.

'Did you meet Valerie at Hampton?'

She removed a wing bone from her mouth and licked her fingers. 'Uh-huh. In our senior year. It's funny the way we met. We were both seeing the same guy, only we didn't know it at first.'

'Uh-oh.'

She giggled. 'Anyway, when we found out he was two-timing us, we came up with a plan. She invited him to her apartment off campus and I hid in the closet. Popped out while they were making out.'

'The poor guy.'

'Poor guy nothing.' She picked up a wing and broke it apart. 'Served him right.'

'But to gang up on him like that. I'll bet it took him a while to get over that.'

She nodded and laughed. 'That was the whole idea.' In a way, it was fun talking to Charles. Since she wasn't interested in him romantically, she could let down her guard and talk and eat freely. She stuck a wing in her mouth and went to work on it. Maybe she would even go to the tennis match. She'd never seen professional players live. That should be interesting. But after the match, it was going to be good-bye, Charlie. She dropped the meatless bone on her plate.

'You sure do a good job of cleaning them chicken bones,' he said, scooping a forkful of vinegared and hot-sauced chitterlings into his mouth.

'Kind of a family trait,' she said, licking her fingers. She smiled and picked up her napkin. 'We all do it.' She wiped her fingers, then picked up her last wing and broke off the little leg section. She stuck the tip into her mouth and sucked on it.

'Wish you'd do me like that.'

Her jaw dropped and the bone fell out of her mouth. She caught it just before it hit the table and dropped it on the plate. She looked at him, trying to be sure she'd heard him right. The smirk on his face told her just about all she needed to know. She'd heard exactly what she thought she'd heard, and obviously he thought he was being pretty clever. Still, she had to be sure.

'What did you say?'

'Said I wish you'd do me like you do them wing bones.'

She tried to maintain her composure. But it wasn't easy. She wanted to ram her plate down that filthy mouth. From what she'd heard about fat men, his thing was probably about the size of one of these wing bones. When it was erect. She wiped her mouth with her napkin, threw it down on the table, then pushed her plate away. The sudden movement knocked her glass over, splashing Coke and ice cubes across the table.

'Hey, watch it,' he said, snatching a napkin. He caught the Coke just before it reached his lap, or rather, his stomach. Too bad he'd been able to catch it, she thought, watching him blotting the Coke from the table and tossing the ice cubes back into her glass. Would have served him right. She grabbed her coat and shoulder bag.

'Where are you going?' he asked.

She didn't say a word, didn't even look at him, just slipped out of the booth. Enough was enough.

He looked up at her. 'Look, I didn't mean . . .'

She walked away from the booth.

'Hey, what about your part of the bill?'

Pay it yourself, she thought. Serves you right. She made her way through the crowd at the door and out onto the street. Darkness had fallen and it wasn't the nicest of neighborhoods. She'd thought she would be leaving the restaurant with a man, so the neighborhood wouldn't matter. Ha! Fortunately, she'd arrived early enough to get a parking space in the small lot at the side of the restaurant. And right now she was so pissed off, if anyone even looked at her funny she would start slugging.

She rounded the corner of the restaurant and nearly collided with three teenaged boys hanging around the entrance to the parking lot. They parted to let her by – two to her left, one to her right.

'Hey, sister. Where ya rushing off to?' the one on the right said. He was wearing a black cap with a big silver X across the front. His pants were so low on his hips Beverly thought they would drop to the concrete pavement if he moved too fast.

'Sure would like to get me some of that,' she heard from the left just as she passed by them.

She wasn't alarmed. Traffic along Florida Avenue was heavy this time on a Friday evening, and all she had to do was cry out. She was furious, though. What made these little no-count thugs think she'd be the slightest bit interested in them? And they had the gall to wear the Malcolm X caps. It was an insult to the man.

She made her way to her car, being careful to glance over her shoulder a couple of times to be sure they weren't following. She got in the car and locked all the doors, then started the engine and pulled out of the lot.

Obviously, obnoxious men came in all shapes and sizes – mainly dumb and dumber. Jeez, what was the matter with these black men? They seemed to think the way to a woman's heart was through her vagina. Other women could put up with that crap if they wanted to, but not her. She was finished with these walking penises.

19

'Black men better watch out,' Beverly said. 'If they don't straighten up, we'll fly without them.' She was sitting on Charmaine's couch with her bare feet propped on the coffee table. Her Reeboks and socks sat on the floor underneath the table.

Charmaine set a big bowl of popcorn on the table next to a bottle of white wine and sat in the armchair. She picked up the remote control and flicked on the television.

'You know, there was a time when having a baby was the one thing you had to have a man for,' Beverly said. She took a sip from her glass of wine. 'But with science we don't even need them for that anymore.'

Charmaine put her feet up on the table. 'Uh-huh,' she said, flipping the channel to the Redskins game.

Beverly removed her feet from the table and sat up on the edge of the couch, twirling the wineglass between her fingers. She looked at Charmaine. 'So what do you think?'

'About what?'

'What else? About what I've been talking about. Having artificial insemination.'

Charmaine put the remote control on the table and waved her hand at Beverly. 'You're just shooting off at the mouth.' She picked up the bowl of popcorn, her eyes glued to the television set.

'I am not. I'm dead serious. I called Evelyn last night to see what she knew about it. She works with all those women. Turns out this couple she knows did it. So she called them and got me the name of a sperm bank.'

'A what?' Charmaine said, giving her sister a funny look.

'A place where you go to get the sperm. I'm calling the place

221

tomorrow to set up an appointment. Evelyn seemed to think it was a good idea to at least look into it.'

Charmaine turned her attention back to the game. 'Evelyn *would* think that.'

'And you don't?'

'What exactly is this artificial insemination stuff?'

'Well, there's different ways to do it, I think. They can remove the eggs from the woman and the sperm from the man and put them together in a tube to conceive.'

'Ugh! Are you thinking about having that?'

'No. In my case, I would just have them insert sperm from an anonymous donor into my uterus or wherever it goes.'

'You don't need to do that shit. Just get pregnant the normal way.'

'Ha! With who?'

'What's the matter with Vernon? He would make a good father.'

'That's out of the question, Charmaine. You know that. I'm not seeing him anymore.'

'You don't have to be seeing him. Just get together to get pregnant. Then go your separate ways.'

'Vernon would never go for that.'

'Then find somebody else. Somebody else in your past might be willing to do that.'

'You mean just hang around with me until I got pregnant and then disappear? I doubt it. Even if they agreed to do it, how could I be sure they would stick to it? Suppose they decide later that they want to be involved with the child? Then I'd have to deal with them for the rest of my life. Uh-uh. The whole point of having artificial insemination is to avoid that.'

'I still think that would be better. This artificial insemination crap gives me the creeps. Give yourself a little more time before you go do something drastic.'

'I don't have any time left,' Beverly said.

Charmaine jumped out of her seat and pumped her fist in the air as Art Monk caught a picture-perfect pass from the quarterback. 'Did you see that?'

'No.'

'You can catch it in the replay. Monk is a masterpiece.' She sat back in her seat. 'I thought you liked the Redskins. You ain't even watching.'

Beverly drained her glass. 'I love them. But I've got other things on my mind right now.'

'Shoot. You got plenty of time to have a baby, girl. You're barely thirty. What you don't have is patience.'

'I'm tired of waiting for a man who may never come. Or if he does, I'll be too damn old and dried-up to have kids.' She set the empty glass on the table and slouched back into the couch. 'What am I doing wrong? Why can't I meet somebody?'

'You're too damn picky for one thing.'

'I guess you think I should have stayed with Charles Friday night.'

Charmaine laughed and slapped her thigh. 'That was hilarious. No, I admit you probably did the right thing in that case. But not with that other guy you went out with. What's his name?'

Beverly turned up her nose. 'Byron.'

'Yeah, him. He didn't sound so bad. But you didn't give him half a chance. What he did, asking you to go back to his place, a lot of men are like that. That doesn't mean you write them off.' She snapped her finger. 'Just like that.'

'I was offended.'

'That's your problem. You get offended too damn easily. What's the big deal — as long as the dude don't yank your clothes off and try to force you. Nobody's perfect. You got to work with what's out there. You might've ended up liking him.'

'I'm not playing nursemaid or psychologist to some man, Charmaine. Life is complicated enough.'

'It's really going to be complicated if you go through with this artificial insemination stuff. What would you tell the child about the father?'

'The truth.'

223

'Do they tell you who the father is when you go there?'

'No. But Evelyn says they let you pick a donor with the characteristics you want. The physical features, the life background.' Beverly sat up, warming to the topic. 'I like that part of it. I think I'd pick a scientist or maybe a mathematician. Someone intellectual. That way at least the baby would be smart. And he has to be tall, in case it's a boy. And definitely not overweight.'

Charmaine shook her head. 'In other words, you want a perfect baby, just like you want a perfect man.'

Beverly reached for the bottle of wine. 'I don't think that's a lot to ask.' She poured herself another glass.

'What's your rush? That's what I don't understand. Lots of women have babies at thirty-five and up these days.'

'But then they're so old while the children are growing up. I want to be a young mother.'

'Have you thought about being a single mother? That's not easy. Take it from me.'

'My financial situation is better than yours was when you had Kenny.'

'It ain't just the money, honey. You need help around the house. Help with the baby, help with your errands. The baby takes up all your time. And I mean all of it.'

'Like Clarence is a big help around here,' Beverly said sarcastically.

'He's better than nothing. He fixes things, makes sure my car's running.'

'Of course I'd prefer being married. But I can manage alone. I just see one problem.'

'What's that?'

'There's no way of knowing what the father looks like. Evelyn says they can tell you how tall he is, how much he weighs, things like that. They even tell you about the extended family members. But you can't get a picture or anything. What if he's not so hot-looking?'

'Beverly.'

'What?'

224

'You'll never be satisfied anyway, so what difference does it make?'

The fertility clinic was in the Watergate complex, a conglomerate of five buildings housing offices, shops, and apartments on Virginia Avenue. Beverly figured business must be pretty good at the clinic if they could afford this prestigious address. The John F. Kennedy Center for the Performing Arts was right next door. The White House and Capitol and the rest of the federal office buildings were all within a couple of miles. This was the area where cabinet members, Congress people, and other big shots hung around when they were in town.

She parked her car in an underground lot and walked under a covered walkway to the building. It had been raining like crazy all morning, and she had to use her umbrella even under the walkway, the wind was blowing the rain around so wildly. Normally, this area of town was crawling with cars at lunchtime, but the weather had kept most people indoors. She would have canceled just about any engagement besides this one.

She entered the building and made her way up to the fifth floor, then followed the signs down a long, plushly carpeted hallway. It was empty, and she hoped it stayed that way. It would be embarrassing to have someone, even a stranger, see her entering a fertility clinic.

No one else was in the waiting area. The door closed automatically behind Beverly and she walked up and stood beside the glass partition. A white woman in her mid-twenties covered the phone mouthpiece and turned toward her.

'I'm Beverly Jordan. I have an appointment with Dr Meta.'

The woman smiled. 'Wasn't sure you'd make it in this awful weather. Is this your first time here?'

Beverly nodded, and the woman handed her a clipboard with a pen attached to a string. 'Fill this out,' the woman said, pointing to the form on the clipboard.

Beverly completed the form, then sat back in her chair and

placed her shoulder bag in her lap. For the umpteenth time since calling and making this appointment, she tried to imagine her interview with the doctor, what questions he might ask and how she would answer them. She hoped the questions didn't get too personal. Like, why don't you do this the natural way? Why don't you wait and get married before having a baby? Most of the women who came here were probably married but just couldn't conceive for one reason or another. And judging from the location of the clinic, they probably had plenty of money. She'd probably stick out like a sore thumb.

The receptionist called her name and she looked up. The woman had come out of the cubicle and was standing at the entrance to the hallway leading out of the waiting area. 'The doctor is ready to see you now,' she said. Beverly followed her into an office just big enough to hold a desk, a couple of hardbacked chairs, and a lone file cabinet. A short, slender man in his late forties or early fifties with an olive complexion and big dark eyes stood behind the desk. He wore the traditional white coat and a friendly smile. The receptionist introduced them and he extended his hand across the desk. Beverly smiled and shook it as the receptionist backed out of the room and quietly shut the door.

'Sit down, please,' Dr Meta said with a slight accent, indicating the chair across from his desk. The phone rang and he held up his finger, signaling her to wait while he completed his call. Although small, he seemed to be a bundle of energy. At least he wasn't white. She'd always felt uncomfortable around white male doctors, especially when it came to something personal like this. Women, white or any color, were the best, but so very rare. In her lifetime, she'd seen dozens of doctors, but could recall only two women, one white and one black, both dermatologists. She remembered feeling a level of comfort with them that she could never feel with a white man. She'd never, ever, had a black male doctor.

'Yes, splendid,' Dr Meta said into the phone. He hung up and removed a piece of paper from a folder on his desk. 'Now, let's see here. When you called and spoke to the receptionist, you said you were interested in learning more about artificial insemination. Specifically, the sperm donor program. Is that correct?'

'Yes, I wanted to know how it works. How you go about it.'

He nodded. 'Are you interested in this for yourself?'

'Yes.'

'Fine, fine. Let me describe the program and if you have any questions just stop me.'

She nodded.

He folded his arms on the desk and leaned forward. 'Here we process and freeze the sperm, then store it until a woman is ready to use it, meaning her period of ovulation.'

'Where do you get the sperm? I mean, where do the men come from?'

He spread his hands out and smiled. 'From all over the city. We have about fifty donors at any given time, and they come here periodically to donate sperm. It's a short procedure once they get the hang of it, and they're in and out in no time.'

It was all she could do to keep from giggling aloud as she envisioned the donors going off alone, holding their little specimen cups.

'I'll talk more about the donors after I explain the procedure,' the doctor said. 'When you're ready, or a little before, we package the sperm and send it to your doctor's office, where he injects the sperm.'

'You don't do that here?'

'No, no, no. Years ago we did, but not anymore. You have a gynecologist?'

'Yes.'

'He will also help you determine when you are ovulating and help you decide how many times you want to try it.'

'How many times is it usually needed?'

'That depends. How old are you?'

'Twenty-nine.'

'Have you ever been pregnant?'

'No. I've always used birth control.'

'No physical problems?'

227

Beverly shook her head.

'It takes about a year on average. But you must remember that some of the women are older and some of them have had medical problems.' He smiled at her. 'But you are young and healthy, you should have no problem getting pregnant with a few attempts.'

That was a relief to hear. 'How much does it cost each time?'

'One hundred dollars for the sperm. Then you will have to pay for your doctor visit, of course. Whatever he charges. Also, if you elect to have us deliver the sperm to your doctor's office you will have to pay those charges.'

'So, what? We're talking around two hundred each time?'

'Thereabout. You can come and pick up the sperm yourself and take it to your doctor if you want to save money.'

'You mean I can come here and get it?'

'Yes, it will be in a little box. When you pick it up yourself, though, you must sign a form and assume full responsibility for it from there on.'

'I don't think I'd want to risk that. Go on.'

'Once you and your doctor decide on how many times you should have the procedure, you should order enough for all the procedures at once. We will hold it here for you until you're ready to use it.'

'So, in other words, if I want to try it three times, I would need to order enough for all three right away?'

'That's best. We use sperm from a single donor only a limited number of times, for obvious reasons. We can't have any one man fathering too many babies. And you don't want to run out of the particular specimen you've chosen before giving yourself enough time to get pregnant. Otherwise, you'll have to pick another donor later.'

Beverly nodded. The cost was starting to add up, but she thought she could manage it. If she was talking about the potential father of her child, it was worth every penny. This was beginning to sound pretty good.

'Any more questions on that? If not, I'll explain about picking a donor.'

228

That was the part she wanted to hear about. She slid up in her seat. 'Do you have many black donors?'

A forced smile crossed the doctor's face. 'Unfortunately, that's something we must go into. I'm afraid we don't have any black donors at the moment.'

Beverly frowned. 'None?'

He shook his head. 'We get very few of them and happen to have none at the moment. Haven't had any for a while now.'

This city was sixty or seventy percent black. Where were all the black donors? She slumped back in her chair.

'There are ways around it,' Dr Meta said. 'What we do when there are no black donors is let black women choose from a list of ethnic donors with darker complexions – East Indian, Middle Eastern, some of the Italians.'

Beverly frowned. She wasn't so sure about this. 'And black women do this?'

He nodded enthusiastically. 'Some of them do. But some don't. It's up to you.'

'But . . . Why do you have so few black donors?'

'One reason is that we're very particular about the medical and social backgrounds. We test for drug use, sickle cell anemia, and AIDS and the other sexually transmittable diseases. We quarantine the specimen for six months, and test it again to be sure. Also, no criminal backgrounds, and they must have at least one year of college.'

That was good to hear, but unfortunately, it eliminated a big chunk of black men. Still, all the black men here weren't drug addicts or former convicts. 'I would think you'd at least have a few. There are a lot of successful black men in this town.'

'Yes, but it's very difficult recruiting them, and when I do, they'll come once and never return. Although we have had a few very good black donors. The most recent was a black doctor who gave several times.'

'What happened to him?' she asked. Call him up. Get him to come back. 'He sounds perfect.'

The doctor smiled. 'We couldn't keep him because we can only allow one man to father so many children. It was hard letting him go, but I had no other choice.'

Beverly was tempted to try and persuade Dr Meta to get him to come back just one more time. One more child couldn't possibly hurt.

'Besides, he left the Washington area,' Dr Meta added, as if he were reading her thoughts. 'I haven't kept up with his whereabouts.'

Beverly let out a deep sigh. It was beginning to seem like there was no solution anywhere on earth to the black male shortage problem. All the social ills of the outside world had just followed her inside the walls of this clinic.

'There is one more option if you're against using sperm from ethnic donors.'

'I'm not sure I'm against it. It's just that I haven't thought about it.'

'I understand. Take your time to think about it. It's entirely up to you. But the other option I wanted to mention is that you can buy sperm from another clinic. This is the only sperm bank in the Washington area, but some other cities with high black populations may have sperm. I know that Chicago has a few black donors now. A black couple here recently got sperm from them.'

She sat back up in her seat. 'And you would have them send it here?'

'Yes. But there's a catch. The clinic in Chicago charges more than we do, a hundred and fifty dollars, and you would have to pay their fee. Plus you would have to pay shipping charges. That will significantly increase the cost to you.'

So the price creeps up, probably to around a thousand dollars for three tries. She slumped back in her seat again. It just wasn't fair. White women had all the luck. They could come in here and choose from a bunch of donors at almost half the price of what it would cost her. She'd have to settle for a much smaller selection of men and it would cost her dearly. And what if she needed more than three tries? By the time she got pregnant, there wouldn't be any money left to care for the baby.

'How many ethnic donors are there?'

'About ten or fifteen at the moment. I would have to check the list.'

'How would I go about selecting one?'

'If you decide to go through with it, we would set up a time for you to come back. I would give you all the information I have about them – physical features, family medical background, education, occupation, hobbies. Everything. We would narrow it down to four or five. Then I would give you a sheet with the information for you to take home and think about.'

'Could I get the same information about the black donors in Chicago or wherever?'

'You would get some information, but not all of the clinics are as thorough as we are here. They may not collect as much information about their donors, and you would have to settle for what they offer.'

Beverly took a deep breath. Another strike against her. This was going to take some careful thinking. 'I need some time to mull all this over.'

'I understand. Take your time. And if you decide to go ahead with it, give me a call.'

It had stopped raining, but it was still a dreary day, with not a ray of sunlight visible in the sky. She walked to the end of the block and entered the garage. Beverly thought this had to be one of the tightest garages she'd ever been in. It had extremely narrow driving lanes and huge poles between every few parking spaces.

She reached her Mazda and as she put the key in the ignition thought about the madness of it all. She thought she'd found the perfect solution for having a baby while still young, despite the shortage of decent black men – that modern science would be her salvation. But black men were scarce

231

everywhere, even in test tubes or vials or wherever it was they kept the sperm. She would never be able to have a baby at this rate, or at least no time soon.

Her mind flashed back to an episode in her childhood around Eastertime. She was very young, about four. So Charmaine must have been around ten, and Evelyn twelve. It was the first time their mother had let her paint eggs for Easter, and she could remember it all so well. Charmaine and Evelyn thought they were too grown-up to paint eggs, but Charmaine did help her make a mess on their mother's kitchen table. Evelyn helped her clean up, and then they placed the bright pink and green eggs in a big straw basket along with egg-shaped chocolate balls, jelly beans, and other goodies. Beverly thought the basket was the prettiest thing she'd ever made with her own two hands. So pretty that she put it on the dresser in her room and refused to eat any of it. She wouldn't let anyone else touch it either.

A few days later their mother told her she was being ridiculous and disposed of the eggs. Beverly hadn't objected too much, since they were starting to rot and smell bad. But when her mother tried to get Beverly to eat the chocolate candy, it was hopeless. Charmaine teased her to death, threatening to eat the candy if Beverly didn't. 'What's the point having them if all they're going to do is sit there?' Charmaine asked her. 'Pretty soon they'll be rotten, too.' Still, Beverly refused, and to keep Charmaine from getting her greedy little paws on them, she hid the basket on the window seat behind the curtains.

The rest of the family forgot about the candy, much to her delight. Easter came and went, and every day for weeks thereafter she would peek at the little egg-shaped chocolate balls and colorful jelly beans just to make sure Charmaine hadn't found them and carried out her threat. Even after all that time, the basket stayed bright and beautiful. She thought she was pretty clever, outwitting everyone like that.

Then one hot July afternoon she took a peek, only to discover that the sunlight had melted all the chocolate eggs into shapeless blobs. She was upset but too embarrassed to say anything to anyone. Charmaine would never let her hear the end of it if she found out. So she just moped around the house all afternoon. That evening she tried stuffing the whole basket in her bedroom trash can but realized the basket was too big to go unnoticed. So she put the basket on the window seat and left it. The next time she remembered to look behind the curtains, it was gone. To this day she didn't know what had happened to it.

Well, now she wanted to use her eggs before they got rotten or she didn't have any left, but it was beginning to seem hopeless. What was the matter with these black men? Couldn't they do anything right? No matter what she did, where she turned, they managed to stick it to her.

She turned the key in the ignition and released the hand brake. The city was seventy percent black. Where were all the black male donors? All it would take was, what – a couple hours of their time once a month? And they would make a lot of their sisters real happy. But no, they couldn't even do that right. She pressed lightly on the accelerator as she turned to look over her shoulder.

Bang!

She felt and heard it just as her eyes reached the rear window. Something was sitting there behind her, some kind of truck or something. And she'd just hit it. Damn, damn, damn. Her car hadn't moved much more than a few inches. What the hell were they doing so close to the back of her car?

She opened the door and squeezed out. A man was standing at the rear of her car inspecting the side of a new red Ford Explorer. He was tall, about thirtyish, with a thick, dark mustache and a very white complexion. She walked up behind him, and he turned and looked at her. 'Didn't you see me?' he said in a not-too-nice tone of voice.

Wasn't the answer to that question obvious? 'No. And what were you doing just sitting there right on my tail?'

'That has nothing to do with it,' he snapped. 'You should have seen me.' He turned away from her and stooped down to examine his sport utility. What an ass. After all she'd just been through, now she was going to have to deal with this jerk.

But she was just as angry with herself. Why hadn't she paid

more attention before backing up? Fortunately, the only damage she could see was a small dent in the bumper of her Mazda. She probably wouldn't even bother to get it fixed. His car looked fine. She didn't know why he was stooping down all over the place looking at the thing. All he had to do was get out of the way so she could leave.

He stood up. 'I need to see your driver's permit.'

That startled her. 'What for? There isn't any damage to your car.'

'You're wrong about that. If you look closely you can definitely see a dent.'

He stepped aside and Beverly walked to the side of his Explorer to look. She didn't see anything, so she bent over and looked more closely. Yep, there it was. A scratch about half an inch long and a centimeter deep. She stood up. 'You can barely see that.'

'Still, this is a brand-new sport utility. Do you have your permit?'

She rolled her eyes skyward and went to her car, squeezed in, and got her purse. Just what she needed now, she thought, removing her wallet. Some fanatic who's going to bother about an invisible scratch on his car. She pulled out her permit and handed it to him.

'I'm going to the pay booth and ask them to call the police,' he said, taking it. 'You wait here.'

She looked at him like he was crazy. 'You're going to do what?'

'Call the police. I'll be right back.' He started to walk off.

'Wait a minute, buddy.' She stood there with her hands on her hips. Who did this obnoxious bully think he was? 'You're not going anywhere with my license.'

He stopped and turned to face her. 'I need to hold onto it to . . .' Suddenly, he looked almost shy. 'Well, you know, to make sure you're still here when I get back.'

It was all she could do to keep from shouting. 'And just where in tarnation am I supposed to go? I'm surrounded by cars on four sides.'

He looked at the situation as he twirled his mustache with his forefinger and thumb. 'That's true. Okay, maybe I'll just jot down some of this information.' He reached inside the pocket of his sports jacket and pulled out a pen. Then he fished around, patting his jacket and slacks. Finally, he stopped and looked at her. 'Do you have a piece of paper, Beverly?'

She sneered at him, but went back to her car to look for a slip of paper. Anything to get rid of this man. She found one and handed it to him and watched while he wrote, trying to size him up. He was dressed in a dark wool sports jacket and a tie. The shirt obviously had a lot of polyester in it and the slacks were a little high-watered. But his necktie was beautiful, silk and obviously expensive. Probably his wife or girlfriend picked it out for him. All in all he wasn't bad-looking, just totally obnoxious. Maybe she should try a kinder, gentler approach. 'Look, ah, what's your name?'

'Peter.'

'Peter, do you really have to call the police about this? I'd rather not get my insurance company involved.'

He looked up from his note-taking. 'What are you saying? How do you plan to pay for this then?'

'All it needs is a drop of spray paint. That can only cost so much. I'll pay you out of my pocket.'

'It's probably more damage than it looks like to you.'

'Don't worry. I'm good for it. Whatever it comes to.'

He shook his head, unconvinced. 'I still think I should call the cops. You can work out the details with your agent later.'

'Come on. You've got all the information from my license. The police are going to think we're crazy bothering them for a scratch.'

'So. That's their job.' He held her permit out to her. 'They won't —'

'What are you trying to do?' she shouted, snatching the permit from him. 'Deliberately raise my insurance rates?'

He held out his hands defensively. 'Calm down.'

Beverly glared at him. He looked over at his Explorer, and she followed his eyes. From this distance you couldn't even see

235

the dumb scratch. 'Okay. I won't call them. But I need your number to get in touch with you.'

Beverly sighed with relief and gave him her home number. 'Get an estimate and just let me know what it is. I'll send you a check.' She started for her car.

'Wait a second. What about your work number?'

She gave him that. 'Anything else?'

He pocketed the sheet of paper. 'Nope. That should do it for now. You'll hear from me by the end of the week.'

'I don't doubt it for a minute.'

They both went to their cars and climbed in, and she waited to hear him pull off. He seemed to be taking an awfully long time, so she turned to look out the rear window. He was sitting there writing. Probably getting her license plate number. She turned back around and tapped her fingers on the steering wheel, trying not to explode. Finally, he pulled off. Honestly, she thought. These fools came in all brands.

20

'I'm going out with a white man,' Beverly said, sifting through the rack of pullover sweaters in Woodies. It was the season 'to be jolly,' and she was downtown shopping with Valerie. Both of them were laden with shopping bags. She'd said it casually, like it was the most common thing in the world. But actually she was surprised at how hard it was to muster up the nerve to tell her best friend she was seeing a white man. Valerie was the first to hear the news. She hadn't even told her sisters.

Valerie paused at a nearby rack of blouses and looked at Beverly. 'What do you mean, "going out"? As in dating?'

'I've only gone out with him once, to lunch last week. But I'm going to see him again tonight. A movie.'

'I see,' Valerie said. She went back to her clothing rack.

That was it? She drops this bombshell and all her best friend had to say was 'I see'? Valerie? The walking mouth? 'So, what do you think?'

'What do I think?' Valerie shrugged her shoulders. 'I'm surprised. No. In shock would be a better word. You've never done that before.'

'First time for everything.'

'He must be awfully good-looking. This . . . What's his name?'

'Peter. Why do you say that?'

'Well, I always thought . . . Well, you know, whenever we talked about white men, we always said how they'd have to be super fine before we'd step out with one.'

'When I first met him, I didn't even think about whether he was cute, given the circumstances. I mean, I had just run into his car, and he wasn't in the nicest frame of mind. Neither was I. But his looks kind of grow on you. He's cute, but not drop-dead cute.'

'Is he tanned? You know, one of those white people with darker complexions?'

Beverly thought Valerie sounded almost hopeful. Like a tan would make up a little for his being white. 'No. He's lily-white.'

'Then he must have a body to die for.'

'No. Pretty much average. But he's tall. About six feet.'

Valerie looked at Beverly strangely. 'How did you say you met this guy?'

Beverly laughed. 'What you really wanted to ask was what I'm doing going out with an okay-looking, average-built, very white man.'

'Well, that too. I mean, I just can't believe it. I'm speechless.'

'Then you must really be in shock. Let's go. I don't see much here, and I wanted to look at jewelry for my sisters.'

'Fine.'

They gathered all their packages and headed down the aisle. 'You remember the accident I had last week?'

'This is the guy from that accident?'

Beverly nodded. 'He's an accountant for a firm on Connecticut Avenue, and he came by my office to pick up the check to get his car fixed. We got to talking and he asked me to have lunch with him.'

'Sounds like he doesn't waste any time.'

'No. He's very direct. But he seems sweet. Wants to take me camping in the spring.'

'Camping? Since when did you start to like camping?'

'I've never been. But I'll try anything once.'

'This is too much. First a white guy. Now you're going camping. And knowing how you hate spiders.'

'Doesn't everybody hate spiders? Anyway, why not date a white man? I've gone out with just about every other kind of man. Including fat slobs.' She gave Valerie a pointed look out of the corner of her eye.

Valerie giggled guiltily. 'Okay, you got me there. But honestly, I had no idea about Charles.'

'Last time I'll ever let *you* set me up with someone.'

238

'Believe me, that's the last time I'll try to play Cupid. I'm just glad it was you who got stuck with him and not me.'

'Thanks a lot.'

'You handle these things better than I do.'

'Ha. There was only one way to handle him.'

'Yeah. I'm glad you walked out on him, the way he acted. I called Andrea and asked her about him being overweight. She claims she hadn't seen Charles in more than a year and that the last time she saw him, he had put on some weight but not that much. She was shocked he was so out of shape.'

'Not nearly as shocked as I was.'

'Well, it's over. Now you've got your little white guy.'

'Oh, please. I've only had lunch with him. We'll have to see what happens.' She stepped on the escalator and Valerie followed her.

'Do you ever hear from Vernon?' Valerie asked.

Beverly shook her head. 'He sent me flowers. Did I tell you that?'

'No. That was sweet of him.'

'Beautiful red roses. But I try not to think about him too much.'

'It's obvious you still have feelings for him.'

'Hurt feelings. Betrayed feelings.'

'That means you must still care. I always thought the two of you would get back together despite what he did.'

'I thought you were against it.'

'Well, according to your charts, you're perfect for each other.'

'Chart or no chart, that's not going to happen. You're just bringing him up because I'm seeing a white man.'

'No, I'm not. Tell me more about this Peter. When's his birthday?'

'I was waiting for you to get around to that. January twenty-eighth. He'll be thirty-five next month.'

'An Aquarius, like me. This should be interesting. You've never gone out with an Aquarius before, at least not since I've known you.'

239

'I guess that makes two firsts for me, then. White, Aquarius.'

'He's probably going to seem weird to you, Beverly.'

'You mean like you do.'

'Very funny. But really, you're so down-to-earth, and Aquarians, well, we're out there sometimes. I'd have to see his whole chart to be sure about him, though.'

'That couldn't be farther from the truth about Peter. He seems very sane and practical. He owns a house in Reston, Virginia. When he told me that, I realized he was the first man I'd ever gone out with who had his own house.'

21

This was going to be tricky. She was holding two stuffed shopping bags in her right hand and juggling a big box containing a toy truck for Kenny in her left arm. She had managed to shut the car trunk and make it up the walkway and the stairs to the front door. Now all she had to do was figure out how to open the door without dropping everything on the porch. She thought about ringing the bell, since Clarence was there watching Kenny for her. Miracle of all miracles that she'd been able to get him to do that even for one Saturday afternoon. But she could see that just reaching the bell was going to be impossible with all this stuff in her hands.

She set the box on the porch and struggled to open the front door. She decided to put everything upstairs and come back to shut the door after her hands were free. She walked across the carpeted living room to the bare dining-room floor, where the clacking of her heels signaled her arrival. Clarence was brushing something off one end of the glass table with his hand, while Kenny sat at the other end eating a hot dog and drinking a glass of milk.

'Mama,' Kenny shouted when he heard her. He squirmed off the chair and ran and hugged Charmaine around the legs. She nearly dropped the box. 'Wait a minute, Kenny. You'll make Mama fall.' She looked at Clarence, who seemed fixed on wiping some invisible dust from the table. 'Clarence, of all the times for you to decide to do some housecleaning. Don't you see me struggling with these bags?' Clarence smiled and moved around the table. He took the box from her.

'Is that for me?' Kenny asked.

'No, honey, this is just some stuff for the house. You finish eating your lunch.'

241

Kenny scrambled back up in his chair, and Charmaine shut the front door, then followed Clarence upstairs to their bedroom. He took the steps two at a time and had already put the box on the bedroom floor by the time she entered the room. 'Did you fix the toilet in the downstairs bathroom?' she asked, dropping the packages on the bed.

'Uh, not yet.'

'Clarence, the thing's been stopped up for two weeks. When were you planning on getting around to it?' She slipped out of her heels and unbuttoned her coat.

'I'll do it today. But I got to get a part from Hechinger's. Couldn't do that and watch Kenny at the same time, could I?'

'You could have taken him to Hechinger's with you.'

'That's the problem. See, my car's not running and . . .'

She threw her coat across the bed. 'Not again, Clarence. I wish you'd get rid of that piece of junk.'

He plopped down on the bed and stretched out his legs. 'You gonna give me the money for a new one?'

She pursed her lips in answer to that question and unzipped her skirt.

'Then quit nagging me about getting rid of it.'

'You never have the money for things we need around here. But I notice that you got on a new pair of slacks. Where did you get the money for those, huh?'

'I been had these.'

'You're lying. How come I've never seen them before?'

'We gonna sit here arguing about a pair of pants? My car needs fixing. So does the toilet. I was going out now to get the parts I need.'

She shook her finger at him. 'Before you even ask if you can borrow my car, the answer's no. I have to take Kenny to a birthday party at three. That's why I got back early.'

He jumped up from the bed. 'That's almost two hours from now. I can be back way before then. It'll only take me an hour at the most.'

She moved to the closet in her underwear and pulled out a

242

pair of jeans and a sweatshirt. 'Forget it. You never come back when you say you will.'

'Aw, c'mon, Charm. You want me to fix the damn toilet, don't you?'

She didn't answer him. She wasn't about to waste her time telling him something he already knew.

'How am I supposed to fix it if I can't get the part? You want to go get it?'

'Take a cab.'

He laughed. 'You can't be serious? By the time I pay for a cab, I won't have the money for the parts I need.'

Charmaine hummed a tune as she squeezed into her blue jeans.

'Fine, then. I guess we can manage with one toilet.' He started for the door.

'You're driving me crazy, fool.' She threw the sweatshirt on the bed and picked up her shoulder bag. 'You're worse than a kid. Can't you do anything on your own without bugging me?' She removed her car keys and threw them on the bed. He grinned and grabbed them. Then he walked up to her and tried to put his arms around her, but she pushed him off. 'Get the hell away from me.' She picked up the sweatshirt from the bed and pulled it over her head. 'And you better be back here in an hour, you hear me? Or you'll never see those car keys again. I mean it.'

He backed out of the room, still grinning broadly. 'One hour tops, Goldy.' He turned around and disappeared.

She zipped up her jeans. Honestly, if that man didn't beat all. She removed the birthday present for Kenny's friend from the shopping bags and hid the rest of the things under the bed. Kenny was at that age where he would open anything he saw if he could reach it. She carried the birthday gift downstairs to the dining room, where Kenny was finishing his hot dog.

'Is it time to go to the party now?' he asked, jumping down from the table.

She smiled at him. 'Almost.' She held up a toy fire engine. 'Look what I got for you to give to Carl. Want to help me wrap it for him?'

243

He smiled and nodded vigorously.

'Go downstairs and look on that bottom shelf where I keep the wrapping paper. Pick out the color you want, but don't get anything with Santa Claus or trees on it.'

'I know,' he said. 'That's for Christmas.' He ran to the basement stairs.

She set the fire engine on the dining-room chair, then picked up Kenny's plate and glass and carried them to the kitchen. She returned with a dishrag and wiped the end of the table where Kenny had eaten his lunch. The thing about these glass tables was that you could see every speck of dirt and dust.

Kenny came back up the stairs with a roll of wrapping paper and started to put it on the table near Charmaine.

'Wait. Let Mama finish wiping it first.'

'Daddy already cleaned off all the salt.'

'Daddy cleaned off the what?'

'The salt he put on the table.'

Charmaine straightened up and frowned. 'You mean he spilled salt on the table?'

'He shook it on the table.'

A red flag went up in Charmaine's head. She remembered Clarence brushing off the other side of the table when she'd come in. She walked to the end where he'd been standing and looked down but could see nothing on the glass. 'Kenny, go upstairs to my room and look in my night table for the scotch tape. Can you do that?'

He nodded and placed the roll of wrapping paper on a chair. She watched as he ran off, then she bent over to look at the table closely. Her heart pounded in her ears as her eyes roamed the glass. Still, she saw nothing. She was about to stand back up when she spotted a few specks of a white powdery substance. She straightened up and tried to catch her breath. Her heart was pounding a mile a minute.

She wasn't sure what to do. She wanted to taste it to see if it was salt or something else from the kitchen, but was afraid of what it might do to her if it wasn't, especially in her condition. Then she remembered all the times she'd seen cops and detectives on TV taste a little cocaine on their fingers. It didn't seem to do them any harm. She decided to try it.

She licked her forefinger and ran it over the white specks. It damn sure didn't feel like salt – it was more powdery. She brought it toward her lips but hesitated. She hoped those cops on TV knew what they were doing. She stuck out her tongue and licked the finger. She smacked her lips. Definitely not salt – it was kind of bitter. But coke? She found it hard to believe Clarence would snort that in her house, right in front of her son. She'd seen and smelled signs of marijuana around the house a few times before, but never coke. That was too much, even for Clarence.

Kenny came back into the dining room and put the tape on the table. 'Ready to wrap it now?' he asked.

'In a minute.' She bent over him and took him by the shoulders. 'Do you remember when Daddy shook the salt on the table?'

Kenny nodded.

'What did he do after that? Before he wiped it up.'

Kenny stared at her blankly.

'Did he wipe it up right away?'

Kenny shook his head.

'No? Then what did he do?'

'He sniffed it with his nose.' Kenny puffed his chest up and inhaled deeply. 'Like that.'

She let him go and straightened up. Tears stung the rims of her eyes. She swallowed hard. 'Have you ever seen him do that before?'

Kenny nodded and picked up the fire engine from the chair. He put it on the table. 'Can we wrap it now?'

She was so upset she couldn't answer him. She sank into a chair and put her hand over her face, partly to think, but mostly to stop the tears. She'd told that man a hundred times, no drugs in her house. And what does he do? Snorts coke right in front of her son. She was going to kill him until he begged for mercy.

* * *

245

Killing Clarence was going to have to wait. At three o'clock there was still no sign of him. Kenny was dressed in his little jacket and bow tie, trying to sit still on the living-room sofa like she'd told him to so as not to mess up his clothes. The fire engine, wrapped in bright red paper and a big bow, was next to him. Charmaine had changed into a black calf-length wool skirt, white turtleneck sweater, and black high-heeled boots.

She heard a car coming up the street and jumped up from the chair. She looked out the window for what seemed like the hundredth time. Not Clarence. She could take Kenny on the bus, but it had started snowing lightly about an hour earlier and she didn't want to drag Kenny through bad weather on the bus. She had tried calling one of her girlfriends who lived nearby to see if she could get a ride, but the friend was out. So was Beverly.

She sat back down. She'd made up her mind. This was going to be Clarence's last day in this house. She was going to tell him to pack his things and get out tonight. She didn't care if he had to sleep on the street in the snow. She never wanted to see his face again. Not ever. She could put up with the silliness, the childishness. All men were big babies. But this she could not deal with.

She stood up. 'I'm going to try to get Aunt Beverly again. You stay here. And don't get those clothes messed up.' She went to the kitchen and dialed Beverly's number. This time, Beverly picked up on the first ring.

'Beverly,' she said with relief. 'You finally came home.'

'I just got back from shopping with Valerie. It's snowing.'

'I know. How is traffic?'

'Not bad now. It's supposed to get worse later, though. What's up?'

'My whole world is falling apart, girl.'

'What's wrong?'

'Well, to start with, Kenny was supposed to be at a birthday party at three. And Clarence . . .' She paused and closed her eyes. Just saying his name made her blood pressure rise. 'That bum is out with my car. He should have been back an hour ago.'

'Oh. I'll bet Kenny is disappointed. You want me to take you?'

'Would you? I hate to drag you out in this weather, but it's not far from here. Only about ten minutes by car. I'm supposed to stay at the party and help out. I'm sure I can get a ride back from one of the kids' parents.'

'I'm on my way.'

Beverly arrived with Valerie fifteen minutes later, and the four of them piled into her Mazda. Beverly and Valerie chatted about their Christmas shopping, while Charmaine sat silently in the back with Kenny, staring out the window. She barely heard what they were talking about. She was too busy planning revenge. It was too bad she had to occupy herself with getting Kenny to this party just now. She wanted to be in the house throwing every thread of clothing, every piece of furniture, every personal item Clarence owned out the door.

'Have you finished your Christmas shopping?' Beverly asked, glancing back at Charmaine.

'Huh? Uh, no.'

'Did Beverly tell you about her new boyfriend?' Valerie asked.

Charmaine shook her head, still staring out the window. 'No.'

'He's white,' Valerie said.

That got Charmaine's attention. She turned to look up front. Beverly hit Valerie playfully. 'He's not my boyfriend. I only went out with him once.'

'So far. She's got another date with him tonight.'

Charmaine turned back to the window. 'That's nice.' Out of the corner of her eye, Charmaine could see Beverly turn and stare at her, surprised at her indifference. But it was only one date and the chances were that Beverly would find something wrong with the man before things got serious, anyway. Even if she didn't, Beverly was a grown woman, and what she did was her business. Charmaine had too many of her own troubles to be worrying about her sister.

It was clear what she had to do, and that was get rid of Clarence. It was going to be hard managing alone. Especially with this baby on the way. But the man was no good. No good for her, no good for her children, no good for nothing. So here she was, back to square one, back to the way she'd been just before she'd had Kenny – pregnant and with no man to help out. That had been the absolute worst time of her life. All those evenings sitting alone in her apartment, getting too fat to do anything but put her feet up.

'Will you need me to pick you up later?' Beverly asked, turning onto the street where the party was located. 'Or do you think Clarence will be back by then?'

'Don't say nothing to me about that 'Bama. I'll get one of the parents at the party to take us back.'

Beverly and Valerie exchanged looks. 'What's wrong with you?' Beverly asked, looking at Charmaine through the rearview mirror. 'You were so quiet on the way over here.'

'I've never seen her so quiet,' Valerie said.

'I got things on my mind,' Charmaine said.

'Are you upset because Clarence didn't come back with the car on time? It's not like it's the first time he's done something like that.'

'I wish it was as simple as that.'

'Do you want to talk about it?'

Charmaine hesitated. She wasn't that worried about Valerie knowing. Beverly's girlfriend had a lot of mouth, but they didn't know the same people, and Valerie was rarely around the family. But she had to be careful with Beverly – she and Charmaine had always been close and told each other pretty much everything. After what happened about the baby, though, Charmaine wasn't sure Beverly could be trusted to keep her mouth shut.

'There's not enough time to go into all of it. We're almost there. But to make a long story short . . . And I don't want you telling a soul, Beverly, you hear me? Nobody. Including family. If you do, I swear I'll never tell you another thing. Got that?'

'Fine. My lips are sealed.'

'Yeah. Like they were about the baby.'

'Sorry about that. But I mean it this time.'

'Clarence has been using c-o-k-e,' Charmaine spelled out. 'Right in the house, right in front of . . .' She nodded in Kenny's direction.

'Oh, no,' Beverly said.

'You're kidding?' Valerie added.

'I wouldn't kid about something like that.'

'What are you going to do?'

'He's out. As of tonight, that sucker is on the street. I've had it with him.'

'I don't blame you. He's a double Pisces. So typical.'

'You definitely can't have that going on around the house. I didn't think Clarence would go that far.'

'Does he have anywhere to go?' Valerie asked.

'I don't know and don't care. He should have thought about that before.'

'I agree,' Beverly said. 'But I don't understand why you have to keep it quiet. People are going to have to know why he left sooner or later.'

'I know that. But I'll tell them when I'm ready. Don't you go telling nobody.'

'Including Mama and Daddy and Evelyn?'

'Especially them.'

'If that's the way you want it.'

'I mean it, Beverly. If you say one word, one syllable, so help me . . .'

'I hear you, I hear you.'

Carl's father dropped Charmaine off in front of her house at seven. Kenny had asked to spend the night at Carl's house, and she let him, thinking it was a good idea considering what probably lay ahead at the Perry household.

She walked to the door carefully. It was dark now and the snow had turned to freezing rain, leaving the streets and sidewalks slick and mushy. Her car was sitting at the curb in front of Clarence's old beat-up Ford, and the lights were on in the back of the house. That meant he was home, probably messing up her kitchen trying to fix himself some dinner. Well, she hoped he enjoyed it because it was the last meal he'd ever eat in her house.

She no longer had the urge to throw out all his things. He wasn't worth the time and energy. But she was still going to kick his butt out. Knowing Clarence, though, he wasn't going anywhere without putting up a good fight on his own behalf, and she dreaded the shouting match she knew lay ahead. She was glad Kenny wouldn't have to witness any of it.

She stepped into the house and stomped her feet to get the snow off her boots. Then she marched straight through the house, removing her coat as she walked. She tossed it and her bag across a dining-room chair and stopped at the kitchen door.

Clarence was standing at the stove in his stockinged feet watching a pan filled with frying chicken. He had a cooking fork in his hand and a More dangling from his lips. If there was one thing the man could cook, it was some fried chicken. It was about the only thing he could cook, but it was always good. He left the kitchen a complete disaster area whenever he cooked, though, and this time was no different. Loose flour was splattered all over the countertop and opened bottles of spices were everywhere. The stove top was covered with grease.

He turned and started to smile when he saw her standing in the doorway, but changed his mind when he saw the expression on her face. He put the fork down on the stove and walked toward her. 'Now I know you mad with me and all and you got every right to be. But I tried my best to get back here before three. I swear.' He paused. When she didn't respond, he shrugged his shoulders and smashed his cigarette out in an ashtray on the kitchen table. 'It just couldn't be helped. That's why I'm doing all this cooking here now. Trying to make it up to you and Kenny.' He paused again and looked around her. 'Where's the little tyke anyway?'

'That's none of your business.' She was surprised at how calm her voice was. 'I want you, Clarence William Perry, to pack everything you can fit in that lame car of yours and get the hell out of my house tonight. For good. What you can't fit in there tonight you can come back for tomorrow. But you're never sleeping in this house again as long as I'm breathing. You got that?'

He looked at her like he thought she'd flipped. 'What's this all about? I was just a little late. I got back here about three-thirty but you had left.'

'You're lying, Clarence. You're always lying and I'm sick and damn tired of it. I tried to call here an hour ago and there was no answer.'

'I was probably up at the corner store.'

He was doing it again, lying his head off. But it didn't matter. 'Just leave.' She turned on her heel and walked back into the dining room. He followed her.

'Wait a minute, Charm . . .'

She swung around so abruptly that he jumped back. 'Don't you wait a minute me. Don't you go getting me started. Just get out.'

'But I told you I got back here as fast as I could.'

'Save your breath. This is not even about that.'

'Then what's it about?'

She pointed to the dining-room table. 'It's about what you did at that table earlier this afternoon in front of my baby.'

Clarence followed her finger to the table, then looked straight at her. 'What you talking about? I wasn't doing nothing at no table.'

She knew he would deny it. He never accepted responsibility for anything. And he could lie with the straightest face. 'I'm not going to waste time arguing with you, hear? I just want you out of here.'

'But . . . I mean, what are you talking about? I got a right to know why you're doing this.'

'You already know what I'm talking about.'

'How would I know what the hell you're talking about? I can't read your mind. Something about the dining-room table. That's all I know.'

'Clarence, I don't see how you can stand there and tell the biggest, baldest lie anybody ever told with a straight face.'

251

'I'm not lying. I —'

'I'm talking about you snorting coke on my dining-room table while my son was eating his lunch.' Her voice was shriller now, but she couldn't help it. This phony innocence of his was disgusting. 'That's what I'm talking about.'

Clarence looked at her like he was shocked. 'He told you that?'

'Nobody had to tell me. I saw it with my own eyes. You didn't do much of a job wiping it up.'

'You're wrong. I don't even touch that stuff no more.'

'What are you trying to say? That Kenny left it there?'

'Don't be silly. But maybe somebody else left it there.'

Oh, so now he was admitting it was there. 'Was anybody else here while I was out shopping?'

'No, just me and Kenny. I'm talking about before today. You had that table a long time, before you met me. Could have been there before we got married.'

She frowned at him. He sounded like he'd just sniffed a line with that crazy talk. He must have realized how ridiculous he sounded, too, 'cause an embarrassed smile crossed his face. 'You know what I mean. Just 'cause you saw it this morning don't mean I put it there.' He lowered his eyes and went back into the kitchen. She followed him and stood in the doorway while he turned the chicken.

'Look, I don't want a confession from you 'cause I know I'll never get it. I just want you out of my house. Tonight. And I'm not changing my mind about that.' She turned and walked away. He followed her.

'Aw, c'mon, Charm. You don't mean that.'

'Oh, yes I do,' she said, picking up her purse from the dining-room table.

'Where am I supposed to go?'

'That's your problem.' She headed for the stairs.

'Charm, you not being fair.'

She wheeled around on the stairs. '*I'm* not being fair? That's the problem. I been too got-damn fair. I let you walk all over me. And that's fine. But nobody messes with my baby.

Nobody. I told you I simply would not tolerate drugs in my house, around my baby. And what do you do? You not only bring them in here, you use them right in front of him. So I want you out of here.' She turned back around and walked up the stairs. She expected him to keep following her, but he didn't.

'Fine,' he yelled from the bottom of the stairs. 'If that's what you want. Maybe I will leave for a couple of days. You need time to cool off and get some sense into your head. Soon as I finish eating, I'm coming up there to get a few things, if that's what you want.'

She stopped at the top of the stairs and turned to face him. 'You just don't get it, do you? You're packing more than a few things. You're moving out. And not for a few days. For good.'

'Yeah, yeah. Boy, women.' He stomped off to the kitchen.

She started to call after him because she still didn't think he'd gotten it. But never mind, she thought. She was tired of using words to try to make this dim-witted fool get the point. She would just have to show him she meant business.

She ran into the bedroom and threw the closet door open with so much force that the knob banged against the wall. She wrapped her arms around a bunch of Clarence's suits and lifted the hangers off the pole. She walked to the banister in the hallway and flung the suits over, hangers and all, and watched as they fluttered down and hit the bottom stairs in a heap. God, that felt good.

She went back to the closet and got some of his shirts, then ran back to the hallway and threw them on top of the suits. She gathered several pairs of his best shoes in her arms and tossed them over, too. They hit the floor with a thud. She went to his chest of drawers and was snatching up his undershorts and socks when she heard him screaming and cussing at the bottom of the stairs. She quickly grabbed as much underwear as she could and ran to the hallway, dropping several pairs of socks on the floor along the way. She flung the underwear over the banister just as he raced up the stairs two at a time. He reached the top all out of breath and turned toward her, his

253

face filled with fury. She ran down the hallway to the bedroom with him right on her heels. She slammed the door shut and locked it quickly, just before he got there.

'Open this goddamn door,' he said banging with his fist. She ignored his banging and ranting and raving and went to the two bottom drawers where he kept his prized cashmere and silk sweaters. She yanked the drawers open and gathered as many as she could in her arms. Then she went to the window and tried to open it with one hand. All the windows in the house were old and in need of repair, so it wouldn't budge more than a few inches. She went to the bed and threw the sweaters down, then went back to the window. Grunting and groaning and using both hands, she pushed and pulled at the window. It finally jerked up with a loud squeak.

'What the hell are you doing in there?' Clarence yelled outside the door.

She gathered the sweaters from the bed and threw them out onto the soggy lawn. They looked like little rags against the wet snow. She went and stood by the door. 'Why don't you go outside and see what I'm doing?' she yelled.

'Woman, you better open this fucking door now or I'm kicking it in.'

'You just try it.'

The door shook with a loud bang, and she jumped back. He really was kicking the door in. She couldn't believe it. 'Clarence Perry, you better stop kicking my door before you break it.'

'Then open it so I won't have to.'

'No.'

'Then you better stand back.'

'Wait a minute, Clarence.' If he broke the door off the hinges, she would be the one having to get it fixed. No way was this bum coughing up the money. And she was going to have to face him sooner or later. Might as well get it over with now. She unlocked the door and backed away. He opened the door and burst into the room, his eyes growing wider by the second as he took in the open drawers and clothes spilled all over the floor and bed. She slipped around him into the hallway while he surveyed the scene. She didn't want to be trapped in that bedroom when he looked out the window.

'Goddamn it,' he yelled. She couldn't see him but heard the window slam shut. He raced out into the hallway and threw her a look of pure hatred. He rushed forward, shoving her aside with so much force her back slammed against the wall. She moved to get away from him but needn't have bothered. He ran past her and raced down the stairs. Damn him. How dare he push her around like that. She heard the front door open and ran to the bedroom window and looked down at the lawn. He was running around through the mush in his stockinged feet, trying to recover his precious sweaters.

'I'll bet he gets it now,' she said aloud, massaging her sore shoulders.

22

'Thanks for coming at the last minute like this, Beverly.' Charmaine took her sister's coat and hung it in the closet. 'Clarence been calling me every day since I put him out last weekend, trying to get me to change my mind. This morning he called and said he wanted to come get the rest of his things. It's probably just an excuse to come and try to talk me out of this, and I don't trust myself to stick with it face-to-face with him.'

'Then get the locks changed, and your phone number, too, while you're at it. Otherwise, he'll never stop bugging you.'

'I will. Just help me get through today.'

'Why didn't you just come over to my place while he gets his things?'

'Shoot. You crazy? He's supposed to be bringing a friend's pickup. He'd probably try to make off with half my stuff.'

'I don't see what he needs a truck for. I thought most of the furniture was yours. You had it before you even met him.'

'All of it is mine. Except the CD player. But he's got two closets full of clothes up there. And a zillion coats. And I told him he could have that big old TV 'cause I don't want to have to finish paying for it. Plus some linen and other things we got when we got married.'

Beverly shook her head. 'You're being too generous, Charmaine. After what he did, you don't have to let him have a thing.'

'I still feel bad about kicking him out two weeks before Christmas.'

'He deserves it. Where's Kenny? Upstairs?'

'I dropped him off at his friend Carl's after church so he wouldn't have to see Clarence moving his things out.'

'Good idea. Where's that husband of yours been staying the past week?'

'With his brother Jimmy and his wife until after the holidays. Then he's going to look for a place. Or so he says.'

Charmaine padded into the living room in her slippers and robe. 'Oh, Beverly. How did I get myself into such a mess?'

Beverly followed her and sat on the sofa. 'You don't need to feel one drop of pity for him. I couldn't believe it when you told me he snorted coke in front of Kenny. What time is he coming?'

Charmaine sat in the armchair and looked at her watch. 'He said about now. Around eleven so he can finish up before the game. But knowing him, he'll be late.' She put her slippered feet up on the coffee table one at a time.

'How have you been feeling?' Beverly asked.

'Other than this nightmare I been going through the past week, fine. A little tired. Oh, Lordy me. I just hope I can manage all this by myself.'

'You'll be fine. We'll all help out.'

'It won't be the same as having a man around the house.'

'Oh, wake up. Sometimes you can be so exasperating, Charmaine. How much help has Clarence been? You always said he was like having a second child.'

'He helped in his own way. He cooked sometimes. And he was good at fixing things when I could get him around to it.'

Beverly waved her hand at Charmaine. 'Call a plumber. You don't need a husband for that.'

'He was good at other things you can't get the plumber or anyone else to do.' Charmaine smiled and crossed her feet on the table. 'God, he was too good at that. The man could get me climbing the walls.'

'That's why you're pregnant now.'

'True.' Charmaine looked at her sister. 'Tell me about this new dude you're seeing.'

'What do you want to know? He's an accountant. Never been married. No kids.'

'How old is he?'

'Thirty-five.'

'And never been married? I always wonder about men like that.'

'Said he's never found the right woman. I can understand that.'

'Where did you meet him?'

Beverly smiled. 'A car accident, believe it or not. I hit him and he acted so irritable at the scene, I never wanted to see him again. A real ass. But then he asked me out to lunch and I had a nice time with him.'

'Have you screwed him yet?'

'My, aren't we modest today. No, I've only kissed him.'

'Well, go on. Come on out with it, so I don't have to ask all these questions. How was it?'

'Mmm. They feel different. You know how black men are hard but real smooth?'

Charmaine's eyes lit up. 'Don't I though.'

'I'm talking about the texture of their skin, Charmaine.'

'Oh, yeah, that too.'

'His skin, Peter's, is sort of soft, almost mushy.'

Charmaine turned her nose up.

'It's not bad, just different. I can definitely get used to it.'

'Has he tried anything besides smooching?'

'Please. He's no different from black men that way. But we've only gone out a few times, and with all the stuff going around these days, I'm taking my time.'

'I don't blame you. But aren't you curious?'

'Hell, yes. It's been almost two months since I've been with a man. But times have changed. You have to be careful now.'

Charmaine frowned. 'I know. That's another thing I'm going to miss about having a steady man around the house. I didn't have to worry about these damn diseases.'

'I can't argue with that. It's a jungle out there now. Sometimes I think about getting myself tested for AIDS.'

Charmaine's eyes widened.

'Well, why not? I've been single and active for more than ten years. This stuff goes way back. And they say every time

258

you sleep with somebody you're sleeping with all that person's partners from the last ten, fifteen years.'

Charmaine shuddered. 'I know. But there's nothing wrong with you. Just be careful from now on.'

'That's easy to say, but . . .'

The door opened and they both looked to see Clarence step in. He was freshly shaven and had a new haircut. And as usual he was dressed nicely from head to toe. He came into the living room, removed his black leather coat, and swung it across the arm of the sofa. He nodded toward Beverly. She nodded back. Charmaine stood up. 'You bring the truck?'

'Nah. Couldn't get it.'

'How you going to get all your things then?'

'I'll load what I can into the car. I can come back for the rest next weekend.'

'Next weekend is Christmas.'

'Well, the week after that then.'

Charmaine exhaled. 'I hoped you could get it all today. Well, go on and get what you can. You want to get the CD player and stuff now?'

He shook his head. 'Too much trouble.'

'What are you going to get, then? The rest of your clothes?'

He looked at Beverly, then back at Charmaine. 'Can I see you in the kitchen for a minute?'

Charmaine glanced at Beverly as if to say, 'I told you he was going to pull some shit like this.' Beverly looked at Charmaine disapprovingly. Charmaine looked back at Clarence. 'I don't think so. Say what you got to say here.'

'I could do that, but it would be better if we talked in private.'

Charmaine shook her head.

'C'mon, Charm. It'll only take a minute.'

Charmaine looked from him to her sister. Beverly mouthed the word no. Charmaine looked back at Clarence and took a deep breath. 'All right, but you better make it quick.' Out of the corner of her eye, she saw Beverly fold her arms across her chest and make a face as she followed Clarence into the

259

kitchen. As soon as they were out of Beverly's eyesight, Clarence turned to face her and took her gently by the arms. She shook him off.

'What's the matter? I can't touch you no more?'

'If this is what you wanted to talk about I'm leaving.' She turned toward the door.

He backed away. 'All right, all right.'

She faced him. 'So go on.'

He took his pack of Mores from his shirt pocket and stuck one in his mouth.

'I wish you wouldn't smoke. The smell makes me sick now.'

He took the cigarette from his lips and put it back in the pack. 'You sure this is what you want? Us to separate like this?'

'Yes.'

'Why?'

'I made myself perfectly clear how I felt about drugs in my house and . . .'

'But see there. I never used no coke in the house. And I damn sure never used no coke in front of Kenny.'

'You're lying.'

'No, I'm not. What you saw on the table probably was salt or something from the kitchen. Flour or something. I don't know. But I know it wasn't no coke.'

'I see you've taken the time to get your story straight. You probably realized how stupid that stuff about somebody else leaving it there sounded. Well, I don't want to hear it.'

'What I got to say to make you believe me?'

'There's nothing you can say. It's not just the drugs, anyway, Clarence. You're always doing things to drive me crazy. Like taking my car and not coming back, knowing I had to take Kenny somewhere. That's not right.'

'Aw. Let me tell you about that, okay? See, I was on my way back when Lem got sick.'

'Lem?'

'I stopped there on my way back from the hardware store.'

'That's your problem. You can never do what you say you're going to do.'

'Well, I should have that day. Lem got sick on me. Started throwing up and all. It ended up just being something he ate. But I had to take him to the hospital. Couldn't help that, could I?'

'If it's the truth. Which I doubt.'

'It's the truth. I swear.' He held up his hand, Boy-Scout style.

She waved her hand at him. 'It doesn't matter. I still want you to leave.'

'Charm, you making a big mistake here. I love you, baby. Why you want to do this?'

'I don't want to hear that now. Just get your things and go.' She walked out of the room.

'Charm . . .'

She ignored him and went into the living room. She sank into the chair and closed her eyes as Clarence came out of the kitchen. He paused in front of Charmaine, but when he saw her with her eyes shut tight, he smiled awkwardly at Beverly and walked on up the stairs.

'What did he say?' Beverly whispered after he disappeared.

Charmaine opened her eyes. 'Just what I expected. Tried to talk me out of it. If you weren't here, he'd be following me all over the house.' She let out a deep breath of air. 'I don't know. He said he was late getting back Saturday 'cause a friend got sick on him and he had to take him to the hospital.'

'Charmaine, you're not going to fall for that, are you?'

'It's possible.'

'Gimme a break. Did he say anything about the drugs?'

'He insists he didn't do it. Maybe Kenny was mistaken. He's only four years old.'

'I don't believe I'm hearing this. No four-year-old child could make up something about someone sniffing something off a glass table. Where would he get that from unless he saw it?'

'TV maybe?'

'Charmaine!'

'Yeah, yeah. You're right.'

261

'And if Clarence didn't put it there, who did?'

'I'm not sure it was coke, you know. I assumed it was because of what Kenny said. But I don't know coke from the man in the moon. Even if it was, that don't mean Clarence put it there. It could have been one of those no-good friends of his, that Lem and the others, and Clarence could be trying to protect him. I think Lem deals, anyway. I always thought if I could just keep Clarence away from those bums he'd be alright.'

'Stop trying to talk yourself out of this. You're doing the right thing.'

'I sure hope so.'

Kenny ran up and down the aisles of Toys R Us so fast that Charmaine could barely keep up with him. Now he was trying out some giant water guns and explaining why one was better than the others. She'd tried to get her sister to join them after Clarence left, but Beverly had said that only a fool would go shopping a week before Christmas. Besides, she had a date with that white guy tonight and wanted to go home and get ready. Charmaine couldn't imagine getting all worked up about going out with some average-looking white dude. But at least Beverly was going out with somebody. That was better than sitting at home with no man around, which was exactly the situation she was in now. A week before Christmas and her family was all broken up.

Clarence didn't pick up much of anything while he was at the house. A few of his clothes and toiletries, that was all. He seemed to be taking it pretty hard. Harder than she would have expected. The man was never around the house when he lived there, always out in the street. So why was he making such a big deal about leaving?

Charmaine let Kenny pull her around the store from one toy that he wanted Santa to bring to another. It was a good way to see exactly what he wanted for Christmas. She already had most of his presents hidden away at the house, but noticed him playing with a couple of items she hadn't bought yet. She'd come back tomorrow to get them. She loved the crush of the Christmas crowds and the bright decorations, and almost always found an excuse to come out on Christmas Eve – some last-minute toy to buy for Kenny or something extra for Clarence or one of her sisters.

Kenny ran around a corner and down another aisle, this one filled with electric train sets, and she followed him. He wasn't old enough for one of them yet, thank God. They cost an arm and a leg. She looked up the aisle to see what else might interest him and noticed a familiar-looking man getting a big box off one of the upper shelves. She squinted her eyes, trying to remember where she'd seen him before and then it hit her. It was Vernon, the lost love of Beverly's life. He sure was looking good in what appeared to be a beige cashmere coat.

'Vernon?' she called to him.

He turned and looked around at the sound of his name. She waved, and he walked toward her with the big box in his arms.

'Do you remember me?' she asked as he approached. 'I'm Beverly's sister.'

He smiled. 'Charmaine, right?'

She smiled and nodded. He looked down at Kenny seated on the floor at Charmaine's feet, playing with a train set. 'And this must be your son.'

She bent down over Kenny. 'Kenny, say hi.'

Kenny looked up and waved. 'Hi.'

Vernon bent down to him. 'Hi, Kenny. That's some train set there. That one of the things you want Santa to bring you?'

Kenny nodded his head enthusiastically, then looked at his mama.

'We'll see about that,' Charmaine said. She looked at Vernon. 'It's good to see you. How have you been, Vernon?'

He placed the box on the floor and straightened up. 'Pretty good. I'm doing some last-minute shopping for the nieces and nephews.'

She nodded toward Kenny. 'Same here. Your family is in Virginia, right?'

He nodded. 'Charlottesville. I'm going down day after tomorrow. How have you been?'

'Oh, I'm managing.' But just barely, she thought.

'You're looking good. And Beverly? How is she?'

Charmaine thought about telling him about Beverly's new boyfriend, but decided not to. 'She's fine. She told me about the flowers you sent her.'

His eyes lit up. 'Did she like them? I've tried to reach her so many times, but she never returns my calls. I sort of gave up.'

Kenny threw one of the toy trains across the floor, and Charmaine bent down over him. 'Don't do that. You'll break it, then Mommy will have to pay for it.' She looked back up at Vernon. 'You shouldn't give up so easily.'

He shook his head. 'A man can take only so much rejection. It's obvious she doesn't want anything more to do with me.'

'She was pretty upset about, ah . . . what happened that night.'

'She told you about that?'

Charmaine nodded. 'We tell each other just about everything.'

He looked uncomfortable. 'I screwed up. I admit it. But it wasn't as bad as it looked. And the person who was there is completely out of the picture now.'

'You should tell Beverly that.'

'How can I? She won't talk to me. I thought I at least deserved a second chance. We had a pretty good thing going, and . . . Well, I do miss her.'

Charmaine's heart went out to the man. She could kick her sister for being so stubborn. 'Beverly's not so big on second chances.'

'Tell me about it.'

'But that doesn't mean you should give up. I know she still has feelings for you.' Beverly would kill her if she could hear this conversation.

He smiled, obviously pleased. 'What makes you so sure about that?'

'Trust me. I know.'

'Did she tell you that?'

'Not exactly.'

The smile fell from his face. He had looked so hopeful a minute ago, and she wanted to encourage him. 'But she doesn't have to. I know my sister.'

'Is she seeing anyone else now?'

'Uh, she's gone out with a couple of guys. Nothing serious though.' True enough now, although it could change any day.

'Maybe I'll go by there. Make her talk to me.'

She nodded enthusiastically. That's the way to handle it, she thought. But he'd better get a move on before this latest thing *did* get serious.

'I'd better get going.' He picked up the box. 'Maybe I'll drop by Beverly's after the holidays.'

She wanted to tell him it might be too late then. That he should go soon, this week even. But she'd already meddled enough for one evening. 'I'll put in a good word for you when I see her.'

He touched her arm. 'Thanks, Charmaine. It was good seeing you again. Tell her I said hello.'

'I will. 'Bye, Vernon.'

He hoisted the box over his shoulder and walked off. A nice man, she thought. And he obviously still thought about Beverly a lot. Charmaine was more convinced than ever that Beverly was making a big mistake in writing Vernon off. Look at the things she was getting into now. Artificial insemination, white men. Vernon was a man she could have a future with, but Beverly was so stubborn, so wrapped up in her anger and self-righteousness that she couldn't see the big picture.

Charmaine wondered if she might be doing the same thing with Clarence. The fool made her so angry sometimes that it was hard to remember the good things about him. Like the sex and . . . What else? Well, he helped around the house once in a while. But the biggest thing, she supposed, was just knowing he was there. The past few nights she'd found herself going around the house double- and triple-checking the locks on the doors and windows. She jumped at every sound in the night.

She hadn't done that when Clarence was there. Her husband ran the streets like a madman sometimes, but he came home and slept in their bed every single night.

She bent over and stood Kenny up on the floor. 'C'mon, let's go.'

'I'm not finished,' Kenny protested and sat back down.

She picked him back up and stood him firmly on his feet. 'Yes, you are.' Kenny pouted, and she bent over and kissed him on the top of his head. 'We can come back another time.' She buttoned his coat and took him by the hand. She wanted to go home and think about what to do about Clarence real carefully. She had to be sure she wasn't doing something she'd regret later.

23

The day was finally here. They'd even gotten several inches of snow, unusual for Christmas in D.C. Charmaine wore her new red silk dress, a Christmas present to herself that she'd picked up at Hecht's, and black patent-leather heels. The dress cost almost a hundred dollars, even on sale, but Charmaine figured she deserved it after what she'd been through. Kenny was dressed in a new gray wool suit and red bow tie. Her charge card bills were going to be out of sight after the holidays. Thank God Christmas only came around once a year.

It had been a battle getting Kenny up from under the tree to get dressed for dinner at Grandma Pearl's house. The only thing that worked was the promise of more presents at Grandma's and Granddaddy's. Now here they were, all dressed in their Christmas finery and knocking on Grandma's door – including Clarence.

It was Clarence's first time at a family get-together since the year they were married. Sometimes he would stop by toward the end of a gathering to pick up Charmaine and Kenny, but that was about it. He was in the doghouse now, though, and trying to be on good behavior. For the past few days since Charmaine let him come back home, he'd been the perfect little hubby. Coming home right after work, helping around the house. This morning, he'd even given Kenny his bath and dressed him. Still, Charmaine wasn't fooled into thinking he'd changed his ways just yet. She planned to keep a sharp eye on him. One more slipup and his ass was out for good.

They entered the house and removed their coats and boots. Kenny headed straight for the living room and the Christmas tree, dragging Granddaddy along with him. Charmaine told Clarence to go along with them and put the presents they'd brought under the tree, she'd be there as soon as she put the potato salad she'd made with the other food. She entered the kitchen to find Evelyn standing at the counter in an apron placing rolls in a pan. She looked up and smiled when Charmaine entered the room. 'Hi. Merry Christmas,' Evelyn said, wiping her hands on the apron. She walked around the counter and gave Charmaine a hug.

'Merry Christmas,' Charmaine said, hugging her sister.

'What did you bring?' Evelyn asked.

'Potato salad.' Charmaine set the dish on the table. 'Where's Beverly?'

'Probably on her way.'

'Uh-huh.' Charmaine watched as Evelyn carried the rolls from the counter to the oven. Under the apron she was wearing a red velvet suit with black embroidery. 'That suit is beautiful.'

Evelyn placed the rolls in the oven and looked down like she'd forgotten what she was wearing. 'Thanks. I've had it a while. Picked it up during a sale at Lord and Taylor, oh, must have been a couple of Christmases ago.' She looked at Charmaine. 'That's a pretty dress. We have on the same color. Where did you get yours?'

Charmaine suddenly felt cheap in her little hundred-dollar dress. Evelyn probably spent three or four times as much on that suit. 'Bloomingdale's.' Charmaine wasn't sure why that lie popped out of her mouth. She'd never set foot in the store much less bought anything there.

'Bloomies?' Evelyn said. 'Which one do you shop at?'

There was more than one? Oh hell, now where was Bloomingdale's? 'Ah, White . . .' What was the name of that fancy mall?

'White Flint?' Evelyn asked.

'Yeah, that's it. White Flint Mall.'

'I'm surprised.'

'Why?'

'I'm surprised you'd go out that far to shop. Must take you almost an hour to get there from your house.'

Charmaine shrugged her shoulders. Truth was, she didn't know how long it took to get to White Flint 'cause she'd never set foot there either. Not because it was too far, but because all the shops out there were too damn expensive. Bloomingdale's, Lord and Taylor, Ann Taylor. Those were Evelyn's digs. Even when they had sales they were beyond her.

'It's only fifteen minutes from me,' Evelyn said. 'I shop there all the time.'

How nice, Charmaine thought.

'Next time you go, give me a call. Maybe we can meet.'

'I certainly will.'

Evelyn removed the apron just as Beverly entered the kitchen. 'Hi, gang,' she said, dropping several shopping bags filled with wrapped gifts on the kitchen floor. She kissed Charmaine, then Evelyn, on the cheek.

'You should put those in the living room with the rest,' Evelyn said. 'They're all out there getting ready to open them.'

'I will. Just let me catch my breath first.' Beverly plopped down in a chair at the table and unbuttoned her coat. She fanned her face with her hand.

'Why are you all out of breath?'

'I was rushing because I was running late.'

'I love your haircut,' Evelyn said.

'Thanks.'

'You mean this is the first time you've seen it?' Charmaine asked. 'Where have you been? She's had it like that almost a month.'

'I haven't seen her since Thanksgiving. You either. It's not my fault you two never come out to visit me.'

'You shouldn't live so damn far,' Charmaine said.

'I've been meaning to get out there,' Beverly said. She removed her coat and dropped it across the back of a chair. 'But I've been so busy.'

'Excuses, excuses,' Evelyn said.

Charmaine sat at the table and plucked playfully at the wool sweater Beverly was wearing over her slacks. 'What's with this getup? It's Christmas Day. That the best you could come up with?'

Beverly waved her hand at Charmaine. 'It's only family here. I hate to get dressed up, you know that.'

'What the hell took you so long then? Couldn't have taken you more than fifteen minutes to put that on.'

'Ha, ha. Very funny, Charmaine. It took me forever to wrap all those presents. Thought I'd never get out of the house.'

'You waited until today?' Evelyn asked.

Beverly moaned. 'I'll never do that again. But I was out late last night. And the night before.'

'Sounds like it's getting serious,' Charmaine said. She wondered if Evelyn had heard about Beverly's new dude.

'What's getting serious?' Evelyn said, joining them at the table.

Charmaine guessed that answered her question. 'You mean she didn't tell you about her new boyfriend?'

'No.'

Charmaine looked at Beverly in mock disapproval. 'Shame on you, Beverly.'

'I've only been dating him a couple of weeks.'

'But you were out with him last night and the night before?' Evelyn asked.

Beverly nodded.

'Two nights in a row,' Evelyn said. 'This does sound heavy. What's he like?'

Charmaine and Beverly looked at each other. Go on, tell her, Charmaine thought.

'He's nice,' Beverly said. 'Fun to be with.'

'Tell her the good part.' Charmaine was dying to get Evelyn's reaction to this.

'What's going on?' Evelyn asked. 'Why didn't you bring him here so we could meet him?'

'It's a little too soon for that.'

Ha. Charmaine wondered if it would ever *not* be too soon to bring a white man around here. 'Go on. Tell her the rest.'

'What rest?' Evelyn said, looking from Charmaine to Beverly.

'There's really nothing –'

'He's white,' Charmaine said.

'White?'

'You know, as in Caucasian.' It was all Charmaine could do to keep from laughing at the funny expression that crossed Evelyn's face.

Evelyn looked at Beverly. Beverly smiled and nodded.

'How did you meet him?'

'A car accident.'

'This is the guy from that accident you had? The one you said was so rude?'

Beverly nodded.

'Why didn't you tell me you were dating him?'

'Because I wasn't at first. Now I am and I'm telling you.'

'Do Mama and Daddy know about this?' Evelyn asked.

'I doubt it,' Charmaine said.

'Gimme a break here, I just started going out with the man. I'll tell them eventually.'

'What are you waiting for?' Charmaine said. 'You never waited with other guys.'

'I agree she should hold off,' Evelyn said. 'This one's different. There's no point in getting them all worked up when it might not last.'

'What makes you so sure it'll bother them?' Charmaine asked.

'Because none of us has ever done that before. I'd be surprised if it didn't.'

'You don't approve?' Charmaine asked.

'It's not that I don't approve. Society doesn't. I've had women in my therapy group who dated men from other races. I think she's asking for trouble.'

'Well, 'scuse me.' Charmaine said. 'I thought you'd be for it a hundred percent.'

'You mean *you* think it's okay?' Evelyn asked Charmaine.

Charmaine shrugged her shoulders. 'If it's what she wants. A man's a man. Long as he's got that vital organ, what difference does it make what color it is?'

'You're so disgusting. It's not that simple. What if it gets serious? There'll be all kinds of complications.'

'So? There's complications in any relationship. When are you going to get that in your head?'

'But this will be even more complicated than usual.'

'Times are changing, Evelyn. Get with it.'

'They haven't changed that much.'

'Look. She didn't plan –'

'Hey, you two,' Beverly said. 'Stop sitting here talking like I'm some child who hasn't got a clue.'

Evelyn shook her head. 'I do wonder if you know what you're getting yourself into. How do you feel when you see a black man with a white woman?'

'I don't love it, but I don't let it bother me.'

'I can't stand it,' Charmaine said, banging her hand on the table. 'I know it's a double standard, but I can't help it.'

'See?' Evelyn said. 'That's what I'm getting at. We hate it when the opposite sex does it. Beverly says it doesn't bother her, but I don't believe that for a minute.'

'It's only natural for black women to feel that way,' Charmaine said. 'There's not enough brothers to go around as it is.'

'That's part of it,' Evelyn said. 'But we also get angry because we feel rejected. We've been put down for so long about our looks. Our hair's too nappy, our lips are too full, our behinds too big. It was years before we had a black Miss America.'

'Yeah,' Charmaine said. 'And look at the first one we got. She didn't even look black.'

'They corrected for that the following year,' Beverly said. 'We got a dark-skinned one. And then another one. I think one of them was Miss U.S.A., though. I get them confused.'

'One of them was really pretty,' Charmaine said. 'I think it was the third one.'

'People just think that because she's got Caucasian features,' Evelyn said.

'She's as dark as they come,' Charmaine protested.

272

'But she's got a thin nose and lips. The one before had more African features, and some people were saying she was ugly. It just goes to show you that society still hasn't accepted black women as beautiful beings, at least not the way they do white women. So, it's hard to see our men with white women. We feel like we're being shunned by our own men.'

'All that may be true,' Beverly said, 'but it's got nothing to do with me.'

'You're fooling yourself if you think that,' Evelyn said. 'Black men feel the same way when they see you with a white man. They think you think black men aren't good-looking enough for you. Or maybe not successful enough.'

'I don't care what they think. That doesn't have anything to do with it. At least not for me.'

'Why are you dating a white man, then?'

''Cause that's what I met.'

'I don't see why you don't just wait until you meet a black man.'

'And just how long should I wait to meet one of this endangered species, Evelyn? Forever?'

Charmaine was getting a kick out of seeing these two argue. Usually she was the one having to put Miss Perfect Nosy Body in her place.

'You have to be more patient,' Evelyn said. 'You just broke up with your last boyfriend. What was his name?'

'Vernon,' Charmaine said. 'By the way, I saw him.'

'You saw Vernon?' Beverly asked, her eyes popping open like two balloons.

'Uh-huh.'

'Where?'

'At Toys R Us.'

Beverly frowned. 'What was he doing there?'

'Picking up something for his nephew or somebody. Said he was going to Virginia for Christmas.'

'Oh.'

'I know what you're thinking. But he said it was over with her.'

273

'He said that?'

'Uh-huh.'

Beverly folded her arms across her chest. 'It doesn't have anything to do with me.'

'Oh, girl. You are so stubborn. He's still got the hots for you.'

'That's *his* problem.'

'And it's obvious you still have feelings for him. Or you wouldn't get all worked up whenever somebody mentions his name.'

'It doesn't matter.'

'He's a nice guy. Why you got to be so hard on him?'

'Maybe you are being a little hard on him,' Evelyn said.

'I don't need him anymore. Who says the right man's got to be black?'

'It would make things a lot simpler,' Evelyn said.

'Like my relationships with black men haven't been screwed up.'

'That's my point. Relationships are difficult enough as it is, Beverly. You're just throwing mud in a swamp.'

'You let me be the judge of that, okay? Everyone's life can't be as simple and perfect as yours is, Evelyn.'

'Amen,' Charmaine said.

'My life isn't simple, not by a long shot.'

Beverly picked up her coat and stood up to leave the room. 'There really is no point in discussing this . . .'

Clarence walked into the kitchen, and they all looked at him. 'They're ready to open the presents.'

'We're coming,' Charmaine said.

Clarence left the room, and Beverly turned to face Charmaine. Her eyes looked like they were about to pop out of their sockets. 'What's he doing here, Charmaine?'

Charmaine knew this would be coming as soon as Beverly saw Clarence. But she didn't want to discuss it in front of Miss Perfect Nosy Body, so she just looked away, hoping Beverly would drop it.

'It is surprising,' Evelyn said, standing up. 'I can't remember

24

It started snowing lightly again that Christmas evening. Not hard, but enough to slow down the traffic. As Kevin drove through their neighborhood, the clutch to his Saab kept coming out of gear, making a loud click.

'What's wrong with the gear, Pops?' Andre asked.

'I think the clutch is about to give,' Kevin said, shifting back into second.

'Will we make it home?' Rebecca asked.

'We'll make it. It's not that bad.'

'Why don't you get it fixed?' Evelyn asked.

'I will. I just haven't had time.'

Evelyn was tempted to remind him that this was the kind of thing that would be a problem if he quit his job – unexpected things like car and home repairs that cost money. But she thought better of it. She reached over to turn down the heat and opened the collar on her mink coat. The fur had been a gift from Kevin for her thirty-fifth birthday. She only wore it on special occasions.

The children were in the backseat discussing their plans for the Christmas break the following week. So Evelyn felt she could broach a subject that had been on her mind since they'd left her parents' house. 'I think Charmaine's marriage is about to come out of gear,' she said in a low voice.

'What makes you think that?'

She spoke softly so the children would not hear. 'She caught Clarence using cocaine around Kenny or something like that.'

'You're kidding? Crazy as he is, I can't believe he would do something like that.'

'Charmaine wouldn't talk about it. And she's barely speaking to Beverly now for telling me about it.'

'I thought the three of you were acting strange back there toward the end of the evening. Kind of avoiding each other.'

'Charmaine's mad at Beverly for telling me. And she's always mad at me for one reason or another. Beverly said Charmaine put him out of the house for a while, but then she let him come back. Can you believe it?'

'Maybe she wants to try to work it out with him.'

'That's impossible, Kevin. He's got a drug problem.'

'I doubt he's addicted. He just needs to grow up some.'

Evelyn shook her head vigorously. 'It doesn't matter whether he's addicted. You can't have someone like that around children. I wouldn't even want him around me.'

'You never did like Clarence much.'

'It's not that I don't like him. He's just all wrong for Charmaine. He's so immature and undependable. What's the point in being married to someone you can't depend on for anything? She'd be better off alone.'

'She obviously wants to stick it out.'

'But why?'

'Charmaine's one of those women who need a man around, so she's willing to bend a little to keep him.'

'She's bending way too much. There's a limit, you know. And Beverly . . . you're not going to believe this. Beverly's dating a white man.'

Kevin smiled and kind of turned up his nose. 'Now that does surprise me.'

'I was shocked.'

Kevin shrugged his shoulders. 'To each his own, I guess. She's probably just experimenting.'

'It's a dangerous experiment. What if it gets serious?'

Kevin chuckled. 'Then I guess you'll have a white brother-in-law.'

'This is serious, Kevin, and you're making jokes about it.'

'It really bothers you, huh?'

'It's not me I'm worried about. It's Beverly. And think about the children. They wouldn't be black or white. It just causes too many problems. I've seen it in my work.'

278

'You think everything causes too many problems, Evelyn.'

She turned to look at him. 'What's that supposed to mean?'

'One little thing gets out of sync and you think the whole world is going to come crashing in.'

'That's not true, and I don't call integrated marriages "one little thing."'

'Why are we even talking about this? It'll probably never come to that.'

'That's not the point. You're saying I take things too seriously. Like my being worried because you want to start your own firm. Is that what you're saying?'

'I don't want to get into that now.'

'You never do, Kevin.'

'I'm just not ready to discuss it yet.'

'When will you be ready? After you hang up the sign, "DuMont and Malone"?'

Kevin shook his head, and they rode in silence until he turned slowly onto their snow-covered driveway and stopped the car. Evelyn got out and opened the back door, and the kids jumped out and ran into the house, their arms filled with boxes of Christmas gifts from their grandparents and aunts. Evelyn followed them until she noticed that Kevin was still standing near the driver's door. She turned and walked carefully back to the car to keep her feet from getting wet in the snow. 'Don't tell me you're going back out tonight?'

'I need to make a run.'

Her arms dropped to her sides. 'But it's Christmas.'

'I'm supposed to talk to someone about a loan.' He opened the door.

'On Christmas Day?'

'I won't be long.' He got back into the car and started backing out of the driveway. Evelyn ran along beside the car, ignoring the icy snow creeping into the sides of her heels. She tapped on the window. 'Kevin.'

He hit the brakes and opened the passenger window. She balled her toes up against the wetness in her shoes and pulled

279

her mink collar up to keep the falling snow off her neck. She bent down and looked at him through the open window.

'I wish you wouldn't do this on Christmas Day. Who in the world wants to talk business today?'

'A friend.'

She stomped her foot on the pavement. 'When are you going to talk to *me* about what you're up to?'

'Soon.'

'How soon?'

'Soon enough. There's really not much to talk about at this point. It's still in the planning stages. I'm trying to raise the money.'

'I want to know what the plans are.'

'Why? So you can try to talk me out of it? I'll tell you when the time is right.' He started backing up again and she stood up straight.

'Kevin . . .' She watched as he approached the end of the driveway and turned onto the road. She let out a deep breath, then turned and walked quickly to the house. In the kitchen, she kicked off her wet shoes so hard one of them flew across the linoleum floor and banged against the wall. She yanked off her fur coat and threw it across the back of a kitchen chair. She had a special silk hanger for the coat but it would have to wait. What she needed now was a nice, hot bath. This business with Kevin and the law firm was sapping all her energy.

She went upstairs to the master bath and turned on the Jacuzzi. She stripped down while waiting for the tub to fill, then stepped into the soothing water. She leaned her head back and closed her eyes. What could she do to get Kevin to stop this? Maybe she should just give in and go along with it, resign herself to the idea that there could be rough days, months, even years ahead while Kevin struggled to get his business going. She shook her head. No, no, she couldn't do that. Not without putting up a fight. So much could go wrong. Kevin was thinking of borrowing a lot of money, and they had the house and cars to pay for, the kids' schooling to

think about. She had to find a way to get Kevin to see . . .
Someone knocked on the door and she sat up.

'Come in.' The door opened and Rebecca stuck her head in.
'Mama . . .'

'Come in and shut the door,' Evelyn said, frowning. 'You're letting all the heat out of the bathroom.'

Rebecca stepped in, with Tabitha the cat trailing behind her. 'Where's the Barbie dollhouse Aunt Beverly gave me?'

Evelyn let her head fall back again. 'I'm afraid it's still in the trunk. And your father took the car and went out.'

Rebecca looked surprised. 'Daddy went out?'

Evelyn nodded.

'But it's Christmas,' Rebecca said, whining like the eight-year-old she was. 'And he promised to help me set the house up.'

'Well, he can't now. He's not here.'

Rebecca stuck her lip out and pouted.

'He'll be back soon to help you set it up.'

'But it's already almost nine o'clock. If he gets back too late, it'll be time for me to go to bed.'

Evelyn closed her eyes. If she could just have some peace and quiet so she could think. 'Rebecca, there's nothing I can do about it. Did you give Tabitha the little ball and other things from Aunt Charmaine?'

'Not yet.'

Rebecca sounded so disappointed. Evelyn opened her eyes and looked at her daughter. 'Come here.' Rebecca came and stood next to the tub, and Evelyn touched her cheek. 'I know you're disappointed, but there's nothing I can do about it. I'll tell you what. You can stay up until ten. Then maybe your father will get back to help you set up the house. If not, we'll do it first thing in the morning.'

'Promise?'

Evelyn held up her hand, Girl-Scout style. 'Promise. Now scoot. Go play with Tabitha.'

Evelyn closed her eyes as Rebecca opened the door and ran out. But something was wrong. A huge draft of cold air floated over her shoulder. Evelyn opened her eyes again. The door was wide open.

She sat up. 'Rebecca, come back and close the door.' She waited a few seconds. The door did not budge. 'Rebecca,' she called out. Still no response.

'Damn it.' This family was driving her insane. She stepped out of the tub and slammed the door shut.

Evelyn lounged on their king-size bed, flipping through the pages of the latest issue of *Essence* magazine. It was after eleven o'clock and Kevin was still not back. And both of the children were upset with her.

Rebecca wanted her dollhouse and blamed Evelyn for leaving it in the trunk of the car. Evelyn had just put her very disappointed eight-year-old daughter into bed more than two hours past the usual time. She was upset with her father, too, but of course, he wasn't around to hear about it.

Andre was off somewhere sulking because she wouldn't let him go to a party. Who in the world let their child have a party on Christmas night? she'd asked him. Children were supposed to be with their families on Christmas, not with friends. Andre pointed out that his father was out with friends. She reminded him that his father was a grown man, whereas he was still just a child, even though he thought otherwise, and would do as she said. Andre gave her a dirty look, stormed off to his room, and slammed the door shut. He was probably in there watching something on cable TV he had no business seeing, or listening to some of that obscene rap music through his earphones. But she was too tired to go in there and argue with him.

It wasn't fair. She was always having to be the bad guy these days because Kevin was never around. She threw the magazine down on the bed. What was taking him so long? She hadn't insisted he tell her who he was going to see because she was sure it must be that Jeremy, and lately she was getting tired of hearing the man's name. He and Kevin had been

282

inseparable the past few months, planning this new business venture. All Kevin's other friends were married and no doubt with their families. Who else would it be besides Jeremy?

But now she thought of Thanksgiving Day, when she'd called Jeremy looking for Kevin, and Jeremy had said he hadn't seen Kevin all day. She'd never gotten a satisfactory explanation for that mix-up from Kevin. Something about driving over to Jeremy's but changing his mind at the last minute and not going in because he wanted to get back home for Thanksgiving dinner. That didn't make a whole lot of sense to Evelyn, but he got so upset when she tried to question him about it that she eventually just dropped it. As ridiculous as it seemed for him to drive that far and not knock on the door, she supposed it was possible. In all their years of marriage, Kevin had never given her any reason not to believe him and she wasn't going to start now. She couldn't, wouldn't, live that way. She had to be able to trust her husband. That was why she hadn't called Jeremy's place tonight, even when Rebecca kept asking for her father and the dollhouse. Besides, he was so touchy lately that he would probably think she was checking up on him.

She still considered herself a lucky woman. Whenever she got down on herself, all she had to do was think about other women, especially the women in her therapy group. Kevin might be difficult these days, but he was still a good husband and father. Somehow she had to make him realize that starting his own firm was not the best thing for his family. But that was not going to be easy – whenever she brought it up he was too busy or too tired. Or they had been arguing. She was going to have to find a nice quiet time, probably away from the house. Maybe she would take him to dinner or . . .

The phone rang and she was pretty sure it was Kevin saying he was going to be later. Who else would call this late on Christmas night? She picked it up at the end of the first ring. Stay calm, she told herself. Avoid arguing. 'Hello?'

'Evelyn.'

'Yes, Kevin.'

'The clutch gave out.'

'Oh, no.'

'I'm having the car towed and then I'll be home.'

'It's so late. Why don't you leave it and wait until morning?'

'I'd rather get it over with tonight. They'll take it and drop it off in front of a car-repair shop so it'll be there in the morning.'

'You want me to pick you up?'

'No, I can get a ride home.'

'From Jeremy?'

'No. You don't know this person.'

'Oh. Is it someone else involved in this . . . this thing with you?'

'Yeah, sort of. She may contribute some money.'

She? She? 'This person is a woman?'

'Uh-huh.'

'Is she an attorney too?'

'No. Just someone who may help us out. Look, I've got to run. I see the tow truck coming.'

'Oh . . . I'll see you when you get home, then.'

Evelyn held the receiver in her hand after Kevin hung up, as a million thoughts ran through her mind. A woman? Contributing money? Who was this person?

She hung up the phone and got up from the bed. She turned on the TV. She had no idea how long Kevin would be – maybe an hour or two, maybe longer. But she had to stay awake until he came home. She wanted to know who this woman was and just what was going on.

25

Tuesdays were always long days for Evelyn since she had a late therapy group. But this one was even longer, coming right off the worst Christmas break she could remember. First the fight with her sisters – although that was nothing new. They always argued, then the next time they saw each other they'd carry on as usual. That's how sisters were.

But the last argument with Kevin, that she was worried about. Although when she thought about it, she couldn't really call it an argument since she never got Kevin to do much talking. When he arrived home the night after his car broke down, he was tired and edgy and so was she. About the only new information she'd been able to pry out of those stubborn lips was that he and Jeremy had rounded up two other lawyers who wanted to go into business with them. Each of the four would have to pledge twenty-five thousand dollars, fifteen thousand to start and ten thousand later if needed. The woman had agreed to loan him ten thousand, which meant all Kevin had to come up with was five thousand to start.

Who this woman was and where she'd come from was anybody's guess. Kevin was so vague about her – said he'd known her for years and had come across her from time to time in his business dealings. Obviously she had money to burn. But that was all Evelyn could get out of him. He was too tired to talk, he said. But not so tired that he wasn't up and out of the house at eight the following morning.

Things were starting to fall into place for him, it seemed, and she was the last to know the details and had to pry them out of him. Now he was talking about borrowing huge sums of money from some mysterious woman, and leaving her in the dark. Well, it would take her money, too, to pay it back. She had a right to know exactly what was going on, and she was going to make him tell her tonight.

' . . . Evelyn.'

She jumped and looked up when she realized Dora was trying to get her attention. She'd been so far gone that she hadn't even realized that most of the members of the therapy group had arrived and had taken their seats opposite her.

'Are you ready to start?' Dora asked.

Five of the women were there, seated in the usual semi-circle. Evelyn looked around and realized Wanda was missing. She looked at her watch. It was 5:30 on the dot.

'Let's wait a few more minutes for Wanda. If she's not here by –'

'Oh,' Merlinda said, interrupting her. 'I forgot to tell you. Wanda called me at work this morning and said she wouldn't be coming. Said she's got a hot date tonight.'

'With the married man?' Laverne asked.

'She didn't say. And I didn't ask.'

'Why didn't she call me?' Evelyn asked.

Merlinda shrugged her shoulders. 'We talk on the phone from time to time. She asked me to tell you.'

'If it *is* with him,' Dora said heatedly, 'I think you should kick her out of the group. We don't need a woman like that around here.'

'Calm down, Dora,' Evelyn said. 'We don't know who she's with. Besides, we don't pass judgment here. We try to help.'

'A woman like that don't deserve to be helped. That's the kind of woman most of us are having problems with.'

Evelyn smiled. 'Moving right along. We'll only be meeting until six o'clock today instead of the usual hour. I need to leave early. But we can make up for it on Friday by meeting from five-thirty to seven.'

They all nodded in agreement. Good, she thought. She would be able to carry out her plan as soon as the meeting was over. Kevin obviously was not going to tell her any more than he thought she needed to know, and when he thought she needed to know it. But it was partly her fault. Every time she questioned him, it was either late at night and they were both tired or they were in the middle of an argument. Well, as soon as this meeting was over she would call home and check on the children, then go to Kevin's office and offer to take him to dinner. She'd thought about calling him first but decided it would be nice to surprise him. He rarely left the office before 6:30, and these days he usually met with someone after work about starting the firm. But she would insist he put off all other plans and have dinner with his wife tonight. They would go to a nice restaurant near his office and have a long, civilized talk.

Driving to Kevin's office, Evelyn thought about how to handle this. Kevin could be so determined when he wanted something badly. She remembered when he'd first decided to go to law school. Andre had just been born about a year earlier, and they had moved into a new house in P.G. County. It was a struggle just to make ends meet. Then, out of the blue, Kevin had decided he had to quit his government job and go to law school. He found part-time work in the evenings, enrolled at Georgetown, and worked like a dog for four and a half years until he'd finished.

At first she'd thought they'd never make it with him working part-time. And it *had* been a long, hard road for several years. She hardly ever saw him and practically raised Andre by herself in those early years. That was the reason for the five-year age difference between Andre and Rebecca. She had always thought two years was the ideal age spread between siblings, but when Kevin was in law school she didn't even see him enough to get pregnant. Then there was money, or the lack of it. Their tiny first house was practically empty for five years because they couldn't afford to furnish it. They had to borrow money from her parents on more than one occasion just to pay the bills. Yes, they'd gotten through it – were even better off for it. And no one had been prouder of Kevin when he marched across the stage and got that degree than his wife. But she never, ever, wanted to go through anything like that again if she could help it. Maybe she could understand it if they were younger. But here she was thirty-seven years old and Kevin almost forty. They had built a nice, secure life together. This was the time to start enjoying the fruits of all that hard work, not throw everything out the window and start all over. She hoped she could convince Kevin of that.

She parked her car in the garage below Kevin's downtown office building and took the elevator up to his floor. It had been eons since she'd last been here. The law firm always had its gatherings at one of the hotels in the city or at one of the partners' homes.

She entered the suite and greeted the receptionist, then continued on to Kevin's office. Betty, a black woman who had been Kevin's private secretary for several years, stood and smiled when she saw Evelyn. Betty was a grandmother now, having raised two sons and a daughter of her own.

'Mrs DuMont. It's nice to see you again.'

'Nice to see you, too, Betty. How have you been? And the grandchildren?'

'Oh, I'm fine, they're fine. Just got my third one last month. A girl this time. How are Andre and Rebecca?'

'They're fine. Although I don't have to tell you what it's like having a thirteen-year-old son.'

Betty laughed. 'Goodness, no. I went through it twice, so I don't envy you.'

'Thank goodness I'll only have to go through it once.'

'I'm sure Andre will be fine. Last time I saw him, he seemed to be growing into such a nice, polite young man.'

Evelyn smiled. 'Oh, he can lay on the charm when he wants. So far, though, I've really had nothing to complain about. He's a good boy.' She nodded toward the closed door to Kevin's office. 'Is Kevin in?'

'I'm afraid you just missed him.'

'Oh?'

'He left early to meet someone for dinner.'

'I had planned to surprise him, take him out for dinner myself.'

'He would have liked that. I'm so sorry you missed him.'

'Do you have any idea which restaurant he went to?'

Betty shook her head. 'I'm afraid not. Although I think it was somewhere near here.'

'Mmm. Well, thank you, Betty. Guess I'll just have to go on home and wait for him.' She started to turn and leave, then an idea struck her. 'Do you keep Kevin's calendar?'

'No. He's always kept that himself.'

'Do you think he might have written the name of the restaurant on his calendar?'

'Maybe. I'll go in and check it for you.' She picked up a ring of keys from her desk, but the phone rang and she held the keys out toward Evelyn. 'That's the one to his office,' she said, holding one out from the rest. 'His calendar's always right on top of his desk.'

Evelyn took the keys as Betty picked up the phone. Just as Betty had said, the calendar was on top of the big mahogany desk standing in the middle of the floor. She set her purse on top of the desk and looked over the page for this week. Bingo. In the slot for Tuesday he'd written the '6:30' and 'Marriott.' Kevin had mentioned going to the hotel's restaurant before.

What caught her attention, though, were the two letters he'd written next to the word Marriott — C. C. Those initials rang a bell. She'd seen them somewhere not long ago. Then she remembered where — on a slip of paper in Kevin's personal phone book on Thanksgiving Day. It had fallen out of the book when she was searching for Jeremy's number. Evelyn flipped the calendar back several pages. It seemed Kevin had been meeting this C. C. for lunch or dinner about once a week since early November. She also noticed that Jeremy sat in on a couple of the early meetings with this C. C., so it could be one of the lawyers thinking of going into this business deal with them. Or it could be the anonymous female contributor.

She turned the page back to this week and put the calendar in its place on his desk. First she would see if Jeremy was in, and if so, she would ask him who this C. C. was. If Jeremy wasn't here, she'd march right over to that restaurant and see for herself. Kevin wouldn't appreciate her popping up in the middle of a business meeting, so she would just walk over there and see if she could spot him. If he was with a group of businessmen in suits, she would try to slip away unnoticed. But he'd been seeing an awful lot of this C. C., and Evelyn had to try and figure out who it was. She closed the office door and locked it just as Betty hung up the phone.

'Did you find what you were looking for?' Betty asked.

She handed the keys to Betty. 'Yes. He's at the Marriott.'

'Oh, good. That's not far at all.'

'No. Is Jeremy still here?'

Betty shook her head. 'Jeremy went to a conference in Chicago this morning. He won't be back until next week.'

'I see.' She was tempted to ask Betty if she knew who C. C. was but didn't want to seem like the prying wife being left in the dark, even though that was the reality.

'Are you going to go meet him?' Betty asked. 'If so, I can call and tell them to let Kevin know you're coming.'

'That's alright. I want to surprise him.'

She left the office and headed up Pennsylvania Avenue. Even though the Marriott was a good six blocks away and it was bitterly cold that evening, it would be better to walk. Parking on the streets of downtown was nearly impossible at this hour, so she'd just be moving it from one garage to another. She turned up the collar to her coat and shoved her leather-gloved hands into her pockets.

She passed several office buildings, the main post office, and finally the National Theater, right next door to the sprawling hotel. She entered through a glass side door and rounded a corner. She wasn't sure where the restaurant was, so she stopped and asked in a small shop on the ground floor that sold sports memorabilia.

She followed the salesman's directions through a glittery lobby to the open entrance of the restaurant. It was dimly lit and looked huge. People sat on stuffed armchairs and couches around tables. A wide stairway led up to a second level. A woman holding a small, empty tray walked up to her and asked if she'd like to be seated. She explained that she was looking for her husband and described him — a very tall black man with a dark brown complexion, wearing a suit. The waitress smiled and shook her head. 'There's a lot of men like that here. Why don't you have a look around?'

Evelyn turned down the collar to her coat and entered, squinting her eyes to adjust them to the darkness. Most of the patrons appeared to be business people, dressed in suits and silk dresses. It was obviously a popular after-work gathering place. She looked toward the buffet, since that seemed to be the best-lit area. A small group of people stood around filling up their plates.

She walked in that direction and noticed a shapely red-haired woman wearing a tight green dress who looked familiar. The woman's back was facing Evelyn, so she couldn't be sure. Then the woman turned to leave the buffet area, and Evelyn caught her profile. It was Wanda from her therapy group. Evelyn smiled. So this was where Wanda's hot date was tonight. Evelyn wove through tables and chairs trying to catch up with Wanda. It wouldn't do to call out her name. She'd have to shout to be heard over the din in the restaurant.

She followed Wanda past the buffet, all the while keeping an eye out for Kevin. The part of the restaurant where Wanda headed was a separate room isolated from all the activity in the main area. It was quieter and even darker. A black baby grand piano sat in a corner, but no one was playing it. It was a nice spot for a romantic dinner, Evelyn thought. She stopped and followed Wanda with her eyes. Maybe she shouldn't bother her. If Wanda did have a 'hot date' with that married man she was so crazy about, her therapist was probably the last person she'd want to run into. Besides, Evelyn had more important things to do, like finding her husband.

She had started to turn away when Wanda stopped at a table and put her plate down. Evelyn just couldn't resist the chance to take a peek at the mystery man. As Wanda sat down and leaned across the table to say something to him, Evelyn took a step forward to get a better look at his face.

291

It was Kevin.

Evelyn stopped dead in her tracks. Her whole body froze. Her feet, her face, her mind. Her mouth fell open. Then the questions flooded her brain. How in the world had her husband come to be sitting across from Wanda? How did he know her? How did she know him? What were they talking about?

Evelyn collected herself and did the only thing she could. She headed for their table even though every fiber in her body was reluctant. She felt so odd approaching them and couldn't understand why. Even though she had on a coat and gloves, a chill raced up her spine. It was a crazy feeling, and she tried to shake it off. This man was her husband, for goodness sakes, had been her husband for almost fifteen years. All he was doing was having a meal.

But she couldn't shake the creepy feeling. And as she got closer to the table and saw them talking and smiling at each other, she began to realize what it was. For the first time since she'd been married to Kevin, Evelyn felt threatened.

She walked up to the table and stood there looking down at them. She managed a smile but it was hard. Her lips felt stiff. Kevin was the first to notice someone hovering over their table. He looked up and his fork practically fell out of his mouth. Wanda glanced up at her, and that half-white face turned beet red. Wanda quickly composed herself, though, and looked coolly in Kevin's direction. Kevin stood up.

'This is a surprise,' he said. 'What are you doing here?'

Evelyn ignored the question. With the smile still frozen on her face, she looked from Wanda to Kevin. 'Looking for you.' She looked back at Wanda. For some reason, the woman couldn't or wouldn't look at Evelyn. She kept her eyes on Kevin and played with a clump of raw broccoli on her plate. Evelyn wanted to tell the woman to take those catty eyes off her husband.

'Uh, Chrissy, this is my wife, Evelyn,' Kevin said.

Chrissy? Evelyn frowned and looked at Kevin. Why was he calling her that?

'Evelyn, this is Christine Cardinale, an old friend of mine.'

292

The smile fell off Evelyn's face. Christine Cardinale? So this was C.C.? Now Evelyn was more confused than ever. She stared at Wanda, or who she thought was Wanda. 'You told me your name was Wanda Green.'

'You two know each other?' Kevin asked, looking astonished.

'I know her as Wanda Green,' Evelyn said.

Wanda gave Evelyn a cool smile. 'Hello, Evelyn. Christine's my middle name.' She looked back at Kevin and smiled warmly. 'Kevin's always called me Chrissy for short. He's the only one who still does that.'

Oh, is he now? Evelyn thought, giving Kevin a look. Kevin shifted uncomfortably from one foot to the other. 'Green is her married name. But since she was married for less than a year, it never stuck with me. I knew her for the longest time in Atlanta as Christine Cardinale. So I still call her that.'

Evelyn wanted to ask him what he was doing calling her anything. Then something hit her. Christine. Atlanta. Kevin had dumped a woman named Christine living back in Atlanta after he moved here – a woman from a prestigious family with a lot of money. This must be that woman. And Evelyn realized something else. Kevin was the married man Wanda always talked about in all those group therapy sessions, the man Wanda was still in love with after all these years.

Evelyn thought she would pass out then and there. Instead, she gave Wanda the dirtiest look she could come up with. 'I think I get the picture now.' The sneaky, conniving little hussy. This Wanda or Christine or whoever the hell she was had used every trick in the book and had even invented some new ones in trying to steal her husband – setting herself up as a therapy client, befriending Kevin, and she was probably the one who was lending him the money.

'How do you two know each other?' Kevin asked.

'She's a client of mine,' Evelyn said. 'Supposedly.'

A look of horror crossed Kevin's face as his eyes passed from Evelyn to Wanda. Now maybe he was beginning to get the picture, too. Evelyn certainly hoped so. This woman had

293

committed a serious breach of ethics. Kevin stared at the woman seated across from him. 'Is that true, Chrissy?'

How dare Kevin double-check on her by asking that poisonous woman anything? And she wished he would stop calling her Chrissy. It sounded like some pet name. The woman was a snake.

'Is it true?' Kevin repeated when he didn't get an answer from Wanda. 'Have you been seeing my wife as a client?'

The woman looked at Kevin. The bitch wasn't smiling now, Evelyn noticed. 'I had no idea she was your wife, Kevin. I'm just as surprised as you are.'

Evelyn didn't believe that for a minute. 'Then how did you get my name?'

'The Yellow Pages.'

'I'm not even listed in the Yellow Pages.'

'Well, I . . . I mean I got the name of a referral service from the Yellow Pages. They gave me your name.'

'You mean, of all the psychologists in this city, they just happened to refer you to me?'

'It's possible,' Kevin said.

Evelyn looked at him in shock. He wasn't going to fall for this sick charade was he? 'You don't actually believe that, Kevin? She probably called a referral service and specifically asked for me.'

'Why would she do that?' Kevin asked.

'That's just it,' Wanda said, her gray eyes pleading with him to believe her. 'I would never do something like that.'

'Kevin,' Evelyn said. She couldn't take this feigned innocence one minute longer. She had to get out of here before she slapped this woman silly. 'I need to talk to you. Alone.'

Kevin was about to object until he saw the look on Evelyn's face. 'Excuse me a minute, Chrissy.'

They moved away from the table, over near the piano.

'That woman is crazy,' Evelyn said.

'I know it seems strange, but it's probably all just a coincidence.'

'You don't really believe that, do you? She's lying.'

'But why would she do something like that? It's too far-fetched.'

'Do you know what she talks about during our sessions? A man she was engaged to back in Atlanta who left for a job and then met and married someone else.'

Kevin shook his head adamantly. 'That's not me. We were never engaged. We kept dating after I moved here until I met you, but that was it.'

'Maybe she doesn't remember it that way. Maybe she's suffering from delusions. Anyone who would do something like this is not right. I'm telling you, Kevin, she's up to no good.'

'But she's given no indication of still being interested in me.'

'Are you blind? It's written all over her face.'

'I think you're imagining things because of the circumstances – she being a client of yours and now knowing she's an ex-girlfriend of mine. But it's all just coincidence. Our meetings these past few weeks have been all business.'

'Is she the one giving you the money?'

'Lending me the money, not giving.'

'You should have told me it was one of your ex-girlfriends.'

'I didn't think it was necessary. It's strictly business and to be quite blunt, you haven't been very supportive of my business dealings lately.'

'Kevin, you simply cannot take money from this woman or go on seeing her. What do I have to say to make you see what she's up to?' Evelyn racked her brain, trying to think of something that would convince Kevin that this woman was up to no good, that she was scheming behind both their backs. As a psychologist she was not supposed to reveal what her clients told her, but neither were clients expected to try to cop her husband. She didn't care, they could take her license if they wanted, but this woman was not getting her claws on Kevin. 'She said the man moved to the D.C. area. Now how many men do you think moved to D.C., then broke up with this woman?'

Kevin gritted his teeth.

'She also said he was now happily married with two children.'

'She said that?'

'Yes.'

Kevin inhaled deeply. 'That does seem like a lot to be a coincidence. But it's still hard to believe Chrissy would do that.'

'Believe it. She was supposed to come to group therapy tonight. But she called one of the women in the group and said she couldn't make it because she had a hot date.'

'A hot date?' Kevin said, looking surprised.

'Her words.'

'Maybe she's meeting someone after we finish here.'

'Kevin!'

'Okay, okay,' he said, putting out his hands to calm her. 'Let me go talk to her. You go on home, and I'll be there shortly.'

'If you think I'm leaving you here alone with that woman for one more minute, you must be as crazy as she is.'

He smiled. 'It'll be alright. I can't just walk out of here and leave her sitting there.'

'Why not?'

'Evelyn, there's nothing to worry about. I just want to question her about this —'

'You're still hoping to get the money from her, aren't you?'

'I didn't say that.'

'But it's true. You want to find some way to believe her because you want that cash so badly. Don't you see what you're doing? You're so blinded by this idea of yours, you can't see this woman for what she really is. If you take money from her, you'll have to continue dealing with her until you pay it back. That's what she wants.'

He gently took her elbow and tried to lead her away. 'I'll handle this.'

She yanked her arm free. 'You haven't done a very good job of handling things so far.'

'Look, I didn't want to have to do it this way. I wanted us to come up with the money. It would have been difficult but not impossible. But you refuse to go along with that. You think I'd be ruining your future, the kids' future. So I'm doing the best I can, okay? There's nothing wrong with borrowing money from a friend.'

'Where is she getting all this money from, anyway?'

'She's got money invested. Her family has always had a lot of money. Her father's one of Atlanta's most prominent black businessmen. She won't even miss it. So I can take my time paying her back.'

Evelyn couldn't believe how hardheaded Kevin was being about this. He had to at least suspect this woman's motives, but he didn't seem to care. He was so desperate to get his hands on that money, he would do anything. And that scared her. Maybe he already had done more than he should.

'Is anything else going on between you two besides business?' She didn't expect him to admit it if there was, but she wanted to get his reaction.

He rolled his eyes heavenward. 'Absolutely not.'

'Are you sure about that?'

'You've been married to me all these years and you have to ask me something like that?'

'Lately you haven't been acting like the man I married.'

'I'm still the same man. I just . . .'

'No you're not. And I'm going to tell you something else. I'm tired of trying to persuade you to come around to your senses. I'm going home, just like you want me to. But if you continue to deal with this woman after tonight, so help me, Kevin, I'll . . . I'll . . .' She stopped. It was hard to say what she was thinking. It was hard to even think it. But right now she didn't think she could live with Kevin if he continued with this nonsense.

'Or you'll what?'

'Think about it.' With that, she turned to walk away, but he grabbed her arm so hard that her bag fell from her shoulder down to her elbow.

'Or you'll what? You'll leave me?' His eyes flashed in anger as he tightened his grip. 'Is that what this is coming to?'

'Let go,' she said, pulling her arm out of his grasp. She

rubbed it with her hand, surprised that Kevin would grab her like that, especially in a public place. She glanced around at the other people in the restaurant to see if anyone had noticed their little scene. The couple sitting at the table closest to them was staring outright. They averted their eyes when Evelyn stared right back. She put her bag back on her shoulder and tried to calm herself. This was embarrassing. Kevin seemed to have noticed others staring, too. He shoved his hands in his pockets and looked at the floor.

'Don't you think you're overreacting?' he asked, his voice calmer.

'This is not the time or place to talk about it. I'm leaving.' She paused, hoping he would say he was coming with her, but he just stared at the floor. 'What are you going to do?'

He looked at her. 'I'll be home later.'

'Fine.' She turned to leave, and he walked off in the direction of the table, where Wanda waited for him.

Before Evelyn knew it, she was back out on the street. She was so upset that she couldn't even remember walking back through the restaurant or crossing the hotel lobby. All she could think of was Kevin grabbing her arm. He'd never, ever, touched her in anger like that before. Once, when they were first married he'd dunked her head under running water because she'd gotten on his case about something. But that was different. Afterwards, they had both laughed about it until their sides hurt. She didn't think they'd be laughing about this anytime soon.

She pulled her coat collar up around her neck and headed toward the parking garage. She still couldn't believe she'd been had like that. This woman, this Wanda or Christine or whatever the little bitch called herself, sat right in her office, right under her nose, and went on and on about how she'd left Atlanta to follow a married man to D.C. And Evelyn never suspected a thing. Not a damn thing. But then why should she have been suspicious? The whole thing was so absurd.

Sure, she and Kevin were going through a rough period. But their marriage was sound, or so she'd thought. She shook her head with frustration. She should have paid more attention, should have realized something was going on before now. Wanda had said time and time again that her mystery man was happily married with two children. That they had a nice life in the suburbs. And she still didn't see it.

Well, she wasn't about to let this scheming, conniving woman destroy their lives. She could blame herself for not seeing things sooner, but her eyes were wide open now.

26

Beverly snuggled a little tighter into the crook of Peter's arm and rested her hand on his bare chest. Well, she'd done it. She'd had sex with a white man. And it was the best she'd ever had. Well, no, not exactly. Vernon was the absolute best. No one could touch Vernon. And Michael wasn't so bad either. And Lamont, her boyfriend in college, was no slouch. Well, then, Peter was one of the best. That was for sure.

She turned her head up to look at his face. He was fast asleep on his back, with that sexy little mustached mouth hanging open. She smiled. In that way, at least, he was no different from most black men. Right after doing it, they all slept like babies.

She stretched leisurely, then threw back the covers on her side of the bed and slipped out. She padded naked down the dark hallway to the bathroom and switched on the light. The first thing that caught her eye was a giant centipede sitting in the middle of her tub. Its long brown body and hairy legs stood out like a sore thumb against the white tub. Ugh! She ran hot water in a glass from the sink and poured it over the bug until it fell down the drain, then she turned on the hot water in the tub full blast. She let it run for several seconds then turned it off and sat on the toilet. She really didn't need to do this, since Peter used a condom, but old habits died hard.

Tomorrow she and Peter were going to spend the day together – check out a couple of galleries downtown, pick up a bite to eat. She'd visited more galleries in the past several weeks than she normally went to in a year. Usually she would check out the African Art museum at the Smithsonian and a couple of others. Vernon was always finding small exhibits of African and African-American art in the city. But Peter was

300

into everything that could be propped up on a pedestal or hung on a wall, from Michelangelo to Matisse.

At first she'd felt a little uneasy about being out in public with a white man, thought everybody would stare at them. But she began to realize that most people couldn't care less. Oh, they'd gotten a few looks she could do without, but she was learning to ignore them. The only time she still felt a little uncomfortable was when they were in places with mostly black people. At the Frederick Douglas House, this one black guy seemed to be paying more attention to her and Peter than to the exhibits. That had given her the creeps, so she told Peter they should leave. He hadn't even noticed anybody was staring at them, he was so absorbed in the exhibits.

She was first in the bathroom the next morning and tried to finish up faster than usual so Peter could have his turn in the shower. They'd hung around in bed the way new lovers always do on Sunday mornings. Now they had to rush to get to the gallery.

She wrapped a towel around her body and yanked the shower cap off her head. Then she opened the door and rushed down the hall to her bedroom. She nearly collided with Peter coming out. What she saw was the strangest thing. He was fully dressed.

'You're not taking a shower?' she asked.

'I'm going to go in and wash up.'

'That's all? Just wash up?' She couldn't believe it. He wasn't going to wash all the muck off from the day before?

'There wasn't much point in showering when I had to put the same clothes from last night back on.'

'Right. Then we'll go to your house first, so you can shower and change.'

'That's too far out of the way. We won't have time for that.'

We'll make time, she thought. Vernon would have had a fit if he couldn't get cleaned up to start the day. 'I don't see how you can do that.'

301

'Do what? Not shower?'

'Yes.'

'You shower every single day of the year?'

'Yes. Well, baths. Sometimes if I'm not going out, I just wash up, but I can't stand to go out without bathing.'

'You're going to wash all your skin off. Not to mention all that water you're using up. Every other day or so is enough.'

She shook her head and went into the bedroom, and he went into the bathroom to do his washing up. It was really surprising, because Peter was so picky about most things, almost to the point of obsession. Especially about the outside of that Ford Explorer of his. It was always spic and span, gleaming from top to bottom. He washed it at least once a week. The inside was a different story, though. The back was always cluttered with odds and ends, mostly small pieces of wood. When she asked him about it, he said it was for a project he was working on around his house. He hadn't taken her to his place yet, but knowing him, she bet it was just like the outside of his car, neat from top to bottom.

She dressed quickly and casually in slacks and a sweater, then went to the front door to get the Sunday paper. Peter was in the kitchen making coffee. By now she was used to the way he did things, so she knew there would be time to read a couple of sections of the paper before the coffee was ready. He'd measure out exactly two and a half scoops of coffee grinds, using a knife to level off the measures. Then he'd carefully pick up any spilled coffee grinds from the countertop with the tip of his index finger and put them back in the coffee container rather than wipe them away with the dishcloth. He hated wasting anything.

He'd discovered that the right amount of water for her coffeepot, allowing for evaporation, was two and three-eighths cups. So he'd fill the coffeepot up to the two-cup line and then add the rest using a tablespoon. Somehow he'd figured out just the number of tablespoons involved in three-eighths of a cup. All of this was in the name of preventing waste. The first time she saw him do this, after dinner one night, she thought it was

302

funny and kind of cute. Now it just got on her nerves, so she stayed out of the kitchen when he made coffee.

By the time Peter came out with two mugs of steaming coffee, she had the paper spread out all over the dining-room table. She pushed a section away so he could set the mugs down.

'Where's the sports section?' he asked, sitting across from her.

She found it buried under the comics. She'd already read the sports section and it was a bit of a mess, so she quickly folded it back up and handed it to him. He set his mug on the table and opened the section flat, then carefully refolded it on its original creases. Then he picked up his mug and began reading the front page. She was used to seeing him do things like this by now, so she didn't say a word. 'We should get moving if we're going to catch this exhibit before it closes,' she said, taking a sip from her mug.

He laid the paper on the table and pointed to an ad. 'I want to stop at Track Auto to get a part for my car. They're having a sale this weekend.'

'Where is it?'

'There's one in that small shopping center up on Rhode Island Avenue. We usually pass it on the way here.'

Beverly shook her head vigorously. 'You don't want to go into that place. It's not a very nice area.'

'What's wrong with it?'

Jeez. Couldn't he tell by looking at it? Thieves and thugs shopped up there. Or stole up there. They had gang fights, for goodness sakes. 'Trust me. It's not safe. We'll go somewhere else.'

'That's the only Track Auto I've seen between here and downtown. There's one near my house in Reston. But that's too damn far.'

'Does it have to be Track Auto?'

'They're having a sale.'

'Well, I'm not going in there. That place is too dangerous-looking.'

He laughed, apparently finding this funny. 'Why are you afraid to go in there? You shop in other places in this neighborhood.'

'I go to some of the small shops up on Twelfth Street. But that's different from Rhode Island Avenue. And if they see you and me in there together . . . Well, I don't think it's a good idea.'

'Then you stay in the car while I go in.'

'You'll do anything to save a buck, won't you?'

Beverly twisted nervously in the passenger seat of the Explorer, keeping a wary eye on the goings-on around the parking lot. She thought there must be more people hanging around outside than there were in the shops. Groups of young guys standing in front of the drugstore, old men who looked like they were on their last legs going in and out of the liquor store, and women with babies standing at the bus stop in front of the shopping center.

She realized that she didn't feel much safer sitting in the parking lot alone than she would have felt getting out and going into Track Auto with Peter. She looked out the passenger window toward the store just as a skinny young man dressed all in black swaggered by the Explorer. He looked in the window at Beverly and smiled. She looked away and glanced down at the door handles to make sure everything was locked. The man shrugged his shoulders and strutted off.

Beverly didn't understand why Peter couldn't tell the difference between this shopping center and some of the other nicer ones in the neighborhood. He seemed to think the people were the same at all of them – probably because they were all black – and nothing could be farther from the truth. Either that or he was the bravest man in D.C. She'd never come near this place the whole time she'd lived in the area.

Peter came out of the store empty-handed and strolled over to the Explorer like he thought he was in Rock Creek Park. His was the only white face in a sea of black ones, and it didn't seem to faze him one bit. Beverly noticed a couple of the guys in front of the drugstore checking Peter out, following him with their eyes as he walked toward the Explorer. She wanted to roll down the window and yell at the crazy fool to get his butt over to the car instantly.

He opened the door and got into the driver's seat. 'They didn't have the brand I wanted,' he said, twirling the corner of his mustache between his forefinger and thumb. 'I'm trying to think of where another one might be that's near . . .'

'Peter.'

He looked at her.

'Put the key in the ignition, start this thing, and let's get the hell out of here.'

Peter laughed. 'This place really gives you the willies, huh?'

'Just go.'

He started the car and pulled out of the lot, and she began to breathe easier. 'Did you say there was one near your house?'

'Yeah. But that's too far if we want to make the exhibit.'

'We can go there after we leave the museum. The store is probably open until nine. Then we can stop by your place. I still haven't seen it.'

'Nah. The store probably closes early on Sunday. I'll just wait until they have another sale. They have one almost every month.'

'When am I going to get to see your house, Peter?'

'Soon enough. Just be patient. It's so far from here, and I'd have to bring you all the way back. That's such a waste of time, not to mention gas.'

'Why'd you buy a house in northern Virginia, anyway?'

'Good question. But you know how prices are in and around the city, and I was determined to buy a house for the income tax breaks.'

'I could drive my car and follow you. That way, you wouldn't have to bring me back.'

'That's an idea,' he said.

'I think it's perfect.'

He raised his hand and twisted his mustache. 'We'll see. It might be pretty late by the time we see the exhibit and get something to eat. I was going to suggest we get take-out Chinese and rent a video this evening.'

Beverly looked out the window. He always did that. Whenever she suggested they ride out to his house, he came up with something else to do.

'Charmaine,' the boss lady said, entering the suite at 5:30. 'Could I see you in my office for a minute?' Without waiting for an answer, Susan swept past Charmaine's desk and into her office. Shit, Charmaine thought. Why'd they have to go through this dumb routine at least once every week? Just when it was time to get out of here, this woman had to find something, anything, that just couldn't wait until the next day. Susan *knew* she had to pick up Kenny from the day care center by six every evening. And she'd let Clarence take her car this morning since his wasn't working. He was probably double-parked downstairs waiting to pick her up right this minute. Charmaine grabbed her shoulder bag from under her desk – it would be a signal to Susan that she was on her way out, so make it snappy.

Susan smiled brightly as she entered the office. 'Shut the door,' she said.

Uh-oh, Charmaine thought. Susan only asked her to do that when something really serious was up. Usually something bad. Charmaine tried to think where she might have screwed up as she shut the door and turned to face Susan.

'Sit down,' Susan said.

Charmaine sat in the chair facing Susan's desk and let her shoulder bag drop to the floor. She'd typed all the reports on time and double-checked all the figures in the tables. What could be wrong?

'When's the baby due, again?' Susan asked.

Charmaine frowned. What was this? Trying to soften the blow? 'In four months. July.'

'And have you been doing all right?'

I been coming in here everyday, working my butt off for you, haven't I? 'I'm fine.'

'Good.' Susan held a small slip of paper toward Charmaine. 'Here. This should help out some when the baby comes.'

Charmaine's face lit up. By now, she was familiar with this routine. That little slip of paper always brought good news, not bad. She took the paper and looked at it. On it was her old salary and her new salary. She was getting a raise. It was a big one, too. Hot dang. She looked up with a big smile on her face.

'That's a twenty percent increase,' Susan said.

'Oh, man. I thought everybody was being held to six percent or something this year.'

'They are, so keep quiet about this. I had to do a little arm-twisting. But I just came from a meeting upstairs and everything's been approved. And you're getting a promotion, too. Your job title is being changed from secretary to administrative assistant.'

Charmaine's mouth dropped open. This was getting better and better. She held the slip of paper to her breast. 'Thank you, Susan. This is about the best news I've had in a long time. I kid you not.'

'You deserve it. You do great work here, Charmaine. I don't know how we would manage without you.'

'Thank you.' Charmaine was grinning from ear to ear.

Susan began shuffling through some papers on her desk. 'Now, you have a kid to go pick up, right?'

Charmaine remembered that Clarence was waiting for her downstairs. She grabbed her bag and stood up. 'Right, and I'm running late. Clarence is probably downstairs waiting for me. But it was worth it to get this news. See you tomorrow.'

'Okay. And keep up the good work.'

Charmaine stepped out of the office and closed the door. She paused to look at the precious slip of paper again. This was the biggest raise she'd gotten in the three years she'd been here. And she was now an administrative assistant. She pumped her fist in the air. That woman sure did come through this time. She tucked the slip of paper into her bag and patted it reassuringly. Tomorrow she was going to come in at eight. Get an early start on the day's work. Fridays were always sweet, but this one would be even sweeter.

She grabbed her leather jacket from the closet and flew through the suite — it felt like she was moving on wings, even with all the extra weight she was carrying around these days. She pressed the elevator button and waited, still grinning from ear to ear. She tried to look a little more serious. If someone saw her standing here by herself grinning like this, they would think she'd lost it. She pressed the button again. Damn thing was taking too long. Clarence would probably get a ticket waiting for her.

She decided to take the stairs — it was only four flights up from the ground level. She rounded the corner to the exit sign and went down the stairs as fast as she could, putting on her jacket as she went. She opened the glass doors onto the street. A lot of cars were double-parked, but none of them was Clarence. He must have gotten held up in traffic.

She closed the door against the early spring chill and stepped back inside the lobby. She couldn't wait until he got here so she could tell him the good news. A raise. A promotion. First thing she would do was pay Evelyn back the money she'd lent her to pay the TV bill. Then buy some things for the new baby and some summer things for Kenny. That boy grew a mile a month. Hopefully, the new baby was a boy so he could wear some of Kenny's old clothes.

The more she thought about all the things they needed, the more she realized it might not be such a hot idea to tell Clarence about the raise just yet. Every time she got one, he expected a handout. Or he'd run off and buy something they didn't need and expect her to foot the bill. Like that big color TV he'd bought last summer. If she was careful, maybe she could finally get enough money together to go back to school. She'd majored in sociology before, but this time she would take up accounting. Lord knows she'd picked up enough about the subject these past few years working with Susan. With a degree, one day *she'd* be the one sitting behind the door giving out orders.

She looked up and down the street again. Still no sign of Clarence. She looked at her watch. 5:50. What was taking him so long? Normally, she would have started assuming the worst by now, but Clarence had been pretty much behaving himself ever since she'd put him out just before Christmas. He wasn't perfect, still ran the street more than she would like, but not as much as before. And she hadn't seen any signs of drugs around the house. She wasn't foolish enough to believe he'd stopped using them altogether, especially since he was still hanging with that no-good Lem. But at least he wasn't bringing them home anymore.

She tapped her foot on the floor and looked up and down the street. He could have *walked* from his office faster than this. She opened the door and stepped outside to the sounds of the downtown rush-hour traffic – cars, buses, pedestrians. Everyone in the city was going home at the end of a long day, everyone but her. She looked at her watch. Six o'clock. Damn. She would wait fifteen more minutes. If he still wasn't here, she'd go back upstairs and call him.

By 6:30 Charmaine was scolding herself. She should have known better than to trust Clarence with her car. Give that man an inch, he takes a thousand miles. Just couldn't be nice to him without him taking advantage of it. When would she finally learn that?

There was no point sitting here fussing at herself. She took one more look up the street, then went back inside and rode the elevator up to the fourth floor. Inside the office, she didn't bother to sit in her chair, just leaned on the edge of her desk and picked up the phone. It was a long shot that anyone was still at Clarence's office at this late hour, and she would probably get the answering machine, but she didn't know what else to do. She let the phone ring, expecting to get the recorded message after the third ring. Instead, it rang a fourth and then a fifth time. She was about to hang up when a man answered.

'Yeah.'

'Is Clarence Perry there?'

'This part of the library is closed. Everyone's gone home. You'll have to call back in the A.M.'

'This is kind of urgent. Do you happen to know what time he left?'

'Sorry, miss. I'm just with maintenance. Normally they have an answering machine on after hours. But I guess the secretary forgot to set it up.'

'I see. Thank you.' She started to hang up.

'Wait a minute.'

She put the phone back to her ear. 'Yes?'

'Did you say you were looking for a Clarence?'

'Yes.'

'Tall black guy in his thirties? Works stocking books?'

'That's him.'

'I know him. See him sometimes in the afternoon. But as far as I know, he's part-time. Doesn't come in on Tuesdays and Thursdays. So he wouldn't have been in today nohow.'

Charmaine frowned. 'You must be talking about somebody else. This Clarence works full-time.'

'Only one black man in his thirties works stocking books. The rest are a lot younger. Of that I'm sure.'

'But that can't be right.'

'Look, miss. That's all I can tell you. Like I said before, call back in the A.M.'

'Are you —' The phone clicked before she could finish. She held the receiver in front of her face and stared at it. What was going through her mind at this second was all those mornings Clarence slept late. She'd thought he couldn't get up because he stayed out all hours of the night, and she was always getting on his case about it. But if this man on the phone was right, he wasn't going in late those days. He wasn't going in at all.

'. . . Charmaine?'

She snapped out of it when she heard her name being called and turned to see Susan standing there in her navy suit, holding her matching Coach shoulder bag and briefcase.

'I thought you'd left.'

310

'Um, no. Not yet.' Charmaine dropped the receiver in the cradle.

'Is something wrong?'

'Not really.'

'Is Clarence here yet?'

'He, ah, got held up.'

'My husband's downstairs waiting. Can we drop you off somewhere?'

'No, I can get a cab.'

'Are you sure?'

Charmaine nodded. 'I have to stop and pick up Kenny. But thanks anyway.'

'Okay, if you're sure. Don't forget to turn out the lights before you leave. You're the last one here.'

Charmaine nodded and Susan left.

The maintenance man was right, of course. That would explain so many things. Why Clarence was always broke. Why he was almost never at work when she called. He had probably sweet-talked the secretary into covering his ass.

She took a deep breath. She didn't feel so light on her feet anymore. In fact, she felt damn heavy. She moved around her desk and sank into her chair. Clarence was wearing her out. While she worked her tail off trying to get ahead, he seemed to put in double time trying to knock her back. Well, she wasn't putting up with this shit one more day. This time she meant it. Wherever he was now, she hoped he was having the time of his life, 'cause it was the last time he was getting over on her. Tomorrow – no, tonight – his ass was going to be out on the street. And this time for good.

Evelyn took the handwritten pages from her daughter and carried them to Rebecca's bed. Outside the window she could hear the sounds of the basketball beating the pavement as Kevin and Andre challenged each other at the hoop in their driveway. Evelyn sat on the bed and read the brief report while her daughter sat at her desk and waited patiently.

When Evelyn finished, she looked up and smiled proudly at Rebecca. 'That's very good, Rebecca. I'm sure your teacher will love it. Especially the part about how you help take care of Tabitha.'

Rebecca took the paper and turned back to her desk. 'I'm going to copy it over.'

'Why? It looked fine to me.'

'But I crossed out two words. See?' Rebecca held the report out to her mother and pointed. 'Mrs Stone doesn't like any mistakes.'

'Then it's probably a good idea to copy it over.' Evelyn stood and picked up a black Barbie doll and some clothes from the carpet and placed them on a shelf with the others. She straightened a few things on Rebecca's dresser, then turned to her daughter. 'If you want me to read it again, I'll be downstairs cleaning up the dinner dishes.'

'Okay,' Rebecca said, already hard at work copying the report onto clean sheets of paper. Evelyn stepped out into the hall and nearly collided with Andre rounding the corner from the stairs.

'Whoa,' he said, grabbing his mother to steady her. Evelyn couldn't believe how the boy was growing. He only had a few inches to go to catch up to her. And she was pretty tall for a woman. 'How did the game go?'

'Okay. Pop's in pretty good shape for such an old dude. But don't tell him I said that.'

Evelyn smiled. 'Did you finish your homework?'

'I'm about to wrap it now.'

'Where's your father?'

'In the den. Said he was going to work on his resumé.'

Evelyn frowned. His resumé?

'Ma?'

'Yes, Andre?'

'Does that mean he's not starting his own gig?'

'I don't know. He hasn't said much to me recently one way or the other.' But he *was* spending more time at home these days. Maybe he was finally coming to his senses.

'Damn. I hope that's not what it means.'

'Watch your mouth.'

'Sorry, Ma. But that's screwed up. You know what I'm saying? That would have been something else. Him having his own firm and all.'

'Something like that takes a lot of money, and we just don't have it. Maybe your father's starting to realize that.'

'Can't you borrow it?'

Evelyn shook her head. 'You think your parents are rich? We need the money for other things. You want to go to college, don't you?'

Andre shrugged. 'Seems like we should have been able to work it out somehow.'

'He tried. But I guess he just couldn't.'

'Did you help him?'

Evelyn was surprised by her son's question. 'There's only so much I can do. Now go finish your homework. Scoot. I'll be up to look at it after I clean up the kitchen.'

She walked down the stairs and into the kitchen, then paused and poked her head into the den. She expected to see Kevin typing on their MacIntosh computer but instead he was sitting sideways in the chair with his back to the door, staring out the window.

'Kevin?'

He started when he heard her voice and glanced at her out of the corner of his eye. Then he turned to face the computer and pushed a few buttons.

'Andre said you're working on your resumé.'

He continued his two-finger typing without looking at her. 'That should make you happy.'

She decided to ignore his sarcastic remark. She didn't want to argue. 'Does that mean you're going to look for a job at another law firm?'

'Obviously.'

'I know you're not happy where you are now, Kevin, but I'm sure you'll find something you like eventually. Lots of firms in the city would be glad to have you.'

313

He shrugged his shoulders, pecking at the keys with his forefingers. In the past, whenever he needed some typing, he always came to her. 'Do you want some help?'

'I can manage.'

He obviously wanted to be left alone, but she was bursting with questions. 'So you and Jeremy and the others decided not to go through with it?'

'They're still going through with it.' He stopped typing and looked up at her. 'But I probably won't be involved.'

She smiled thinly as he turned back to the computer. 'What made you change your mind? Or almost change your mind?' Had to be careful how she worded things. He did say he *probably* wouldn't be involved.

Kevin stopped typing and let out a deep breath. 'The money, mainly.'

'What happened with your friend?' It was hard to even think her name, much less say it.

He looked at her. 'Chrissy?'

'Yes. Her.'

'I told you weeks ago that I wouldn't be taking her money, since the idea is so repellent to you. Remember?'

Of course she did. That night she walked in on the two of them in the restaurant had to have been one of the worst in her entire life. Partly because it was the first time she'd ever felt threatened by another woman, but also because of the frustration she could see on Kevin's face when he returned home. By that time, he'd already decided not to accept the loan. He still wasn't convinced Chrissy had deliberately set things up the way Evelyn suspected, but he admitted it was possible. And he said he could never take that kind of money from someone Evelyn distrusted so strongly. She'd been so relieved to hear that.

But it was obviously bitterly disappointing for him, and Evelyn couldn't help feeling his pain. He told her he hadn't given up, though, and had spent the past few weeks calling all over the place trying to come up with another financial source. And in an odd way, Evelyn found herself partly hoping he might pull it off. She didn't tell him that — the idea of him starting his own firm still frightened her, and she couldn't find it in herself to encourage him outright. But she knew how Kevin hated to fail at anything, and rarely did. That was as much a source of pride for her as it was for him. So she rooted for him secretly, quietly, to herself. Apparently, he hadn't been able to work things out, though, which was probably for the best.

'What I meant was do you still talk to her?'

'Not since about a week after what happened at the Marriott.'

'You still don't believe she was after more than just a business relationship, do you?'

'I doubt it seriously.'

'Then you believed her, not me.'

He blew air from his mouth. 'Look, I'm trying to work. Can't you see that?'

'Just answer the one question and I'll leave you alone. You think I made all that up?'

'Of course not. But I think you mistakenly convinced yourself she was after more than she really was.'

'Why would I do something like that?'

'So you could justify in your own mind insisting I not take money from her to start the firm, I guess. How would I know? You're the psychologist. You tell me what your motives were for fantasizing the whole business.'

'You're the one fantasizing, with all these crazy ideas about starting your own firm.' The minute it came out of her mouth, she regretted having said it. He was up out of the chair so fast that it fell back and hit the floor.

'You're never satisfied. My dream of starting my own firm has gone up in smoke, thanks to you and your foolish fears, so worried you'll lose a few of your precious possessions, and still all you can do is complain.'

'That's not fair. Is it so terrible that I want to keep things secure for our family? That I don't think we should take a chance on losing what we've worked so hard for.'

'Well, you're getting exactly what you wanted. Are you going to stand here bugging me half the night or will you let me work?'

'Lately, all I do is bug you. Whenever I try to talk to you, you shut me out.'

He jabbed his finger in her face. 'No. You're the one who's been shutting *me* out.' He walked around her and out of the room.

She closed her eyes and took a deep breath. She should never have come in here. She had thought that since Kevin was working on his resumé, he was finally coming around and they could patch their relationship up. But things were worse between them now. He was so bitter and blamed her for everything that had gone wrong. She was beginning to think he might never bounce back, that things would never be the way they had been. She walked around the desk, picked up the chair, and placed it where it belonged.

When Charmaine heard the front door open that night, it took every ounce of restraint she could muster to keep from charging down the stairs and attacking Clarence. Instead, she calmly lifted Kenny out of the tub and sat on top of the toilet to help him dry off. Or tried to, anyway. Kenny grabbed the towel from her and announced that he could dry himself off.

'Okay, okay,' she said. She folded her arms and watched patiently as he wiped his stomach like it was his only body part. She tried to sneak a corner of the towel to wipe his back, but he snatched it and moved away from her. She threw her arms in the air. 'Okay, you do that while I get your pajamas out.' She stepped out of the bathroom just as Clarence came bounding to the top of the stairs. He stopped in front of her.

'Charm, baby, what happened to you?'

She glared at him. 'Get out of my face.'

'I was there at your office waiting for you. What happened?'

'I said get out of my face. I'm putting Kenny to bed and I don't want to start arguing now.'

He stepped aside and she walked by him. 'Okay, but there's nothing to argue about. Like I said, I showed up, but you must have left before I got there.'

She wheeled around to face him. 'What the hell time were you there? Eight? Nine? You were supposed to pick me up at five-thirty.'

'Come on. It couldn't have been nine o'clock, it's only nine-thirty now. Sometime after six.'

'I was there until after six-thirty, and you were nowhere around.'

'Okay, maybe it was closer to seven or seven-thirty.'

'That's two hours late.'

'I can explain. See –'

'I don't want to hear your damn excuses. You can just pack your things and . . .' She stopped when Kenny came out of the bathroom, dragging his damp towel behind him.

'I'll deal with you later,' she said.

'Shit, Charmaine. You can't be throwing this stuff at me, then walk off.'

'Stop that cussing around my son. I said I'll deal with you later.' She picked Kenny up despite his howling and squirming and carried him into his bedroom and sat him down on the bed. He jumped up as soon as she turned her back to get his pajamas and made a beeline for the door. She ran and grabbed him and tossed him back on the bed. 'You sit there and behave.' He pouted as she helped him into his pajamas – as much as he would let her – then tucked him in and kissed him good night. She turned out the light and shut the door behind her. Normally, she left his door open but she didn't want him to hear what was bound to happen next.

She entered her bedroom to find Clarence emptying his pockets on his bureau. 'Don't bother to do that,' she said. 'You're not sleeping here tonight.'

'Aw, come on, Charm. I was trying to tell you the car battery died on me. I had to call Lem to take me to get a new one. That's why I was late. By the time I got there, you was already gone.'

'The battery on my car died? I don't believe you one bit.'

'It's the truth. How did you get home?'

'I got a cab, you bastard.'

He shook his head. 'I'm sorry about that. But what else could I do?'

'You have the receipt?'

He stared at her blankly. 'The what?'

'The receipt from getting my car fixed.'

'Oh. Yeah. Just a minute.' He reached inside the pockets to his jeans and came up empty-handed. Then he searched through the things he'd just put on his bureau. 'It's got to be here somewhere.'

She stood there watching him with her hands folded across her chest. He turned to face her with an embarrassed smile on his face. 'I must have left it in Lem's car.'

'That's what I thought.'

'But I can go by there tomorrow and get it.'

'Save the energy, Clarence. You'll need it to explain how long you been working part-time.'

He squinted at her. 'Say what?'

She lunged at him but stopped short of attacking him. 'You know damn well what I'm talking about.'

He backed away and held up his hands in defense. 'Okay. Where'd you hear this?'

'I called your office and they told me you only work part-time. How long has this crap been going on?'

'Who did you talk to?'

'Not the secretary. She's been covering your ass all this time.'

He smiled guiltily and wiped his hand down his face.

'Answer me, Clarence. How long you been part-time?'

'Uh, about a year.'

'Why would you change to part-time? *Knowing* how much we need money.'

'I didn't do it. They did it. Budget problems.'

'You're lying. You probably reduced your hours yourself so you could have more time to goof off.'

He shook his head. 'It wasn't my choice.'

'Then why didn't you tell me?'

''Cause I knew it would upset you. Look at you now.'

'The main reason I'm pissed off is because you didn't tell me. I should have known something was up, though. For the life of me, I couldn't understand how someone could stay out all hours of the night and then work a full day five days a week.'

He shoved his hands in his pockets. 'I wanted to tell you but kept thinking I'd find something else any day.'

'Have you even tried to find something else?'

'Of course. I got applications out all over the city. But it's hard to find a job now.'

She shook her head. 'I don't know what to say about you, Clarence.' She sank down on the bed. 'Lord knows I've tried to work with you. But you don't make it easy.'

He sat down beside her. 'Look, I know we've had some problems lately, and I've done some things to upset you. But I couldn't help it about the job. Something else will come along soon. I know it.' He reached out to put his arm around her, but she jabbed him in the gut with her elbow and slid away from him.

'And, like, about the car today,' he said. 'That couldn't be helped. It broke down about five o'clock, in the middle of rush hour when I was on my way to get you. I was running around trying to get it started. By the time I thought to call you, it was after six. I figured you was outside waiting for me by that time, and I know the receptionist puts that answering machine on in your office after five-thirty.'

That was true. Even though Susan was there, he wouldn't have been able to get through because of the answering machine. And it was also true that a lot of people were losing their jobs now. She supposed she should be thankful he was at least working part-time – as meager as the money he brought home was, it was better than nothing. With anybody else it would be easy to understand and forgive something like this. But Clarence always seemed to be screwing up one way or another. And he lied so much she didn't know when to believe him.

She stood up. 'I'm going to wash up and go to bed. I'm tired.'

He stood up. 'Anything you need done? The kitchen been cleaned up?'

'There's nothing I need now. When I needed you earlier you weren't there.'

'I'm here now. Anything you want me to do now?'

'Yeah. Stay out of my damn way.'

27

'This strawberry ice cream is delicious,' Valerie said, smacking her lips. They were curled up on opposite ends of Beverly's sofa with the TV on, though they weren't really watching it. 'Almost as good as that cherry-chocolate chip you always have.'

'It's not ice cream,' Beverly said. 'It's frozen yogurt. Supposed to have fewer calories.'

Valerie frowned into her bowl. 'It's not?' She took another spoonful, twirled it around in her mouth and swallowed. 'I can kind of tell. Not as rich.'

Beverly kicked Valerie playfully with her bare foot. 'You can't tell nothing. A minute ago you thought it was the best ice cream since that cherry-chocolate chip.'

Valerie giggled. 'These days you can't be sure what you're getting, can you? By the way, how are things going with the snow prince? I've been here half an hour and you haven't said a word about him. With all your other boyfriends, I couldn't get you to shut up about them, but you never talk about Peter unless I ask.'

'It still feels a little funny talking about him. I remember how we always used to say we'd never date a white man, and here I am doing just that.'

Valerie waved her hand at Beverly. 'That was back when we were young and dumb. In our teens and early twenties. There were a whole lot more black men to choose from, so we could afford to be picky. Or so we thought. We also said we wouldn't date any men under six feet who didn't have good jobs, or this or that. Ha. Between the two of us, we've done all that and then some. And that reminds me. You got a birthday coming up next week, old woman.'

Beverly made a face. 'Valerie, please. Don't remind me.'

'Any special plans?'

'Peter's planning a camping trip to upstate New York. He's renting one of those pop-up campers.'

'Sounds romantic.'

'Yeah, it does.'

Valerie looked at her friend. 'You sound about as excited as my daughter does about doing her homework. I've always fantasized about making love under the stars.'

'Peter's a lot of fun to be with. It's just . . .'

'Well, what? Come on. Tell me what's on your mind.'

Beverly set her empty bowl on the coffee table and leaned back on the couch. 'When we first started doing it, you know? I thought it was fantastic. He was so gentle and, well, it was just nice.'

'And?'

'It's still nice . . .'

'Yeah, go on. But?'

'But, you know.' Beverly turned up her nose. 'It's getting kind of boring.'

'Boring?'

'Maybe boring's not the right word. It's just that Peter is so meticulous, even mechanical, no spontaneity whatsoever. Not only in that but in everything he does. He counts every dime he spends. And you should see him in the kitchen. God. At first I thought his attention to details during lovemaking was nice. The lighting had to be perfect, the music just right. But now . . . How can I put this?'

'Just spit it out.'

Beverly chuckled. 'I'm beginning to see that the routine is always the same, you know. A certain amount of foreplay, in a certain order. First he does this, then I do that. We use about two positions. Me on top and him on top.'

Valerie giggled. 'Tell him you want to try different things.'

'I tried to hint around about it. But it hasn't done much good.'

Valerie put her bowl on the table and rubbed her hands together. 'Sounds like Peter's history already.'

'No he's not.'

'I know how you are, Beverly. It doesn't take much for you to toss somebody into the rejection heap.'

Beverly shook her head adamantly. 'This time I'm going to try to work things out. I really like being with him. He's all the other things I've been looking for – successful, considerate, honest. He's even got his own house. Although I have yet to see it.'

'He still hasn't invited you over?'

'Reston is so far from everything. We never seem to have time to get over there. And when we do have some time, he always says the place is a mess and he wants to clean up before I see it.'

Valerie looked skeptical. 'I don't know about that. You sure he's telling the truth about owning this house?'

'He's telling the truth. If nothing else, Peter's honest.'

'Then why doesn't he take you over there? You say he's so meticulous about everything, yet his house is always too messy to take you to see it. It doesn't make sense. I would watch that. He sounds like some of these brothers out here.'

'It's probably just not up to his standards. Which would be spic and span, floor to ceiling.'

'You just make him take you over there real soon. I wouldn't . . .' Valerie paused at the sound of the doorbell. 'You expecting company?'

'No,' Beverly said. She went to the door and looked through the peephole. When she saw who was standing there, she jumped back, covering her hand with her mouth. She looked at Valerie. 'Shit. It's Vernon.'

'Vernon?'

'You heard me right. Vernon. Is my hair okay?' she said, pushing the top into place.

'Your hair is fine.'

'You sure?' Beverly turned toward the bathroom. 'Maybe I better go check it.'

'Beverly, your hair looks fine. Open the damn door before he goes away.'

'Right.' Beverly turned back to the door and undid all the locks. 'I wonder what he wants.' She opened the door and smiled. It had been months since she'd seen Vernon, but he was looking as sharp as ever. No. Better. He'd grown a mustache that made him look so distinguished.

'Hi,' he said. 'Is this a bad time?'

'No. Come on in.' She'd forgotten just how good-looking this man was. Even after all this time, he still had the power to turn her stomach inside out without even touching her. It had been a long time since she'd been around a man who could do that.

'You remember Valerie?' Beverly said. He smiled and Beverly thought his lips looked too sexy for words under that mustache.

'Hi, Valerie. How have you been?'

'Fine, Vernon. How about yourself?'

'Pretty good.'

'Sit down,' Beverly said.

He sat on the sofa next to Valerie, and Beverly sat in a chair facing them.

'I'm not staying. I just thought I'd stop by to see you before I go. My firm is transferring me to Charlottesville. I'll be moving the first week of May.'

Beverly tried to keep a straight face, but it was hard. Vernon was leaving D.C.?

'That's next month,' Valerie said. He nodded, and Valerie looked at Beverly, but Beverly couldn't speak. Her lips felt like they'd been glued shut with cement.

Valerie turned back toward Vernon. 'Are you excited about the move?'

He nodded. 'I requested it.'

He was probably moving to be near that woman she'd caught him with, Beverly thought. Charmaine said he'd told her it was over, but that just went to show you. She'd been right about Vernon and that woman all along.

'You don't like D.C.?' Valerie asked.

'It's not that. This is a good opportunity for me. Things are not as competitive back there since it's a much smaller town. I'll have a better chance of getting into management.'

He'd probably be sending out wedding invitations any day now, Beverly thought. She looked up to see Valerie staring at her again. And now Vernon was, too. She tore her lips apart. 'I hope you'll be happy.' There. That was all she could manage. She stood and picked up the empty yogurt bowls from the table.

His eyes followed her as she moved around. 'I'll be staying with my mother until I find a place of my own. I'm trying to find a house since the prices are more reasonable down there than they are here.'

Valerie gave Beverly a 'did you hear that?' look. Beverly returned it with a 'so what' look. It was probably for his bride to be.

'That's nice,' Valerie said to Vernon. 'Sounds like a smart move.'

Beverly went into the kitchen and set the bowls in the sink. She put her hands on the edge of the countertop and pressed down hard. Even though they weren't seeing each other anymore, it wouldn't feel right knowing Vernon was no longer just a few miles across town. Charlottesville, Virginia, was a two-and-a-half-hour drive from D.C. But she was acting silly. She'd barely spoken to Vernon for almost six months now. Why should she care if he was leaving, if he got married? She shouldn't even be surprised. Vernon was a good catch in so many ways. Maybe this woman had tamed him. Maybe she was able to get him to settle down. If so, she deserved to have him.

When she went back into the living room, Vernon was standing near the door.

'Vernon's leaving,' Valerie said.

'I see.'

'I just wanted to let you know where I could be reached. You still have my mother's address and phone number?'

Beverly nodded even though she wasn't sure. But it didn't matter, because she wasn't going to be needing it. They said their good-byes, and Vernon was gone just as quickly as he'd appeared.

'That was a surprise,' Valerie said, sitting back on the couch. 'He looks good, too.'

'Why is it surprising? I'm not one bit surprised he's ending up back there with that woman.'

'I meant it was surprising he showed up.'

'Oh.'

'You think he's moving back to Charlottesville because of that woman you caught him with? He told Charmaine he wasn't seeing her anymore.'

'Obviously he lied.'

Valerie gave Beverly a look of exasperation. 'If that's the case, why would he come to see you before he left?'

'Ask him. Don't ask me.'

'You're jumping to conclusions. I think he's still interested in you. And you still care about him, even though you won't admit it.'

'I admit I still have feelings.'

'Then do something about it.'

'What am I supposed to do now? He's leaving town. Even if it's not to be with that woman, he's leaving in what? A couple of weeks?'

'Well, he said he requested the transfer. Maybe he can unrequest it.'

'Oh, like he'd do that for me. Just let him go. I've got to get on with my life.'

'You sure a big part of your life didn't just walk out that door?'

Beverly glanced at Peter sitting behind the wheel of his Explorer, driving with one hand, twirling his mustache with the other. He'd been awfully quiet the last ten minutes of the drive. They usually talked constantly when they were together – about politics, traveling, their jobs. All this silence was so unlike him. She reached over and ran her hand across the top of his head. It was soft, like a baby's hair. 'Penny for your thoughts.'

326

He looked at her and smiled. 'Well, to tell you the truth, I was kind of wondering how you're going to react to this when you see it.'

'Peter, your house can't be all that messy. And if it is, so what? We don't have to stay.'

'Yeah, right. Look, there's something I need to explain. Lately, I haven't really been staying at my house all that much.'

She tapped his head playfully with her knuckles. 'Well, I know that. You've been at my place.'

He smiled. 'Right. That's over the past couple of weeks. But even before that, I was almost never there. I stayed in town a lot during the week with a friend.'

Beverly removed her hand from his head. She wasn't sure she liked the way this conversation was shaping up. 'I don't get it. You trying to tell me you're seeing someone else?'

'No, not that. Of course not. It's a guy friend.'

She relaxed. 'Oh.' Then she frowned. 'Why are you staying with a friend when you have your own house?'

'It's kind of a long story.'

'Go ahead. I've got nothing but time.'

'I'll just give it to you straight.' He paused and took a deep breath, then let the air out slowly.

Jeez, she thought. What was this leading up to?

'A while ago, the fire marshall put a padlock on my door.' He stopped and looked out his side window, waiting for her reaction.

Beverly turned and looked at him. Who in the world was the fire marshall and what was he doing at Peter's house? 'I don't understand.'

'You know how I told you I collect things?'

She shook her head. 'No, I don't remember you telling me that.'

'I told you.'

'Well, if you did, I don't remember. But go on. It's not important now.'

'I distinctly remember telling you. Anyway, the things were

kind of starting to pile up a bit in my house, and the fire marshall claimed it was a fire hazard. He told me I had to –'

'Wait a minute, Peter,' Beverly said, holding her hand up to stop him. She had a zillion questions. 'What in tarnation are you collecting? And how did the fire marshall know what was inside your house in the first place?'

'Let me back up.'

'Please do.'

'At first most of the stuff was outside the house, in the front and back yards. I guess a neighbor complained, because the police came by originally. They told me I had to get the things out of the yard.'

'Why, if it's your property?'

'That's what I asked him. He said it was a public nuisance or something. He never did explain that to me so I could understand it. I think this whole thing has been a violation of my rights from beginning to end. Anyway, I started moving it into the house over the next few weeks, until I could find a way to carry it all off. In the meantime, this cop's coming by the house about once a week checking on my progress. About the third or fourth time he came by, for some reason, he ended up inside. Oh, boy. That was a mistake. I never should have let him in my house. When he saw I had moved it all inside, he hit the roof and called the fire department. They came by and told me it was a fire hazard and that I couldn't stay there until I got rid of the stuff. They put the padlock on that night.'

'Whew,' Beverly said. She was out of breath just listening to that story. 'What kind of stuff is this, Peter?'

'Mostly old stuff.'

'What kind of old stuff?'

'Bikes, kitchen appliances. Just stuff.'

'C'mon, Peter. It must be more than that for the police and fire department to get on your case about it. Where do you get it?'

'From different people. Like someone will be about to throw out a bike that's in perfectly good shape except for a small part that needs replacing. I'll get it and fix it and then give it away or donate it to charity.'

'That sounds fine. But if you're repairing these things and giving them away, why is it piling up to the point where the fire marshall put a lock on the house?'

'I'm not always able to fix it and get rid of it as fast as I would like.'

Beverly shook her head. 'I still don't understand why the fire marshall got involved. I mean, why would he care about a bunch of old bikes and toasters?'

'I honestly don't know why the fire department's making such a big fuss. What I do on my property is nobody's business but my own.'

'But if it's really a fire hazard, you're endangering the neighbors. Is it an attached house?'

'It's a town house. But a fire's no more likely to start there than in anyone else's house. I think this guy's probably not getting anything from his wife, so he's picking on me. I'm thinking about getting a lawyer and suing them for invasion of privacy or something.'

'Are you serious?'

'Yes, I'm serious. I hate spending the money for a lawyer. But what am I supposed to do? This guy has been around the house bugging me at least half a dozen times for six months now.'

'You've been locked out of your house for six months?'

He smiled thinly, obviously embarrassed that he'd blurted that out. 'Well, yeah.'

Beverly shook her head. 'Jeez.'

'What is it?'

'This sounds so strange. How are we going to get inside if it's locked?'

He banged the steering wheel so hard Beverly jumped. 'That's another thing,' he said. 'Whenever I want to go by there, I have to go to the fire department in the morning and get the key to the padlock, and return it that evening. It's not fair. This is my house, not theirs. I'm suing.'

'Don't you think it would be easier to just clean it up?'

'What the hell do you think I'm trying to do?' he shouted.

She looked at him. It was the first time she'd heard Peter yell. His face was all flushed.

'Calm down, Peter. I'm not the enemy.'

'Sorry. But it's my own house and I have to get permission to go inside. That pisses the hell out of me. I tried to explain that I could clean it up much faster if I could stay there. But nothing doing. They want to make this as difficult for me as possible.'

Beverly leaned her head back on the headrest. It did sound like they were being hard on Peter. She couldn't imagine his house – or anybody's house for that matter – being so bad the fire department had to put him out. Peter had probably lashed out and gotten on the wrong side of some official, and they were trying to make his life miserable. Peter could be difficult when he thought his rights were being violated. She remembered how he'd acted when they'd had that accident and how mad he'd made her. He was a pure asshole about it. But if he cleaned the place up, got it spic and span, they might leave him alone. Probably all it needed was a mop and broom and some muscle power. And some big trash bags. Normally, she'd run a mile from something like this. But this was the new Beverly. She would try to get him calmed down and help him clean it up.

They turned onto a side road and drove up a steep hill lined with neat little red brick town houses. In the second block, he pulled over and parked. The houses were smaller than those in the first block but just as well kept. Peter directed her to the second house from the end, and Beverly looked around as they walked up the steps. At least it didn't look bad out here. The hedges around the house needed trimming and the windows could have used a little soap and water, but otherwise it looked fine. Then she stepped onto the small front porch and saw the padlock on the door. It was a big, clunky thing. She also noticed a large green sign with bold white letters posted on the door. She tried to read it, but Peter blocked her view as he opened the padlock. It was obvious he was doing it intentionally. All she caught were the words, 'by order of the fire marshall.'

330

Peter opened the door, then moved aside for her to enter first. She stepped in but couldn't make out much in the early evening light, except that they were standing in a narrow hallway that had a doorway to the left. Peter flicked on the light switch. What jumped out of the darkness sent a chill up her spine. This was much more than a few bikes and kitchen appliances. Boxes upon boxes were stacked up against both walls, literally from floor to ceiling. The hallway wasn't as narrow as she'd first thought. It was just that the boxes were eating up most of the space. There was just enough of a path down the middle of the hallway to squeeze through.

She took a couple of steps and looked through the doorway on the left. It took her a few seconds to realize that this was the kitchen. The countertops were piled with all sorts of odds and ends — cases of canned food, jugs of bottled water, piles of dishes and pots and pans, a couple of broken fans. On the kitchen table was a stack of old magazines two feet high. Several of them had fallen on the floor near the table.

She took a few more steps and found herself standing on a carpet in . . . She didn't know what to call this room. She could make out the edges of a couch and a chair, a table. But every inch was covered with more boxes and all sorts of loose gadgets — lamps, clocks, picture frames. The floor was layered with old papers, phone books, magazines. And you couldn't see the walls. They were hidden by tall piles of old wood. It was everywhere, even running up the stairs. In one corner sat what looked like a complete set of cabinets that had been ripped out of somebody's kitchen.

She turned and looked at Peter. He glanced down, suddenly preoccupied with his feet. Talk about seeing someone out of different eyes. In her wildest dreams she would never have conjured up this mess. The way she saw it, the fire marshall had done him a favor by kicking him out.

She was almost afraid to see the rest of the house. 'What's upstairs?'

He hunched his shoulders. 'Pretty much the same thing, I guess. You want to go up and look?'

331

'Uh-uh.' No siree. She'd seen more than she cared to and was afraid she'd trip and break her neck trying to navigate around all the junk on those stairs.

He smiled weakly. 'Pretty bad, huh?'

She raised her eyebrows. That was the understatement of the year. 'Why, Peter? Why'd you let it get like this?'

'I don't know. A hobby that got out of control, I guess.'

Another understatement.

'I mean, I started out with good intentions. But before I knew it –' He threw his arms into the air.

'Where do you find all this stuff?'

'Like I said. Different places, different people. Sometimes from people I know. If I see someone throwing something out that's still serviceable, I pick it up.'

That explained why the inside of his Ford Explorer was always such a mess. She looked around at the piles of wood with rusty nails sticking out, the three-legged chairs, the worn appliances. That was probably the strangest part. That he thought somebody could still use this junk. The Salvation Army wouldn't take most of it. 'Why don't you just throw it out? Then maybe the fire marshall will let you back in.'

'I *am* throwing it out. It's already better than it was before.'

Beverly decided to ignore that comment because it was too much to even think about the possibility of it ever being any worse. 'Why is it taking so long? You said the fire marshall came by six months ago.'

'It takes time to go through this stuff.'

'Why waste time going through it? All of it's junk. Just toss it.'

He tightened his lips. 'It's not junk. Look, you've seen my place. You want to leave now?'

She picked up a copy of the *Washington Post* sitting on the top of a stack on a table. It had turned yellow with age and looked like it had never even been opened. She checked the date. It was almost a year old. She held the paper out toward him. 'Why on earth are you saving *this*?'

'I'm going to clip the articles and file them away.'

'In that?' She pointed to a banged-up metal file cabinet standing in front of the wood. It was leaning over so far to the side that it had to be braced against a chair to keep it from toppling over. The chair was piled high with old telephone books.

'Yeah, maybe. It just has to be repaired.'

This man's brain needed repairing. She looked around for a place to put her purse and finally settled for a spot on the floor. 'Peter. Let me show you how it's done.' She picked up the pile of newspapers from the table. He looked alarmed. 'What are you doing with that?' He reached out to take them from her, but she turned away from him and marched into the hallway. She'd seen a wastebasket in the kitchen. It was the only thing that wasn't filled with junk. No surprise there, since he never threw anything out.

'Where are you taking that?' Peter demanded, following close on her heels. She didn't say a word, just walked into the kitchen and dumped the whole pile in the trash can.

'Oh, no,' Peter said. He gave her a dirty look and reached into the can and retrieved some of the papers. He was clearly upset. 'Now look what you've done.'

'What? I threw away some ancient newspapers.'

'You messed them all up. Now they're all out of order.' He made some room on the countertop and restacked the papers as he removed them from the can, one by one.

She grabbed his arm. 'Peter, leave it. You need to clean this place up.'

He shoved her hand away and gave her a cold look. 'I'll do it myself, when I'm good and ready. I don't need you meddling. I knew I shouldn't have brought you here.'

She stepped back and watched as he got the rest of the newspapers out of the trash can and piled them neatly on the countertop. Then he began to put the sections back together, slowly, meticulously. It was like he was in a trance. Suddenly, Beverly realized that this man – the man she'd been spending all her free time with, the man she'd been sleeping most nights

with, eating with, drinking with, and thought she was falling
in love with – was a nut.

'I'll wait for you in the car, Peter.'

28

Beverly looked around the Szechuan Gallery restaurant for her sisters. They were all meeting for lunch in Chinatown in celebration of her birthday. The official day wasn't until tomorrow, but Beverly didn't want to celebrate on that date. She was turning thirty. Why revel in that? Charmaine and Evelyn were determined to do something for her, though, so Beverly agreed to let them take her to lunch the day before. Beverly spotted Charmaine waving across the room and headed that way.

'Sorry I'm late,' Beverly said, sitting at the table. 'At the last minute an author called complaining about some changes I made in his manuscript. I had to calm him down. Where's Evelyn?'

'Probably stuck in traffic on Connecticut Avenue.'

Beverly leaned over to get a better look at Charmaine behind the table. 'You're really starting to show now. How many months is it?'

'A little over six.'

'You never did get that test to find out if it's a boy or a girl, did you?'

'Nah. I wanted to, but Clarence wants to be surprised.'

'I don't see how you can go nine months without finding out, when it's so easy to these days.'

Charmaine shrugged her shoulders. 'No point in me knowing if I can't tell Clarence.'

'I guess you've got a point there.'

'So what was this you were telling me on the phone last night about Peter's house, girl?'

Beverly rolled her eyes to the ceiling. She hated to even think about that mess. It was so depressing. 'Oh, Jeez. His place is a nightmare. I couldn't begin to describe it. Junk all over the place.'

'That bad, huh?'

'Worse. I've never seen anything like it.'

'Then help him clean it out. Men are such big babies, got to lead them by the hand.'

'That's the biggest problem. He won't let me touch the stuff. It's like he's got some kind of fixation. It's weird. I don't think I want to get involved with it.'

'Knowing you, that's probably the end of the relationship.'

'I didn't say that. But I *am* having second thoughts.'

'You probably thought you'd found a perfect little man, 'cause he's white. Just goes to show you.'

'I'm not dating Peter because he's white or because I expected him to be perfect. For your information, I happen to like him.'

'I believe you,' Charmaine said. 'All I'm saying is that all men have problems. I don't care what color they are.'

'Believe me, I'm beginning to learn that. But that doesn't mean I have to put up with it. Sometimes I think I'd be better off alone.'

'No, no, no. You're never better off alone.'

'But I'm tired of fooling with these jerks. If it's not one thing, it's another. How'd they get so screwed up? All of them. Black, white. Makes no difference.'

'That's life, sis.'

'Not my life. Peter is either going to get himself together, or I'm getting out of it.'

'See? I told you. No patience. Go ahead and spend the rest of your life by yourself, then. See if I care.'

Beverly started to protest, then stopped. She looked at Charmaine and laughed. Here they'd barely been together five minutes and already they were arguing. 'Is this supposed to be a birthday celebration or what?'

Charmaine smiled thinly. 'You the one getting all hot under the collar. I'm just trying to give you a little sisterly advice.'

'I know. It's just that lately I've been thinking . . .' Beverly paused and pointed her finger at Charmaine. 'If I tell you something, you have to promise not to say "I told you so" and not to tell anyone.'

Charmaine held up her hand. 'I promise. And I'm better at keeping them than you are.'

'Yeah, sure. The whole Jordan family will probably know by tomorrow. But anyway, sometimes I think, well . . .' She knew Charmaine was going to get a kick out of this. 'Maybe I made a mistake letting Vernon go.'

Charmaine jabbed her finger at Beverly. 'I knew it. What did I tell you?'

Beverly put her hand on her waist and looked at Charmaine in mock indignation. 'I thought you weren't going to say that.'

Charmaine laughed. 'Sorry, but I couldn't resist. That's what I've been trying to tell you for the last six months.'

'I know, I know.' Beverly shook her head. 'He is starting to look good to me now, despite what he did.'

Charmaine waved her hand. 'What he did wasn't all that bad.'

Beverly's eyes widened.

'I mean, considering the circumstances. He wasn't married to you or anything. Shit, you're not even sure he went all the way with her. He said he didn't.'

'Maybe he did, maybe he didn't. It's getting so I don't even care anymore.'

'Even if he did screw her, there's worse things he could have done. Like, like . . .'

'Some of the stuff Clarence pulls.' Beverly couldn't resist slipping that in.

'You're right. Clarence can be a real ass.'

Beverly blinked. 'Am I hearing things?'

'I admit the man's got problems. Lately, he's really starting to get on my nerves. He can't be trusted for a second. But that's enough about Clarence. Let's get back to Vernon. It's probably not too late to do something about him, you know.'

'Yes it is. He's moving to Charlottesville next week.'

'What?'

'For his job.'

'Damn, Beverly. You wasted all that time, and now he's leaving. I still think you should call him. Charlottesville's only a few hours away. Long-distance relationships can be nice, as long as you're not *too* far away.'

'Maybe I will. We'll see.'

A young Asian woman came to the table to take their orders.

'Should we go ahead and order or wait for Evelyn?' Beverly asked.

'Go ahead and order. Evelyn always gets that shredded chicken Szechuan style. We can order that and two more things and share like we usually do.'

'Okay.' They ordered and handed their menus to the waitress.

'Wonder what's holding Evelyn up?' Beverly said. She looked across the room toward the entrance and noticed the back of a man who looked familiar leaving the restaurant. When the man turned and Beverly could see his face clearly, she realized it was Evelyn's husband. 'There's Kevin,' Beverly said.

Charmaine followed Beverly's eyes. 'It sho' is. What's he doing here?'

'He doesn't work far away,' Beverly said. 'Right over on Pennsylvania Avenue.' Just then, Beverly noticed a tall, pretty woman with reddish hair walking in front of Kevin. 'Is that woman with him?' As if in answer to Beverly's question, Kevin put his arm around the woman's waist and escorted her out the door. 'Guess so.'

'Oh, my Lord,' Charmaine said. 'I don't believe it.'

'Now don't go jumping to conclusions. I'm sure she just works with him or something.'

'Hmmph. I hope you're right, looking like that.'

'She was attractive but . . .'

'She was drop-dead gorgeous.'

' . . . Kevin would never do something like that.'

'You never know with these men,' Charmaine said. 'Lord knows I'd be suspicious if I saw Clarence with a woman looking like that.'

Beverly smiled. 'Uh, Charmaine, I don't think you can compare Clarence and Kevin.'

'Why not? A man's a man.'

'I think it was all perfectly innocent.'

'Maybe so,' Charmaine said. 'You think we should mention it to Evelyn?'

'Why not? There's nothing wrong.'

'Maybe we shouldn't say anything, just in case it wasn't so innocent. Wouldn't want to start something.' Charmaine stretched her neck, looking back toward the entrance.

'Will you stop acting like this? I'm sure there's nothing to it.'

'Maybe we won't have to mention it.'

'What do you mean?'

Charmaine nodded toward the entrance. 'Evelyn just walked in. She probably ran into them outside.'

They waved to Evelyn and she came to the table.

'Traffic was a mess,' Evelyn said, sitting down. 'I should have known better than to try to drive across town during lunchtime. Should have taken the subway. Have you ordered yet?'

'We ordered the shredded chicken for you,' Beverly said. 'That okay?'

'That's fine. So.' She looked at them and smiled. 'What did I miss?'

Charmaine and Beverly looked at each other. Charmaine, with her wild suspicions, made Beverly hesitant to mention that they'd seen Kevin with another woman.

'Did you see Kevin outside?' Charmaine blurted out. Jeez, Beverly thought. So much for her not wanting to say anything.

'Kevin? He was here?'

Charmaine nodded. 'He left just before you came in.'

'No, I didn't see him. Was he with anyone?'

'A woman,' Charmaine said.

'He's always taking clients out to lunch. Or it may have been someone from his office.'

Charmaine raised her eyebrows doubtfully. Beverly tossed Charmaine a 'drop it' look, but Charmaine was having none of it. She leaned across the table as Evelyn opened her napkin and spread it over her lap. 'Any of them shapely, pretty black women with gorgeous red hair?'

Evelyn looked sharply at Charmaine. 'She had red hair?'

Charmaine hesitated for a moment. She seemed startled by Evelyn's reaction. Charmaine nodded.

'About how old was she?'

Charmaine shrugged her shoulders. 'Young. Mid- to late twenties.'

'Or early thirties,' Beverly said.

Evelyn's lips tightened. 'Very light complexion?'

They both nodded.

Evelyn grabbed her napkin from her lap and threw it on the table. 'Damn. That whore.'

Beverly and Charmaine exchanged wide-eyed looks. Beverly couldn't remember the last time she'd heard Evelyn curse.

'And that bastard.'

'Whoa,' Beverly said. 'Who is she?'

Evelyn's lips got tighter and tighter as she looked around the table. Beverly thought she was trying to find something to pick up and throw.

'Who is she?' Beverly asked again.

Evelyn let out a long breath of air. 'An ex-girlfriend of Kevin's who's been meddling in our lives. Kevin swore he told her to get lost.'

'Hmmph, I declare, I . . .' Charmaine stopped when she saw Evelyn glaring at her.

'What?' Evelyn snapped.

'Nothing,' Charmaine said.

'Go ahead, say what you're thinking.'

'I just never would have figured anything like this with you two, that's all.'

'I know you wouldn't. You thought everything was la-la land with us. I don't know where you got that impression.'

'From you 'cause that's the impression you give.'

'I do not. Kevin and I have always had disagreements.'

'Yeah, but I always thought they were more like, you know, whether to put in a new pool or deck.'

'Very funny,' Evelyn said bitterly. 'Now you know better. The last several months have been pure hell if that makes you feel better.'

'Why the hell would that make me feel better?'

'What's going on with you and Kevin?' Beverly asked.

'He's got this crazy idea in his head about starting his own law firm.'

'What's wrong with that?' Beverly asked.

Evelyn's eyes widened as if she couldn't believe she was hearing the question. 'Everything. We can't afford something like that at this point in our lives.'

'Get out of here,' Charmaine said. 'All that money you two have?'

'We don't have that kind of money.'

'Then why does Kevin think it can be done?' Beverly asked.

'Oh, I don't know,' Evelyn said. 'You know men. Always up to something.'

'Uh-huh,' Charmaine said. 'Just what I been trying to tell you two all along.'

'But the difference is that I put the brakes on Kevin's nonsense,' Evelyn said, pointing her finger at Charmaine. 'Or try to, anyway. You let Clarence get away with murder.'

'Why you got to drag him into this? Kevin's the one fucking . . .'

'What does this woman have to do with it?' Beverly asked, interrupting before they could go at it again. These two would argue about the color of the sun if you let them.

'She wants to lend Kevin the money he needs to get started.'

'Sounds like that's not all she wants,' Charmaine said.

'You're right. It's not.'

'You mean she's after Kevin?' Beverly asked.

Evelyn nodded. 'Only Kevin doesn't see it that way. He thinks she's all business. I thought I had finally gotten him to see what she's up to. He dated her just before we met, and she never got over him.'

341

So the perfect marriage wasn't so perfect after all, Beverly thought. If Evelyn was having problems, everybody must be. 'I can't believe I'm hearing this,' Beverly said.

'And that's not the worst of it.'

'You mean there's more?' Beverly asked. She thought she was about to go into shock.

'The woman joined my therapy group. She pretended . . .'

'She what?' Beverly and Charmaine cried in unison.

Evelyn nodded. 'Before all this came out, she pretended to be somebody else. Used a different name. She was coming to one of my biweekly therapy groups, talking about some man who left her years earlier and married another woman.'

'That man was Kevin?' Beverly asked.

'And the other woman was you?' Charmaine asked.

'Yes. Only I didn't realize what she was up to at first. She was good. I have to hand it to her. She deserves an Academy Award. After all this broke out, she stopped coming, of course.'

'How did you find out?' Charmaine asked.

'That's a long story.' Evelyn told them about catching the woman and Kevin in a restaurant.

'That woman's crazy,' Beverly said, with a look of horror on her face.

'She's a nut,' Charmaine said.

'Here we thought Evelyn was leading this charmed life and she's got a little soap opera going on in the wings.'

'Is this bitch rich or something?' Charmaine asked.

'Kevin says her family's got money.'

'You think anything is going on between them?' Charmaine asked.

'You mean are they having an affair? Of course not. I wouldn't still be living with him if I thought otherwise.'

'Might not be nothing going on now,' Charmaine said. 'But men can be so weak when it comes to that kind of thing. And with the way she looks, honey, I'd be real worried. What if she keeps going after him?'

'I'll admit I'm worried now. Especially after what you just

saw. What am I going to do with him? I've tried being patient. I've tried putting my foot down. Nothing works.'

'Go on and let him have the money to start the business or whatever it is he wants to do,' Charmaine said. 'Hell, anything but let him think he needs that scheming bitch.'

'I like the idea of Kevin having his own firm, anyway.' Beverly said. 'Why is it you think you can't afford it?'

'That's what I want to know,' Charmaine said. 'Always thought you two were loaded.'

'Well, we're not. We've got savings, but we need that money for other things, like the kids' college. And we want to buy another house. Kevin thinks we can put that off, but I don't want to.'

'Another house?' Charmaine asked. 'What's wrong with the one you already got?'

'Nothing. But we never planned to stay there forever.'

'I'm sure he doesn't intend to put everything off permanently,' Beverly said. 'Just until he gets on his feet.'

'Well, the whole idea gives me the creeps. What if he never gets back on his feet? I like being stable and secure, the way we are now. Mama and Daddy never took chances like that with us.'

'Things are different now,' Beverly said. 'It was so hard for their generation just to get decent jobs that they were afraid to strike out and take chances.'

'Yeah,' Charmaine said. 'But times have changed.'

'Not that much,' Evelyn said. 'It's still harder for black people to get loans, even when they're financially secure. We would probably have to use everything we own as collateral, then we could lose it. I don't know. Maybe I'm just being old-fashioned.'

'You're going to end up with a bunch of possessions and no husband. I don't understand you, or Beverly either. I swear the two of you are never satisfied. Did Beverly tell you about Peter?'

Evelyn pursed her lips. 'No. You two never tell me anything.'

343

'We're telling you now,' Charmaine said. She turned to Beverly. 'Tell her about the house.'

Beverly told Evelyn about her visit to Peter's junkyard.

'She's probably going to dump him now, knowing Beverly,' Charmaine said.

'I didn't say that.'

'I wouldn't blame her,' Evelyn said.

'I'm sure you wouldn't. You never did like Peter, 'cause you don't want your baby sister going out with a white guy. You'd have her all alone waiting forever for the perfect black man before doing that.'

'No I wouldn't. If she wants to date a white man, that's up to her. I just don't like to see her go through the problems black women have when they date white men.'

'Funny,' Charmaine said. 'Her problems with Peter don't seem to be because he's white, but because he's a man. Most of 'em are no good, black or white. But he's better than having nobody.'

'That's the wrong attitude,' Evelyn said. 'She should —'

'Will you two cut it out,' Beverly said. 'This is supposed to be a celebration.'

Evelyn and Charmaine looked at each other.

'You didn't even want to celebrate,' Charmaine said to Beverly.

'Well, I'm here. So let's get on with it.'

Charmaine raised her water glass. 'I want to propose a toast.'

Beverly raised her water glass. 'That's more like it.'

'Maybe we should order some champagne,' Evelyn said.

'If you want to order champagne, fine,' Charmaine said. 'But for now can you just get that fucking water glass up?'

'Okay, okay.' Evelyn raised her glass.

'To our dear baby sister,' Charmaine said. 'May we share our wisdom and experiences with you over the next thirty years, just as we have over the first thirty, as a lesson on how *not* to run your life.'

The three of them laughed.

'Amen,' Evelyn said.

'I'll drink to that,' Beverly said.

'Oh,' Charmaine said before Beverly and Evelyn could get their glasses to their lips. 'We have something else to celebrate. I got a raise and a promotion.'

'All *right*,' Beverly said.

'Congratulations,' Evelyn said.

'And she's been talking about going back to school to get her degree,' Beverly said.

'That's wonderful. What are you getting it in?'

'It's not definite yet, but if I can pull it off – accounting.'

'That's perfect for you,' Evelyn said.

They all took sips from their water glasses, just as the waitress came to the table with the food. As soon as she left, Evelyn turned to Beverly. 'What did you finally decide about the artificial insemination?' she asked, picking up her chopsticks. 'Are you going to go through with it?'

'Oh, that. Probably not. I'll –'

'Have a baby by Peter,' Charmaine said.

'Charmaine, please,' Evelyn said. 'Where do you get these ideas?'

'What's wrong with that? For the life of me, I don't understand why anybody would go through this artificial insemination shit. At least she'll know what the daddy looks like.'

'That's true, but I –'

'But Peter's white,' Evelyn said, interrupting Beverly.

'So? The baby will be black. One drop of black blood and you's one of us.'

'The father will still be white. It would be complicated enough for her trying to raise a child alone, but to have to explain to the child the father was white. That just gets more complicated.'

'You don't think it's complicated to have to tell the baby it came from a damn test tube?'

'It wouldn't be a test tube baby,' Beverly said. 'The baby would be conceived inside me. It's just that the sperm is injected from a needle.'

'Same difference,' Charmaine said, waving a hand.

Beverly rolled her eyes and took a deep breath. 'Would you

345

approve of me getting pregnant by a man I didn't plan to marry if he was black, Evelyn?'

Evelyn looked at her. 'It would depend on the man. Who do you have in mind?'

'Well, nobody. I was just asking hypothetically.'

Charmaine chuckled sarcastically. 'Hell no, she wouldn't approve. So don't even bother asking her. She wouldn't approve of nobody unless she thought they were perfect. Clarence may have his problems. Sometimes he makes me so mad I could kill him. But it's better than going home to an empty bedroom, especially with another baby coming along.'

'Not after what he did around Kenny,' Evelyn said. 'That man would never come back to my house after that. Are you serious about this, Beverly?'

'Like I said, I was just . . .'

'He promised it won't happen again,' Charmaine said before Beverly could finish. 'I think he deserves a second chance.'

'He's already had a hundred chances,' Evelyn said.

'He means it this time.'

'Obviously he's convinced you of that.'

'Look, I don't think you're exactly in a position to be giving anybody advice in the personal affairs department now. Clarence may not be the most dependable man in the world, but at least I never had any problems with him lying to me about some other woman.'

Evelyn's jaw tightened.

Uh-oh, Beverly thought. This was really getting out of hand. 'That was uncalled for, Charmaine.'

'She had it coming. I'm sick and damn tired of her getting on me about my marriage. She ought to worry more about what that husband of hers is up to instead of worrying about me. Maybe then she wouldn't be having these problems.'

'Look you two, I've had it with all this arguing. I'm having trouble believing we're celebrating something here. If you don't cut it out, I'm getting up and walking out. I mean it.'

Charmaine and Evelyn clammed up.

'That's better.'

29

As Charmaine walked from the restaurant to her car, she couldn't help but think about Evelyn and Kevin. Unbelievable. But it proved a point. No man on this here earth could be trusted. Not even a supposed Goody Two-shoes like Kevin.

She bet all this had taken Evelyn completely by surprise. Shit, in some ways Evelyn was worse off than she was because Evelyn was so damn trusting of her husband. She, on the other hand, was always suspicious, looking under every rock for trouble. At least when something crawled out, though, she was prepared for it. But a man like Kevin got women feeling all comfy and secure and then, wham. Evelyn probably didn't have a clue about how to handle this. Probably acting all righteous and indignant, driving Kevin straight into the bitch's arms.

She got into her little Chevy and turned the key in the ignition. The engine grunted a bit, then died. She turned the key again, this time pumping on the accelerator. She heard a click, then silence. Damn it, she thought, frowning at the steering wheel. She tried again, this time pumping faster. Still nothing. She waited a few minutes and tried again. Zero, zilch. She smacked the steering wheel. Shit. Now what the fuck was she supposed to do? She thought about looking under the hood, but what the hell good would that do? She wouldn't have the faintest idea what she was looking at.

She got out of the car and looked up and down the street. There was a filling station about two blocks up. Maybe they could help her. She slammed the car door shut and locked it, then walked toward the station. She hated dealing with these things – soon as mechanics saw a woman, dollar signs flashed through their brain cells. They'd tell her anything to make a bigger buck. But she had no choice. She couldn't call Clarence since he got off work at one o'clock on Fridays, and there was no telling where he was. A lot of good that man was.

After asking around at the station, she found one of the mechanics, an older black man who reminded her of her father. Still, she didn't trust him one bit.

'Where's the car?' he asked, wiping his hands on a greasy rag.

'About two blocks up the street.'

'Is it parked?'

Charmaine nodded.

'So there's no hurry. Give me a minute and I'll go take a look at it. But I can't make you any promises.'

It was more like fifty minutes before the mechanic got to her car. He looked under the hood while she turned the key in the ignition, then he told her to stop and fiddled around a few seconds. He came to the window on the driver's side, where Charmaine was sitting. She braced herself, fully expecting him to tell her it was some major shit that would empty her bank account.

'It's the battery.'

'The battery?' That was impossible. 'But it's a brand-new battery.'

'No way. That battery's several years old. And we don't carry 'em at the station. We might be able to jump-start it, though. Then you can drive it somewhere to get a new one.'

'But it's not the battery. My husband told me he had a new one installed a few weeks ago.'

'Your husband told you that?'

Charmaine nodded.

'Lady, I don't know what to tell you. Except that there's no new battery. Come here, I'll show you.'

Charmaine got out of the car and followed the mechanic. She looked as he pointed to all the signs of wear and tear. Each time he pointed to a spot of corrosion, Charmaine's blood pressure rose a point. It was all she could do to keep from screaming at the top of her lungs. Damn that no-good bastard.

The mechanic straightened up. 'I hate to say this, but either your husband's not telling you the truth, or he's the biggest sucker in the world letting somebody sell him this battery.'

Charmaine looked at him. 'I'm the one who's the sucker.' But that was about to change.

Evelyn was having trouble concentrating on what her client was saying. Her mind kept wandering back to what Beverly and Charmaine had said about seeing Kevin with a red-haired woman. Evelyn was almost sure it was that 'Wanda.' And if it was her, then Kevin hadn't kept his promise not to see her anymore. That was so unlike him it was hard to believe, but then Kevin wasn't his old self. It felt like she was living with a different man.

Even though he was spending more time at home now and sending out his resumé, they still didn't talk much. And forget sex. How could two people make love when they couldn't think of what to say to each other? Her days of hoping he would snap out of it were over – he just seemed to be slipping farther and farther . . .

' . . . Evelyn?'

She snapped out of it to see her client, a blond woman in her late forties, staring at her strangely. They were seated on opposite sides of a coffee table in Evelyn's office, the woman on a small couch, Evelyn in a stuffed armchair. Evelyn sat up straight. 'Uh, Katie, I'm sorry. What were you saying?'

'I was asking what you thought about face-lifts.'

'You're thinking of having a face-lift?'

'Maybe.'

'I see.' Evelyn thought a minute. She knew Katie had lost a lot of confidence when her husband of twenty-four years had walked out a couple of years back. She was a quiet woman, kind of shy, and had built her whole life around this man. Now she was having trouble getting out to meet new people. 'It depends on why you want to do it. It's usually much better to try to improve your life from the inside out.'

'But impressions are important. Sometimes I think I'll never attract another husband with these bags under my eyes.'

'Some people would say they add character to your face.'

'I'm not sure I need character. I need a man. And if that takes a pretty face, then that's what I want.'

Evelyn smiled. 'There's nothing wrong with your face. I'm not knocking cosmetic surgery and I'm not plugging psychology. But . . .'

Katie laughed.

'So many women spend all this money on face-lifts and breast implants and tummy tucks thinking those things will change their lives, only to find in the end that they don't really. They're just as unhappy or miserable as they were before, for whatever reason. The change is that now they've got this huge medical bill to pay off. Focusing on a superficial thing such as a few lines on their faces, they neglect the really important things, like working on their personalities so they can become better people and building up their relationships with those around them. That's what really matters in the long run.'

'It seems easier said than done.'

Evelyn smiled and looked at her watch. 'You're right, it is. Unfortunately, our time is up, but we should talk more about this when you come back in two weeks.'

'Fine,' Katie said, standing up. 'But I wanted to ask if you can recommend anyone.'

'You mean a plastic surgeon?'

Katie nodded.

Evelyn smiled teasingly. 'Sounds like my little sermon didn't make a whole lot of difference.'

Katie shrugged. 'I'm not sure I'll go through with it, but I think I'd like to talk to somebody, you know. See what they say.'

'Fine. Ask my secretary on your way out. If she doesn't have the name of a doctor, she can put you in touch with someone else who can recommend one. Maybe one of the medical referral agencies. But let's talk more before you go through with it.'

'Thanks. I'll see you in two weeks.'

After Katie left, Evelyn moved to her desk. Here she was worried about losing out on a new house and getting her Ph.D. If she didn't watch it, she was going to lose her husband. Without him, that other stuff was meaningless. What he wanted to do scared her, but right now she was more alarmed about the changes in Kevin.

He said he was leaving the office early today to do some yard work before it got dark. Well, she was going home immediately and tell him he could start his own law firm and that she would back him every step of the way. Just the thought of it made her nerves tingle, it was so radically different from anything they'd ever done. But there was some comfort in knowing that it would be Kevin leading them down this strange new path. If anyone could pull it off, he could.

She picked up the telephone and dialed her secretary. 'Judy, cancel my evening group session. Call all the members and tell them we'll meet at the usual time next week.'

'Okay.'

She hung up and removed her shoulder bag from a bottom drawer. She let out a deep breath of air as she turned off the light switch. In a way, it was a relief to have come to this decision. She should have done it sooner.

She was about to shut the door when the phone rang. She was going to ignore it and let Judy take a message, but a button on the phone told her Judy was trying to reach her. She switched the light back on and picked up the phone.

'Evelyn, Merlinda from the group session is on the line.'

'Put her on.'

'Hello? Evelyn?'

'Yes, Merlinda.'

'Hi, I was calling to let you know I won't be able to make it tonight. I have to work late. But then Judy said it's been canceled anyway.'

'That's right. I just told Judy to call all of you.'

'Oh, I'm glad. I hate to miss our sessions. But I also wanted to tell you about Wanda. You remember her?'

Evelyn sank into her chair at the mention of that name. 'Yes.'

'She moved back to Atlanta.'

Evelyn couldn't believe her ears. 'How do you know that?'

'She told me. She said things didn't work out with that married man. He told her she had to get over him, and there was no way she was coming between him and his wife. So she decided to move back to be with her family. I went over there yesterday to help her finish packing. She seems to be handling it pretty good. I think she's finally given up on him. I hope so, for her sake.'

If this was true, then who was that with Kevin in the restaurant? 'When did she leave?'

'Her flight left late this afternoon. She said the guy was taking her to lunch and then the airport. She was worried about how she would hold up saying good-bye to him.'

Evelyn closed her eyes. She wanted to thank Merlinda but couldn't speak for the moment. The lump in her throat was too big.

'I thought I would tell you that,' Merlinda said. 'She was something else, wasn't she?'

Evelyn swallowed hard. 'Yes, she was.'

'Anyway, I've got to get back to work. See you next week.'

'Thanks for calling, Merlinda.' Evelyn hung up the phone, then leaned back in her chair and closed her eyes.

Charmaine couldn't get the stuff into the suitcases fast enough. She finished packing one, then opened another and threw it on the bed and went on throwing things in. Underwear, socks, shirts. She even tossed in his shoes. Right on top of his good shirts, the shirts she'd ironed herself with loving care. The lying, cheating, sniveling fucker. She wanted it all out of here. Including him.

God, he'd played her for a fool. Well, she didn't care if she never saw that 'Bama face again. A white undershirt fell out of the pile she was carrying to the suitcase, and she nearly tripped over it. She threw the rest of the pile into the suitcase, then stomped all over the shirt on the floor. Then she picked it up and threw it on top of the other things. Half of the stuff was sticking out of the edges when she set it by the door next to the other suitcase.

She got his duffel bag and went back to his chest of drawers. The only stuff left was his toiletries on top. She took her arm and raked everything into the bag. Then she went to his night table and emptied the contents of that. She set the full bag near the other two, then went to the closet. God, she'd filled two suitcases and a duffel bag and had barely made a dent in this man's things. How'd he get so much shit? She had a mind not to give it all to him. It was her money that paid for most of it anyway. But she didn't want anything around to remind her of the sorry sucker. She gathered an armful of his slacks from the closet and went and dumped them on top of the suitcases. Then she went and got another armful. That was when she heard him come in.

She threw the clothes in her arms on top of the others and raced down the stairs as fast as her bloated body would allow her to. She was screaming before she hit the bottom. 'I've packed most of your junk. I want you to get it and get the hell out of here. Right now.'

He rolled his eyes to the ceiling. 'Here we go again.' He saw the rage on her face and held up his hand. 'Okay, what did I do this time?'

'I'm not even going to talk about it, 'cause I don't want to hear any more of your damned lies. Just get out.' She marched toward the front door.

'Wait a minute, Charm . . .'

She wheeled around. 'Don't call me that.' She screamed the words so loud it hurt her throat. 'Just get the hell out of my house, you bastard.' She turned back toward the front door.

'All right,' he yelled after her. 'If that's the way you want it. See if I care. I'm getting damn tired of this shit myself.'

She went out to the porch and plopped down on the glider. She crossed her legs at the ankles and tapped her foot. She could hear Clarence upstairs carrying on about his clothes being all over the floor, but she didn't give a damn. Served the sorry bastard right after what she'd gone through with the car. She'd had to leave it parked in Chinatown and get a cab back to work. Tomorrow she would have to deal with tow trucks and batteries and all that stuff.

But she didn't want to think about that now, or the man ranting and raving upstairs. It was a beautiful spring evening — so cool and crisp — and she wanted to focus on the future. Clarence was a part of her past. Tomorrow, right after she got her car straightened out, she was going around to all the universities in the area and picking up applications. Howard, American, George Washington, Catholic, Maryland — hell, she'd even try tony old Georgetown. Why not?

The first thing Evelyn noticed as she turned the Benz onto her block was the bike sitting in the driveway. She smiled to herself. Some things never changed. The second thing she noticed was Kevin's car. That meant he'd come home early, just like he said he would. She pulled her car partway onto the lawn and walked up the driveway. In the kitchen, Andre was hanging up the wall phone. A basketball sat at his feet.

'Yo, Ma.'

'Hi, honey.'

'You're home early, aren't you? I thought you had that group thing tonight.'

She placed her purse on the table and picked up the mail. 'I canceled it.'

'Oh.' Andre picked up his basketball. 'Well, I was just about to go out and move my bike.'

'Take your time,' Evelyn said, sifting through the mail.

Andre did a double take. ''Scuse me?'

'There's no rush. I can move my car up later. Did you eat yet?'

'Yeah, we just finished. See how nice we cleaned the kitchen up for you?'

354

Evelyn looked around. They had done a good job, which was surprising, and a nice change. 'Looks good.'

'Mostly it was the old man. I was going up to the court to shoot some hoops. I already told him.'

'Just be home by dark.'

'See ya when I see ya.' He headed for the door.

'Wait a minute.'

Andre stopped and turned to face her. 'What?'

'Give me a hug.'

Andre scrunched his face up. 'Huh?'

'You too big for a hug from your mama?'

Andre shrugged. 'Guess not.' He stepped forward and she gave him a big hug. Andre backed away smiling, but looked at her funny.

'That's better,' she said. 'Where's Rebecca?'

'She went over to Naomi's. That sleep-over thing that girls do.'

'Oh, that's right. The pajama party's tonight. How'd she get there?'

'One of the girl's mothers picked them all up in a van.'

'And your father?'

'He was out cutting the grass a few minutes ago, but I don't hear the mower now.'

'Okay, I'll see you when you get back. Just remember to be home by . . .' She stopped. Andre was already halfway down the driveway, dribbling the ball as he ran. As she rounded the house to the backyard, she saw Kevin in his sweats stooped down over the lawn mower. He had a screwdriver in his hand, and some of the mower's parts were sprawled out on the grass. He stood up when he saw her approaching. 'You're home early.'

'I canceled my evening session.'

'I can't remember the last time you did that.'

Evelyn looked over at her garden. She'd planted a few early vegetables, but not nearly as much as usual. So much was going on around her that she hadn't been able to summon the time or the inspiration. 'I need to get moving on that thing if we're going to have any kind of garden this summer. And the weeds. Seems I can't get them under control.'

'I'll help you out after I get this thing working and finish mowing the lawn.'

'Not today. Maybe tomorrow.'

'Fine. I'll be in all weekend.'

She looked at him. 'You're going to be here all weekend? I can't remember the last time *you* did *that*.'

He stooped back down over the lawn mower and stuck the screwdriver in somewhere. 'There's a lot to do out here. The hedges need trimming. And I want to clean out the shed. Never got around to any of it last fall.'

'No more meetings? No all-day planning sessions?'

'I think I've had enough of those. Don't you?'

'Depends.'

He looked up at her, then went back to the mower. 'Oh, I see,' he said, chuckling. 'You were glad to have me out of the house all winter.'

Evelyn smiled. 'No. What I meant was if you're going to start your own law firm, you've got to plan every detail carefully.'

The pleasant look on his face disappeared. 'If that's your idea of a joke, it's not funny. We both know that probably won't be happening.'

'I'm not joking. Why won't it be happening?'

He stopped his screwing and stood up again. 'What do you mean, why won't it be happening? You've done everything you could to thwart it. And it would be impossible without you backing me. I may be stubborn but I'm not crazy.'

'That makes two of us.'

'Huh?'

'I can be pretty stubborn, too. Look, I'll back you if that's what you want to do.'

He stared at her with wide eyes. He seemed speechless and confused. He looked at the ground, then back at her. 'Come again?'

'I think you should go ahead with it.'

He eyed her suspiciously. 'Where would I get the money?'

356

'From our savings. A second mortgage. Whatever. I'm sure you'll come up with something.'

'Hold on a minute now, 'cause I don't believe I'm hearing this. What about the new house? The kids' education and yours?'

'If we can't save enough by the time the children are ready for college, we'll have to borrow the money. Or they can work to help pay for their schooling. As for the house and me going back to school, that can wait. Our happiness is more important.'

The look of bewilderment on his face slowly changed into one of joy as he realized what she was saying. Evelyn thought it was the nicest look she'd seen on his face in a long while. She'd gladly give away the store to see it more often. He laughed nervously, as if he still wasn't sure to believe it. 'Are you serious?'

Evelyn nodded. 'Very.'

'Oh, man.' He rubbed his hand over his face. 'I don't believe it.' He wrinkled his brow. 'What brought on the change of heart?'

Evelyn thought about Wanda, and yes, she had to admit she'd felt more than a little threatened by the woman. But the biggest factor was the husband standing in front of her. He was faithful, honest, hard-working. And before all this had happened, he was also very loving. They had been a happy family, and she wanted that back. 'You brought on the change.'

'Me? What did I do?'

'It's not what you did. It's who you are. You're good to me, Kevin. And I want you to be happy 'cause that's what makes me and the children happy.'

He dropped the screwdriver on the ground and pulled her into his arms. He planted a big kiss on her forehead, her nose, her lips. 'You won't be sorry. I promise you that.'

She shook her finger at him playfully. 'But once the firm turns the corner, it's my turn. I'm going back to school to get my Ph.D. Agreed?'

'No question.'

'And if it hasn't turned the corner in a few years, we'll have to rethink it. Maybe you'll even have to go back to working for someone else.'

'Fair enough.' He took her hands. 'Evelyn, about Chrissy, that woman I knew from Atlanta . . .'

The one who was going to stay in Atlanta if she had anything to do with it. 'Mm-hmm.'

'You were right about her.'

'You mean about the way she felt about you?'

He nodded. 'She finally admitted it. I still find it hard to believe she felt like that all those years and I never suspected it. But anyway, she moved back to Atlanta.'

'So I heard.'

'You knew that? How?'

'Another woman from my therapy group who kept in touch with Wanda, Chrissy, whoever.'

'Damn. You know everything.'

She jabbed a finger in his chest playfully. 'You'd better remember that, too.'

'Hmm.'

'Kevin? How long were you, ah . . . communicating with her after she moved here?'

'Not long. I probably got together with her for lunch about half a dozen times over two years. A little more after she offered to lend me the money.'

'And Thanksgiving night, when you went out for juice and stayed forever . . .'

'Oh, yes. That night.'

'You were with her, weren't you?'

'She called me at work the day before and invited me to stop by. I thought since she didn't have family here . . .' He shrugged. 'I only intended to stay a few minutes but that was when she offered me the money, and before I knew it an hour had gone by.' He shook his head. 'I should have seen what she was up to, but I guess I just didn't want to.'

'And Christmas night?'

'Same thing, pretty much, only that night she brought me

358

home after my car broke down. All we did was talk about the money and the firm.'

Evelyn nodded. 'I believe you.'

'Do you want to know what the plans are for the firm?' he asked. 'What we came up with before I dropped out?'

'Definitely. We're in this together. And I must admit, I'm starting to get excited about the idea.'

'In a few years, you'll look back and wonder why you were so reluctant.'

'I hope you're right. But I'm still nervous about it, and you're going to have to be patient with me if I get cold feet from time to time. Our lifestyle will probably change, for a while, anyway. And it's not going to be easy for me.'

He smiled. 'I understand. I think if you knew how well we were planning it, you'd feel better. As soon as I get this lawn mowed, I'm going to call Jeremy and get caught up. Then I'll go over everything with you.'

'I've got a better idea.'

'What?'

'Andre is out of the house for the next couple of hours, Rebecca all night. The lawn can wait – there's something more important we need to catch up on.'

He looked at her and understood immediately. 'That's going to take much more than a couple of hours to get caught up on,' he said, peeling her clothes off with his eyes. That was another look she hadn't seen for a while, and she'd forgotten how sexy it made her feel. She stuck her hand under his sweatshirt and ran it across his chest. 'Then we'd better get started, don't you think, Counselor?'

He started pulling the shirt over his head. 'Lead the way. I'm right behind you.'

30

When Beverly's eyes opened, the first image that popped into her head was the number three-oh. It was spread out before her mind's eye like a neon sign, taunting her, teasing her. She rubbed her eyes and stared at the ceiling, then turned her head to look at the clock on her night table. Damn, only six in the morning and she was wide awake. She'd often heard older people say they had trouble sleeping late. Was this a sign?

She sat up on the edge of the bed and stretched and yawned leisurely. She slipped her feet into her bedroom slippers and sat there. What the hell she was getting up for she hadn't the slightest idea. She didn't have anything special planned and here she was getting started at six in the morning. Last night, she'd had her final dinner with Peter. She'd canceled their date for tonight, their camping trip for next weekend, their lives together. Call her whatever you wanted. Picky, a quitter, a perfectionist. She didn't care. But she just couldn't keep dating someone when she knew there was no future. Now that the novelty of dating a white man had worn off, she had to admit to herself that Peter was just plain dull. Not to mention weird. She couldn't be bothered.

She stood up. What she needed was a nice, long, hot soak in the tub. Then maybe she would crawl back into bed for a couple more hours. She padded to the bathroom, dragging her bathrobe behind her. She went through her ritual of filling up the tub with hot, hot water and adding bath oil. She tucked her hair into a shower cap, eased in, and closed her eyes.

That number popped into her head again. Go away, she thought, sinking deeper into the tub. She tried to push the thoughts of her birthday out of her mind, the thoughts of breaking up with Peter, and the lonely days and weeks ahead.

She tried to think of more pleasant things. It was about this time last year that she'd first met Vernon, when he'd shown up at her office with an article he'd written for her magazine.

She wondered what he'd been up to all these months. They hadn't really talked when he stopped by, and it had been more than six months since they'd broken up. Maybe she would give him a call. Why not? It was her birthday, she deserved some excitement. And he was leaving town soon. It was too early now, but after she read the paper and had some breakfast, she would do it.

She read the *Washington Post* from cover to cover while eating a breakfast of bacon, toast, and coffee. By the time she finished it was still only 7:30, too early to call Vernon, so she started cleaning up the apartment. She vacuumed and dusted. Then she carried her dirty clothes to the laundry room in the basement of the building. She came back and scrubbed down the kitchen appliances. By the time she brought up the load of clothes from the dryer, it was 9:30 and she'd done more housework in a single morning than she normally did in a month. But at least the place was spic and span. And it was late enough to call Vernon.

She went into the bedroom and dumped the clean clothes on the bed. Should she fold them before or after she called him? Better fold them now. No telling what kind of mood she'd be in after talking to him. She sat on the bed and folded the clothes slowly, trying to think of what she would say when she called him. Would he remember that today was her birthday? Probably not. They'd only been together five or six months. She could always say she was calling him to see how his move to Charlottesville was going.

She stood up and put the clothes away. Then she went to the nightstand and stood by the phone. She stared at it a minute, trying to shake off the butterflies darting around in her stomach. She took a deep breath, picked up the phone, and started dialing. In the middle of the number she paused, exhaled deeply, and slammed the receiver down. She couldn't do it. She just couldn't. Everybody thought she should, but

361

they hadn't gone through what she did. The humiliation, the aggravation. She might be alone now, but she'd never felt more lonely than after breaking up with Vernon. She was just starting to get over him. Why drag all that muck back out of the gutter?

Even if she didn't call Vernon, though, she wasn't going to sit around all day on her birthday. She looked at her watch. She had an appointment to get her hair done at one, then she was supposed to stop by her parents'. But how was she going to occupy all the hours before and after that? She'd brought work home but didn't feel up to it. It was her birthday, for goodness sakes. She was supposed to have some fun. She was sorry she'd told everyone she didn't want to celebrate today. She needed to get out of this apartment.

Maybe she could still get somebody out to do something. Shopping, a movie, maybe even a club. She dialed Valerie's number. 'Hi. What are you up to?'

'Beverly?' Valerie said. 'How are you?'

'Oh, bored mostly. I woke up at six this morning and cleaned the place from top to bottom.'

'You must *really* be bored. I thought you were going out last night with Peter and again tonight.'

'I did. But we broke up and I got home early.'

'You called it off?'

'Yes.' She knew what was coming but might as well get it over with.

'Like I told you, your charts are totally out of whack. And knowing you, I must say I'm not surprised.'

'What do you mean, "knowing me"?'

'Well, after what you told me about his house. You know how you are about men screwing up.'

'Yeah, I know. I don't like it.'

'Don't I know it. Well, it's probably for the best. Are you okay about it, though?'

'I'm fine, I guess. But it would be good to get out. Want to go out for dinner or to a club?'

'Tonight?'

362

'Yes, tonight. Or do you have something else in the works?'

'Since you said you didn't want to do anything special for your birthday, I made other plans.'

'Jeez. If I have to stay in this house tonight, I'll scream.'

'Go shopping. Always works for me.'

'I don't want to go alone, not on my birthday.'

'Sorry. Oh, by the way, happy birthday. How's it feel to be thirty?'

'Unbelievable. Seems like only yesterday I wanted to be older so I could stay out late and buy wine.'

'Believe me, those days are gone forever.'

'I know. It's all downhill from here.'

'It's not that bad. What about Charmaine or Evelyn? Have you tried them?'

'I'll probably drag one of them out of the house. Talk to you later.'

Beverly hung up and immediately dialed Charmaine. Her sister sounded like she was still in bed.

'You're still sleeping this late?'

'I had a long night,' Charmaine said. 'What time is it?'

'Almost ten.'

'Shit. How'd I sleep so late?'

'I've been up since six this morning.'

Charmaine moaned. 'What the hell for?'

'Couldn't sleep. I broke up with Peter last night.'

'I don't blame you. Let him deal with his own problems.'

Beverly couldn't believe she was hearing right. 'What did you say?'

'If the man is bugging you that much, maybe it's for the best.'

'You been drinking or something? This doesn't sound like you at all. I expected to get the third degree and I had my arguments all ready.'

Charmaine chuckled. 'Well, I guess if I can get rid of my husband, you can break up with a boyfriend.'

'Come again?'

'I kicked the sucker out last night.'

'Clarence?'

'What other suckers do you know of living around here? Of course, Clarence.'

'What did he do this time?'

'Everything, Beverly. It's the way he breathes.'

'I sure hope it's for good this time.'

'If I let that bum back in this house ever again, I want you to slap the shit out of me.'

'I'm taking you up on that.'

'Fine. But you won't get the pleasure 'cause that 'Bama's never moving back. He's coming to get his things tonight, and that's it. I'm tired of it.'

It wouldn't be right to ask Charmaine to come out and cheer her up tonight. If anything, Charmaine was the one who needed uplifting. 'Want me to come by and give you support?'

'No. I got to handle this by myself.'

'Okay, if you're sure. I'll call you tomorrow to see how it went.'

'Thanks, sis. Let me go check on Kenny. And happy birthday.'

Beverly hung up. So she'd kicked the bum out again. Amen. But would she stick to it this time? There was no way of telling, really. It depended on which was more important to Charmaine, having a man around or living in peace and harmony. For Beverly, there was no contest. She'd pick peace and harmony any day. If a man couldn't at least give her that, it was time to send him packing. There were too many battles to fight out there in the world to have to come home everyday and fight more of them.

She picked up the phone again and dialed Evelyn's number. Evelyn wouldn't want to go to a club, but maybe she'd be willing to go to one of the shopping malls in Maryland. Boring as shopping was, it was better than sitting at home on your birthday.

Rebecca answered the phone. 'Hold on a minute, Aunt Beverly. She's out back with Daddy.'

As Beverly waited for Evelyn to come to the phone, she thought about the previous day at the restaurant and wondered what Evelyn had said to Kevin. It was hard for her to believe that Kevin was up to no good, but not impossible. Men could be so spineless when it came to resisting an attractive woman, especially when the woman was doing the pursuing. But unlike with Charmaine, Beverly had no doubt that Evelyn would get Kevin straightened out.

'Hi,' Evelyn said. 'How's the birthday girl?'

'Hanging in there. You're not going to believe this. I just spoke to Charmaine and guess what? She put slicko out.'

'I'm almost afraid to ask what he did this time.'

'Your guess is as good as mine. She didn't go into it.'

'I don't know about those two.'

'I hope she sticks with it this time,' Beverly said. 'She's better off without him.'

'Maybe she will. She got that big raise and promotion.'

'Yeah. Did you talk to Kevin?'

'You mean about that woman in the restaurant?'

What else? 'Uh-huh.'

'We had a good long talk yesterday after work. It was exactly who I thought it was. But he was taking her to the airport. She moved back to Atlanta.'

'Jeez, Evelyn. You are so lucky.'

'Lucky? What's luck got to do with anything?'

'I don't know. Everything always seems to work out for you. I think that's why Charmaine's so jealous of you. Me too, come to think of it.'

'I don't get it. Everyone thinks we have the perfect relationship. But we don't. Kevin can be so stubborn when he wants something, and difficult when he doesn't get it. The same goes for me, too, I guess. But he's a good man. Clarence only thinks about himself.'

'But how do you find a decent man? Every time I meet somebody I think, "This is it." This is the one and only I've been waiting for all my life. And then, wham! He does something dumb.'

'You're asking the wrong person. Kevin is always doing things, not dumb things, but strange enough to throw me off balance.' She laughed. 'One thing I'll say, it's never boring with him.'

'You're so lucky. I envy you.'

'We're going to need a lot more than luck the next few years. I told him to go ahead and start the law firm.'

'I declare. You two are going to be rolling in the dough. I won't be able to talk to you.'

'Ha. If anything I'll probably be coming to you begging for a loan or something.'

'Pity on you, if you need to come to me. But I doubt it'll come to that. Knowing you two, you've got a million bucks stashed away somewhere.'

'That's ridiculous. It's going to be tough for a while trying to make ends meet. We were up half the night talking about it, trying to figure out how we'll manage, and we started in again when we woke up this morning. One of his future partners is coming by later and we're going over the plans. I'm tense about it, but it's exciting in a way. And Kevin is being so sweet and patient about making sure I understand everything.'

Of course it was exciting to her. She had her husband back. Obviously, this was not the time to ask her to go shopping. 'I just called to see how things were going. I won't keep you.'

'You and Peter doing anything exciting tonight?'

Peter? Oh, yes, Peter. 'No. I called it off with him last night.'

Evelyn was silent.

'Go ahead,' Beverly said. 'Say "I told you so."'

'You said it, not me. I'm not going to judge anymore. It's your life. Was it because of the house?'

'More than that. The man was starting to bore me. When the only excitement in a relationship is a man's weird habits, it's time to call it quits.'

'Sounds like you got over your excitement of being with a white man.'

'It wasn't about that. Well, maybe, in a way.'

'Uh-huh.'

366

'I honestly thought things would be different with Peter. But if anything, I found out white men can be just as disappointing as black men.'

'I'm sorry this had to happen on your birthday. Does that mean you don't have any plans for tonight?'

'Looks that way. I'm going to get my hair done later. Stop by Ma's. But that's about it.'

'You can't stay home alone on your birthday.'

Why not, Beverly thought? Wouldn't be the first time. The year she and Michael started having problems, she spent her birthday by the phone waiting for his call. It never came. 'It won't be so bad.'

'Why don't you come by here?'

'What am I going to do out there? Help you and Kevin plan your business? No thanks.'

'The man who's coming by, Jeremy, is divorced. Maybe . . .'

'Uh-uh. I'm through with blind dates for the rest of my life.'

'He's not bad-looking.'

'Forget it.'

'He's a lawyer. You should at least meet him.'

'Thanks, but I don't care if he's president of the United States.'

'I don't like the idea of you spending your birthday alone.'

'I'll be fine. Maybe I'll stop at the library for a book on my way back from Ma's.'

'Are you sure?'

'I'll be fine.'

'Okay. Well, let me get back to Kevin.'

'Fine. I'll talk to you later.'

Some birthday it was turning out to be, she thought as she dropped the receiver in the cradle. Looked like she'd be spending another one by herself. At least it wouldn't be as bad as it was that year with Michael. She was alone now, but not depressed and sitting around moping about some guy. She was man-free, worry-free. Why, there must be a million things she could do around the apartment tonight – like curl up with a book, maybe that one by Marita Golden that she'd never gotten around to reading, and some cherry-chocolate chip ice cream. Or she could rent a video or finish the work she'd brought home from the office.

How dreary it all sounded, she thought. Was this the way she was doomed to spend the rest of her birthdays?

31

Beverly hadn't been back at the apartment ten minutes before the doorbell rang. She was standing in the bathroom stark naked with a shower cap on her head and one toe in the tub. Damn, she thought. Somebody would have to show up unannounced now. She shook the water off her foot and removed the cap, being careful not to mess up her hair, newly permed and styled. She pulled on her robe and shut the bathroom door behind her.

She glanced into her bedroom as she passed by. She could barely see the clock behind all the shopping bags piled on her bed, but it was seven o'clock. Whoever this was, she was getting rid of them fast. She looked out the peephole expecting to see a salesperson or something, but instead saw both her sisters and Valerie. She laughed. What in the world? She opened the door, and the three of them stood there, all smiles. Evelyn was holding what looked like a cake box from the bakery. Valerie was carrying a bottle of wine.

'What is this?' she said, standing aside as they piled in.

'Happy birthday, old lady,' Valerie said, poking her playfully in the ribs.

'Couldn't let you celebrate the big one all alone, could we?' Evelyn said.

'I thought you-all had other plans. Whose crazy idea was this anyway?'

'Well, Evelyn called me,' Charmaine said. 'Said you were sounding all depressed on the phone.'

Beverly put her hands on her hips. 'I was not.'

'And Charmaine called me,' Valerie said. She put the wine bottle on the coffee table.

'We talked back and forth,' Evelyn said.

369

'And decided we could all put off our plans.'

'Come and cheer you up some, girl.'

'For the last time, I'm not depressed. In fact I was getting dressed to . . .'

'Well, depressed or not,' Evelyn said, placing the cake on the coffee table, 'here we are.' She held her hands in the air, palms up.

'Wait a minute,' Beverly said. 'We're going to have to make this snappy.'

'Aw, c'mon, Beverly,' Valerie said, pulling the strings off the cake box. 'Turning thirty's not the end of the world.'

'It's not that,' Beverly said. 'I've . . .'

'You got any ice cream to go with the cake?' Charmaine asked, heading toward the kitchen.

' . . . got a date tonight.'

They all stopped, turned, and looked at her.

'With Peter?' Valerie asked.

'I thought you said you broke up with him,' Evelyn said.

'Lordy me,' Charmaine said. 'And I thought *I* was fast about forgiving and going back.'

'It's not with Peter.'

'Then who?'

'Vernon.'

'Vernon?' all three said at once.

Beverly smiled and nodded. There, she'd said it. And yes, she'd done it. She'd called him, and they'd had the best time talking. They got so involved in catching up with each other, she was almost late for her hair appointment. He'd remembered right away it was her birthday. And when she'd told him she wasn't going to be doing any celebrating, he insisted on breaking his plans for a night out with the boys to take her to Blues Alley, a popular jazz spot. Good music, good wine, a good man. How could any woman possibly say no to that combination?

'You called him?' Evelyn asked.

Beverly nodded again.

Valerie sank down on the couch. 'I don't believe it.'

'It's about time you came to your senses, girl.'

'So if we're going to have cake and ice cream we need to get started. He's coming in an hour and I have to get ready.'

'We're not doing nothin' or going nowhere 'til you tell us what happened.'

'It's simple, Charmaine. I called him. We got to talking and he asked if I'd like to go to Blues Alley.'

'That's nice,' Valerie said.

'Look at her, trying to act all cool about it,' Charmaine said. 'I'm getting the ice cream and some plates. Don't say another word 'til I get back.' She dashed off to the kitchen as fast as her swollen feet would carry her. Valerie followed. 'I'll help you.'

'What made you change your mind about calling him?' Evelyn asked as she removed the cake from the box.

Beverly sat on the sofa. 'Oh, I don't know. After I talked to you, I just got to thinking. Luck doesn't just happen – you've got to bend a little.'

'I'm really glad you called him.'

Charmaine came back carrying a half gallon of Edy's Grand Cherry-Chocolate Chip Ice Cream and four plates. Valerie had the utensils and glasses.

'I want to hear every last detail about that conversation,' Charmaine said. 'What's Romeo been up to? Is he moving to Charlottesville?'

Beverly stuck her bottom lip out. 'Yes. He leaves next weekend.'

'Oh, damn.'

'But we're going to stay in touch. He wants me to help him pick out a house. Who knows? Maybe I'll end up living in Charlottesville someday.' She paused and watched as Evelyn cut the cake, Charmaine dished out the ice cream, and Valerie opened the bottle of wine. 'This is so sweet of you-all.'

'Skip the bullshit,' Charmaine said. 'Get on with what happened.'

Beverly giggled. 'Oh, God. I was so nervous when I first called him, I could hardly say a word. But he was so sweet. Before I knew it, we were laughing and talking like nothing had ever happened.' She noticed Charmaine piling a mountain of ice cream onto her own plate. 'Charmaine, didn't you get any dinner?'

Charmaine sat back on the sofa. 'I got two mouths to feed now.' She scooped up a spoonful of cake and ice cream and shoved it into her mouth.

'Where's Kenny?'

'My car's in the shop, so Evelyn brought Andre and Rebecca over to watch him and picked me up.'

'And Tabitha,' Evelyn chimed in. 'Rebecca never leaves the house without that cat, if she can help it. I suggested Kenny ride back with me and the kids after I drop Charmaine off. He can stay at my house until Clarence gets all his things.'

'Good idea,' Beverly said.

'He doesn't need to be there with all the fighting and carrying on me and Clarence will be doing these next few days.'

'So it's for good this time?' Beverly asked.

'It's for good. I've got a locksmith coming first thing Monday morning. But I swear I'm worried about being alone with the baby coming and all.'

'You're not alone,' Beverly said. 'You have us.'

'Kenny can stay at my house as long as you need. And we'll help out after the baby is born.'

'You can do it,' Valerie said. 'You've got family support. I raised Olivia without a husband.'

'You make more money than me, Valerie. Believe it or not, I got a little help from Clarence with the bills.'

They all looked at Charmaine doubtfully.

'I did. Although I also got more bills because of him.'

'And more headaches,' Evelyn said. 'With him out of the way, you can start thinking about things like going back to school for your degree.'

'That's the *first* thing I intend to do,' Charmaine said. 'I don't care if I end up living on the streets trying to pay for it, I'm getting my degree.'

'Don't worry,' Beverly said. 'If you can't pay your bills, you can always move in with Evelyn. She's got more than enough room.'

'She can move in with me, but she might be living in a tent.'

'That'll be the day,' Charmaine said.

'I'm not kidding. Kevin will have to quit his job, and we're going to take out a second mortgage on our house. That scares me with only one steady income.'

'Sounds like you may be coming to live with me,' Charmaine said.

They all laughed.

'Well, this has been wonderful, ladies,' Beverly said, placing her empty plate on the table. 'But I need to start getting dressed.'

'Listen to this,' Valerie said.

'I'm telling you,' Charmaine said. 'Just yesterday she didn't want to have nothing to do with the man. Now she's ready to kick us out for him.'

'You're not going to put us out so soon, are you?' Evelyn asked.

Beverly smiled at them. 'Yes, I am. But don't go far. No doubt I'll need some warm bodies to lean on again someday real soon.'